PRAISE FOR *IN THE ABSENCE OF MIRACLES*

'Beautiful, lyrical prose takes the reader through a perfectly constructed, often harrowing tale' Denzil Meyrick

'Engrossing, hard-hitting – even shocking – with a light poetic frosting. Another superb read' Douglas Skelton

'A chilling tale of secrets, lies and the ultimate betrayal' Theresa Talbot

'Emotional. Brave. Dark. Raw. Utterly beautiful' Louise Beech

'Challenging and emotional, *In the Absence of Miracles* enthrals as it corkscrews to a shocking, yet ultimately rewarding end' LoveReading

'*In the Absence of Miracles* is a captivating mystery, a heartbreaking look at family and a triumph of emotional storytelling that all combine to create a powerful and poignant story' The Tattooed Book Geek

'Malone strikes the right balance and has produced a masterpiece; it's subtle, sensitively written, wrought with emotion and has to be one of my most captivating, heartbreaking reads EVER' The Book Review Café

'Beautifully written, substantial and heartbreaking, it is an astonishingly powerful novel for our time' Live and Deadly

'Harrowing, emotional, realistic (unfortunately), and leaves you feeling a little off-balance at its conclusion. Emotional excellence' The Big Fat Bookworm

'A thriller, the darkest domestic noir, a family drama. A captivating, mesmerising, engrossing, at times poetic story about creating a future am̲̅ ⋯ ok Love

'Absolute literary perfection that left me catatonic within a vortex of emotion! I can't recommend it highly enough' The Reading Closet

'Michael J Malone has this extraordinary talent to write about difficult subjects in such a beautiful way. He is not afraid to tackle sensitive subjects that are usually kept quiet. A book that resonated with me on many levels and one I won't forget' Madeleine Black

'Powerful yet tender, and an emotional masterclass in how to write about harrowing and difficult issues' Hair Past a Freckle

'Quite the dark and twisted family tale that uncovers secrets that are truly shocking! There's an undertone of such sadness in the uncovering of child abuse that just breaks your heart' Laura Rash

'Poignant, raw and breathtaking, *In the Absence of Miracles* will break your heart … I reckon he is going to have to set up a retreat for emotionally distraught readers' Chapter in My Life

PRAISE FOR MICHAEL J. MALONE

'A stark, gripping storyline' *Scots Magazine*

'Malone tackles the taboo subject of female violence against men with insight and compassion (for Anna is no one-dimensional witch), while creating all the hallmarks of a fine, page-turning psychological thriller' *Daily Mail*

'Exceptional' *Publishers Weekly*

'A complex and multi-layered story – perfect for a wintry night' *Sunday Mirror*

'A beautifully written tale, original, engrossing and scary' *The Times*

'An expert plotter; twists and turns feel properly embedded in the story. It's a tough high-wire act, balancing believability with surprise, but the author pulls it off with aplomb' *Big Issue*

'Vivid, visceral and compulsive' Ian Rankin

'Michael Malone has twisted the marriage thriller into a new and troubling shape, creating a story that, with its bristling unease, feels all too real. This is domestic noir at its very darkest' Eva Dolan

'Disturbing but compulsive' Martina Cole

'Emotionally intelligent and engaging' Caro Ramsay

'Moving and compelling … Malone perfectly balances storytelling with a brutal commentary on a dysfunctional relationship' Sarah Ward

'Hits you like an express train' Mason Cross

'A chilling tale of the unexpected that journeys right into the dark heart of domesticity' Marnie Riches

'Malone is a massive talent … get on board now so you can brag you were reading his books long before the rest of the world' Luca Veste

'A tightly wound page-turner with real emotional punch' Rod Reynolds

'Dark, disturbing and peppered with his trademark humour … a fantastic read, and, as a writer, Malone just gets better and better' S.J.I. Holliday

'A disturbing and realistic portrayal of domestic noir with a twist … a shocking yet compelling read' Mel Sherratt

'This searing depiction of an abusive marriage with the conventional roles reversed nonetheless manages to radiate warmth and integrity' Anya Lipska

'Funny and brutal, heartfelt and compelling. Highly recommended' Craig Robertson

'Beautifully crafted and colourfully descriptive … keeps the reader gripped by an uneasy presence, a chill, literally, down the spine, as you become absorbed into the experience of the main character' *Undiscovered Scotland*

'The story twists and feints, pulling us along with it at every turn, the edginess of its central character making every development even more unsettling' *Herald Scotland*

'Terrifying exploration of lust and betrayal' *Sunday Post*

'Brilliantly creepy, with a dash of Glasgow humour, I couldn't turn the pages fast enough. A spine-tingling treat' *Daily Record*

'A thought-provoking read – well researched, well written and well done!' Off-the-Shelf Books

'It certainly keeps its reader on the edge of their seat throughout with its twists and turns … I truly cannot get enough of this author's writing. Another brilliant read from Michael J. Malone' Have Books Will Read

'This is a great psychological thriller with a gripping storyline … Well written and intuitive, this is another great read by Michael J Malone' My Chestnut Tree Reading

'A well-written, character driven, gripping thriller that held my attention throughout the whole book' Nicki's Life of Crime

In the Absence of Miracles

MICHAEL J. MALONE

**ORENDA
BOOKS**

Orenda Books
16 Carson Road
West Dulwich
London SE21 8HU
www.orendabooks.co.uk

First published in the UK in 2019 by Orenda Books
Copyright © Michael J. Malone, 2019

ISBN 978-1-912374-79-3
eISBN 978-1-912374-80-9

Typeset in Garamond by MacGuru Ltd
Printed and bound by CPI Group (UK) Ltd, Croydon CR0 4YY

For sales and distribution, please contact *info@orendabooks.co.uk*
or visit *www.orendabooks.co.uk*.

IN THE ABSENCE OF MIRACLES

'Pain that is not transformed is transmitted.'
—Richard Rohr

1

My mother's face had haunted me since I'd last seen her, almost two weeks ago. Her one good eye staring. A string of saliva stretching from the corner of her mouth. Her right hand frozen into a claw as she struggled to reach for the warmth of mine.

This would be the first time I had seen her since she'd been transferred from the big hospital in Glasgow to Lennox House – a nursing home in the village where she'd spent most of her adult life.

The driveway was just wide enough for one car – there were a few passing places dotted along its length. The grass verges were neatly trimmed and a mix of large-leafed trees and giant rhododendron bushes broke the view over a wide, closely clipped lawn.

I followed the long curve of the drive and a couple of minutes later we were pulling up in front of a large ivy-covered Victorian mansion. There were three rows of tall windows set into stained, blond sandstone. In the centre, a grand portico, supported by four Greek pillars, stood over a large glass door.

'It's lovely,' Angela said to me from the passenger seat, as she craned her neck to look up at the building. 'The village seemed nice as well. A nice place to grow up. I've only ever known the city,' she added wistfully.

I studied her expression to check if she was having a go at me. Despite the fact we'd been together for around two years – by *around* I mean we've been as much 'on' as 'off' over that period – I'd never brought her to the village where I'd grown up.

Inside, I was struck by the elegance and grandeur of the place. This impression was followed by the recognition of the subtle smell that hung in the air. It clung to my nostrils and filled my lungs. It was the smell of incontinence, dying breaths, and fading memories.

The flowers spilling from vases on every available surface did nothing to mask it; their perfume only added to the cloying smell. We approached an imposing desk, and the receptionist looked up from her paperwork and offered us a smile. She had dark, straightened hair and was wearing a black jacket over a white shirt. The name badge on her lapel read *Donna. Receptionist*. 'Morning. How can I help you?' She looked from me to Angela and allowed her gaze to rest on her as if she judged Angela the more important.

'I'm here to see my mother, Donna,' I said. 'Mrs Lorna Docherty.'

Donna smiled over at me, then looked down at her screen and punched a few keys on her keyboard.

'Room twenty-two, first floor.'

I nodded my thanks, turned and walked over to the staircase. As I looked around, the doctor's words from the last time I spoke to him echoed in my mind: 'Your mother has had a massive stroke, Mr Docherty. And sadly she didn't get to a hospital quickly enough. Our tests indicate…' He went on speaking but I couldn't really take it in. Lots of big words and serious expressions. '…We remain ever hopeful of course, but despite her relatively young age we expect she will see her days out under assisted care…'

And this place would cost money. A lot of money.

I'd need to sell her house.

Angela reached for my hand. 'You okay?' she asked.

'Got a bit of a sore head,' I replied, offering her a smile, aware my tension was causing it to fray at the edges.

Together we walked over to the wide staircase and started to climb its plushly carpeted steps. The oak panelling on the walls matched the banister and was hung with large portraits of grim-faced Lennox men and women. The men all wore some form of army uniform and the women were dressed in dark, no-nonsense garments, the only flesh on show their pale hands clasped firmly on their laps.

Finding the door marked *22* I paused before it, steeled myself against the upset of what I would see on the other side, knocked on it with a single knuckle and entered.

My mother's room matched the scale of that part of the old house we'd seen so far. Immediately on entering we were greeted by a wide space, her bed against the wall to the right, so that she was afforded a spectacular view out of the large bay window, taking in the rooftops of Seamill, a wide strip of sea, and the outline of the sleeping warrior on the horizon: the Isle of Arran.

'...ohn,' my mother tried to say my name and reached her good hand out to me.

With a churning stomach I rushed over to her, praying I was convincing in my effort to hide my shock at her appearance. Each time I visited her in hospital the jolt I experienced at the change in her didn't lessen. I felt it again as I attempted a reassuring smile.

'Whe ... you ... been?' she asked, squeezing out the words with considerable effort, her mouth making almost impossible shapes.

I used the time it took to pull a chair over to her bed to compose myself. To force my mind to accept what I was seeing as her new 'normal'.

'I was here just the other week,' I lied, struggling to meet her gaze.

'I know ... s'not easy...'

I leaned forwards and kissed her cheek, and in response I could feel her stiffen as she inhaled, as if she had caught the scent of something.

'You ... drinnkinnng?'

'Goodness sake, Mum. Give it a rest, eh?'

I distracted myself again for a moment by reaching for a tissue from the box on her bedside cabinet and then wiping at the dribble sliding from the side of her mouth and down to her chin.

'Hi there,' said Angela as she moved to the other side of the bed. Leaning forwards she gave my mother a peck on the cheek. 'I hope they're looking after you.' I envied her apparently casual and natural demeanour. Thinking that I'd never get used to this version of my mother, I once again composed my features into an expression that suggested everything was normal.

But it wasn't. My mother was a stricken, haunted version of herself. Always slim, she was alarmingly thin now, the weight loss exaggerating the lines on her face and the size of her one good eye.

Her hair, which she had always taken great care over, was flat and lifeless on her crown and was pressed to the side of her head by her pillow.

'I think we should get in touch with Marie at your salon. See if she'll do an outside visit,' I said, forcing some energy into my voice.

Mum's face looked like it was being pushed to one side as she worked on a smile. 'Would be … nice.' Then she turned her attention to Angela and I could see a wariness there. Mum had never taken to any of my girlfriends.

Mum made a sound that could have been a thank-you. Or it might just have been her trying to clear her throat. Angela took the kinder interpretation, smiled in response and continued talking. Her chatter was warm and unaffected, and eased the tension in the room. I couldn't have been more grateful for it.

Back in the car, Angela reached across and held my hand. 'You okay, honey?'

I craned my neck and looked up at the old house. 'She's in a bit of a state, isn't she?'

Angela's face formed a reassuring expression. 'She's in the right place.'

'I know. It's just … she's not long turned sixty. She's way too young for this to have happened.'

'Can happen at any age,' Angela said. 'A man at my work had one when he was only fifty-six.' She stroked my hand, her eyes warm with sympathy. 'You OK? Can't be nice seeing your mum like that?'

'I envy your … you were just so calm with her. And she's hardly been the most welcoming…'

Her smile was pained but accepting. 'Mothers and sons,' she sighed. 'Lots of mothers struggle with another woman in their son's life.'

'I should really go to Mum's, have a look and work out what needs to get done before I try and sell the place.'

'Good thinking,' Angela replied. 'And you need time on your own to process all of this. Why don't you drop me off at the train station and I'll make my way back home? I need to get back up for the wee one, and it strikes me that you could do with some time on your own.'

As we made our way back up the drive, I looked in the rear-view mirror. A glint of evening sun against a window caught my eye and I stared up at the building. Ivy leaves the size of hands clung to it, lifting and shifting in the determined breeze, giving an illusion of movement, a deception of life.

2

Grateful for Angela's sensitivity I dropped her off then made my way to my childhood home. I let myself in and stood in the small hallway for a long moment as if letting myself settle back into the space.

Although Mum had been hospitalised weeks earlier, the air felt fresh. I wondered if the next-door neighbour had been coming in now and again to open the windows. From where I stood I could see into the kitchen, the sitting room to my left, my bedroom at the back, downstairs. As I expected, the place was spotless. Looking at the bare cream-coloured walls and the hoover track marks on the carpet it felt as if Mum had just popped out for some shopping.

The last time I'd seen my mother before she had her stroke was on the anniversary of my father's death, a few months earlier. Mum wasn't bothered either way about Christmas and refused to acknowledge her birthday, but was adamant that each year on the date my father died I should make the trek down to my childhood home and spend an hour or two with her.

For some reason, on this particular visit I was more reflective than normal.

'I never got the sense that you and Dad really loved each other,' I said, thinking out loud.

Mum recoiled. 'What a horrible thing to say,' she said, her expression tight. 'Your father was the love of my life.' She crossed her arms and stared defiantly at me.

I held her gaze while I debated arguing the point. My comment was thoughtless, but to argue about her revision of her marriage would have been a waste of energy. If she coped with her grief by reframing her marriage more positively, who was I to challenge her?

Shaking my head as if that might rid me of the way my thoughts were going, I made for the kitchen and the cupboard where my dad used to stash his whisky. Bingo. Behind Mum's almost-empty bottle of port I found a single malt that only had a couple of measures taken from it. I poured myself two fingers, threw that back. Savoured the melt across my shoulder muscles and poured myself another. This one I nursed in my left hand as I walked through the house.

Minutes later I was walking towards my old bedroom. I stopped at the threshold and allowed the memories to flood in. I'd spent hours lying on that bed, on that very red, grey and black bedspread – a colour scheme I once thought was so grown up – hands under my head, earphones in, listening to all sorts of music.

I never played the music too loud. I needed to hear what was happening in other parts of the house. And as if memory had layered echoes in my mind, I could hear Chris charging upstairs, Mum shouting after him, Dad telling us dinner was ready, Mum calling to say that my mate Paul was at the door. Chris running in and jumping on top of me, making sure the bony saucer of each knee hit me in a tender spot.

There were also times when it was deathly quiet, when Dad's silences lay heavy in the house. When he was working a murder case we knew to tiptoe around him, that he would be quick to fury, to lash out, but just as quick to apologise.

I found him once, asleep at the kitchen table, an almost-empty bottle of whisky at his right hand. I couldn't see a glass and guessed he'd drunk straight from the bottle. Breathless with anxiety, certain he was dead, I studied him in the gloom, ears primed for the sound of his breath. Then he'd woken himself with a snore, lifted his head off the table and with one eye still shut he'd shouted at me to get back to bed.

He'd followed me to my room and stood on the very spot I did now, watching me as I got into bed. I pulled the quilt up around my neck as if I was protecting myself and pretended to sleep, wondering what on earth he was doing as he lingered there.

A deep grumble issued from his throat. It sounded like, 'Sorry, son. Not your fault.'

That was the pattern of our relationship. Shouts, long silences, and apologies.

I gave myself a shake. And another sip of whisky. I had a job to do. But where to begin? I climbed the stairs and looked up at the access door to the loft. That had been Dad's space. No one was allowed up there but him. I suspected it would be covered in a thick layer of dust – I couldn't think of anyone who might have gone up there since he died.

There was hardly any room for my feet because of the amount of junk in the spacious attic. Boxes, trunks and piles of old clothes almost reached the sloping roof. Paintings and books lay in front of me along with an open box, which, from where I stood, looked as if it was filled with black cloth. The cardboard was clean and firm as I pushed back the flaps to discover what lay within. The rough, heavy wool gave it away instantly. It was my father's police uniform. I fingered the black serge and tugged at the epaulettes my father had proudly worn throughout his career. Emotions vied for attention in my mind; guilt argued with logic, rejection played with fear, love yielded to loss.

Who was the man who wore this material? His strong face appeared in my mind, wearing a hint of a smile. My throat tightened as I replaced the tunic and closed the dust-free box.

Far into the corner, deep in the shadow I came across a couple of small boxes, hidden under a stack of books. Each box had been carefully wrapped in brown paper and tied up with string. Untying the first box I found a small camera and two rolls of film. Under that was a pile of photographs of varying shapes and sizes, some in colour and some in black and white. They were all portraits of children. There were several of both Chris and I, naked in the bath. In one, I sat sombrely on one side while Chris displayed all of his teeth to the camera. What age would I have been? Five? Six?

Then there were some photographs of me in my early teens. In one I was holding a toddler in my lap, sitting in front of a dark-green car. I recognised the background, the pattern of rocks and the small ruined castle off to the right. That could only be down by Portencross. Chris was nowhere to be seen, which was unusual. In most family pictures we came as a package. And why was I holding a baby? And whose car was that? I couldn't remember Dad having one that colour.

Dismissing this, I placed the photographs to the side and picked up the other box. It was lighter than the first and with a strange sense of excitement, I opened it up. It held a single item – a stained sand-shoe; rubber sole, white canvas upper. A boy's shoe? I picked it up by the laces and holding it closer to the light, I squinted to identify the stains. The green was unquestionably grass, but could the splash of rusty, almost brown colour be blood?

3

My mobile phone rang, echoing through the dust and dark of the loft space. Without looking at the screen I answered it.

'How's it hanging, big guy?' A voice said. It took a moment for the owner to register.

'Paul,' I said. 'How the hell are you?'

'A wee bird tells me you're in town. Fancy a pint down at The Lion?'

'How did you—?'

'My mum misses nothing, mate. You should know that.'

I laughed. Paul's mother lived in a house at the far end of our street, on the opposite side of the road.

'She was on the phone to me seconds after you arrived.'

Paul's mum never quite took to me and didn't bother to hide the fact, so I was surprised to hear she'd alerted him.

'The call did come with a government health warning,' Paul said, clearly reading my pause. '"That Docherty boy is at his mother's",' he added in a falsetto. We both laughed, a noise that felt good among the murk and secrets of the attic.

We arranged a time and with a sense of pleasure, I hung up. Paul had been one of the casualties of my move up to Glasgow. I really should have made more of an effort to keep up with him.

The photograph had fallen from my hand when I answered the phone. I picked it up, looked around me at the mess and with a sigh decided there was no rush. I could sort this all out some other time.

Paul watched from his stool at the far end of the bar as his old friend ducked inside the door and then looked around the room for him.

He stood up and gave a wave. 'John,' he shouted over the music. 'Over here.'

John gave a sharp nod, flicked a smile and walked towards him, meeting him at the bar, hand out. They shook, and with his free hand Paul clasped his friend by the shoulder.

'Been a while since you've been in here, eh?'

John's face bloomed into a smile and Paul thought, there he is, the guy who had been by his side as he negotiated the world of boyhood. His face was puffier, his belly was pushing his shirt out, but the boy peeped out of that smile, and Paul found himself feeling the years since he'd seen his old friend. John's smile was full of warmth, but its edges were traced in sadness. Paul wondered what John had been through since they last spoke.

'Years, mate,' John answered Paul's question with a nod. 'Years.'

With that he took the stool beside Paul at the bar, looking around himself as he did so. It would be, Paul guessed, as if time had frozen. More than likely it was the same music – Whitesnake – bouncing from the tiny speakers in the ceiling; the same copper-topped bar at their elbows, and if not exactly the same people, similar figures were dotted around the room as if part of some colourful but ageing frieze. The walls covered in murals depicting scenes from the poems of Robert Burns.

'Will we grab a table up the back?' Paul asked after they'd both ordered a drink, trying not to cast a judgemental expression when he heard John order a pint and a double whisky chaser.

A few people gave the men a nod as they walked across the low-ceilinged room towards a small table in the far corner, just by the dartboard.

'Good to see you, man. You're looking well,' John said as he sat, stealing a glance at the pale two-inch scar that ran across his cheek below his left eye. Paul gave the skin there a scratch. His scar was ancient history, at least to him, but he could see a flare of guilt when John's eyes strayed there.

'How's your mum?' Paul asked, recalling what his mother had told him.

'She's not looking quite so poorly as the last time I saw her.' John replied.

'Getting old's rubbish, eh?' Paul commiserated. 'How are you dealing with it?'

John took a long drink and after he swallowed gave a long, slow sigh as if that was his best moment of the day. 'Man, I'd forgotten how shitty that road is down from Glasgow.'

'Tell me about it,' Paul replied, thinking if his friend didn't want to talk about his mother that was fine by him.

For the next few minutes they caught up on the machinery of their everyday lives – work and relationships. Surprised at how easily they slipped back into each other's company, Paul heard himself tell John that he and his wife were considering fertility treatment, something he'd not even told his mother.

'I don't mind kids,' John said. 'But more than one in a burger is a bit too chewy.'

'Says the teacher,' replied Paul with a grin.

'Spend all day with the wee shits and that would soon cure you of your desire to procreate.'

'But weren't you promoted to head of department last year?' Paul asked crossing his arms with mock outrage.

John laughed. 'How did you hear about that?'

'Your mum told my mum soon as it happened,' Paul answered. 'You must be doing something right to be moving up the ladder.'

'To be fair, most of the kids are cool. They speak my language.'

'Aye, cos you never really grew up.'

John gave a nod of recognition. 'Maybe that's why I don't want any. I'm still just a big wean myself.'

They both took a drink, mirroring each other's actions and Paul smiled.

'What?' John asked, his cheeks plump with a grin. And Paul was back on day one, year one in primary school. A boy, his dark hair cut in almost exactly the same short style it was today, was sitting on his own by the school wall, chewing the strap of his backpack, his eyes heavy with tears. Paul had already been going to nursery for a couple of years so leaving his parents and going to school didn't faze him, but something in him recognised the emotion the other boy was battling to hide. Then an older boy walked over, kicked John's foot. 'Poof,' he snarled.

John was up in the bigger boy's face. 'Shut it,' he shouted and pushed out.

The older boy didn't expect the speed of John's response and fell back. Then in the manner of all bullies who are called out on their actions, he scurried off. Paul decided there and then that this was a boy he would like to be his friend.

'What?' John asked again.

'Just remembering that first day in primary school.'

They both chuckled. Then John grew sombre and looked to Paul as if he was trying to come to a decision.

'When I was over at Mum's I found this in the loft.' John pulled what looked like a photograph out of his pocket.

Paul picked it up. 'Look at you with the weird haircut.' He looked at John. 'I don't remember your hair ever being like this.'

John looked like he couldn't either and moved the subject on. 'What's strange is it says on the back "the boys". That was always how Dad referred to me and Chris – who's only two years younger than me, whereas this child is little more than a toddler. Who the hell is he?'

After two hours in which we'd almost talked ourselves dry, while drinking too much, we left the pub and walked the first hundred yards in companionable silence. The cool night air brushed my cheeks as I examined my shoes scuffing along the pavement.

'I'd forgotten how good it was to talk to you, John. You always seemed to be able to draw me out of myself.' Paul's voice slurred slightly into the night air, and I realised he'd probably drunk more tonight than he had in a long while.

'Aye,' I said, while thinking, *I did?*

'I'm sorry I wasn't there for you, John. I can't help feeling that I could have been a better mate to you.'

'Yeah,' I said and punched out at his arm. 'Twat.' We both giggled. 'Don't worry about it, buddy,' I said. 'You can hardly help if I don't let you know when you're needed.'

'True, but I should have made more of an effort to keep in touch.' Paul stopped as if unsure of himself. 'Ever since you went away to uni we've let things slip.' He paused. 'Women are much better at this friendship shit, eh?'

'I was in such a hurry to get away from this place, and coming home was like admitting I hadn't made a success of leaving.' I wasn't sure this even made sense. My mind knew what I wanted to say but the connection to my tongue was frayed by booze.

'I never understood the big rush to get away. What's so awful about this place?'

'And you know,' I said as I looked up at the stars. 'It was a total waste of time. Wherever I go, there I am.' I rubbed at my forehead. 'Who said that? Some eejit probably.' Eyes up, looking ahead, I saw the green telephone junction box at the end of the street. There was one of these at the end of the street where we grew up, and we'd arrange to meet there almost nightly after dinner. 'Green box at seven' was the cry.

'Look,' I shouted. 'Let's go and sit on the green box.'

I ran across the road, jumped up onto the box and promptly fell over the other side. Laughing, Paul helped me up.

'You're a clown, Docherty.'

Several clumsy attempts later we managed to perch on our improvised seat. There we sat, with legs kicking the side. The years fell away and we were twelve years old again. We looked at one another and an unspoken message passed between us. A message of mutual affection, one we both understood but felt too constrained to acknowledge.

'Shame about your mum, mate,' Paul said, momentarily lost in reverie. 'I had a massive thing about her when I was a kid.'

'Fuck off,' I said and punched his arm again.

He grinned. 'All the guys did.'

'No way,' I said in disbelief. 'You sure you're talking about my mum?' That wasn't how I remembered her at all.

'If the term MILF had been coined back then she was it. She was always happy to buy cigs and drink for kids loitering outside the Co-op. Always winking at the lads. Connor Davidson said she felt his arse one day and was totally up for it.'

'As if,' I replied. 'Connor Davidson was always saying women liked him.' Then I withdrew from Paul's comment. It felt like we were moving into disrespectful territory.

Paul read the shift in my mood and apologised.

'That was the drink. Ignore me,' he slurred. 'Jesus, I've got no class.'

We were silent for a while as if we were both wondering how to shift back into a more agreeable mindset.

'So, what now?' Paul asked.

'I'm going home to sleep. I'm absolutely knackered,' I answered as I brushed dirt from my knees.

'That's not what I mean,' Paul studied me. 'One shoe in a box in the attic, and it's covered in blood? That's weird.'

I looked off into the distance. From above pockets of diffuse electric light illuminated a series of cars, hedges and houses all the way down the street. But I saw nothing, my mind held by the mystery.

'And I'm too tired to think about it anymore.'

We hopped off the green box and began the last leg of the journey towards Mum's house. I stopped at the gate before I pushed it open.

'Want to come in? One for the road?' I hoped he was going to say yes. I didn't want to carry on drinking into the night on my own.

'Thanks, mate,' Paul grinned. 'I'm too old for this shit. I'm practically craving my bed.'

'Bollocks. We're still youngsters. And so is the night.'

Paul snorted. 'Thirty is the new eighteen.' He stepped into the space I had studiously kept between us and wrapped me in a bear hug.

'Cheers, Paul,' I said into his neck, at last trusting myself to speak.

'Aye,' he said, his throat sounding as if it was too tight. He let me go, and stepped back. 'You'd better keep in touch, Docherty.'

I looked at him, my eyes straying down towards his scar.

'I'm sorry,' I said. 'I've never stopped being sorry.' And I braced myself for any recriminations.

'I know,' he said quietly. 'That's why I still love you, man.'

And we were back in that moment. Two fourteen-year-olds walking home from school, arguing about a football game. We'd been on opposing sides. Paul was convinced I'd handled the ball before scoring. I hadn't, and he wouldn't shut up about it.

Instead of laughing it off, which I usually did when faced with Paul's keen competitive streak, I grew angrier and angrier. And angrier. The next few moments were a blur, but I came to with him at my feet, a large stick in my hand and Paul holding his face.

Thankfully, giving vent to my anger in such way left an indelible mark on my conscience, and I never again lost my temper to such a degree.

'He could have lost an eye,' both my mother and Paul's shouted at me after he'd been stitched up at the local hospital.

'I forgave you a long time ago,' Paul repeated now.

Unable to meet his gaze, I reached across and patted his shoulder.

'That anger,' his voice raised in a question, 'had to come from somewhere – did your dad ever … hurt you?'

'What?'

'You always seemed so angry at him. Always complaining about him.'

'I was?'

He nodded.

I turned to my memory but there was nothing.

'He was a good man. Mostly,' I said, hearing a strange note in my voice. What was it? Denial? 'He loved us. Would have done anything for us.'

The photos of Chris and I in the bath imposed themselves in my mind. The clear skin, freshly painted trust in our eyes…

'Anything,' I repeated, wondering who I was trying to convince. 'He would have done anything for us.'

4

My mother's good eye sparkled when she saw me when I went for a visit the next morning, and her mouth moved to the side in her new version of a smile.

'Okay, son?' she managed to ask.

I nodded, and regretted the movement, which fired off a pulse of pain in my head. Faking a smile, I debated for a moment if I should ask her about what I had found in the attic. Then I spent the next thirty minutes breaking up long spells of silence with chat about what Paul and I had been up to the night before, detailing the various people I'd seen in the pub.

'You know I'm going to have to sell the house,' I said before I'd thought through how I was going to address this issue.

She didn't respond. At first. She just stared at me with her one functioning eye. Her scrutiny was unbearable. It felt like I had failed her.

'Sss'okay, son,' she said. Then she closed her eye and her small frame shook with emotion.

'There's no way round it, Mum. You deserve the best of care and I'm…'

She reached for my hand and squeezed. A movement that had all the power of a leaf landing on my skin.

'Don't worry … be fine.' She swallowed. 'Always loved … that house.'

'So sorry, Mum. There's no other option. I can't see any other way.'

I felt a little more pressure bear down on my hand from hers. 'Always dreamed of … of living by sea,' she said, her face tight with concentration as if she was struggling to find the right words. 'Away from the city. Away from…' She looked at me and for a moment it felt like she was about to tell me something momentous. Then she turned away and focused her gaze out of the window, towards the North Ayrshire seascape. It was a grey early-winter's day and in the weak light cloud blended into the mountains of Arran, which in turn seeped into the sea. Solid lines made hazy as nature coalesced and blurred.

Leaving the nursing home, I felt drained. There was barely enough strength in my thighs to negotiate the stairs. It felt horrible telling Mum that I'd have to sell the house.

I phoned Angela, told her how Mum had been, and with the promise of a nice dinner ringing in my ear we arranged a day to meet.

Seated in my car I considered what I should do next. I toyed briefly with the idea of going back to Mum's to carry on clearing out the loft. But that required an energy I didn't possess. Finally, I decided I needed some distance from all of this and aimed my wheels at the road that would take me back to Glasgow. School was back tomorrow and I had some marking to do.

Home was a two-bedroom Georgian flat in an area of the city inhabited predominately by students. The rooms were enormous – high-ceilinged and draughty, and they proved near impossible to heat in winter. When I moved in the walls were dotted with Blu Tack, the only remnant of legions of homesick students who had surely toiled over their books while they struggled to keep warm under a mass of blankets.

Parking my car, I was not too happy to see that someone had stolen my usual spot – right in front of the entrance to my flat. Nice car though, I thought, appreciating the sleek lines of the black BMW.

There was someone sitting in the driver's seat. As I walked by the car, I slowed my step and attempted to peer in through the tinted window. I was rewarded with a flash of white teeth. Then the door opened and the driver jumped out and bellowed, 'How's it hanging, big brother?'

It took me a moment to register who was standing in front of me. 'Chris. What the hell are you doing here?'

'What kind of welcome is that for the prodigal?' Chris demanded with a grin.

Before I could answer, he was round my side of the car and had enveloped me in a hug. Still resenting him for leaving me to deal with Mum on my own, I self-consciously pulled away from him, but not before I got a good nose full of whatever wacky substance he'd been smoking.

'Well, you'd better come in,' I smiled, trying to hide my confusion.

I fumbled with the key and opened the security door, then led the way upstairs to my flat on the first floor. When we got into the living room, he bounded across the room and dumped himself onto one of the armchairs.

'Cool place you've got here, man. But what's with the Marvel poster?'

'It's in a frame,' I said defensively. 'That makes it more grown-up.'

He snorted an 'Aye, right' and was then on his knees in front of my TV, examining the pile of PS4 games that lay there. 'Still into all this shit?' he asked.

'It's a great way to unwind after dealing with kids all day, and it helps keep an old man relevant.'

Chris nodded slowly as if he saw the sense in what I said. 'Cool.'

I ignored the transatlantic sheen he rolled over his vowels and gave him the once-over.

'You're looking well,' I said. He was broad-shouldered, slim-waisted and perhaps taller than I remembered. And he was expensively dressed, tanned and his long, sun-bleached hair reached almost to his shoulders.

'Thanks,' he replied. 'You look like shit.'

'Hang on a minute,' I laughed. 'The usual routine is half an hour of pleasantries, then the insults begin.'

'Why waste time…' he grinned. 'Sorry I didn't reply to your email. Reception was patchy where we were.' He paused 'How is she?' He asked the question as if out of a sense of duty rather than a need to know.

'Oh, you know,' I grimaced. 'Shit.' I smiled. 'When you going down to see her?'

Chris joined me on the sofa, leaned forwards in his seat, elbows on his knees. 'I'm sorry I wasn't home in time to help out, John. It sounds as if it was really rough.'

'Will be good to get your help when we go down to clear out the house.'

'Yeah…' he said, looking away from me. There was a strong reluctance there.

'I need your help, Chris,' I said. 'I'm tired of dealing with her all on my own.'

His shoulders slumped, and he sat back in his chair. Then, as if he'd made a decision, he slapped a hand on his thigh and jumped to his feet.

'Where's my manners? And where's the nearest off-licence? How about I get some wine in?'

I stood in front of him. 'What's going on, Chris?'

'I'm thirsty, brother. Tell me where the nearest offy is and I'll be back in a jiffy.' He stretched into the pocket of his jeans and pulled out a smart phone. 'Never mind. I can find it on this. And I'll be back before you can rinse off the manky glasses in your kitchen.' He gave me the full glare of the Chris smile. All teeth and sparkly eyes. 'Great to see you, man.' And he was out of the door before I could say anything more.

Twenty minutes later he was back with two bottles of red wine and two massive bags of crisps. He held them before him as he walked back in the door.

'Since when did Scotland get with it on the fancy flavour front? Thai sweet chilli, or sea salt with balsamic vinegar? So cool. I couldn't decide which to get so I bought both.'

'When was the last time you were back in the country, Chris? We've had these for ages.' I registered a note of irritation in my voice and fought to temper it with a smile as big as his. But gave up. There was no way I could compete with him on that, and his high-energy act was already getting on my nerves. 'And dial down on the enthusiasm, will you? You're giving me a headache.'

'Okay, okay,' he said as he walked towards the kitchen. 'I hear you. It's all those grey skies,' he said. 'Makes you a miserable bastard.'

'Wanker.'

'Fannybaws,' he shot back and his Scottish accent was back in full play. I laughed. He joined me.

'Just two bottles?' I asked as I walked into the kitchen and pulled out a couple of glasses. 'What are you going to drink?'

Chris rolled his eyes and then followed me as I walked through to the living room. We settled down on the sofa with a bowl of crisps each and a glass of wine.

'In your last email you were six months into a relationship with a rich American. How's that going?'

'See that BMW I arrived in?'

'She's that rich she bought it for you?' I was incredulous.

'Eejit. She rented it.'

'So, you're a kept man?'

He sipped at his wine. 'That noise is the penny dropping.'

'Nice work if you can get it,' I said.

'She's amazing,' he said, his eyes shining.

'What? Is little brother in love?'

He raised his glass.

'Name?'

'Marjory.'

'Not very American. Just how rich is she?'

'None of your business.'

'Where is this amazing lady just now?'

'She's back at the hotel.'

'Why didn't you bring her to meet me?'

'Because I wanted to see you on my own first, we've a lot of catching up to do.' He grew solemn. 'I've missed you, you know.'

'Yeah right,' I answered, feeling myself shrink into my seat and away from the implied affection, but simultaneously pleased at his response.

'You're the only brother I've got.' He looked deep into my eyes. Assessing. Probing. It made me feel uncomfortable. 'I don't want us to be strangers anymore, John.'

I was touched, perhaps it was time for both of us to grow up. But not quite yet. There was still some undealt with resentment on my part.

'How long are you and Marjory staying in Glasgow?' I asked.

He laughed. 'After me saying I no longer want us to be strangers, we're leaving tomorrow. We're on Marjory's version of the Grand Tour.' He spoke the last two words in a self-mocking tone. 'We're going all around Europe. Driving down to London tomorrow – hence the car. Then flying across to mainland Europe and Paris, Madrid, Prague. Should be a lot of fun.'

'Good for you.' I couldn't disguise how disappointed I felt.

His expression slumped, then darkened as he read my tone. He held his hands out to the side. 'I can't do it, John. I can't.' There was a sense of deep pain in his eyes.

'You didn't come back for Dad's funeral. And now you're leaving me to cope with family stuff on my own again. Fucksake, Chris. Doing the drug and beach tour thing while you were still a kid was fine, but it's time to grow up.'

I looked away from him, out of the window. Then I put my glass down and, crossing my arms, folded into myself. It was great to see him again, but the realisation that he was only here by accident and on his own terms hurt.

'Really? You're giving me the "grow up" line?' He looked around. 'This flat is like the space where boys' toys go to die.'

'Shut up. You love it.'

'True,' he grinned. He closed his eyes, exhaled. Then he looked over at me with a conciliatory smile. 'We've got a table booked at the hotel for dinner in an hour. Join us? Marjory would love to meet you.'

'Sorry,' I said feeling a little spiteful, then instantly regretting it. 'I've got a busy night. Lots of papers to mark and hand over to students in the morning.' I was caught between resentment of him and pleasure that he wanted to spend the time with me.

'My bad,' he said. 'I should have warned you we were coming.' He clapped hard down on his thighs. 'But I wanted it to be a surprise.'

'Yeah, well.' I fought to keep my tone even. 'All the time with Mum over the last few days means I'm behind on my work, so I need to spend the evening elbows deep in teen angst.'

'I hear you,' Chris said as if he was acknowledging how let-down I felt. 'Next time I'm over you and I will really talk.' His blue eyes pierced mine.

'What's that supposed to mean?' I asked with a sinking feeling. The words 'really talk' were heavy with importance. At least to him. What did he need to talk to me about? I'd had enough of revelations. Life could get back on an even keel any time soon.

'Never mind; it will keep for now.' He stood up, indicating it was time for him to leave.

I had a thought. 'Can you hold on a minute? There's something I need to show you.'

'Sure,' he replied with a quizzical look on his face. I pulled the photo out of my jacket pocket and handed it to him.

'What's this?' he asked, looking from me to the photo. He squinted, then smiled. 'Eeesh, when did you ever have a haircut like this? Flat-top boy. And who's the kid?' He looked over at me. 'I recognise Portencross. Some family outing that, eh? Half a mile down the road.' Then, back down to the photo: 'Hang on … That car has a weird number plate. Whose car was that?'

'I'm guessing Dad's. Why would he take a photo of me leaning against someone else's car?'

He turned the photo over and read what Dad had written there.

'That's his writing.' He made a face. 'Why am I not in this picture? It says "the boys" here. That was always how Mum and Dad referred to us two.' He paused. 'This makes no sense.' He looked back to the photo. 'And the car – it's old.' He looked back up at me.

I read the look and knew instantly where he was going. 'That was always Dad's thing, wasn't it? A new car every two years,' I said. And he had a thing for Fords.

'This is a Ford Sierra,' Chris said.

He was always a bit of a petrol-head so I took his word for it.

'And look at your hair … and Jesus, that shell suit. When did you ever have a shell suit?'

I shook my head, utterly mystified.

Chris brought out his phone, and tapped on the screen as he mumbled about Ford Sierras.

'Right,' he read. 'Those cars were phased out in 1989. No way did Dad have a Sierra when you were a teenager. He would have gone on to the Mondeo by then.' He went back to the photo. 'The smaller kid though…' He looked at me, his mouth hanging open.

'What's going on?' I asked, feeling the world shift around me.

His face was pale with the realisation. 'You're the infant here, John.'

'What?'

'Look closer at the older boy. Sure, he looks like you … but he doesn't quite … Jesus.' He put the photo down on the sofa as if burned. 'Now that I've thought about it, how could I possibly think that's you? The hair, the tracksuit … the face. It's almost you … but not.'

I shoved my hands in my pockets as if afraid to touch the thing, but still bent over to get a better look. Chris was right. The older boy wasn't me.

'Fuck,' I said. 'There could be more.' I told him about the shoe.

He rubbed at his scalp and stared across at me. 'What the hell have you stumbled onto?'

5

For minutes we sat in silence, each of us struggling to process the implications of the photo.

'But…' Chris began, then shaking his head he lapsed back into silence. Moments later: 'It explains why I'm not in the photo.'

'The resemblance is weird.'

'Uncanny,' Chris agreed. 'And Dad wrote "the boys". He has to be our brother.'

'That's quite a stretch.' I shook my head and made a face. Chris had always been the imaginative one. 'He could be anybody.'

'"The boys". Not "John and cousin whoever". "The boys".' He paused. 'And what cousins do we have, anyway?'

I considered what I knew about our parents' extended families. Dad was an only child. His parents struggled to have children, we were told, and had him when they were in their early forties. They were both long gone. Mum had two sisters. I couldn't remember much about them.

'Do you remember Dad having any mates that would bring their kids round to ours for a wee trip?' I asked.

'Harry Bone? But I don't remember him ever popping round with his kids.'

'Aye, Harry's a good bit older than Dad. His kids would have been almost grown-ups by the time we were born.'

Chris pulled his phone out and thumbed at the screen. I heard it dial out.

'Hey babe,' he said. 'Something incredibly…' he paused as if trying to find the word '…strange has come up. Mind if I miss dinner tonight? I'm sorry, I hate the idea of you eating on your own, but this is…'

I could hear a tinny voice coming from his phone. Not clearly enough to work out what was being said, but the tone sounded supportive.

'Thanks, babe. I'll be back as soon as I can. Love you.' He hung up. Then without pausing he asked. 'And how come no one in the village ever asked us about him? I mean if we had a brother, and presumably something happened to him, why did *no one* ever talk about it?'

'That's small towns for you. Closed ranks. Displayed collective amnesia. Our parents didn't want to go there so no one else did?'

Chris made a face. 'I can see lots of people complying with that. But all of them?'

'There's a simple explanation, surely.'

'When did Mum and Dad move down here?' Chris asked. 'I can remember stories Dad telling us about the characters he grew up with in Glasgow – the gang stuff, the tenements and how he was desperate for a bit of sea air.'

'The place in the photo is definitely Portencross.'

'Maybe that was a wee day trip. Maybe they came down here all the time for holidays and stuff, and that's why they ended up moving here. And maybe that's why nobody we grew up with knew.'

I could see the sense of that. Something happens and they move to get away from the memories. 'Jesus,' I said. 'I can't take this in. What the hell's going on here?'

6

When Chris went back to his hotel, I brought out the hard stuff, had a few more drinks and phoned Angela to tell her what we'd discovered.

'What's wrong, babes?' she said when she answered, her voice tinged with alarm. 'It's the middle of the night.'

I looked at my watch. It was 2:25 a.m.

'Shit. Sorry,' I said. 'I thought it was only about midnight.'

'Midnight's still a bit on the late … Have you been drinking?' she asked. 'Haven't you got work in the morning?'

'Just had a wee party with my erstwhile brother.' I giggled at how I managed to mangle the word erstwhile. 'Have I told you lately that I love you?'

'John, that's lovely.' I could hear her shift in her bed. 'But really? I've got work in the morning. You've got work in the morning.' She yawned, and I got a picture of her stretching, and felt a surge of affection.

'I didn't thank you for coming with me to see Mum the other day. That was kind of you.'

'You're welcome, John, but can't we do this in the—'

'So kind. You are a sweetheart, you know that?'

'I'm a sweetheart, thank you.' I could hear her smile despite her tiredness. 'But you didn't phone at this ridiculous time to tell me that.'

'No, no, no,' I said. Then I told her about the box with the shoe, and the photo.

'You thought the photo was you at first?'

'It was the hair style that gave it away. I never had a mullet.'

At this Angela started laughing. 'You with a mullet. That would be hilarious.'

'And a shell suit.'

She snorted. 'Who is this boy then?'

'Chris is convinced he's our brother, but I don't know. That's a massive thing to keep from your kids. There must be another reason for this boy's stuff being in my parents' house.'

'From what you've said in the past, Chris tends to be a wee bit dramatic.' She yawned again. 'I'm sure there's a plausible explanation.' I could hear the swish of cloth on cloth as she moved on the bed. I would have given anything to be with her.

'Postcard moment: wish I was there,' I said.

'A postcard would read *wish you were here.*'

'You know what I mean.'

She was silent, and in her silence I knew where her mind was going. The debate surfaced regularly. We led separate lives. I was selfish. I was commitment-phobic. I was a bachelor. And if I really wanted to be there, I could be.

'Anyway, I just wanted to talk to you. Big news, eh? I could have had another brother.'

'I'm sure there's another more plausible explanation, John,' she repeated and stifled another yawn.

'Sorry I woke you,' I said in a whisper. 'But you shouldn't have your phone by your bed, so it serves you right.'

'Idiot.' She laughed, and hung up.

My mother's eye was large. And accusatory. Her fingers curved into a claw, as she stretched towards me. Imploring.

'You don't love me. You've never loved me. How could you leave me in here?'

Words like barbs.

'You never cared about me … I gave you everything and you do this to me?'

Shame and guilt covering me, weighing on me like thick, black oil, my answer, my weak attempt at justification, dying in my throat.

Silenced by my remorse, my tongue lay as still as a corpse in a drawer at the morgue.

'I gave you all the love I had and you leave me here…

'Just like your father…

'Just like your father…

'Just like…'

I shot up out of bed so quickly my head spun.

What was that noise? Light blasted through my barely open eyelids. Must have been the postman. I felt sick. I made it to the bathroom just in time.

When I pushed myself back up from the pan, I remembered with a squirm of embarrassment being in here during the night, for the same reason. After thoroughly washing my hands I made my way back to bed. There, I sank into the pillows. No way could I go to school in this state. The head would smell the drink on me, order me home and write me up.

'Disappointed in you, Mr Docherty,' I could hear him say.

Again.

I needed to get my act together or I'd be out of a job. And I would have no one to blame but myself.

Invoking a silent promise to do better, I reached for my mobile. I read on the screen that I'd made a call in the middle of the night to Angela. Shit. What nonsense did I spout to her? I'd call later and apologise. In the meantime I had a school secretary to call and convince I was ill.

That wouldn't be too difficult in my current state.

By noon, however, I was feeling almost alive and decided I should make use of my day off. I'd go see my dad's old mate Harry. If anyone knew our family secrets it was him.

Gravel popped and crunched under the car, and the branches of the trees that lined the drive seemed to surge and whisper at me in the strong wind as I made my way up to Lennox House.

In a corner of my mind a voice intoned that this was a mistake. Let dormant secrets lie, it said. But I was on a track and couldn't stop.

As I parked in front of the house I considered my conversation with Chris the previous evening. He appeared genuinely sorry that he was having to leave me at that moment; but he reasoned that this mystery had existed all our lives, so waiting a few weeks or even months until he got back to help wouldn't make much difference. This was a trip Marjory had been planning for a long time and he didn't want to let her down.

'I get it,' I had said. 'It's not a problem. Perhaps it's best we don't go diving into this anyway. Who knows what we might find out?' I gave him a hug as he left. 'Have a great time on your trip, and if anything else pops up…'

'What, like a link to the royal family?' He grinned.

'Knowing our luck it would the relative with the hunched back, locked in the tower.'

We hugged again before he jumped in his car, and that felt good. A reassurance. I wasn't entirely on my own.

Rain sparked against the windscreen as I released my seatbelt. I should stop. Go home and put this behind me. I shrugged off the thought, climbed out of my car, and ran the ten steps to the front door regretting that I'd left my jacket at home.

Inside, the receptionist took a moment before looking up from her paperwork,

'How can I help you?' she asked.

'I'm looking for Harry Bone,' I replied, taking in the cloying smell from the flowers on her desk, and feeling a little guilty that I wasn't going to see my mother first.

'Oh … and are you a relative?' Her smile came and went in a flash.

'No,' I answered, surprised by her question. 'I'm a family friend.'

Harry and my dad were not only colleagues, they'd been great mates. Surely on one of their long night shifts, while they waited for the local miscreants to get busy, they'd shared a few secrets? And it was no surprise that he and Mum were both in the same nursing home. There was only one other in the area, but it had been taken over by a new company, and in a place like this people took a while to accept newcomers.

'Room thirty-two, second floor.' Smile. 'There's a lift just round the corner beyond the stairwell.'

I walked over to the wide staircase and started to climb its carpeted steps. But now that I was here I started to question my reasoning. Would Harry remember me or my family? Would he be able to tell me anything? Would he want to see me? And what the hell was I doing here? That picture couldn't be my long-lost brother. I was kidding myself on. Looking for something to distract me from my worries.

I was so lost in this chain of thought I almost walked by Harry's door. Slightly out of breath, I paused before knocking. I should go. I was wasting everyone's time.

Then a loud voice ordered, 'Ye can come in.'

I hadn't yet knocked, but feeling like a schoolboy ordered to see the headmaster I entered the room. The space before me was huge. It had high corniced ceilings, wide walls and an expanse of grey carpet. The only furniture, a television set, a small desk, a massive wardrobe and a bed tucked away in a corner. Apart from a different view, this could have been my mother's room.

The owner of the commanding voice lay propped up on his pillow. 'I could hear you breathing even through a closed door,' the man said. 'You need to take up jogging, son.'

'I'm sorry…' I offered while thinking he was right. I was badly out of shape. 'I think I've come to the wrong room. I'm looking for Harry Bone.'

'Aye, well, you've found him.'

Astonishment loosened my jaw and I gaped at the man before me. I expected the years to have altered him somewhat, but this? Trying to hide my shock, I corrected my expression and smiled weakly at the dried-up apple core of a man propped up on the pillows.

Harry's bald pate was pale and liver-spotted, with a monk's tonsure of sparse silver hair. His skin was paper thin and almost translucent, and the long, thin lump under the sheets hinted at the damage that disease and old age had visited upon him.

'Jings, if it's not young Docherty.'

'Hello, Mr Bone.'

'Come in, son, come in and sit down, and for fuck's sake call me Harry.'

I smiled. A memory of Harry in my mum's kitchen. My mother giving him a row for swearing in front of us kids.

'To what do I owe this pleasure, young Docherty?' And without waiting for a reply he continued, 'Sit down, son. My, you've filled out. That's polite speak for "you're a bit of a fat bastard", by the way.' He cackled, then a deep cough rattled his frail form and pain clouded his eyes. 'Oh son, old age doesn't come by itself. So…' he said, piercing me with his grey eyes, '…what's up?'

Not wanting to get straight to the point I said, 'I was visiting my mum and somebody mentioned you were also a patient here.' I coughed. 'Thought it would be nice to say hello.'

His eyes were rheumy and bloodshot but they missed nothing. 'Whatever your reason is, son, it's fucking good to see you,' he said kindly. 'How's that mother of yours?'

'She's…' I wondered how much to tell him. 'She's just been given a room in here, Harry.'

'I fucken know that, son. I'm old, no' stupid. I'm asking how she is.'

'Feels like she's getting better every time I see her,' I lied.

'Illness is a bastard, eh? Fine woman, so she is. If she hadn't been married to your old man, I would have run away with her years ago.' This was arrant nonsense, as anyone who had a pair of eyes and had spent any time with Harry and his wife could see that he was hopelessly devoted to her.

'How's your wife keeping, Harry?' I asked.

'Oh son, she passed away six months ago,' he answered with the matter-of-fact compassion that only the old can muster. 'Aye, she was done in looking after her old man.' He paused, his eyes distant. 'Six months, that's how long I've been in this place. Anyway, that's enough about me. Tell me about you. What's happened to you in the past few years? Married? Working? Kids?'

While I answered his questions Harry's eyes never left my face. He nodded at appropriate times and in a voice that resembled the purr of a tiger he punctuated my sentences with a series of 'Aye's'.

'And how's that young brother of yours doing? Still working for that newspaper?'

That newspaper was a local newspaper based in Bermuda, the only real job Chris got following his journalism degree at Napier University. Mum hid her disappointment over Chris going to the other side of the world to work by bragging to everyone she knew that her son was an international correspondent in the Caribbean. She never quite forgave him when he binned that in favour of soft drugs and beach-hopping.

Soon the subject came around to the real reason for my visit and I handed Harry the photo and told him about finding it and the shoe among my father's stuff in the attic. I halted in my speech and with a churning stomach I waited to hear if he could shed any light on the boy in the picture.

He looked at the picture. Looked at me. And then back to the picture. Then he sucked on his teeth, and produced another hacking cough.

'Where did you say you found this?' he asked, when he recovered, his expression inscrutable.

'In the attic,' I replied, feeling a sense of strong disappointment when I realised he wasn't going to tell me anything. 'I was clearing my dad's stuff out—'

'I'm feeling awfy tired, son.' Harry slumped back onto his pillows, and with a note of regret said, 'You should go now.' He studied my face and then his gaze slid away from me. It may have been my imagination but his energy levels had completely faded and there was a defeated tone in his voice.

'Can you tell me anything about the boy in this picture?' I asked, trying to hide my desperation. I was beginning to feel that this task was beyond me.

'Aye. It's you.'

'But…'

'But, sorry, son,' he puffed. 'I'm fair wrung out. Need my sleep.' He shoved the photo back at me, as if it might burn him. Then he closed his eyes and turned from me.

What the hell just happened?

Harry had been delighted to see me, but the second I brought out that photo he shut down. He knew something, I was certain.

'Harry?'

He stared out of the window.

Realising that I was going to get nothing from him, I sighed, turned and walked towards the door. When I reached out for the door handle I heard a rustle from the bed as the old man moved. I turned back, hoping he was about to offer me something.

'If you'll excuse an old man for speaking out of turn…' He paused while another cough wracked his frail form. He spat onto a tissue and then wiped his lips. 'I loved your old dad like a brother. He was a fine, fine, man,' he said as if he was keen to offer me something, without breaking any promises. 'You need to go, son, before I say too much. But think on this: only an eejit runs away from the present by burying himself in the past.'

7

I left Harry's room, crushed by disappointment. The old man knew something. Of that I had no doubt. But why was he being so tight-lipped? Who was he protecting?

Standing with my back to his closed door I considered going back in and having one more attempt at getting him to open up. But the way he'd turned over on his bed, presenting his back to me, was too strong a signal to ignore. If I returned to the room, I'd surely only alienate him.

Perhaps the next time I came to see Mum I could try him again.

My feet felt heavy as I made my way downstairs and out to my car. I'd called in sick for nothing. It was all a waste of time. And there were still all those papers to mark and a head teacher who would be scrutinising every sick day I had from then on.

Almost on automatic, I drove to my parents' house instead of going back up to the city. Once inside, I wandered through the downstairs rooms as if searching for some sign of them.

In the living room, I sat in my mother's seat facing the TV and looked around the room, trying to see it as a prospective buyer might. It could do with a fresh coat of magnolia and a reduction in the number of flower-based patterns, but like the kitchen everything was in its place.

As I shifted in the seat my right foot connected with something on the floor. I looked down to see an opened TV magazine lying there. That was out of character, I thought as I leaned over to see down past the arm of the chair to the stand where Mum kept her reading material, which like this one, was mostly magazines report-ing and dissecting what was on the telly. Mum loved soaps, and when the programmers made *The X Factor* and *Strictly* overlap she had a strop. How could she miss even a minute of one of them? This was compounded by the fact she couldn't cope with technology and had no idea how to record anything.

It occurred to me that Mum might have been reading this magazine when her stroke happened. It really would take something that major for her standards of tidiness to lapse.

Mum.

I felt a tightening in my throat at the thought of her lying in that bed in the nursing home. Her hand reaching for mine. Just like in my dream. And felt shame that I wanted to move away before she touched me. Her disintegration after the stroke was just too difficult to witness. I could hardly bear any contact with her.

Enough. I got to my feet, feeling the purpose in my thighs, reminding myself I was here for a reason.

The air in the attic was thick with dust, and although the floor space was mostly covered a tidiness had been imposed. Order in the chaos of experiences and lives shed. Nothing had simply been thrown up here. Instead, it felt like everything had its own space.

Perhaps it was Dad who'd been the clean freak? Was Mum's work in the house her effort to appease her husband?

The small box with the shoe in it was still on top of the larger box, where I'd left it previously. I picked it up and brought it to my nose, hoping my brain would pick up some signal from its scent. But sadly there was nothing there but the stale smell that permeated the room.

I continued sifting through the detritus of my family's life, but instead of thinking about what could be recycled to charity shops, or what should be taken to the town dump, my question when I touched something was, would this offer up any clues?

The ceiling was low so I'd alternate between standing up and bending at the neck, or bending my knees and stooping over. After what felt like several hours of this my neck was sore and my back was aching so much that I was on the point of giving up. There was nothing of note in this attic that would teach me anything about this other boy. Just the photo and the stained shoe.

It was then that I found something in the furthest corner, and it felt like everything else had led to this moment. Looking back over my shoulder to the ladder I noted there was even a sort of path, as if this was a natural route my father had taken every time he'd been up here.

The light shifted. The room grew even darker despite the small bulb. The building creaked. A gust of wind, and I could hear a loose slate on the outside of the roof above me clicking back down into position.

I reached out to the box, and with the index finger of my right hand I drew a line across the thick dust that had settled on the top. How long had this been here?

The box had been sealed with brown tape, but the adhesive was no longer effective, and the tape came off with little effort. Feeling trepidation about what I might find, I pushed the box leaves out of the way and peered inside.

The first thing I spotted was a pair of football boots – black with three white stripes. I plucked one out and compared it, sole to sole with the solitary shoe. They were a match. Next I saw a Scotland football scarf and a football programme. Scotland versus Spain in November 1984. Someone had written the score across the cover – 3–1 to Scotland, as if they couldn't believe it.

Pushing those to the side I noticed a mix of vinyl, CDs and cassettes – U2, Bruce Springsteen and Prince.

Tucked away in the bottom corner was a paperback. Michael Moorcock's *Elric of Melnibone and Other Stories*. It looked like it had been a much-loved read. The paper seemed to warm to my touch as I leafed through the pages, noting where they'd been turned down at the corners, and where the spine had been cracked.

On the first page I saw the sticker for a library. It had been taken out of the Mitchell Library in Glasgow numerous times. The last entry was for the 10th March, 1986.

I felt shock, and an ineffable sadness. A living, breathing boy had handled this book. It had been in his bedroom when he'd left my parents' lives – and my life too – and it felt like I was following in this boy's footsteps. Who was he? Did Mum have another child before she had us? Dad was a little bit older than Mum, so perhaps he'd been married before and this boy was from that relationship. Or maybe he was the offspring from another relative? His resemblance to me was striking.

Jesus.

This was like something from a movie.

And again I wondered: if he was my brother why would our parents keep this from us?

Now he was more than a mysterious image in an old photograph. He played football, listened to music, read books. He'd possibly lived in this house. So what had happened to him, and why had my parents never mentioned him? I imagined all of this stuff strewn around one of the bedrooms downstairs. And felt with certainty that I had to carry on looking into this. Regardless of who it might hurt.

Then it occurred to me that this was my father's space. This was his way of remembering his son – whatever had become of him. And if he had his space where he would sit quietly in remembrance, surely my mother had hers?

8

As kids we were never allowed into our parents' bedroom. We were told, if we wanted something while our parents were inside, to knock and wait for an answer. This rule was so heavily imprinted on my psyche, even with one parent dead and the other in a nursing home, it took a solid effort to cross the threshold of their ground-floor room.

Two single beds about a foot apart were the focal point of the room, the covers were hotel-smooth, and with the soft purple throw at the foot, and masses of pillows and cushions at the head of each bed, it looked as if it had just been staged for a boutique hotel photo-shoot.

As a kid, knowing my parents slept in single beds didn't seem odd. It was just the way it was. But viewing this through adult eyes does suggest a lack of intimacy and reinforced my thought that there was an emotional distance between them.

Under the bed nearest the door, sat a pair of red-velvet slippers, my Christmas present to my mum two years ago.

With a heavy sigh, I walked over, picked them up, felt the lightness of them and wondered how much use she'd get from them in future. I shook that thought from my head and put them back. I made a mental note to take them with me next time I visited. Mum was certainly far away from placing her feet on the ground, but ... you never knew.

I got to my knees and checked under the bed. Nothing. Not even a suggestion of dust. Then I checked both bedside cabinets. Apart from some TV magazines, three pairs of reading glasses, a basket of heated rollers and a selection of shampoos, make-up and perfumes there was nothing worth further investigation.

Inside the wardrobe, under rows of her skirts and dresses, I found an old suitcase tucked into a far corner. I pulled it out. Judging by its lack of heft, it was empty, but I needed to be sure, so I placed it on the bed, zipped it open and had a look inside.

Nothing.

Once I'd checked every available corner of the room, I stepped back to the doorway and scanned it all. There had to be something; who loses a child and keeps nothing of them? There was something, somewhere, I was sure.

I looked back at the wardrobe. There was a space of about twelve inches between the top of it and the ceiling. Could there be something stashed up there?

Pulling over a chair, I placed it in front of the wardrobe and stepped up. And there, just within reach were two small shoeboxes. I picked them up carefully, and one at a time placed them on the bed.

I stared at them for a long moment, feeling a little nervous, suddenly filled with the importance of what I might discover. Did I really want to find out? My hands were sweating, my mouth dry, and my pulse was heavy in my throat.

Taking a breath I sat beside the boxes, telling myself it was probably just going to be a lot of receipts and financial stuff. I picked up the heaviest one, sat it on my lap and lifted the lid.

Paper. Lots of it. Cards displaying sympathy. I picked one up and opened it. It was addressed to Mum and was signed 'with love from Dave and Mandy Collins, and all the gang at Maryhill', in an expansive and curly script.

I flipped it over and looked at the front. It all looked very grown up, not a card for a lost child. And it was only addressed to Mum, so must have been sent to her when Dad died.

There were another twenty or so cards in the box. All of them variations on a theme. Sympathies and condolences, with doves, butterflies and flowers. All with verses sweet enough to cause tooth decay.

Only twenty? I could remember the house being strewn with

flowers and cards. Did Mum just keep those from the people important to her?

I recalled a tall man at Dad's funeral, puffy-faced with deep wrinkles and a head of white hair. David Collins, he introduced himself
as. His handshake was strong enough to crush bone, which made
me think he must be a bit of a dick. Only weak men feel the need to
display their strength when they first meet you. 'Worked with your
dad back in the day,' he said.

The woman I took to be his wife placed a hand on my shoulder.
'He was a lovely man, your dad,' she said. 'Just lovely.'

I mumbled my thanks, trying to work out why I'd never met these
people before.

'God, you're his spit,' Mandy said, almost under her breath.
She was silenced by a look from her husband, and before I could
ask her what she meant, someone else stepped in and offered their
condolences

You're his spit, she'd said. She couldn't have been comparing me
with my dad. Everyone said we looked nothing alike.

Mandy and her husband must have known my brother.

I replaced the cards in the box and set it to the side. Then I placed
the other box on my knees and opened it.

A newspaper headline blared up at me.

'Boy, 14 Disappears. Parents Appeal for News'.

With trembling fingers I picked the excerpt up and read:

> A city-wide search is underway for a missing boy, fourteen,
> who disappeared after going out on an errand for his mother.
> Thomas Docherty was last seen riding a sports bike towards
> Duke Street. He has dark-brown hair, and was wearing a navy-
> blue shell-suit top with a white panel on the chest.

Below the article was the same image I'd found among my father's
things, except the lower half of the picture, where I was, had been
cut off.

With reverence I placed the cutting back in the box and took a breath.

Holy shit. I was right.

I pulled my phone out of my pocket, thinking I should send Chris an email. He needed to hear about this. But just as I keyed in my screen password a knock sounded at the door.

It was Paul.

'Hey, big guy,' he smiled. 'I've got a Chinese meal here for you.' He held up a white plastic bag.

'How did you…?'

'Mum. Who else?'

I stepped to one side to allow Paul entry. He walked past me towards the kitchen speaking over his shoulder. 'Sweet 'n' sour chicken?'

'Does it go with whisky?' I asked as I followed him.

Paul served up the food, and I tucked in.

He looked over at the box. 'What's this?'

Swallowing a mouthful of chicken, I told him everything I knew so far.

'We had this brother,' I finished. 'And our parents told us nothing.'

His chin dropped. He looked down at the newspaper cutting and then back at me. 'This is mental. Like something out of a movie.'

'Real life, mate.' I pushed my plate away from me. I'd talked for so long the food was cold.

'Mind if I have a look?' Paul asked, pointing at the shoebox.

I nodded. Paul pulled the box closer, wiped his hand on his trouser leg and stretched inside. He took out a small black jewellery box that must have been tucked into the corner and opened it. Inside there were three little milk teeth.

'Do you think that's one for each of you?' he asked.

'Would make sense.' I reached over and carefully pulled one out then cradled it in my palm. It was tiny. Like an absurdly shaped pearl, with a jagged edge and a stain of blood.

'And, wow. Look at this…' I could hear the reverence in his voice.

It was a form of some kind. He read silently. Then he looked over at me. 'Thomas Docherty. Born in Glasgow in 1975. Father, William Docherty. Mother, Lorna Docherty...' He slid the paper across the table. 'All the proof you need, mate. Your brother's birth certificate.'

9

Paul studied John from across the kitchen table, wondering how he would react if this was his family secret being brought out into the open. 'What are you going to do?'

John looked over at him, mouth hinged open, held in a mute state by the enormity of it all.

'How could your parents not let you know?' Paul asked. 'You got nothing from them? No hints?'

John worked at a knot in the surface of the table, circling it with his index finger.

'Things are starting to make sense,' he said. 'Mum was always terrified when we were late. A minute beyond the time agreed and she was on to the local police station.'

Paul recalled John stealing glances at his wristwatch. 'Yeah, you used to get a bit fidgety when it came close to hometime.'

'There's only the one article about his disappearance in here...' He pulled everything out and scanned through it, paper rubbing against paper whispering in the quiet. 'There's nothing to say what happened next. Did they continue appealing for witnesses? Did the police keep the case open?'

'You mentioned the sandshoe with the blood on it...'

'Aye.'

'Perhaps they accepted that as proof that something horrible happened?'

'Jesus,' John said and leaned back in his seat, crossing his arms as if he was guarding himself against the thought. 'And I can't say anything to my mother.' John sent Paul a warning glance. 'Imagine what that would do to her. How does anyone get over the disappearance of their child? She would have gone through enough at the time ... and I don't want to set off another stroke.'

Paul pursed his lips. Opened his mouth to speak and then closed it again.

'Go on. What were you going to say?' John asked.

'Well, if you're not prepared to ask her … is there any point in you looking into this at all?'

'I can't explain why, Paul.' John said, his expression held in certainty. 'I just need to know.'

Next morning, I phoned in sick again, not before I noted I'd had another late-night call with Angela. My sore head and dry mouth suggested it was another drunken one.

I dialled her number, and before I could say sorry, she started talking.

'Can't talk. I'm getting Cathy ready for school … *and we're running late, Cathy.*' She shouted this last part, aiming it at her daughter. 'Got to go.' She hung up.

As I showered and dressed I considered the tone of her voice. Just how pissed off was she at me? I vowed to keep my phone out of the bedroom so late-night drunken chats were less likely to happen. I must have phoned to tell her about the birth certificate. I prayed I hadn't made a pest of myself.

I drove back over to the nursing home, really wanting to see Harry, but first I had to call in on my mother. A nurse was coming out of her room just as I reached to pull open the door. She smiled at me and spoke quietly. 'Your mum had a troubled night's sleep, Mr Docherty, but she's just settled down now.' She stepped to the side. 'If you want to sit quietly with her, I'm sure she'll appreciate it.'

'Thanks,' I said. And with a stab of guilt I tried to ignore the feeling of relief at what she'd said. It meant I wouldn't have to try and work out what to say to Mum while I was there. I could simply sit in the chair and work out what I was going to say to Harry.

Half an hour later and my mum was still asleep. Her head was turned to the side, away from the weak light coming in from the window, and as I watched her I became all but hypnotised by the slight lift and fall of her chest, lulled by it into something approaching relaxation. At one point I leaned over and carefully wiped some drool from the corner of her mouth. I allowed myself a small smile at this. Doubtless she'd be mortified if she realised.

'Don't 'av to sit 'er all day,' Mum mumbled.

'You're awake?' I asked.

'Just,' she replied after a long moment as if she'd been sorting through the appropriate responses in her mind.

'I was just thinking I needed to be going,' I said. 'So I'm glad you're awake before I do.'

'Oh,' she said, and seemed to look a little disappointed.

'I'll be back tomorrow though,' I said, then leaned forwards and lightly pressed my lips against her forehead. A touch that I held for as short a time as was possible before I moved away. And despite telling myself I had a good reason for leaving, I slipped out of the room, hunched over, like a man leaving a church service too early.

Harry was sitting up in his bed when I arrived, working on a laptop placed on his over-bed table. He peered over his spectacles and addressed me with a nod.

'Do you use that Facebook computer thing?' he asked.

'I've got an account,' I answered, 'but I rarely use it, to be honest.'

'Marvellous thing, son. Marvellous. I'm on this … a page they call it, where I can blether with a bunch of retired cops.' He closed the lid. 'Means I can get out into the world while sat within these four walls.'

I took a seat. 'Mum's looking a wee bit better today,' I said.

'That's good, son.' He studied me as if that wasn't what he expected to come out of my mouth.

'The doctors say she'll never be able to live independently again, but if she can at least speak and make herself understood…' I paused. 'Kinda like you with your Facebook page. Making contact.'

We chatted some more about inconsequentials until Harry pierced me with a look. 'You're not for giving up, are you?'

'When I was last here I got the impression you didn't want to betray a confidence…' I began.

'Your old man was a good friend to me.'

'I get that, but if you could just—'

'I can't, John.' His voice held a tenderness I'd not heard from him before.

'I found his birth certificate,' I said, trying to keep the challenge out of my voice. 'So I know Thomas is … was real.'

'Right.' He looked away from me out of the window, and then back. His face was heavy with regret and sadness. 'I came across a quote the other day. Nietzsche, whoever the fuck he was.' He grinned to show me he knew exactly who he was. '"You can judge a man's spirit by the amount of truth he can tolerate."' Pause. 'Can you tolerate the truth, John?'

I felt a massive weight of pressure across my forehead. Resisting the urge to stroke it, or to show I was in any discomfort, I answered, 'I need to know, Harry. I had a brother. My parents lied to me.'

'They were protecting you,' he said, but I could detect a note of uncertainty as if he couldn't quite understand what keeping this from me would protect me from.

I remembered one of the cards I read in the box. *From the gang at Maryhill.*

'They weren't living here when the … my brother disappeared?'

He was surprised by this turn in the conversation. 'No. They had a flat in Partick.'

'And Dad worked in Maryhill?'

He cocked his head to the side. 'My, aren't we the great detective? I believe it was Maryhill, yes.'

I said nothing, hoping Harry would rush to fill the silence.

After a long pause he said, 'Glasgow born, bred and buttered was how your dad used to describe himself. Until Thomas disappeared. Then your mum pushed your dad to get a transfer, said she needed to get away from all of the memories.'

'Who found the shoe? Did it really belong to Thomas?'

Harry nodded as if his head was suddenly too heavy for him. 'It did. And it was your dad who found it. He said there was a grassy area at the corner of his street where the kids used to play. There was a big fence that ran along a railway. The shoe was down by that fence.' Harry crossed his arms as if guarding himself against the memory of the pain his friend had suffered. 'That crushed your dad. That was the point when he decided your mum was right, that they had to move.'

'And they found nothing else?'

'That was it,' Harry sighed. 'It was if he never existed, was how your dad described it. Vanished into thin air.'

'Did he ever talk about leads? Suspects?'

'Only when he'd a drink in him. Usually he kept a lid on it. Which...' he made a face '...is probably what gave him a heart attack at such a young age. It's not good for you to bottle all that shit up.' He began coughing and was looking like he'd never stop. I was about to pull the cord at the side of his bed when he lay back on his pillow, exhausted.

'Can I get you something,' I asked, half out of my chair.

He grimaced in discomfort. 'Can you hand me that box of tissues?'

I did so, and he plucked one from the box and wiped his mouth. 'There was something about the Shows being in town the week Thomas disappeared, but as I recall nothing came from it.'

The Shows. That was an expression I hadn't heard for a while. It was what Scottish people called the travelling fairgrounds that used to pitch up in an area for a weekend or so, with thrill rides such as waltzers, and stalls where you could win a goldfish or a cuddly toy if you knocked over a couple of tins.

'Among the sympathy cards I found at home I found one from David Collins. You recall Dad ever talking about him?'

'Met him a couple of times.' Harry nodded. 'Didn't have time to get much of an impression … enough, mind you, to think he was a bit of a walloper.'

I smiled. 'Heavy handshake?'

'You got that too?' Harry laughed. Coughed. Then he waited until he'd recovered. 'I'm pretty sure Davie was your dad's contact for what remained of the investigation. They'd keep in touch and Davie would let him know what was happening.'

'Maybe I should chase Davie up, then.'

'Gimme a second.' He reached over towards his laptop and opened it up. He typed with an ease that surprised me and then read from the screen. 'Aye, David Collins. He's in this Facebook group as well, would you believe?' Then silence as he read the screen. 'He hasn't posted for a good while. Maybe he's dead. Or maybe he can't be arsed with Facebook.'

'God forbid,' I replied.

'Leave it with me.' Harry acknowledged my sarcasm with a smile. 'I'll track him down for you.'

Something occurred to me: 'About Mum and Dad moving away – wouldn't they have wanted to be there in case he found his way back home? I mean, if he had disappeared, and there wasn't a body or anything. Wouldn't a parent want to stay in the same location in case he returned?'

Harry's expression was heavy, as if he was back in that moment when his old friend accepted his oldest son was never returning.

'The official line was that Thomas was dead. And they didn't want to be reminded of him all the time. Couldn't face their neighbours' faces. Couldn't deal with the questions – *any news yet*, all that stuff. So when your dad heard about a vacancy down by the coast, they went for it. Moved somewhere nobody knew them, where they could make a fresh start.'

'But why the big secret? Why wouldn't they even tell me and Chris?'

'Who knows, son? Speaking about something bad, even years later, can still take it out of you. And when should they have broken it to you? When you were ten? Eleven? When's the right time to tell your kids you've been holding back something that fucking huge?'

I heard the sense in Harry's words, but still felt an injustice in the fact our parents hadn't been honest with us.

'Why are you helping me now?' I asked Harry.

'That cat isnae going back in the bag, son.' He scratched at the side of his face. 'Your dad told me all about it not long after we started working together. Asked me to tell no one in the village that I knew about this. He didn't want the tragedy to follow him down from Glasgow. And that's what I did … but you found out anyway.' He clasped his hands and let them lie on his lap as if satisfied with his decision. 'Your mum and dad were in denial for years, and I saw how it tore at them. Maybe it's time for this mystery to be solved.'

10

Memory is not to be trusted. It's as mendacious as the shimmer on the surface of a placid lake. Providing an illusion of calm, while beyond the sunless depths the sand and silt are littered with rocks and the debris of life. And there within the roots of a drowned tree, a pike lurks with hate in its unseeing eyes.

I'm trapped in sleep and I can't wake up.

I grab for truth but it eludes me. Slips from my grasp like vapour. I see a face distorted, as if plundered from a Picasso painting. I read the anger. Take all of the blame.

I'm in a dream but I enter memory.

I'm looking into a shattered mirror, the pieces scattered at my feet. Pieces of me corrupted to look smaller. Bigger. Incomplete. The corner of an ear here. A knee there. Lines crowing from the side of my eyes.

The mirror repairs. I peer into it, and where my face should be I see ... a steaming bath, blur of a nose, fog that shifts so my eyes can't rest, and an indistinct profile.

My past is there, but it doesn't belong to me. It belongs to memory and it refuses to release anything to a sensible interpretation. For I know making sense of it will make nonsense of me. And I panic, breathing harsh, pulse heavy, but I dig and dig; thoughts are my shovel, callouses grow, I work so long, and I hit ... something.

I'm naked. Aroused. Scored through with shame. Frozen still, and yet in a fever of anxiety.

This is wrong. So very wrong.

I scream, but no one is listening.

11

Harry was as good as his word. I received an email from him within the day, giving me the address of David Collins. Although Collins himself had gone quiet on the Facebook page another cop who knew him read Harry's post asking Collins to get in touch, and provided Harry with the man's address.

'He's retired now, I'm told, so I'd imagine he'd welcome a chance to blether about the old days,' Harry wrote in his email. 'I'm sure it will be a welcome relief from sitting around, scratching his nuts and watching daytime TV.' This characterisation was followed by a smiley face emoticon and a LOL. It felt oddly reassuring that old Harry was keeping up with modern society.

The path I walked down and the small garden surrounding it were beautifully cared for. Not a single weed and any cracks in the paving were filled in with sand. The turf looked good enough to be used as a putting green and the roses under the front window still held on to a pair of red blooms despite the imminent arrival of winter.

The front door opened even before I could lay a knuckle on it.

'Well, if it isn't young Docherty.' David Collins' voice was loud in the late-morning air and held a note of enquiry.

'Hello,' I said somewhat discomfited. 'Mr Collins?'

'The one and only,' he said.

'I'm surprised you remember me.'

'Course I do,' he replied. 'Your old man was a good mate. And you don't forget what happened to him – to his family – too easily.' He looked me up and down.

It had been about ten years since I had spoken to this man – for the one and only time. He still had that stiff bearing, the keen gaze … and yes, the bracing handshake, I thought as he shook my hand, but his hair was almost white and the skin around his eyes was so lined, stretched and heavy that it looked as if his eyes had slipped slightly down his head.

I heard a woman's voice from behind him. 'Well, invite the boy in, Davie. Don't have him standing on the path.'

David laughed and welcomed me in. As I walked past him I thought I detected the slight odour of whisky. It was only around noon, so surely I was mistaken.

Ushered into the living room, I found myself in doily heaven – almost every surface was protected by one. Even the glass table in the corner of the room that held the TV had a couple of white lacy circles to save the gleaming surface from the stand. The air was sweet and perfumed, and too warm, as if the heating was on full and every available plug point had an air freshener.

'Have a wee seat, son,' said David's wife from her throne in the corner. She looked exactly the same as when I met her all those years ago. Her fingers were twitching away on a crochet hook as she spoke. 'My, you're looking well, Thomas,' she said.

Her husband fired her a warning look, and I realised what she'd just called me.

'Cuppa?' he asked, and a few minutes later we were munching Kit Kats and talking about the weather.

'You called me Thomas when I came in, Mrs Collins,' I said, and then offered a smile of apology for changing the conversation so abruptly.

She looked confused for a moment. Had a sip from her cup. Then, 'Did I? You sure? Don't know where I got that from.' She shot her husband a look. 'We know fine well your name's John.'

'It's okay,' I said with what I hoped was a conciliatory tone. 'I know about him … Thomas.'

Neither of them said anything.

'I *know* I had a brother who vanished when I was a baby,' I added,

'Didn't just vanish,' said David as if he'd realised there was no further point in keeping up any pretence. 'He's probably dead.'

'Davie,' Mandy said in a harsh tone. 'Don't be so cruel.'

David looked at me before sending a look to the ceiling. Then said, 'Did your mum finally come clean then?'

'Not exactly,' I replied and felt a churn in my stomach as I prepared to tell them. With each time I talked about it, the seriousness of this discovery was weighing on me more and more. 'I was attempting to clear out the house…' I gave a rueful smile at this admission. 'And I found his birth certificate in a box.'

David said nothing. He took a long drink from his mug before placing it on the carpet just to the side of his right foot. 'Why come and see us?' Whatever joviality was now gone. He was in cop mode.

'I … eh … I came across some sympathy cards among my mum's stuff. Saw one from you guys…' The atmosphere in the room was now decidedly chilly.

'And how did you find me?'

Me not *us*.

'I … I spoke with Harry Bone. He's in the same nursing home as my mum.'

'Ah. Saint Harry fucking Bone.'

'It's getting close to your nap time, Davie,' Mandy said. Her tone was soothing but it held a note of steel. Then to me, 'Davie doesn't sleep well during the night, so he likes a wee nap before his dinner.'

'He was a prick of a man,' said David. 'Coming up here from Ayrshire after your dad transferred. Didn't want the case to go cold, he said. He was a right pain in the arse. If he was in front of me right now—'

'You'd shake his hand, give him some of your whisky and talk about the old days as if they were the best times of your life,' Mandy interrupted.

I examined my mug, wondering if I should just get up and leave.

'Your brother disappeared, John,' David was looking in my direction but his eyes were glazed by the past. 'Was around Easter. We had a cold one that year. I remember frost and stamping my feet on the ground to keep the blood circulating.' He exhaled as if there was a sudden weight in his lungs. 'I didn't really know your family that well, to be honest. We saw you at the odd birthday party, or Christmas do down at the police station.'

It occurred to me that he'd said just moments earlier that he and Dad were good friends. They couldn't have been that friendly if he didn't know Thomas, me and mum that well.

'We've got two kids that were the same age as … your Thomas,' Mandy said. 'Our Sean was in Thomas's class at school.'

'What kind of boy was he?'

Mandy shrugged. 'A nice enough lad, as I remember. Liked his footie.'

'He was a wee shite,' David said.

'Davie,' Mandy remonstrated with him.

'No point in sanitising his memory, hen.' Then to me, 'He was disruptive in class. Acting out. Always getting the belt.'

'We were worried he'd be a bad influence on our Danny,' Mandy admitted.

'He was quite studious as a younger boy,' said David. 'Liked a book. But then puberty hit and he became a bit of an arse.'

'In what way?' I asked.

'Drinking, fighting, the usual stuff. As if he was trying to embarrass your old man. Cops get it all the time, son. Their kids can get bullied by the other weans for having a dad in the police, so they act up to show how tough they are. And your Tommy performed that act with a fair bit of relish.'

'Can you remember much about that night?' I asked.

'Your mum came charging into the station around seven p.m. Your dad was on back shift. She was in a right state. Said Tommy hadn't come home from school.' As David spoke I recalled again Mum's panicked expression whenever I was ten minutes late. 'We visited his usual haunts, checked out his pals, but found nothing.'

'Any leads? Any known paedophiles in the area? Was there anyone out to get him?'

'We did our job, John,' David said, irritation in his voice. 'This wasn't *Carry on Sleuthing*. We knew what we were doing.'

'Sorry,' I said. 'I didn't mean to…'

David ignored my attempt at an apology. 'The community cops had a good handle on what was going on in their patches in those days. All the known paedos checked out … they tend to target younger kids anyway. And none of the local neds had it in for Tommy, as far as we could find out. He tended to save his bad behaviour for those in authority.' He gave me a quick, rueful smile.

'All the mums were talking about the Shows being in town. And how it was probably some sicko that worked there who got him,' Mandy said with a small note of gossipy excitement in her voice.

Harry had also mentioned the Shows, I thought.

'Nothing came from that,' David said somewhat defensively. 'We investigated everyone connected with it. The family that ran it. All the men who worked for them. They were often the subject of suspicion…' he gave his wife a look I struggled to make sense of '… so they ran a very tight ship. Seems we liked to be entertained by these people but we were also quick to blame any incomers if something went wrong.' He leaned forwards in his chair and finished what he was saying with a hard-clipped tone. 'There was nothing there. Nothing.'

I realised that as he'd been speaking I had leaned forwards in my seat too. I exhaled, and sat back, wondering how I could gracefully leave.

As if she read my mind, Mandy spoke: 'You've got to have your nap, Davie. See the boy to the door first, eh?'

With a grateful smile I stood up and walked to the front door with David following me. As I stepped outside he cleared his throat.

'Nothing good can come from raking up the past, son.' His expression was grave and respectful. 'Your parents were certain Thomas died that day. For your own sake that should be the end of it.'

12

The Mitchell Library is an imposing sandstone building that sits proudly in the heart of Glasgow. This grand building would, I hoped, provide some answers to my questions.

Collins was sure Thomas was dead, a certainty he said was shared by my parents, so perhaps I should let this go.

I couldn't.

The library's hushed ambience was soothing, and it occurred to me that this place was some kind of link to my lost brother. He'd been here. He'd walked along the stacks of books and selected something that he might enjoy reading.

I explained to a young woman at the reception area what I was looking for and she directed me to the fifth floor. 'Special collections,' she said. 'They've got all the old newspapers on film up there.'

At the fifth-floor reception, I decided lying was easier: I explained that I was researching a book on local history and asked to look at back copies of the *Evening Times*.

'This way.' She stood up and began to walk across the large room, towards a line of grey, shoulder-high cabinets. 'What time period are you after?' she asked.

'Around Easter, 1990,' I replied. 'March and April. And May as well, please,' I added.

She pulled out the relevant small boxes and then marched over to one of the tables that housed the microfilm readers. She directed me to take a seat and then taking the March film out of its box she fed it through the viewer and explained how to work the reader.

'Thanks,' I said, and with a nod she left me to it.

I sat back in my chair, momentarily reluctant to continue. What if

I found something I didn't want to know? My dad's face flashed into my mind. He and Mum didn't want Chris and me to know about Thomas. Why? Was my investigation betraying his memory?

Looking around me, as if delaying the moment, I took in the rows of Formica-topped tables, four chairs at each cushioned with red cloth. Then down to the orange-and-brown patterned carpet that must have been the height of fashion at one point: a colour scheme that hadn't aged well.

Someone sat in the chair opposite me and their microfilm reader whirred into action.

Right. Get on with it, I told myself.

I pressed the green forward button and words and images blurred across the screen. I released the button and the film stopped on the sports pages. A young man with a Rangers strip was being tackled by another young man in the hoops of Glasgow Celtic. I scrolled on.

A nun aged forty-two had been sexually assaulted in Bellahouston Park.

A man aged twenty-eight was on a murder charge after stabbing his victim repeatedly.

Frank Sinatra would receive a million pounds if his concert were to go ahead in the city that summer as part of the European City of Culture programme.

So far, nothing about my brother's disappearance, or the Shows.

Then I was on to a series of small ads. Sunbeds, caravans in Saltcoats, and singing telegrams were apparently popular with Glaswegians in 1990. I moved on. The financial pages showed the pound at 1.635 US dollars, and the FTSE100 at 2221.6.

The next article was about women receiving tax independence. Their income would now be taxed on an individual basis rather than being aggregated against their husband's.

Married women's financial independence and singing telegrams. This was just less than thirty years ago but apart from the 'anchor' of Celtic and Rangers enmity it was feeling like a different world.

Enough, I told myself. I was here to research my brother's

disappearance, not to get a glimpse into life in Scotland when I was a toddler.

With improved focus, I carried on reading and searching.

Lost in what I was doing, I was surprised to feel a tap on my shoulder. It was the librarian.

'We're about to close.'

'Already?' I asked, looking at my watch. It was almost eight p.m. 'Is that the time?' What had I been doing the last three hours? 'Are you open tomorrow?'

'Yes,' she replied with a distracted smile, suggesting she was keen to be on her way home. 'We're open from nine to five on Fridays.'

The next morning I phoned the school and in a pathetic voice explained that the doctor wanted me to take the rest of the week off. Red-faced with shame at my lies, I squirmed when the school secretary told me to take care of myself.

Friday held more of the same. The same sort of crimes, the same advertisements, the same focus on Glasgow's main football teams. Some hours later, I stretched my aching back, and rubbed at my eyes. I should go home. I was getting nowhere.

Patience, I reminded myself. This 'case' was more than thirty years old. I wasn't going to find something in a matter of hours.

And if I was frustrated after just a few days, how would my parents have felt? It must have been a torment. Was Thomas alive or dead? The agony of the uncertainty, waiting to hear something, anything, must have been unbearable. How did parents cope with that? Their lives would have been on hold. How much sleep did they get? Did they force themselves to eat? Did they share their distress with one another or did they not want to show the other how much they hurt, thinking that would save the other some anguish?

I tried to think about how my parents were with each other when I was a child. My lasting impression was one of remoteness. Two people who had nothing in common other than the building they inhabited, a child-shaped void, and the huge mistake of having a further two love-starved boys.

I couldn't, wouldn't subject any children to that. Having observed plenty of distant parenting in my time in the classroom I knew how damaging that could be to a young person's growing sense of self.

A pain was growing across the back of my skull and down my neck, and my head felt too heavy. I pushed myself away from the library desk and rubbed at the muscles either side of my spine just under my cranium. Of course it did nothing to ease the pain. I crossed my arms, feeling a growing sense of something. Unease. That the things I needed in my life were just moving beyond my control. Angela, work, family. I needed to get a grip. Perhaps a coffee would help to shift my mood.

Down in the café in the large atrium of the library, as I was ordering my drink, my phone buzzed in my pocket. It was Angela.

'I've got a baby-sitter tonight. Fancy going to that Italian place on Bothwell Street? There's something I'd like to chat with you about.'

We arranged a time and hung up. Then after finishing my coffee I returned to my investigation, looking forward to an evening with Angela, and a chance to remind myself how important she was to my sanity.

Over a welcome large glass of red wine in the restaurant, I explained what I'd been doing the last couple of days. As I spoke I was aware of a tremor in my voice and a feeling that something was hovering in my mind, just out of reach.

'Ah, right,' she said. 'Your phone call the other night was a bit muddled.' She paused. 'I love the romantic phone calls, John, but could they not be so late, and could you not be so drunk?' She gave me a look that suggested her patience was beginning to fray. 'So, there's an actual birth certificate?'

'Sorry,' I could feel my face heat in a blush. 'I'll stop that,' I added quietly. 'But yeah, I have, sorry, *had* another brother.'

'That's crazy.' Her mouth fell open.

'And doing the arithmetic, I must have been about two when he died.'

'Bloody hell.' She shook her head slowly. 'Why would your mum and dad keep that from you?'

'I have no idea.'

'How horrible. You must feel so betrayed.'

Betrayal. Such a good word.

'And you can't possibly ask your mum about this now,' she continued. 'Goodness knows how that would affect her.' She reached across the table top and squeezed my hand. 'How awful for you.'

'It explains so much,' I said. 'Why Mum was so pissed off whenever I came home later than I said I would. And why there often seemed to be an atmosphere between her and Dad.'

'God, yeah,' Angela agreed. 'If anything happened to…' She broke off, clearly thinking of her own daughter. 'And you're going all private detective on us?'

'I don't know why I can't let it go,' I replied. 'I need to know what happened, you know?'

The waiter arrived with our food, and as we ate we allowed our conversation to drift to less-demanding topics. But when the waiter delivered our coffees I remembered that Angela had said there was something she wanted to chat about.

'On the phone,' I picked up my coffee and had a sip. 'You sounded like there was something on your mind.'

'Yeah.' She picked up a teaspoon and stirred her drink. She gave a faint shake of her head. 'That doesn't matter. It'll keep.'

'Oh c'mon, honey. It's all been about me tonight. And that's not fair. What's up?'

'I can't,' she said and looked away from me for a second. 'After all the stuff about your brother…' She picked up a sachet of sugar and dropped it again.

'What's going on?' I asked. I was suddenly sure I wouldn't like what was on her mind but felt compelled to force the issue. 'Talk to me.'

'We're going to have to have that conversation soon,' she said slowly after a long pause. She lifted her eyes to meet mine. 'Where this is going…'

The cast of her eyes eased my nerves only a little. She wasn't going to dump me just yet. Provided I offered her some reassurance.

'It will be two years this summer, John. I'm not asking for a ring on my finger or anything, but it's like we lead separate lives. You're in your flat, I'm in mine … I have a daughter you've barely spent any time with.' Her mouth twisted a little and I thought for a moment she was going to cry, but she blinked hard and recovered. 'I'm in love with you, John, but after all this time I barely know you—'

'Honey…' I gripped her hand and tried to interrupt. My head felt light, as if my brain was shifting inside my skull.

'Please, let me finish.' She coughed. 'I'm not sure much longer I can go on like this. I can't mess about. I've got Cathy to consider. I need to know either way if we have a future.'

I studied the table for a long moment. Everything suddenly felt too much. My mum, my new secret brother, Angela's unhappiness … I felt a surge of something approaching panic: a tightness in my chest and my pulse was a weighty thump in my neck.

I should get up and leave.

Go.

But I couldn't move. If I went now I'd never see her again.

Dampening down my anxiety, I forced a long, deep breath and considered what she had been saying. She was right. I had let our relationship run in a way that suited only me. I had an occasional girlfriend and all the space I needed when I wanted to retreat from the world.

I was being entirely selfish. She needed more from me.

Suddenly, I had the answer.

Perhaps it was time to grow up. Perhaps it was time to show that I wasn't my parents' son. I could have a loving, sharing, warm relationship, and this woman was the person to show me how to do that. Besides, life without her in it would lose too much of its spark. And maybe there was a way to help me feel like I was pulling my life back into a shape of my own devising.

Without fully realising I was doing it, I'd pushed my chair back, moved round to her side of the table and got down on one knee.

Her hand was at her mouth. 'John, what are you doing?' Her face was pale, her eyes shining.

'You're right,' I said. 'I love you. I can't go on treating you like this. And I can't live without you.' As I said those words I felt the truth of them linger in my heart.

'John, don't be daft. This was not what I was getting at.'

Even as the words were spilling from my mouth, a voice in my mind was demanding, what on earth are you doing?

'Will you marry me?' I asked.

First thing on Monday morning, I was in the car park, my back glued to the back of my car seat. My pulse thundered in my ears. My mouth was dry. My hands shaking where they rested on the steering wheel. I could make out my chest moving up and down under my suit jacket and tie. What was happening to me?

My heart pounded faster and harder. Even faster, even harder. I tried taking a deep breath to calm myself, but my breathing was sharp and shallow, the air barely reaching my lungs. My vision narrowed, getting darker and narrower.

Shit. I was having a panic attack.

'It's okay,' I said out loud. 'It's not fatal. It's. Not. Fatal.'

I squeezed my eyelids together, hard. Forced a breath. And made myself pay attention to it as air finally flowed into my lungs. I breathed in again and exhaled slowly, saying the word 'calm' over and over again as I did so.

My reaction surprised me. My actions felt almost like a habit.

Jesus, I'd had these before. Of course.

When I was a kid.

And the doctor sent me to a woman. I could see her in my mind. Shoulder-length black hair, an expressionless face and hands clasped on her lap as she taught me to focus on my breath and think of that one word. I said it out loud again.

'Calm.'

How could I have forgotten these attacks had happened all those years ago? And why was it happening again now?

Twenty minutes later, feeling a tremble in my thighs, like a hangover from my panic attack, my heels echoing the pattern of my stride down the long school corridor, I saw Mr White, 'the Headie', as the kids called him, waiting at the door to my classroom.

'Mr Docherty.'

As was usual when confronted with this man I felt my hackles rise.

'Morning, Mr White,' I managed to say.

'In my office, Mr Docherty,' he ordered. 'You and I need to talk.' Without waiting for a reply, secure in his absolute authority, he performed a heel turn and marched down the corridor. I followed in his wake, like a schoolboy preparing himself for ten of the best.

I followed him into his office and sat down. The desk before me was of dark polished walnut and was unadorned save for a pad of pristine white paper and a silver fountain pen.

'Am I to understand that congratulations are in order?'

'Sorry?' How on earth did he know about that?

'I was there, Mr Docherty. In the Italian restaurant where you publicly proposed to your girlfriend.'

'Ah.'

Shit.

I was back in that space, people applauding, Angela wordless with emotion, nodding her answer and drying her eyes with a napkin. Me, wondering if I had just made a huge mistake.

'And...' He cocked his head to the side. 'You made a quick

recovery. What was wrong with you again?' He looked at the pad of paper in front of him. 'Stomach flu?'

'I can explain.'

His eyes drilled into me. 'That would be interesting. Can you also explain what is happening here in school? I've been getting complaints from your colleagues about the noise coming out of your classroom. Whisky coming off your breath. What's going on?' He clasped his hands on the desk in front of him. 'I promoted you to head of department despite your relative youth because of your work ethic and your relationships with your pupils. Don't prove me wrong.'

'I … eh … can explain … em … everything, Mr White,' I stammered.

'I do hope so, Docherty.' Mr White had a formidable weapon in his arsenal of intimidation. He would pause after you had stopped speaking, which had the curious effect of making you say more than you intended.

'My mother had a stroke a few weeks ago and was recently taken into a nursing home…' I opted to go for the truth in the hope he would understand. I looked over at him to assess how he was taking my explanation. I got nothing back. 'I took the time off to meet with the staff there and discuss her care. And I have to clear the house to pay for it all…' I tailed off.

Silence.

I rushed to fill it with a lie, constructing it as I spoke, hoping my words would have the ring of truth. 'And I was feeling a little better. The meal had been arranged for our anniversary. An occasion I felt would work well for a proposal. I'd gone to a bit of effort and didn't want to let Angela down just because I was a bit poorly.'

He raised an eyebrow, the rest of his expression carved from stone. 'I'm sorry about your mother, John, but there are weekends, emails, and you can actually pick up the phone and call people. Why do you need to take time off?'

'But…' I couldn't think of anything that might appease him. He lifted a hand as if to silence what I was about to say.

'Nonetheless, if one of my members of staff is ill, I do not expect to see them eating out … and my real concern is that your colleagues have gone to the extent of dobbing in one of their fellows. We leave our problems at the front door, John. We do not take them into the classroom.' This last sentence was delivered in a more caring tone. Entirely fake, I thought, but the attempt was there. 'There are protocols to be observed.' He was reminding me that only a small amount of self-certified days off were tolerated before a formal attendance interview was arranged. 'I'm giving you an unwritten warning, Mr Docherty. I always prefer to take care of these matters in-house if I can. But your disregard for your colleagues and the young people in your classroom is very disappointing. If this happens again I will have no choice but to take formal disciplinary action.'

'Right,' I shouted when I got back into my classroom to see that children were dotted around the room in clumps rather in sitting at their own seats. 'Everyone back to their desks.' Seeing that I was in no mood to be disobeyed, everyone did as they were told.

I began the lesson for the day.

'I want to talk about the narrative choices…'

Twenty-five teenagers groaned.

'…made by the writers of the second Thor movie.'

They instantly perked up.

'Aye, sir,' somebody shouted from the back of the class. 'That was the worst wan.'

'Why didn't it work?' I asked them all. 'Have a wee think? Write something down and we'll come together as a class to discuss.'

Once they all had their heads down, I took time to consider what Mr White had said. There had been complaints from colleagues? Jesus, I prided myself in my work. If I didn't have that…

Rubbing my aching temples with my fingers I had to grudgingly admit that I hadn't been myself of late, but what had I been doing that had led to other staff members going behind my back to White? Sure, a few comments were made after I was awarded the promoted post, but were noses out of joint solely because of that?

I was really worried about Mum's illness, perhaps that had leaked over into my work. I chewed down on this for a few minutes, and resolved to do better. Aside from everything else the kids under my care deserved better from me.

After the final class of the day one of the kids hung back, wanting a word with me. Norrie McKee. He often waited to have the last word if the topic was something that interested him. But at times he had an ulterior motive.

'That was bang on, sir. What you said about *Thor 2*. It was a pile of shite.'

'We try not to use language like that in school, Norrie,' I said as I packed my lesson materials into my briefcase. His eyes strayed to the bag of food sitting under my table. I'd learned to buy extra sandwiches and fruit at lunchtime, knowing how many of my kids' parents were reliant on food banks, and how many of them went without lunch. 'You got a use for these?' I asked him as I sat the bag on my desk. 'I swear my eyes are bigger than my belly. They're only going to get chucked if you don't take them.'

He claimed the bag with alacrity then asked, 'You going to see the new *Avengers* movie, sir? My cousin downloads them all so we can watch them. That new one looks like a belter.'

That evening I was back in the library, aware that this need for answers was driving my behaviour and was in danger of becoming an obsession. I should have been with my fiancée planning the next stage of the rest of our lives, and as I positioned myself in front of the viewer I sent her a silent apology and prayed that she understood.

The first microfilm I chose displayed the same set of information I'd looked at before. I re-spooled the tape, returned it and jumped a couple of weeks. Back at my desk, with the new tape inserted, and at last there was something of interest.

An advert for a travelling funfair setting up in the East End of the city: waltzers, dodgems and a helter-skelter. Cheap entry on the first day. I assessed the advert and considered how exciting that would have been to the young people in the area. They would have heard of places like Alton Towers, but few families would have had the money to go there.

I scrolled on to the next day.

The front-page headline told of the disappearance of a local teenager. His photo shined out at me. Bright eyes, cropped dark hair, a light strip of fuzz over his top lip and a chipped front tooth. I read down through the article. The boy's family were from the East End. I read the street name, and then scrolled back to the advert to read the address there. My knowledge about that part of the city was sketchy, but I knew enough to realise that the two addresses were only a few streets apart.

Walking distance.

Could this disappearance be a coincidence? Did two missing children – one presumed dead – constitute a pattern? Could there be more? A shudder passed though me. I had hoped to find something, but this? What had I uncovered? Two schoolkids had disappeared round about the same time that the Shows had been in the area. What if there were more?

I was jumping to conclusions, and vowed to keep a clear mind as I ploughed on.

In the news a week later, a body was found. The same picture of the same boy smiled out at me. His death, according the police, was to be the subject of an ongoing enquiry. They had few leads, but would keep looking.

His poor parents. That was not the final answer they'd been hoping and praying for.

I jumped a few months forwards. The fair had moved to a small town called Bridge of Weir – a place I'd never visited, on the outskirts of the city. The same advert was showing, except this time with the new address.

This gave me a new base line. I could go back and forward from this date and see if there were any more missing children. A week or so passed by in a blur on the screen. I noted that my breath was shorter and that my stomach was feeling tight. I needed to calm down and take this more slowly.

There.

Another boy. He was from Lochwinnoch – another place I'd never been to, but I did remember Paul as a kid, talking about an uncle taking him to the bird reserve there. On this piece there was no photo of the boy, but there was an image of the parents outside a police station, the man's arm over the woman's shoulder. Both of them wearing haunted expressions.

Three boys.

All three were in their early teens.

All three lived near a site where the Shows visited.

One I know for certain died.

One was suspected to be dead.

And now a third boy missing.

I took a long breath. They could all be unrelated incidents. The Shows arriving at each area at the same time as a child went missing could be just a coincidence, couldn't it?

Something jumped out at me from the screen. The third child's name was Robert Green. That was Paul's mother's maiden name. And his uncle had lived in Lochwinnoch.

I had to speak to Paul.

13

Paul wasn't at home, but his mother, Dawn let me in. She was as round as she ever was, but her hair held flashes of grey, and her mouth was turned down at the corners, giving her a slightly sour expression which was at odds with my memories of her. Although she had never quite forgotten I'd almost blinded her son, she was always polite, as if her son's ability to forgive me trumped her need to harbour any resentment.

'I suppose you should come in, John,' Dawn said, but she held on to the door frame, her arm barring my entry. Then she took a step back as if she'd just reminded herself this was not her home. 'Paul and his wife pay me to clean once a week. But I think they just want to keep me busy.' She tutted. 'Come in. Sit down and I'll put the kettle on.'

I followed her into the living room.

'Laura's on an evening shift, but Paul should be home anytime.' She watched as I took a seat on the sofa. 'It's tea you prefer, isn't it?'

She returned moments later holding a mug of weak tea.

'What brings you here? How's your mum?'

'She's been better,' I replied as I took the drink from her.

'You just never know the minute, do you?' she said. 'A massive stroke?' she asked.

I nodded.

'Just awful,' she crossed her arms. 'She won't take well to that, eh?' It was more of a statement than a question. 'Your mum always liked getting glammed up. How's she going to cope without managing to do all that?'

This felt like a strange thing to say in the circumstances. Being able to make herself look presentable was the least of her worries.

But then I always had a sense that Dawn didn't quite approve of my mother. Wondering where that came from, I asked, 'Do you remember much about when Mum and Dad moved into the village?'

She looked at me with a questioning look. 'Vaguely,' she replied. 'Your mum always struck me as a bit of a wild child. Bit of a man-eater.' She coloured at that, as if worried she'd gone too far.

'Really?' I asked with a smile. 'You sure you're talking about my mother?'

This seemed to make her relax. 'To my shame I was a wee bit judge-mental where your mother was concerned. Jealous, to be honest. She was a stunner, and didn't hide it. Low tops, long legs. Paul and his dad's eyes were always out on stalks whenever she appeared. The village was always full of gossip where your mother was concerned.'

'Like what?'

'Nobody blamed her, really. It was no secret your dad liked a drink. And…' her gaze was unclear for a moment '…she used to have those episodes, didn't she?'

'Sorry?'

'Paul told me at the time that she used to take to her bed for days. That you'd all be whispering around her till she got better.'

At her words I had a flash of something: Mum fully clothed, on her bed, on her side, knees pulled up to her chest, lying with her back to me. The gloom of the room pierced by a thin, bright strip of sunlight where the curtains hadn't been shut properly.

Dad was absent, on a case or something, and Mum was in bed for about two days. We went off to school without any breakfast, but at dinnertime we were weak with hunger, so in desperation I managed to make Chris and me a meal of mashed potato out of a tin with some beans. I'd then gone in to check she was okay and she beckoned me over to her, asking me to get onto the bed.

Once I was there she inched closer, put an arm over me, and placed her face against my head as if she couldn't get enough of the smell of my hair. I couldn't move for hours. Every time I tried to get off she would start to cry, and eventually the ache in my bladder was too much to contain so I shouted through to Chris to come and take over.

Then it blew over and she was singing and dancing about the house, cooking elaborate meals, and cleaning the place as if she was preparing for some event.

On another occasion she had Chris and I sit on her bed while she 'performed a fashion show'. She'd shuck her clothes until she was only in her bra and pants and then jump into one outfit after another. *Does my bum look big? Am I showing too much cleavage? Do I suit the red or the purple?* Chris and I were clueless and answered yes to everything until she gave up asking. *Why couldn't I have girls*, she then complained.

'You mentioned gossip?' I asked, amazed how such a memory could appear after all this time.

'The rumour was that something terrible happened and that's why they moved away from the big city and into the village. So if she was blowing off steam, who could blame her.'

I perked up. 'A rumour? Like what?'

She waved a hand dismissively. 'Just gossip, really. Nothing to it I'm sure, and nobody was ever able to provide any detail. We prefer scandal to finding a truth that's just a kick above the ordinary, don't we? Mind you, we didn't have the interweb in those days or we'd have been straight on there.' She laughed and made typing motions with her fingers. 'Trying to work out the truth of it all.'

I wondered at this version of my mother, but then reminded myself about the real reason for visiting Paul and realised it was Dawn I needed to speak to after all.

'I came across an article in an old newspaper when I was doing some research for a school project – about a young boy that had disappeared,' I lied, surprised how easily it came to me. 'His name was Green. Robert Green. I wondered if Paul knew anything about him.'

'Oh my.' Her face was long, eyes wide, and she held a hand over her mouth. 'Good lord, I haven't thought about that in such a long time. Hard to believe as it was such a wrench in the family.' Her eyes narrowed. 'Why did you think of Paul when you came across this name?'

'I recognised it as your maiden name, and I remembered years ago, Paul talking about an uncle in Lochwinnoch. This boy came from there, apparently.'

'Paul told you about Lochwinnoch?' she asked in a quiet voice. She waited for my answer as if holding her breath. There was something important going on here and I couldn't work out what it was.

'Yeah, about the bird-watching place and how his uncle used to take him there.'

She nodded slowly. 'Where did you come across this? What kind of project are you doing with these kids of yours?'

'It's about how truth imbues fiction, and how authors often use real-life stories as a jumping off point for their novels.' I hoped this explanation came across as plausible. For some reason I didn't want her to know, just yet, that there might be a connection between my family and hers.

She made a face. 'A bit grim, isn't it? How old are these children you're teaching?'

'Och, they're a hardy bunch nowadays, teenagers. Much more worldly wise than we ever were.'

'That poor boy.' She held a hand to her throat. 'Robert's dad was my cousin, or something, and when he disappeared the whole town was in shock. His parents were inconsolable. You know, they never, ever found a body.'

I shuddered.

'What's wrong?' she asked.

'Nothing,' I answered with a weak smile, but thinking that she clearly wasn't aware of what had happened to my brother, Thomas. 'Does Paul know about this?'

'No, he was just a baby at the time, and there was no reason to tell him when he grew up.

'Did the police ever find out what happened to Robert?'

'They found nothing. As far as I can remember, there were a

couple of other disappearances too. But in only one of them was a body found. As far as poor Robert was concerned, no body, no suspects, nothing.'

14

I tried to curb my excitement as my car wound its way back to Glasgow. I was on to something here, I was sure of it. Everything was pointing to a perpetrator that had never been caught. Driving on autopilot, I speculated on who would have been capable of such vile acts, and I wondered about the last moments of the boys that were his victims. Did they see their killer? Did they know him? Did they see it coming? How terrified must they have been?

By the time I arrived home, therefore, it was a much less excited and much sadder man who opened the door to my flat. My imagination had spooked me.

I phoned Angela, got her up to speed with my search for Thomas and then arranged a date for the following evening. 'We haven't managed to celebrate our engagement properly yet...' I said suggestively.

'Down boy,' she laughed.

'I'm talking about making you a nice dinner,' I replied with a butter-wouldn't-melt tone.

'What? You're going to cook?'

The next evening, after we'd eaten Angela gave me an appraising look.

'Okay, Mr Chef, how did you manage to rustle up such a delicious meal?'

'Are you impressed?' I asked, pleased with myself, mentally reminding myself to make sure that the bin lid was closed and that no Marks and Spencer's food labels were visible.

'Very,' she said as she slowly licked the last drop of ice cream off her spoon. Her eyes closed as it melted down the back of her throat. She groaned, 'That was lovely.' A thousand thoughts, all of them under the title 'Lust', rose unbidden to my consciousness.

'A penny for your thoughts,' she said.

I coughed suddenly embarrassed. 'Would you like to wash all that down with a coffee?'

'Tell you what,' she answered. 'You loosen your belt and I'll make us both a nice cuppa.'

Minutes later Angela brought through the coffee, kicked off her shoes and curled up on one of the armchairs.

'When are we going to go into town to sort out a ring?' I asked, pleased at how certain my voice sounded.

She beamed. 'You don't have to, you know. I don't need a ring to signal to everyone that I'm taken.'

'Call me old-fashioned, but I want to show the world that I love you.'

'John, you are so sweet.' She moved closer to me on the couch and pressed her lips against mine. I swear that my heart actually stopped. I sucked in some air so that it would start again. Angela rested her hand on my thigh and my pulse quickened. I was sure that the people in the flat next door would have been able to hear its pounding.

I felt a flash of doubt. I didn't deserve this amazing woman. What would I do to fuck it all up?

'It's getting hot in here,' Angela said with a small smile as she unbuttoned the top button on her blouse, pulling me out of my thoughts.

'You have a small bit of ice cream on your top lip,' Angela said moving even closer. I tried to lick it off.

'Nope, you missed it completely. Here let me.' She gently took my head in her hands and licked my top lip with her tongue. I had never felt anything so erotic in my life. My pulse roared in my ears.

With my finger, I removed a blob of ice cream from the cereal bowl that I had served dessert in and placed some more on my lower lip. 'Oops, I've managed to get some more.'

She grinned and then slowly licked the full length of my bottom lip. 'I'd better make sure I get it all,' she murmured. She then pressed her lips lightly on mine and we began to kiss. Her tongue darted inside my mouth to touch mine. I groaned. That was delicious.

'Time to get naked,' she giggled. Then gracefully, like a dancer, she divested herself of her clothing, while I struggled with mine, suddenly as clumsy as a week-old puppy. Suddenly aware that this was the first time we'd make love after formalising our relationship.

'Here, let me help you,' Angela said as she slowly pulled down my jeans and my boxers at the same time. I kicked them off the end of my feet, she stepped in close and we then stood clasped together, her full breasts rubbing against the flesh of my chest.

Her eyes were huge and luminous in the dim firelight. We sank lower onto the rug, breathing heavy, hands moving slowly, but constantly in motion.

'Jesus, you're beautiful,' I said.

I stopped moving, and savoured our connection as if it were the first time we were together.

She used her hand to guide me inside her.

Then with the abruptness of a light being switched off, I could feel nothing. It was if all of the nerve ends in my groin had been severed. One second I was in sweating, lust heaven, the next I had as much feeling as an amputee.

Burying my head in the crook of her neck, I willed all negative thoughts from my mind. I was with a sexy woman, we were naked and I was enjoying myself. We'd been in this situation plenty of times, why was this happening now?

But there was nothing.

I rolled off Angela and covered my groin with a cushion. We lay for a couple of seconds that felt like hours in silence, both of us staring at the ceiling.

'What's wrong, John?' she asked in a timid and hurt voice.

'Nothing,' I turned my back to her.

'We need to talk,' Angela said to my back. Then in a small voice: 'It's not a big deal, you know.' She reached for me as if to coax me back to life. But it was if that area was anaesthetised. Her touch barely registered.

I put my hand over hers to still the movement, feeling that every second her hand was on me was adding to my embarrassment.

'Talk to me, John.' Angela got on to one elbow and looked down over me. 'Tell me what's going on in that head of yours.' Her tone was sympathetic. Caring.

I said nothing. It was if the language centre in my brain had been disconnected. Emotions roiled in my head, demanding to be named, but sense was at a remove.

'I can handle … this,' she said as she motioned in the direction of my groin. 'But I can't handle the silence.' I could hear the hurt in her voice but I was feeling too awkward to reassure her.

'No, you're alright,' I managed.

Everything suddenly just felt like too much. I'd never properly grieved for my dad. My mum was seriously ill. And now I knew they'd both lied to me my whole life: I had a secret brother. And then feeling a little bit of pressure from Angela, I had proposed. What was going on in my head? 'God…' I sat up '…I'm a bloody mess.'

'John, it's okay. It happens.' She stroked my shoulder.

'That's not the…' The touch that only moments ago I was craving, now felt like an admonition. I inched away from her hand. 'Get dressed. I'll call you a taxi.'

'John, shouldn't we at least talk about this?' She pulled her top close to hide her breasts. Her eyes limp with pity.

I stood up, covering myself as I did so. All the passion and electricity that was in the room had dissipated. I pulled on my underwear with my back to her. Why was this happening now? We'd made love lots of times without any problems; what was wrong this time?

I could hear her move behind me, and like two people on their way to a funeral we followed the discarded trail of clothes around the living room.

As soon as she was dressed, I stood at the door, my expression hewn from stone. I wanted to reassure her, tell her she was beautiful. That any man would be incredibly fortunate to spend time with her. Tell her it was me. That she was not the problem. But the words remained frozen under the ice of my tongue.

Back in my bed, and with a weariness that surprised me, I slipped off my clothes and lay under the covers. Curling into the foetal position I went over events of the night. How had an evening that had shown so much promise ended so badly?

I relived the successful part of our love-making and tried to assess the moment it all went wrong. What had happened? One second I was fully engaged and more aroused than I'd ever been. The next it was like I had been numbed below the waist.

She was smart, beautiful, empathic. My life was so much richer with her in it. And there was a huge attraction there. An electricity. So why was I feeling this reluctance now that our relationship had a formal basis?

Eventually I slept, and what felt like five minutes later my alarm clock rang.

Followed by my phone. Could it be her?

With a wild churn in my stomach I raced through to the living room and found my mobile. With a sense of disappointment, and some relief, I read the name.

'Hey, Paul.'

'Hey, buddy…' He paused. 'You sound disappointed. Expecting someone else?'

'Nah,' just tired.' I offered a fake yawn.

'Right…' He drew the syllable out as if he doubted me. 'I hoped I'd get you before you went off to work.'

'You okay, Paul?' I wasn't so caught up in my own problems that I couldn't sense something was going on with him.

'Mum said you came round…'

'Aye,' I said as I rubbed at my eyes. The conversation I'd had with his mum had been relegated in my mind after the events with Angela.

'We should talk,' he said, and I heard a note of importance in his voice.

'Sure. When?'

'Tonight? I'll come up to yours.'

15

Paul was pushed to the back of my mind as I worried about how Angela would act towards me the next time we met.

'Sir, what do you mean, sir?' A boy at the front of the class asked, throwing me from my thoughts, and I realised that once again I was allowing my personal life to impose itself on my professional one.

I coughed, and then gave the proper instructions, relieved that I had been doing this long enough that the answers were all there in my mind.

The day wore on. My classroom filled then emptied, filled then emptied. I had one part of my mind on the job and used the remainder to compose a series of apologies for Angela. But how could I explain to her what I couldn't understand myself?

Paul wasn't due to arrive at my house until eight p.m., so, ignoring the mountain of marking I should have been doing for my pupils, I calculated I had a couple of hours to get to the library. But first I should give Angela a call to see how she was. I dialled her number on the way out to my car. She picked up straight away.

'I'm sorry,' I said before she could speak.

'I wasn't sure you were going to call.' She sounded wary.

'I could have handled that situation a lot better, Angela. Forgive me?'

'You weren't yourself last night, John. What's going on? Do you regret proposing?'

'No. No,' I said.

'You sure? You don't sound sure.'

'I'm not sure of anything right now.' Immediately realising how that sounded, I tried to backtrack a little. 'What with pressure at work, my mother in the care home, and this thing with my brother, my head's all over the place…'

'What? Do you want to break up with me?'

'No. Jesus, no,' I said. 'Where the hell's that coming from?'

'I'm confused, John. For a smart guy you don't choose your words very well.'

I nodded. Closed my eyes, and wondered how I could retrieve this situation.

'There's a lot going on right now, babes. Can you bear with me? Please?'

Relieved that things were on a slightly more solid footing with Angela, I went to the library and tucked myself away in my usual corner to continue my research on the Green boy. I couldn't concentrate. My mind was too full of Angela.

We'd arranged to meet a couple of nights later, after she finished work, when she expected she could ask another babysitting favour of her mum and dad, and my relief that she was now talking to me was tinged with fear at what would happen if we got into another romantic clinch. The possibility of a repeat failure crowded my mind. I wanted to see her but I wasn't sure I wanted to go through that experience again.

Eventually, I gave my research up – I was just too distracted – and made my way home to meet Paul.

The doorbell rang, bang on time. From my seat on the sofa I shouted out: 'It's open. Come on in.'

I heard the door open. Footsteps. And then Paul was standing in the doorway as if he didn't quite know where to put himself.

'Have a seat, man. You're making the place untidy.'

He sat. 'Awright,' he said. There was clearly something on his mind, but I thought it was best I didn't force it out of him. I knew how I responded to that kind of treatment.

'Drink?' I asked him as he stretched his legs out in front of him. He looked as if he'd barely slept the night before. He was, as usual, well dressed, in a pair of dark jeans, blue checked shirt and black leather jacket. 'You're allowed to take your jacket off,' I said.

'Yeah. Yeah.' He said as if distracted. 'Coffee's fine, mate.'

'On its way,' I said, wondering what was wrong with him. I went through to the kitchen and came back with a mug of coffee for him and a large red wine for me.

He mumbled his thanks, then cradled the mug on his lap as if he hadn't quite worked out the next step in the process.

It was looking like whatever was on his mind was going to take a while to come out so I thought I'd better get things started.

'I found something in the library and I wanted to go over it with you.' I paused. 'Didn't your mum ever tell you about your cousin?' I asked.

'Yeah.' He exhaled sharply. 'Like several decades too late.' There was a heaviness about his words I couldn't fathom. 'Your brother. My big cousin. What a strange coincidence that is. And neither of us knew anything about either of them.'

'There's something else I found out,' I said.

'What?' Paul leaned towards me as if he was relieved I was about to do more of the talking.

'The Shows were in town when my brother vanished, and the same company was in your cousin's area when he vanished too.'

'Could be just another coincidence,' he said.

'Really? Two boys around the same age vanish a couple of weeks apart, and the same Shows visits both areas.'

'That is spooky,' admitted Paul. 'Growing up I didn't know I had a disappeared cousin,' he said as if still trying to make sense of it. His eyes narrowed as a thought had occurred to him. 'Two missing kids could be just a coincidence. They could just be two runaways. Kids run away all the time. If there were more that would suggest a pattern.'

'But there are more.'

His eyebrows almost hit his hairline. 'Really?'

'This kid was found, though. Well, his body was.' I told him more about my visit to the ex-cop.

'He's sure your brother died as well? Shit.' He crossed his arms, sat back in his chair and studied his feet.

'Three kids disappear all those years ago, and nobody spots a link,' I said.

'What do you think we should do with this?' he asked as he returned from wherever he had gone in his mind.

'I'm really not sure. Go back to the newspaper? Speak to the actual reporter – or even contact the police? Say there might have been some sicko following the Shows, or even working for them.' I paused. 'And these kind of people don't just stop with two or three. There's bound to be more.'

We sat with that for a moment. I shuddered at the thought of what I might have uncovered. Then I shook my head. I was jumping to conclusions. I could be way off.

Paul looked away from me, out of the window. 'I never told you…' he began. 'I never really told anyone … until recently.' His eyes were swimming with tears.

'Paul, what's wrong?'

'That anger when you attacked me with the stick…' He rubbed absently at his scar. 'I recognised it, I think. That's why I stayed friends with you. I was too young to articulate it at the time, but now I can see that I was hoping we could help each other.'

'Paul, what on earth are you talking about?'

16

'Remember me talking about going to Lochwinnoch? My uncle taking me to the bird-watching?' Paul waited for my response. I could only nod. 'That's not all my uncle did.' He left that hanging.

'What the fuck?' I was on my feet.

'Please ... sit down,' he said, waving his outstretched hand. 'This is difficult enough.'

I sat. 'Sorry.' Part of my mind was watching, assessing, while the bigger part was demanding, *What the hell has this got to do with me?* A sense of what he was trying to say crowded me, but I pushed at it. I squared my jaw and fought it down. I wasn't going there.

And I was there in that moment again. A boy with a stick in his hand. Fury, a constant simmer in my mind. There had been a trigger. But what? My anger had boiled over and I had to lash out. Couldn't contain it.

I struggled to quell the questions and forced myself out of my own head, refocussing on my friend.

'I won't go into detail.' He swallowed. 'But Mum just told me the uncle who took me ... birdwatching was the father of the boy who disappeared.'

'Fuck.' The implications of this hit me. 'So you think this boy ... Robert ... ran away to get away from his dad?'

'I wanted to run away. I wanted to die. So many times.' He bit at his bottom lip, then breathed out. His exhalation heavy with a suppressed sob. 'I'm sure my cousin Robert went through what I did.' He held his hands out, an eloquent movement that said it all.

'Your mum knew?'

'She does now. She says she sensed something was off at the time.' His smile was weak and worn through with apology. For whom I wasn't sure. He shook his head. 'Couldn't tell anyone. He said no one would believe me. That I would be carted away to a remand home for lying little bastards. That I would ruin my parents' lives for nothing. It was only after I married that...'

'How did I not know any of this?' I felt like such a bad friend. I moved my eyes from his, shifted in my seat. The pressure in the centre of my forehead was building again.

'I thought silence was helping. If I didn't say anything it hadn't really happened.'

'I feel awful,' I said. 'I should have picked up on something.'

'Don't be daft,' Paul smiled. 'You were just a kid yourself.' He paused. 'With his own issues.'

'What's that supposed to mean?'

'There was a spell when you were angry, like, all the time, mate.'

'I was?'

'Talking about my stuff helped me. I just want to put it out there that anytime you want to talk...'

'Jesus, you think I was abused as well?'

'I'm sorry, John.' His face coloured and he looked like he was admonishing himself for misreading the situation. 'I don't know what I'm trying to say.'

'Because I was angry all the time, that means I was abused? Fucksake, mate. Yeah, I was angry, but if you'd had my dad, you'd have been angry too.'

'You weren't—?'

'Fuck no.' I recalled David Collins' explanation of Thomas's behaviour before he vanished, and recognised the truth of it in me. 'Having a cop as your dad in a small town like ours was a nightmare. I acted out to show I was tough. That I was one of the boys.' I stuffed my hands into my pockets, feeling shame now at the way I had overreacted. What was wrong with me? First I messed things up with Angela. Now I was messing them up with Paul.

'Sorry,' he said. He looked exhausted. 'I'm an idiot. I projected my stuff onto you. Sorry.'

I leaned into his space, my mind full of the agonies he must have experienced, and put a hand on his knee. I needed to be a better friend to him. 'Jesus, mate. What happened to you … Why didn't you tell me sooner?'

He looked off into space as if trying to find the right words, as if that's what he'd been doing most of his life, and for most of his life he'd struggled.

'You pray a miracle will come along. Time will march backwards and undo everything. Then you can stop pretending, cos it never really happened after all.'

17

I was looking into a mirror as if memory was contained there. There was a noise like a gunshot and the mirror shattered and fell around my feet. As I looked down at it, pieces of me were distorted to look smaller. And bigger. And incomplete. A mouth. A knee. My body full length, with blankness where my face, heart and groin should be.

A clock throws its hands over its face.

A tree bends against the wind.

Wherever I place my eyes there is nothing there. A void.

That sense of incompleteness from my dreams hung over me as I woke and dragged myself through to my kitchen to make breakfast. Thanking the gods that this was a Saturday, I forced myself to slough off my mood and vowed to move on with my investigations. If I kept moving, kept putting one foot in front of the other, I was sure I would eventually find a solution to my other problems.

My brother had been killed. That was what was really important. I had to find out who did it and see that justice was done.

Feeling a renewed sense of purpose, I munched through some cereal and determined I would venture back to the library, go through some more old newspapers. My plan was to trace the owners of the travelling fair, and any old employees.

Parking the car on a street behind the library I realised I hadn't brought my notebook and pen with me; so much for my renewed focus. There was a small supermarket at the end of the road, so I made my way there.

From the doorway I could see that the shop was mostly empty apart from a security guard, two sales assistants at the checkouts to my far left, two children, one of whom was in a pushchair, and a woman who was examining the magazines and newspapers.

I quickly found a packet of blue pens and a notebook, and then grabbed some fruit to keep me going while I was carrying on my research. When I got to the checkout I found the pushchair blocking my way. The child fastened into it was about two years old, and judging by the colour of his clothes was a boy. His little fingers and his face were covered in melted chocolate. Standing guard over the pushchair was his big brother. He looked to be about four, and wore a blue anorak and a defiant expression.

The smaller child looked up at me, and his face lit up. 'Daddy,' he gurgled.

Taken aback, I looked over my shoulder. Once again, his little face full of joy, he said, 'Daddy,' and arms wide he strained at his reins to reach me.

'Silly, that's not Daddy.' It was a woman's voice.

I looked up to smile at the child's mother. She was a short, trim woman, in her mid-forties with shoulder-length brown hair, dusted with grey flecks.

Our eyes met and her mouth gaped open briefly, and a strange expression flirted with her face. She almost visibly shook herself and her features assumed a look of polite indifference. She smiled as she turned back to the shop assistant, picked up her shopping and then arranged her two bags of groceries under the pushchair.

'I'm sorry,' she said. 'My youngest is never happy unless he says something to embarrass me. He's at that stage.'

'That's his job, eh?' I said, trying to work out what had just happened. 'To embarrass Mummy.'

With another hurried 'Sorry' the woman bustled towards the exit. The little boy stretched out of the chair to wave to me, and as she scurried by the window I caught the woman taking another quick, almost furtive, look in my direction.

'You nearly had yourself a lovely wee boy there,' laughed the shop assistant as she took my things and scanned them into the till.

'Aye,' I answered. 'I'm glad I missed the sleepless night part, mind you.'

The assistant laughed as I handed over my card.

'Have you seen that family in before?' I asked.

'Oh, aye,' she answered with a lop-sided smile. 'She's in here pretty much every day. I expect she likes to get those wee ones out of the house, eh?' She looked at my puzzled expression. 'Why? Do you think you know her?'

I shook my head. 'Never met her before in my life.'

The woman's face stayed me for the rest of that weekend and over the next few days. Angela even remarked that I was distracted as we lay idly in one another's arms one evening. We'd had one more failed attempt at sex and decided we should just kiss and cuddle for the time being. Her theory was that we should just enjoy the nearness of each other, the physical contact, without any expectation.

'It's that woman I met. For some reason I can't get her out of my mind. The look she gave me was pretty weird.' I shivered. 'As if she knew me? I'll just have to put it down to one of those things and forget about it…' I stretched forwards and placed a kiss on the tip of her nose.

After a pause in the conversation, Angela pushed herself into an upright position, her face betraying an uncertainty.

'John, how do you feel about me?'

'What kind of question is that?'

'Please … just answer me … no games.'

'Okay, okay … I love being with you…' I could feel myself shrinking a little from my own words, hearing the crassness in them. This was certainly not what she wanted to hear.

'See…' She shook her head sadly and crossed her arms. 'You said the L word, but managed to deflect it.'

She looked tiny as she said this, and I squirmed. There was so much going on in my own head I was unsure if I could give her the reassurance she needed. I mumbled something. Made some reassuring noises. Pressure was building behind my eyes. It was as if there wasn't enough room in my head for all the things that had happened to me lately. And if I was being honest, I'd been expecting this, and didn't know how I should react, or even how I wanted to be. All I knew was that I wanted her in my life.

'Apart from the engagement nothing's really changed, John. Cathy's the most precious thing to me on earth. It seems like you want to keep us in different compartments, and I hate that.'

I felt my face heat; it was true. 'I'm glad you brought the subject up,' I said, cringing a little at my lie. 'It's something we needed to discuss.'

'Yes, and it's something that won't go away either, John.' Her expression let me know she was fully aware of my reluctance. 'I want the two parts of my life to come together.'

'She's a lucky wee girl to have you.' As I spoke my mind was back in the fracture that was my own family.

Angela missed nothing. 'I'm picking up some vibes here,' she said. 'You know, you've never really talked much about your dad, your mum, your family … apart from this new thing about your missing brother.'

'Aww, c'mon, I must have.'

'Not much, other than the basics,' she said with hard-eyed certainty. 'It's been over two years, John.' She paused. 'Two years on and off, admittedly, but there are still parts of your life that are a mystery to me.'

'There's not much worth talking about that's why. Typical dysfunctional family, really. As you know, Dad died a few years back. You visited Mum in the care home…' At this she gave me a look, as if accusing me of stalling. 'My brother, Chris, has run away from us all,' I carried on. 'That kinda sums it all up.'

She took my hand and pulled me up from the floor onto the sofa. Once I was there, she arranged us so that she was sitting upright and I was lying down, my head on her lap. She stroked my forehead, running her fingers slowly through my hair. 'Talk to me, John.'

Soothed by the action of her hand, and a little under the spell of my love for her, I began, haltingly, to speak.

'My early childhood was great, a happy time. Nothing bothered me. Life was just one big adventure. Dad wasn't around much. He worked long shifts in the police. Taking as much overtime as he could. And Mum was fun back then.' An earlier discussion with Paul entered my head and I was presented with an image of her dancing to the radio in the kitchen, nails painted, short skirt, earning admiring glances from my friends. How could I have forgotten that? And the resultant emotion. With a jolt, as if I was a ten-year-old again. I was pleased my mates thought she was cool, but simultaneously jealous that she would share that side of her with them.

'My dad used to do that as well,' Angela said. 'When I used to complain that he was always working, he said he was doing it so we could have nicer things, but I knew he was trying to keep out of the road of Mum.'

'I've never thought about that. I bet that's what my dad was doing as well.' We both laughed.

I plucked a cushion from under me and held it over my stomach, absently stroking the velvet fringes as I continued to talk.

'I was a horrible teenager. I used to frighten myself. I had so much anger in me it was incredible. I used to pick fights all the time.' I debated whether I should tell her about the incident with Paul, but decided against it. At this delicate time I didn't want to tell her anything that would make her feel badly about me. 'My parents didn't know how to handle me. It was worse for my father; he was a policeman. I was showing him up and I couldn't have cared less. Looking back, I was probably hitting out at him for not being there enough. Negative attention was better than no attention, you know?'

'What changed? I'm no great judge of people but you seemed to have dealt with that anger. You seem a patient kind of guy now.'

'That's because I keep such control of my emotions.' I held the cushion tight. 'I had to.'

'Why, what happened?'

Before I knew it, despite thinking I couldn't tell her only moments earlier, I told her about that day all those years ago with Paul.

'I went crazy. Screaming and acting like a wild animal … The next thing I remember is Paul's face covered with blood. The way he was huddled away from me like I was some kind of…' I shuddered.

'Aren't you being a little bit harsh on yourself?' Angela said, but her hands had stopped moving and I could feel that emotionally, just for a moment, she had retreated from me. But then her need to reassure me took over. 'We all have episodes like that as a kid.'

'I've never lost it like that ever again.' I shivered. 'Leaving the village and going to uni here in Glasgow helped. A new environment, a new group of people. I could start again, reinvent myself. It was just what I needed.' I craned my head back so that I was looking up into her face. I could see her eyes were moist. 'See, told you. Just your normal, boring childhood.' I laughed.

'It's a real credit to him, to you both, that Paul and you are still friends.'

I thought about the last time I'd seen him. How badly I'd reacted. Understandable, but still, Paul deserved better from me. Could I tell Angela anything of that? I opened my mouth to say something, but she was on the move. With care, she lifted my head from her lap, then she shifted so that we were side by side. She then looked deep into my eyes.

'Kiss me,' she whispered. And I felt our connection stronger than ever. I wanted this woman in my life. I wanted to wake up next to her every morning.

Pressing my lips against hers, I felt myself react. My pulse grew heavy, by breath shortened, and I could feel a tightening in my groin.

I assessed my arousal. Would it be strong enough? Would I embarrass myself again? Should we just stick with cuddling for now?

Panic clutched at my chest. But unaware of my internal battle, Angela reacted to my kiss with the gentlest of touches on my chest, over my heart. Her soft contact soothed my panic a little. I began to move my lips slowly in concert with hers.

My heart began to beat faster again, this time with something approaching passion.

'See, it isn't that bad,' Angela said, inadvertently reminding me of my failures. Then her hand moved to open my shirt. Anxiety snapped at me, and I moved my hand to intercept hers.

'Maybe later?' I said, hating myself.

18

The abatement of the tensions between Angela and me was only temporary. Her reservations didn't lessen over the next few weeks, and in an effort to appease her I agreed we should meet up and take her daughter Cathy to the cinema. In the meantime I threw myself more and more into my investigations.

One Sunday morning, coffee laced with whisky to my right, croissant and jam to my left, I opened up a search engine on my laptop and read up what I could about the Shows and in particular the owner, who I discovered from my research at the library was one Benito Marinello.

According to one source, his father, Leo, came over from Italy in the 1920s, and got a job in a funfair. The son came along, grew up in the life and decided to branch out on his own as soon as he was able.

Most of the entries that came up on my search engine contained nothing of any real note. They were mainly puff pieces saying how Marinello gave this amount to that charity or he attended some big event in the city, or that he had publicly backed a certain politician. It all suggested Mr Marinello was keen to show that he was a concerned citizen. Maybe he was, but it felt to me like someone who was trying too hard.

My attention caught on an article from 2012 in the business pages of the *Glasgow Times*. Mr Marinello had quietly diversified over the previous ten years into a number of other businesses. His portfolio now included children's nurseries, old folks' homes, and a small chain of cafés. Marinello was keen to stress how perspicacious he had been – he'd seen that the writing was on the wall for his fairground business. At the same time, however, he felt it was important to stress to those who loved that institution that it would still be on the road for as long as it was supported, but sadly footfall had declined massively, which he blamed on computer games.

I entered the newspaper's own search system to see if there were any, more recent articles on the him and found one dated just ten months previously, which said Marinello was stepping back from the overall running of the business because of illness and his only daughter was taking over.

This was all very interesting, but it wasn't really getting me anywhere.

Then I hit on something with promise. A blog written by a guy who had been writing a biography of the man. They had had a falling-out and Marinello had withdrawn his permission. And in a note at the end of the first post the blogger noted that due to ill health Mr Marinello had gone to live in one of the nursing homes the family owned. The note felt just a little bit spiteful. Reading between the lines it felt like the blogger was saying, *This guy messed me about and I ain't letting all that hard work go to waste.*

The date on the first post was just a few days later than the article about Marinello stepping back from the business in favour of his daughter.

There were another half a dozen entries on the blog, each of about a thousand words long. The writing was clean and efficient but edged towards the sensational and had a ring of gossip. I could see why Marinello might have stepped away from his deal with this guy. The tone didn't suit the image he had previously presented to the world.

There was some juicy stuff in there though. Aside from the 'immigrant does well' narrative, which Marinello would have enjoyed, there was lots of stuff he would have hated, information I doubted the blogger would have ever shown the old man. Details about affairs with the wives of other fairground bosses, and links with organised crime.

The pissed-off tone of the whole thing made me wonder how much was true. However, it did suggest there was more to the old man than first appeared.

On a whim I looked up which nursing homes the family owned. There was one in Glasgow, one in Stirling, and the same in Edinburgh.

This was all well and good, but what should I do with this information? Might it be worth actually going to visit the old man? Chatting to me might be better than sitting in the common room watching *Homes under the Hammer*, so why not? I thought.

I decided I'd phone the nursing homes to find out which one he was resident in. I hit it lucky with my first call.

'Armadale Retirement Home, how may I help?' A woman answered.

'Is Mr Marinello available, please?' I asked.

'He's with a visitor at the moment,' she replied. 'Can I leave him a message?'

'Actually, I'm going to be in Stirling next week for a meeting,' I lied. 'Would it be okay to pop in and say hi?'

'Might I ask what this is in connection with, sir?'

'I'm doing a piece for the BBC,' I said, and wondered where the ease with which I could now lie was coming from. 'About the demise of the travelling funfair. I thought Mr Marinello would be a great source of information.'

'Let me check with the family, sir, and get back to you.' She took a note of my phone number and promised to reply to me by the end of business that day.

She called back two hours later to arrange a time for my visit.

The following weekend I was on the road to Stirling.

As I turned into the drive of Armadale Retirement Home I could see a wide two-storey building with a red-brick façade, and a high sloping roof covered in dark-brown tiles. It was set among mature trees and large shrubs. A portico at the front was large enough to allow a car or, it occurred to me, an ambulance, to pass under it, park and drop off a client.

The vaulted ceiling in the entrance lobby reminded me of a church. The walls were bare brick, just like the exterior, and the ceiling was high with large windows letting in lots of light.

'Can I help you?' A young woman wearing a light-blue blouse, navy skirt and matching cardigan approached us. It felt to me as if she was dressing for her clientele rather than her own age group.

'Yes, please…' I peered down at her name badge. *Amanda*. 'I arranged a visit with Mr Marinello.'

'Ah right. Mr Docherty from the BBC?'

I mentally retreated from the lie. 'In the flesh.'

'Yes, we're expecting you.' She offered me a warm smile. 'Please come with me and we'll get you settled in with a nice cuppa.' She walked ahead for a few steps and then turned to face me.

'The family agreed on this visit with the proviso that one of them sits with Mr Marinello.' Another smile. 'Miss Marinello, his grand-daughter, actually runs the place, so that makes life easier, but she's been held up. She'll be with us shortly,' she added with a bright smile.

'Great,' I said, wondering when I should just confess to the truth.

'I'm sure Benny will be more than happy to help you with your research if he can…' Her expression grew serious and she continued in a low tone. 'He has his good days and his bad days. Let's hope you've caught him on a good one.'

The walls of the room she led us into were lined with easy chairs, and the far corner housed a giant TV set, which was blank and silent. In the middle of the room, in front of a wall that was floor-to-ceiling glass, sat a man who, judging by the way his clothes hung on him, had recently lost a lot of weight.

'I've got visitors coming, you said.' The man's voice wavered uncertainly.

'And here he is, Benny,' Amanda said with forced jollity.

'Ah.' He looked over at me as if he was waiting for his eye muscles to settle. Then. 'Travelled far?' he asked.

'Glasgow,' I said hoping my answer wasn't a disappointment.

'Yes, yes, yes,' the old man said. 'You must be Danny.'

'No, Benny,' the young woman smiled an apology towards me. 'This is John Docherty. He's with the BBC.'

'Oh dear,' Benny said. 'That's not so good. But who's Danny?'

'Sometimes he gets an idea stuck in his head and we can't shift it,' Amanda said. She indicated I should take a seat beside the old man. 'I'll bring you in a nice cuppa,' she said.

'Have you travelled far?' Benny asked again.

'Benny loves getting visitors and is always extra chuffed if they've come a fair distance to see him,' Amanda said.

'Don't talk about me as if I'm not here, Amanda,' Benny said, each word clipped with irritation. 'I've not totally lost it yet.'

Amanda gave a little smile and in an awkward motion ducked her head by way of an apology.

'I'm from Glasgow, Benny,' I said again, and thinking I might as well dispense with the lie and get to the point, I fished the photo of Thomas and me out of my pocket. 'I wanted to ask you if you ever came across this lad.'

He leaned over and studied the photograph.

After a pause he looked up at my face. 'What's this about?' As he looked at me, I could see the younger man was still in there.

'The older boy here disappeared in 1990, and I've traced the disappearance of a couple of other lads around the same time … in the same locations where your Shows were based,' I answered, trying not to look at the confused expression on Amanda's face.

'But isn't this…?' she began.

'The BBC,' I nodded.

'Is this Danny?' Benny looked over at me, his eyes cast in vagueness. 'You're a nice lad. Got a nice smile. Could do with a haircut, mind you.'

I was taken aback by this and simply smiled in response. The way he was flipping from one state of mind to another was slightly alarming. 'Thanks,' I said feeling like a bit of an idiot, but also feeling that I was wasting my time. This poor old guy wasn't in any state to offer any help.

'Three boys went missing. Each of those dates matched a visit by the Marinello Funfair,' I carried on gamely. 'It's probably just a coincidence, but we need to chase down everything. My dad died never knowing for sure what happened to his eldest son, and I want to make sure the other families involved have some kind of answers.'

'Oh, dear, that's…' Amanda's hand went to her throat. 'Those poor parents.' She leaned forwards. 'Benny, do you recognise this boy?'

'Of course,' he said, eyebrows knitted together. At these words my heart thumped and my stomach twisted. The old man knew him?

'I'm not an idiot.' Benny looked over at me and pointed. 'It's him. He's a lot younger here mind. And he has a daft haircut in this photo.'

He was talking about me. I sat back, deflated. I should have known it wouldn't be that easy.

As if she realised the jump I had made in my mind, Amanda sent me a commiserating smile. Then said, 'Sorry, I was so caught up in this I forgot to go and get us a drink.'

Just then the door opened behind us, and I heard the light tread of someone enter the room.

'Hi, Gramps,' a woman said. I turned around and saw a woman of medium height and slim build, with dark shoulder-length hair. She was wearing what looked like an expensive navy suit with a pale-blue blouse. She was smiling as she approached me with her hand out.

My breath caught in my throat as it occurred to me that she was like an older version of Angela. More grey in her hair, more lines at the sides of her eyes, but Angela was there in the cast of her expression; that intelligent, understanding look I'd come to know and love.

Angela.

Shit.

I was supposed to be going to the cinema with her and Cathy today.

'I'm Gina,' the woman said, and I introduced myself. Amanda repeated that she would go and make us a hot drink.

'I'm sorry…' I opened my mouth to explain my lie and say why I was really here, fighting to ignore the inner voice that was scolding me loudly for forgetting about my previous arrangement with Angela and Cathy.

'This is Danny,' Benny said. 'Needs a haircut.'

'Okay, Gramps,' she smiled at him and turned to me with an apology on her face. 'If you got him on a good day I'm sure he would have been able to help.'

'Every day's a good day,' Benny said. 'I hate it when you talk about me as if I'm not here, Gina.' He looked at me. 'Don't get old, son. Everybody thinks you're a cunting idiot.' He was so angry a few spots of spit flew out of his mouth.

'Right, Grandad, you know we don't like that kind of language in here.' Gina looked back at me as if seeing me for the first time. She paused, a smile lingering. 'He has problems with self-editing.' She narrowed her eyes in enquiry. 'Have we…?'

'When's the tea coming, pet? I hope they've got those Jammie Dodgers.' Benny looked at me. 'You look like you might enjoy a Jammie Dodger, Danny.'

'Grandad, Amanda has just this second gone for the tea. And this is…' She sent me a quick look.

'John,' I said.

'Right. Lovely,' Benny said as he sat back in his chair, holding his hands on his lap. Then seconds later his head slid to the side, his eyes closed and his breathing settled into a slow and rhythmic pattern.

'He goes to sleep that quickly?' I asked.

'He does. Visitors wear him out. But sometimes it's just a bit too convenient, if you know what I mean.' Gina said with a tired smile.

That was a signal that the meeting should come to a close. I doubted there was much point in me staying any longer so I stood to leave.

'I really shouldn't take up any more of your time,' I said. Then I took a gamble and stretched out to touch the old man's hand. 'Lovely to meet you, Benny. Thanks for your help.'

He opened his eyes. Then took my hand, his grip light, and smiled as if taking real pleasure in the contact, the skin crinkling round his pale eyes. 'You must be Danny,' he said. 'You'll be a handsome lad once you get a shave and a haircut.'

19

When I got back to my car I was feeling more and more cheesed off. I'd come all this way, concocted a ridiculous story about the BBC, and I'd managed to forget about meeting Angela and Cathy. Clearly detective work was not for me. Perhaps I should think about engaging a real one and then maybe I'd get somewhere with this situation.

My mobile phone sounded.

'John, where are you?' It was Angela. 'You were supposed to pick us up twenty minutes ago. Is everything okay?' She sounded concerned.

'God, I am so sorry,' I said feeling my face grow warm. 'Something came up.'

'What?' And in that one syllable she somehow managed to convey irritation, disappointment and confusion.

'I found an old man who might know about Thomas,' I replied, hoping that by exaggerating the significance of Marinello's connection with Thomas it might help explain my rudeness.

'And this was the only time he could see you?'

'Well … it was…'

'You forgot, John, didn't you?' She sounded more disheartened than angry.

'Let me explain, please,' I begged.

'Don't bother.' And she hung up.

I tried to call right back but it went straight to her answering service. I left a grovelling apology and asked her to call me back. Five minutes later I did the same. Rather than drive off and be unable to take her call I waited, still in the car park of the retirement home.

A knock sounded on my window. I turned to see Gina Marinello standing there. I climbed out of the car.

'I was looking out of my office window...' she turned back towards the building as if to indicate where her office was '...and I saw you still sitting there. I'm sorry you came all this way for nothing.'

'That's okay,' I said. 'There's really no need to apologise. It was a long shot.'

'I still feel bad. I should have just said no when I found out you'd called to ask for permission to speak to him, but I hoped your visit might stimulate Gramps' brain.'

'I understand,' I said, feeling like a bit of a heel given my subterfuge.

She studied my face as if scanning her memory for a name. 'I'm sorry, but I have this notion that we've met before...' She let that hang, giving me room to answer. Part of me wondered if she was coming on to me, but her expression was all business.

'I'm pretty sure we've never met.'

'Okay...' She looked dissatisfied with that answer. 'It will come to me. I never forget a face.' She took a step back. 'And once again, I'm sorry for your wasted time. If only I could put you in touch with some of the people Gramps dealt with in the past. They might be able to help you, but since I started working for him I've really only dealt with the care side of the business.'

'Thanks,' I said, digging my hands into my pockets.

'There's a couple of guys I can remember. They were always doing stuff for Grandad. Stuart Gillon and Jim...' she reached into her memory '...Dick. Jim Dick. I wonder if Gramps has their details somewhere. Do you have a card? Give me a couple of days and I'll have the details for you.'

'I'm freelance,' I said, hoping my lie wasn't creaking at the seams. 'So the Beeb don't give us any of that kind of stuff. But I can...' I reached into the side pocket of the car door and pulling out a note-book and pen, I tore off a page and wrote down my email address. 'Any details you can provide will be gratefully received.' I offered her my best smile.

'And how could I forget Elsa?' Her expression grew warm. 'Such a lovely woman. She was always very kind to me. Brown. That's it. Brown. She and her husband ran a stall until he died. Poor Elsa was distraught. She tried to make a go of it, but even though I was only a girl at the time I could see her heart was no longer in it. Last I heard she was working as a foster carer in Glasgow.'

It was better than nothing.

'Thanks, I'll see what my researchers can find out.' I almost choked on the word 'researcher' but she was so earnest about wanting to help I felt I had to maintain the lie.

'Gillon and Dick,' she said. 'They're who you really want to talk to. I'll get you their details as soon as.' She waved the piece of paper I'd given her at me.

'It's a start,' I said with confidence. 'Thank you.'

It's true that when you have a time of personal discomfort you seek solace in habit and familiarity. And for me that came from booze. The deeper the discomfort, the bigger the bottle.

I'd let Angela down. I'd let me down. When it came to relationships I was fooling myself. They just weren't for me.

I phoned Paul. 'Want to come out to play?' I asked.

'Long time since I heard that expression,' he replied with a laugh. 'But sorry, mate, no can do. I've got something on tonight.' He hung up after promising we would do something another time.

Didn't matter. It was probably best that I did this on my own.

Sometime later I was in a small bar just around the corner from my flat, elbows planted on a scored and sticky table top, a pint of self-destruction and a chaser of self-loathing in front of me.

A couple of women at the bar were looking over at me. I sent them a wink and shouted over, offering to buy them both a drink.

That was my next mistake of the day.

My phone rang. With a groan I reached for it, and as I opened my eyes a shaft of sunlight pierced my brain with a hot finger of pain.

'Hello,' I said, my voice sounding like my vocal cords had been grated with broken glass.

'John, it's me.'

Angela. I sat up.

'Sorry about yesterday,' she said. 'Even though you were a shit, I was a bit huffy.'

Someone moved at my side, under the quilt. Then she began coughing.

Shit. I'd picked up one of those women at the bar last night. In the momentary befuddlement of awakening from a late night and very little sleep it had slipped my mind.

'Is there someone there with you, John?' Angela asked.

I was mute. How on earth was I going to explain this one? A lie presented itself. I'm in a café. Someone near me must have a cold. Then the woman in my bed sat up, her hair crushed on the one side of her head like a cascade of bleached straw.

'Honey, where's your bathroom. I'm pure bursting,' she said.

'John, do you have someone in your…?' Angela gave a shout of anger and hung up.

20

After two weeks of pleading, Angela eventually agreed to meet up with me. I didn't expect her to want to continue our relationship, and I was too deep in my own brokenness to even hope for such an outcome, but I felt I owed it to her to apologise in person.

I met her outside her office in St Vincent Street.

She approached with her head down, hands in her pockets, and in the light of the streetlamps I could see the cloud of her breath in the air.

She looked up, flicked her hair away from her eyes with a toss of her head, and raised an eyebrow. Breath caught in my throat. She had never looked so beautiful.

I quailed at the thought of what was to come, but I had to do this. My selfishness had made both of us miserable and there was nothing I could do to mend that, but I could treat her with some dignity.

When she reached me she said, 'I don't know what you hope to achieve by this, John. We're over.' Her voice held a quiet strength.

When I tried to speak tears filled my eyes. Angela saw them and made a small sound of sympathy despite herself, moving her hand upwards as if to brush them away. Then she stopped herself and let her hand fall to her side.

'I'm such a dick, Angela. I'm so sorry. You deserved better.'

'Yes, I did.' She took a step back, and crossed her arms across her abdomen. 'I knew this day would come, John. I *knew* you'd hit the self-destruct button.' Her tone was conciliatory. But then her expression clouded and there was anger behind her words. 'Just, for God's sake, don't say that you still want us to be friends.' She looked away as if pulling on her reserves. Then she turned back to face me. 'This is all because I have a child, isn't it?'

The truth of her words cut through me. Her eyes were swimming with tears, and I could feel emotion swell in my throat. I bit down on my lip in an attempt to control my feelings.

'You fool, you still love me.' She spoke without rancour, but with a deep sadness. Then looking deep into my eyes, she said, 'Whatever demons you're wrestling with, John, face up to them, or you'll never be happy.'

21

'Christ you look a mess,' said Chris, when I opened the door to him.

'Hello, yourself,' I said and looked down at my dark-brown towelling dressing gown, stained white T-shirt and green, cotton pyjama bottoms.

Chris, in contrast, looked tanned and fit. He watched with a half-smile as I took in his dark designer jeans, grey full-length wool coat, and plain white T-shirt.

'You'll catch your death in that,' I said, then turned and walked back inside my flat.

'Good to see you too, bro,' Chris said as he followed me inside. In the living room I slumped onto the sofa and regarded my brother.

'What's up?' I asked. 'Didn't think you'd be coming back so soon.'

'Yeah, well. Man plans, God scoffs. Or something.' Chris looked around. 'Life's treating you well, I see?'

'I'll give it a clean later,' I said, feeling my face heat at the state of the place. Over the last few weeks my only concern had been making it into work each day. It was about the only thing I could raise the energy for.

'What happened? I mean, I know you live like a teenage boy, but you don't usually let it get this bad,' Chris said as he looked around again.

'Angela and I broke up,' I replied, finishing off my statement with a weak, I'm-really-okay smile.

'There's an Angela?'

I gave Chris the hard-eye.

'I knew you were seeing someone. I just forgot her name is all.'

'Stop talking American,' I said.

'Shit. Looks like about two months of crap here. How long ago did this happen?'

'A couple of months.'

'Fair enough. A broken heart isn't to be sniffed at.' Chris clapped his hands against his thighs and stood up. 'But time for the pity party to be shut down. C'mon…' He reached for me, grabbed the lapel of my dressing gown and pulled me to my feet. He knew that when his energy levels were high it irritated the life out of me, and I knew he was playing on that. 'It's time to clean this place up.' Chris smiled. 'I'll even give you hand.'

With me trailing behind him, Chris went round the flat like a whirlwind, opening curtains, picking up soiled clothes and flinging out rubbish. After we were done I let Chris sit me down with a can of beer.

'Why did this Angela give you the elbow, then?' Chris asked.

'I was an arsehole. It was richly deserved.' I held my can up and toasted the notion.

Chris assessed me for a moment. 'Still doing the self-sabotage thing?'

'What do you mean, still?' I demanded.

Chris made a *pfft* sound. 'You've only been doing that with women all your adult life.'

'I have?'

'Please,' Chris laughed. 'A string of one-night stands. Three serious girlfriends that I know of. All of whom you dumped when things got too heavy.'

I sat back in my seat, opened my mouth as if I was going to refute the accusation, then sighed. Even I could hear the truth in what he was saying.

'Enough about me,' I said, feeling uncomfortable. I hadn't spent weeks burying my head in the sand to have Chris excavate my feelings after two minutes of being in the flat. 'What happened with you two? I thought you were head over heels.'

'I was,' Chris answered. 'I kinda knew from the start it would have its limits. But silver lining…' He adopted his happy face and rubbed his hands together. 'I've still got her credit card and all the fancy clothes she bought me.'

'I'm sorry,' I said, but I felt just a frisson of pleasure there. It was good to have company in my misery. 'What're you going to do now?'

'Kick around for a little while. See what's what, and then hop a plane. Maybe try the Florida Keys this time. Bag me another rich widow.' Chris studied me and asked. 'Why? You got a use for me? I take it the search for a brother was a bust?'

'Oh, that.' I coloured.

'What?'

'He's real,' I leaned closer. 'We *did* have a brother. Thomas.'

'What? Jesus. Why haven't you been keeping me up to speed, bro?'

'I found a birth certificate. One Thomas Docherty born in 1975 to William and Lorna Docherty,' I said.

'Fuck,' Chris said, emitting one elongated vowel sound as he slumped back into his seat. 'I knew it. The lying bastards.' He shook his head.

But then, as if furious that our parents had kept this from him, he jumped to his feet. 'Fuck,' he repeated, and looked around him as if he was wishing there was something he could kick or punch. He rubbed at his head. Then turned back to face me. 'Why didn't you let me know?' he asked sharply.

'I was going to. I tried…' I paused, studying a spot on the carpet.

'You were so full of your own shit you couldn't even get in touch with your brother. I deserved to be kept informed, John. A phone call. Or an email if you couldn't be arsed actually talking to me.'

'Don't be like that.'

'Like what? Angry my brother would keep something this big from me?'

'Oh, right.' I was on my feet now. 'Play the brother card now, why don't you?'

'Yeah, 'cos you play the martyr so well, brother.'

'Fuck you.'

We stared at each other for a long moment. Faces almost close enough for me to feel my brother's breath on my skin. A dozen comments flitted through my mind, each of them designed to wound. But I forced myself to resist that temptation.

With what looked like a massive effort, Chris moved back to the sofa and took a seat. 'How about Mum? And the house? It sold yet?'

Shit. The house. The money in Mum's account wouldn't last much longer. I had to get it sorted. And at that thought I felt the usual stab of resentment that all of this was on my plate.

'There's an estate agent I was about to contact,' I lied, thinking I'd get on it as soon as possible. Then wondering why I was acting as if I was ashamed at my inactivity, I shot back at him. 'And like you care. Are you even going to see her while you're here?'

His lips were a thin, pale line, as if he was restraining himself from shouting back at me.

'Okay.' He held his hands out. 'It's unfair all of that stuff has been on you. But I promise to help now. Get me the details of the estate agent and I'll take that over.' He paused as if he'd had a thought. 'How can you sell the place without Mum's say so? Officially, like? Can she even hold a pen to sign anything?'

'Not sure.' It hadn't even crossed my mind. I had a memory of people coming to see Dad, asking him as a local professional to witness documents. 'She definitely has the cognitive ability to understand what's happening. Perhaps whatever signature she can manage needs to be witnessed?'

He bit his lip, and I knew he was thinking if he took on this bureaucracy it would mean he'd have to go and see her.

'Okay. Leave that with me.'

'Are you sure?'

'I'm sure.' He leaned forwards. 'In the meantime, how about you take a seat and you tell me everything you found out after I left with Marjory?'

'Sure,' I agreed with a small smile as I sat down. 'Sorry I blew up there. Things have been…'

'Shitty. I hear you.'

Feeling mollified at his evident sympathy, I began to recount the events of the last few months, telling Chris about my library searches, the visit to meet the old man from the Shows, how good-looking his granddaughter was and how she'd given me details of a few of the Marinellos' employees.

'Gina was as good as her word. An email came in from her just the other day with the details of two or three of her grandad's workers. I've just kind of sat on it since.' As I said this, I reached for my laptop, which was sitting on the coffee table. I located the email and read aloud from it.

'Look at you, Mr Private Eye,' Chris said with a grin. 'Dick and Gillon? Sounds like a firm of funeral directors. Maybe I can put that old journalism degree of mine to good use. Want me to try and find out more about them while you're off at work?'

22

The following weekend, Chris and I pulled up in front of a block of flats in Perth. They were three storeys high and looked like new-builds, set alongside a canal and with the air of a retirement village: lots of flowering baskets, satellite dishes, and net curtains.

We located the entry for Jim Dick and knocked on his door. A tall, slim white-haired man, with what looked like a bowling ball under his light-blue cardigan and a face full of acne scars, opened the door and peered out at us from behind thick reading glasses.

'Aye?' he enquired.

'Mr Dick,' I said. 'We're researchers from the BBC and we're making a documentary about Scotland's travelling funfairs.'

'You are, are you?' He raised an eyebrow. 'What's that got to do with me?'

'We understand you worked for a Mr Marinello for a number of years, and we wondered if you might like to talk about that time?'

'That whole thing would have ground to a halt without me,' he said, with a great deal of self-satisfaction.

'Mr Marinello himself suggested you would be worth speaking to,' I said, thinking I could appeal to his evident ego.

'Am I going to be on telly, like?' He stood taller and sucked in his belly.

'We'd need to talk to you first,' Chris replied. 'Lay the ground-work, so to speak, and then if we like what we hear we arrange to come back with a film crew.'

Jim Dick preened a little more at the thought. 'You better come in then.' He directed us into a small sitting room that had a view out onto the slim strip of water of the canal and the shopping centre beyond. 'The missus is out with the girls. At a cancer coffee-morning thing,' he said as he pointed towards the sofa. 'She'll be fair tickled that we're going to be on the telly.' He looked at me and then Chris. 'The BBC you said?'

We sat where he indicated. 'Yes,' replied Chris. 'What can you remember about your time with Marinello?'

Jim sat down, stretched his long legs out in front of him and started talking, telling us boring stories of his days with the Shows, from a seemingly endless supply. And it felt like he would never stop. Eventually he paused, smacked his lips as if they'd dried out and offered us a cup of tea.

'No, thanks,' I said, thinking I didn't want to be in his company for any longer than I needed to. 'What you've been telling us is fascinating and definitely worth using for the show. But it can't all have been good,' I added in what I hoped was a cajoling tone.

'For sure,' Chris interjected. 'Were there any scandals in your time there? Any friction between Old Man Marinello and the rest of the team?'

'He was a good man,' said Jim, huffing to himself. 'I won't hear a word said against him. And if you're going to speak to Stuart Gillon next, don't believe a word you hear.'

'We are indeed going to see a Mr Gillon next,' I said. 'Why shouldn't we listen to him?'

'Hmm.' Jim Dick drummed on the arms of his chair with both hands. 'I suppose I should trust you to see through the wee arsehole. You look like you've got your heads on the right way.' Then he began to talk again about his halcyon days with the funfair.

Finally, sending a look to Chris, I got to my feet.

'Wonderful stuff, Mr Dick. You've given us lots of stuff to chew over.'

'Yeah, we'll definitely be back in touch to work out when to send the film crew over,' Chris said.

Dick bustled after us to the front door, and as we exited he thrust a small piece of paper into my hand.

'My phone number, you know, for when you need to get back to me.'

'Great,' I said. 'Wonderful. The wheels of the TV documentary world turn very slowly, Mr Dick, but you will hear back from us in a few months.'

We waited until we were back in the car before speaking.

'Well, that was a waste of time,' Chris said as he put the car key in the ignition.

'I wonder what he has against the other guy, Gillon.'

'Only one way to find out,' Chris smiled over at me as he fixed his seatbelt and drove off.

Stuart Gillon lived in the neighbouring town of Crieff, in a small bungalow fronted by a large, well-maintained stretch of lawn and some tall fir trees. As we walked up the path, a small, bald man with a long white beard came round the side of the house, carrying a rake and a trowel.

'Gents…' he began, his eyes narrow with suspicion. 'Whatever you're selling I'm not buying.'

Chris gave him the same story we'd given his former colleague, playing on the fake BBC connection.

'You are, are you?' he asked, a copy of his old friend, but judging by his expression, Mr Gillon's suspicions didn't ease any. 'The BBC, aye?' he added as if his question was accompanied with a silent *my arse*.

'The Marinello story is a fascinating one,' I said. 'And given the fondness the Scots have for the Shows, one that's bound to have a big audience.'

'If they have such a *fondness*, as you say, why was I out of a job?' With that, he walked past me to a stretch of border and started pulling out some weeds.

Chris and I looked at each other wondering how to deal with this guy.

'You have no interest in talking about your time with the

Marinellos?' I asked. 'Sounds like they dumped you when you felt you had more work in you.' The way he was attacking the weeds suggested he was still a fit man.

'Something like that,' he said as he wiped his brow with a sleeve. 'Twenty-odd years I gave that mob, and they binned me without a second thought.'

'I hear they went into retirement homes,' Chris said.

Stuart Gillon paused in his actions and looked at us. 'I suspect you went to see Jim Dick before you came to see me?'

'Yeah. He couldn't have been more helpful,' I replied.

'Of course he was. Nothing but an arse-licker.' Then he cocked his head to the side and started to speak as if he was mimicking someone. A certain Mr Dick, I assumed. 'You and me we'll stick together, Stuart. You and me, we'll show them Marinellos what's what, so we will.' He spat. 'Arsehole. A few months after they closed up shop Jim calls me to say he's been asked to do a few wee jobs round the nursing home in Stirling. Did they ask me? No. Did Jim even suggest me to them? No.'

'That's not fair,' Chris commiserated with him. 'Mr Gillon said Marinello was a good guy. Didn't have a bad word to say about him.'

'I'll bet you he talked about him as if he had one foot in the Vatican.'

'Something like that,' I answered.

'If you ask me, anyone who spends that much time trying to look good has a lot to hide,' Stuart said in a quiet voice. Then, as if forcibly distracting himself, he examined the pile of weeds at his feet.

'What do you know, Mr Gillon?' I asked, feeling there was something important this man could tell us. His eyes shifted as if he was contemplating saying more. Then his expression clouded and closed down.

'Listen,' he straightened his back, reaching his full five feet five, his expression unreadable. 'This is the first dry day we've had for ages, so if you don't mind going back to the BBC,' he looked pointedly back down the garden path, 'I've got a lot of work to do.'

23

There was no point in trying to drag anything more out of the old man, so Chris and I trudged back up the path to the car. Feeling despondent, I looked at my brother.

'We're wasting our time here. Why don't we go back to the city and find a proper private detective – let them do the work for us.'

Chris raised an eyebrow as he looked at me. 'You giving up already?'

'Not giving up. It just feels that we're wasting our time doing this ourselves. These old guys are finding it too easy to fob us off.' I looked back down towards the house, where Mr Gillon was transferring his pile of weeds into a large brown bin.

'We've got one more address to try. Elsa whatever her name is. And she's on our way home. Why don't we go there, and if we get the same kind of reaction then look at paying someone to do this?'

Sometime later, Chris and I were pulling up in front of a terrace of small white houses. They each had two windows and a door on the ground floor, and two windows on the top floor. Modest, but with trim lawns and flower baskets everywhere you looked.

My knock on the door earned a high yip from what sounded like a small dog and a female voice shouting, 'Coming.'

A small breathless woman appeared, her thin, lined face pink with exertion. She had a head of thick, wiry, grey and black hair.

'Yes?' she asked. The dog moved back and forth behind her, barking constantly. 'Dolly,' she shouted down at it. 'For goodness sake, I can hardly hear myself think.' She kicked out at it. The dog dodged her leg, but closed its mouth.

'Sorry to trouble you,' Chris said. 'We're doing some research on the Marinello Funfair for a BBC programme and wondered if we could talk…'

'How did you get my name?' she asked as her eyes scanned the street behind us. Then she focussed on me, her eyebrows shot up, and she slammed the door shut.

'What the…?' Chris said as we looked at each other.

He knocked at the door again. That set the dog off.

He bent over and opened the letter box. 'Mrs Brown? Mrs Brown, we just want a quick word with you.'

Nothing.

'Let me try,' I said.

Chris stepped back and I brought my face down to the letter box. The dog kept up its barrage of barks, but I could hear the old woman moving just behind the door. 'Mrs Brown. My name is John Docherty.' I decided we should go with the truth. 'My brother Thomas disappeared thirty years ago. My dad died thinking he was murdered. If there's anything you can do to help us find out what happened we would be very grateful.'

I could hear her breathing, heavy and laboured. Then the door opened again.

'Jesus, you gave me a fright,' she said with a hand to her throat. 'I thought you were someone I hadn't seen for a long time.' She looked up to the sky and crossed herself. 'In the name of the Father…' She bit her lip, held a hand to her throat and in a quivering voice said, 'It's my time for penance.' She shook her head, the movement incredibly slow.

'Thomas, you called him?' she asked.

'Yes.'

'I never knew his name.'

'Thomas Docherty,' I said, hearing a quiver in my own voice now.

'Dear God, you are so like him…' She reached out a hand to touch me, as if needing to verify my presence.

'Mrs Brown, if you could shed any light on my brother's death we would be immensely grateful.' I was trying to keep my voice calm and level, but my stomach was churning. We'd hit on something big here. It was clear from her reaction that this woman had actually met Thomas.

We were invited inside, through a dimly lit hall and into a small living room festooned with lace, cushions and curtains, the small dog keeping up its high-pitched barking.

'Once you have a seat she'll settle down,' Elsa said, sitting herself.

We did the same, and, with a final bark, the small dog leapt onto Elsa's lap and snuggled in.

Elsa's cheekbones and nose were sharp, her lips pale and thin. But despite the slightness of her face and body, her jowls and the skin around her neck was loose, as if at some point she'd lost a great deal of weight. Her eyes didn't settle on one place, suggesting a frantic jumble of thoughts.

With a mind crowded with questions I stared at the small gas fire in front of me. The fire surround looked like it was made from Formica-covered plasterboard and was sitting on a grey, marble-effect hearth resting three inches proud of the carpet. The mantelpiece itself was studded with the metal and glass frames of photos of a legion of teenage boys and girls.

'My penance,' Elsa said following my gaze. 'I fostered each of these kids and gave them all a good start in life.' She dabbed at her eyes with a tissue. 'I've had dozens and dozens of kids in my time. Every one a treasure. Mr Brown and I were never blessed with kids of our own and after…' she looked at me. 'When I left the Marinellos it felt like a way to make up for…' She tailed off as if unsure how to explain what had happened. But she appeared unable to take her eyes off me. 'It's burned into my memory, son. But I had no choice. I really had no choice.' She began to sob, as if decades worth of guilt were now forced to the surface.

Chris and I simply sat there in silence and allowed her to cry herself out.

'Sorry,' she said eventually. Then she blew her nose. 'What did you say his name was?'

I told her again.

'Thomas,' she repeated. Her lips curved up in a weak smile. 'He was a handsome lad.'

'Mrs Brown, are you able to tell us what happened?'

She wiped at her right eye and nodded. 'Give me a minute, son. This has been decades in the making.'

She took a deep breath and there was a long silence.

'This won't go any further? You promise?'

'We promise,' Chris said as he leaned forwards in his seat. I repeated his words.

'You sure?'

I would have sworn on a Bible if it would have made her speak, but she looked from me to Chris and gave a small nod, as if she had come to a decision.

'Confession is good for the soul, they say.' She looked out of the window. 'If I get locked up for my part in this, so be it.'

'We're telling no one, Mrs Brown,' I said.

She sighed and settled down in her seat, as if preparing to give up a dark secret was easing her mind. 'Things were in a bit of a state, to put it mildly,' she said with a grimace. 'Mr Brown borrowed lots of money to pay off a gambling debt, and our stalls weren't doing so well. Kiddies were no longer interested in poxy little popguns when they had all these computer-game things, or so my husband thought.' Her expression slid into sadness. 'Then he ups and dies, leaving me with all this money owed. No life insurance. So the debt was put onto me.'

'How much did you owe?' I asked.

'Just over ten grand,' she replied. 'Might not sound like much now, but thirty years ago it was a tidy sum. And the people my husband lent it from weren't too patient about waiting for repayment.' As she was speaking her hand stopped stroking the dog's head and began gently tugging at its ears. It moved its head out of her reach.

'I just didn't have the money, and they knew it, but it didn't stop them coming round, threatening all sorts. I was terrified. Absolutely terrified.' She held a trembling hand to her mouth. 'I really didn't have the cash to give them and they knew that, so they came up with a solution.' She studied the carpet in front of the fire, before forcing her eyes up to meet mine. 'Any kids who were hanging round my stall, at a loose end, preferably on their own, I was to get them chatting. Find out if they had any issues…' She cleared her throat. 'Basically I'd to find out if anyone might miss them.'

'Then what happened?' Chris asked.

'I was never really sure. Didn't really want to know, to be honest.' She coloured a little at this admission. 'It was mostly boys – teenagers – they were after. Took a couple of girls as well, but because of the boy thing I was sure it wasn't about sex.'

I opened my mouth, about to say to her that boys could be just as much a target of sexual predators as girls, but changed my mind. There was little point in that assertion. The woman obviously felt badly enough.

'They took the kids away?' Chris asked.

She nodded. 'In a big blue van.'

'Who was your contact? Who came up with this suggestion? How were you to get in touch?' Chris asked.

'That's all a bit muddled,' she said and rubbed at her forehead. 'All I can remember is the blue van, and this guy. He had an English accent.'

'What part of England?'

'Somewhere in the North, I think. It wasn't posh English, that's for sure.'

'The north of England has a variety of accents,' Chris said. 'Can you narrow it down a little? Was it Geordie, or from the west of the area?'

'Goodness, I don't know.' She stopped as if she was debating with herself. 'It wasn't a Newcastle accent, I know that much.'

Chris looked from her to me and back again. 'Mrs Brown, your remorse for your part in this situation is very clear. You couldn't be more sorry, and we can both see that.' Elsa looked over at him, her eyes almost drooping with gratitude at the tone Chris was taking. 'However,' he continued. 'Any help you can give us would be huge. Our family has been through enough.'

'I can't say,' Elsa replied. She was shaking, and despite everything I couldn't help but feel sorry for her. Picking up the distress of her owner, the dog focussed in on Chris and gave out a series of barks.

Chris studied her, waiting for the dog to stop. 'Can't? Or won't?' His tone was kind.

'These are dangerous people. There's no saying what they'll do if they find out I spoke about them.'

'How will they ever know?' Chris cajoled. 'We won't tell anyone. This is just for our own sake.'

'I can't. I just…' She started crying again.

As good as Chris's questioning was, I felt that he was backing her into a corner, and once there she was just going to shrivel into herself and give us nothing. We needed a slight change of direction. And I needed to know more about Thomas. This woman could well be my last and only contact with him.

'Mrs Brown,' I said, ignoring Chris's stare. 'Can you tell me more about when you met Thomas?'

24

1990

'So, you want to run away then, boy?'

'Aye,' he answered, squaring his shoulders, sensing that any sign of weakness would be jumped on by this guy. The man in front of him was even taller than his dad; his cheeks were hollow, his teeth yellow even in the weak light, and his eyes radiated a need to satisfy something, an urge that the boy couldn't even try to name.

'What you called, then?'

'Ben,' he lied. He was aware he knew almost nothing. He'd barely been out of his housing estate in all his fourteen years and therefore had little knowledge of the world. But he knew enough to protect himself. A lie was a little bit of safety in this moment.

'I can get you to London, Ben.' The man slowly rubbed his hands together. Lahndun. He pronounced it like they did on *EastEnders*. But as if he was taking the piss. 'You want to go to London?'

London.

He'd seen it on the telly. It was bound to be miles away. Lots of people went there, he knew, to either make lots of money, or to vanish.

'Yes, please.'

'He says please. I like a lad wiv manners.' The man smiled. One of his front two teeth on the top row was half the length of the other. 'Got any money?'

Ben ducked his head. Shook it.

'Not got any money?'

Ben shook his head again, feeling his desperation grow. This man had to help him. He had to get away. And stay away. Going back was just unthinkable. He felt … damaged. And the only way to get away from that damage was to move – away.

''Ow on earth you gonna get to London wivout any money?'

Ben shrugged a dunno.

'Cat's got your tongue and you ain't got no money.'

The man was teasing him, Ben realised. And enjoying his discomfort.

'I can work,' he said rousing some defiance. 'I'm a quick learner.'

'Sure you are,' the man said as he looked him up and down, his face souring as he did so, as if Ben had been judged and found to be lacking. The man sucked his teeth, then scratched at his chin as if making a tricky decision. It was all an act, Ben knew. The decision had been made the second the man saw him.

Ben had approached every stall, every ride in the fair, asking for work. Most looked him up and down and then dismissed him with a sneer, a loud curse or a wave of the hand.

Until the largest woman Ben had ever seen had taken an interest in him. She'd grabbed his arm with a strength that surprised him and pulled him to a small caravan just behind the dodgems. She huffed as she squeezed through the door and invited him inside.

'What are you running away from, son?' She asked. Now that she was inside it felt to Ben that she had changed and was less sure of herself.

'Stuff.'

'Whatever it is it can't be worse than what could be ahead of you.'

'There's no way it could be worse,' he huffed. 'I need to get away.'

'Okay,' she said quietly. Her face darkened, and the expression that formed on her face chilled Ben. It was as if she'd reached a con-clusion that was distasteful but unavoidable. 'I know a guy.'

She got to her feet, her bulk almost enough to block out the light from the window at the end of the van. 'First let me make us a wee cuppa.' She took a step across to the smallest kitchen Ben had ever seen, turned her back to him and started to bustle around.

As she did so Ben looked at the door. He felt the breeze that was coming in and thought about leaving. Whatever he had just set in motion could be dangerous. He had no way of knowing if this woman and the guy she was talking about had anyone's interests at heart apart from their own.

He felt a chill run through him. He should run out. But his feet and limbs were locked into position. Whatever lay ahead of him couldn't be worse than what was behind him.

'Have a seat, son,' the woman said over her shoulder.

The kettle sang its way to the boil and she soon put a hot, milky drink in front of him.

'Go on,' she said. 'Drink up. It won't kill you,' she said in a tone that suggested it just might. Ben reached out for the mug, placed it to his mouth and sipped. It was sweet, and not too hot. Just the way his Mum used to make it. At the thought of his mother, Ben felt a yearning. But quashed it. He wasn't going back home. Not ever. He took another sip and noticed a sourness this time as it hit the back of his tongue.

'I put a little whisky in it,' the woman said as if she'd read his reaction. 'Put hairs on your chest.'

He was almost a grown-up, wasn't he? He could handle a little whisky. And to prove it he took a large gulp.

Prompted by the woman, he continued sipping until the mug was empty. His eyes felt suddenly very heavy. He opened them wide as if to combat the feeling.

'Relax, son,' the woman said. 'Running away is hard work, eh?' Her large bosom heaved as she filled the space between them with her laugh and its hard edges.

He slipped down on the bench he was sitting on, allowing his head to rest on a cushion that smelled of sweat, cigarettes and whisky.

The woman disappeared, but returned soon after. How long she'd been away he had no way of knowing. Could have been minutes. Might have been hours.

Ben felt weight shift in the caravan and tried to pull himself up through the fog that had slowed his mind. He could hear two voices.

'That's us done after this one, Seth.' Ben recognised the woman's voice. 'From now on I owe you nuthin'.'

'Dream on, darling,' Seth snarled. 'The debt's done when we tell you it's done.'

'I'm not doing this anymore. I can't.' She sobbed. 'And what are you doing with these kids? It's not right.'

Ben felt the weight shift on the caravan floor again, and even in his drugged state he could feel the energy in the space heighten. Then the man spoke in a low voice. 'You got any money to give me, sweetheart?'

Nothing.

'Wot's that? I can't hear ya.'

'No,' she said in a tremulous voice.

'So, you'll know what to do about it then, wontcha?'

'Yes.'

The next he knew, he was sitting up in what looked like the back of the van, now on top of a quilt.

The double door was open, and beyond it Ben could see brightly coloured stalls, gaudy signs, and more caravans and large vehicles. He rubbed at his eyes. This wasn't the same place he'd been in before. Where had this guy taken him?

'Don't know what that old bitch gave you but it will soon wear off,' the man said, and Ben could hear the irritation in his voice. 'This has got to be your choice. I ain't hijacking any kids.'

Ben opened his mouth to say, *Well, it kind of feels like it*, but changed his mind. He sensed that kind of backchat wouldn't go down so well. He shifted position as he felt pressure on his bladder.

'Need a piss?'

He nodded.

The man shifted crab-like to the end of the van and hopped out.

'C'mon, before you wet yourself,' the man motioned. 'There's a tree over there. Be quick, while no one's watching.'

When Ben was finished, he turned to find the man sitting on the end of the van's floor space, feet crossed at the ankles as he smoked a cigarette. That he'd been given such leeway relaxed him slightly. The man was apparently unconcerned that he might run for it.

'Hungry?' the man asked.

Ben nodded.

'Mate, this is going to be a long trip if you don't loosen that tongue of yours.'

'Yeah. I'd like something to eat. Thanks,' he added, remembering the man's comment about his politeness.

'I could eat a fucking horse, mate. There's a burger bar further down the fair. Let's go.' And without waiting, he turned and started marching away.

Ben ran to catch up, and as they walked Ben looked around. People were milling around everywhere. Families, groups of boys, groups of girls. Everyone animated. Every face bright with the expectation of fun. And Ben had never felt so alone. This was stupid. He was being stupid. What did this man really want with him? He imagined himself running up to a family and asking for help. But then he imagined the mother grouping her children around her as if saving them from his threat, and heard the father telling him to go away.

The fair was set up in a large field surrounded by houses. Ben had no idea where he was, but judging by the accents of the people around him he was still in Scotland.

The man stopped walking and placed a hand on Ben's shoulder. 'Still hungry?'

'Yes, please,' Ben replied, unsure why he'd added a please to his answer.

'Okay, then,' the man said as he looked around. 'First, a little test.'

He appeared to be scanning the crowd nearest them, clustered round a stall where people were throwing darts at playing cards. He stopped and homed in on a young couple.

'Nothing dodgy, like,' the man said as he looked down at Ben. 'A test. Nothing more. To see what kind of smarts you got. Okay?'

Ben nodded, and then said, 'Yes.' And as the man loomed over him, it occurred to him that there was a threat in the wide hang of his shoulders and the large, heavy hand that rested on his shoulder.

'That couple. The girl with the long, dark hair, and the lad with the Scotland strip. You need to separate them.'

25

Once the woman had stopped talking I could only sit and stare at her. My brother was alive when their paths crossed, and this woman had had the power to bring him back into the bosom of his family. Instead he had been used as part payment of her debt.

I reminded myself it was a debt she didn't accrue.

But then there were the other kids she passed on. Whatever happened to them?

She could have gone to the police and stopped it all.

Would they have believed her?

My mind was a morass, full of contradictory thoughts and emotion. I'd found Thomas and lost him again, all in the one breath. This woman was caught up in that, but she'd been in an impossible situation. I felt sorry for her – it was clear that her confession was relieving her conscience somehow, so much so that she now seemed to be throwing caution to the wind. But at the same time I wanted to scream in her face for thinking only of herself.

A car horn sounded outside followed by a squeal of brakes. Elsa was on her feet, the disturbed dog once again barking as it danced around her feet.

'Who is it?' Elsa asked as she peeked out of the window, as if afraid to get too close. 'Can you see?'

Chris got to his feet and stepped to the window.

'Wait, get back,' Elsa shouted. And I could see she was beginning to regret having opened up to us.

'It's a wee bit late to be worrying about that, Mrs Brown,' Chris said. Then when he read the very real fear in her eyes his expression changed. 'You okay?'

'What have I done?' Elsa cried. 'I shouldn't have let you in. They'll come for me now.'

'No one will come for you, Mrs Brown,' Chris said. 'We'll get in touch with the police. We can tell them to keep an eye out.'

Elsa snorted. 'The police can't stop these people. And I'm not scared of the police anymore. I'll confess to my part in all this if they come for me. It's these others I'm terrified of.' She paused. 'The police are bloody rubbish anyway. Mrs Dawson three doors down was robbed two years ago. She kept her life savings in a biscuit tin. Never saw a penny of it ever again, and the people who stole it were never caught. Not even a whisper of it. The police are next to useless for people like us.' As she spoke, she squared up to Chris showing a bit of the fight that had brought her this far in life.

'Are you really that scared they'll come for you, Mrs Green? This was something that happened a long time ago,' Chris said.

'Do you think it all stopped after your Thomas went missing?' She looked from Chris to me. 'This is not an old crime, son, and I'm certain those involved are still at it.' She fell back onto her chair. 'What have I done?'

'If you're that worried, do you have somewhere else you can go?' Chris asked. 'Visit a relative for a few days?'

'They'll not get me out of my house, son.' As she replied she sat bolt upright. 'Besides, I'm the last in my family. Everyone else is dead.'

'This is not part of an official investigation, Mrs Brown,' I said, trying to offer some perspective. 'We just need to know what happened to our brother.'

'Now that you know this much are you going to stop digging?' she asked, her eyes pleading.

I was tempted to lie to give her some peace of mind, but I couldn't. 'I've got to carry on, Mrs Brown. The people who harmed him need to be caught and punished.'

'Oh, son, you really don't have a clue, do you? These people have been at this a long time. No way will you and your wee crusade affect them in any way.' Bitterness came off her in waves. 'Your brother is long gone. Probably trafficked to some distant country where horrible old men prefer boys with light-coloured hair. Save yourself a lot of pain and just put him out of your mind.' She grabbed at my hand, her voice quivering with fear and shame. 'That I had a part in your brother's demise is a guilt that I'll have to take with me to the grave, son. But not one of those kids they took ever came back. It's best you accept that and move on.'

26

Chris twisted in his seat so that he was facing me. We were sitting on either end of the sofa in my flat.

'What are you thinking, bro?' Chris asked. We'd both been silent the whole journey back across town from Elsa Brown's.

'Jesus,' I said. 'I can't…' I shook my head. 'That woman handed him over as if he was nothing.'

'That's not quite fair,' Chris replied, but sounding like he couldn't quite keep the ambivalence out of his voice.

I exhaled. 'She used a child to help pay off her debts and sold him into God knows what horrific situation.' I threw my head back and studied the ceiling. 'I could do with a drink.'

Chris got to his feet, and threw me a look as if he was thinking that seemed to be my answer to everything these days.

'Don't start,' I said.

'What? Chris asked, throwing his arms wide. 'Stay there. A red wine coming up.'

'Get me a whisky?' I shouted, as Chris sped towards the kitchen.

Moments later he was back with a full glass of red wine in each hand. He offered one to me and I took it with a questioning look. 'I asked for a whisky.'

'Jesus, it's a bit early for the hard stuff, even for you,' Chris said, as if the words were out before he could self-edit.

'What, you're monitoring my drinking now?'

'Oh, for chrissakes rein your neck in,' Chris said half under his breath. 'I'm not sure I can handle this,' he added as he rubbed at his forehead. 'I thought I'd dealt with all the shit my childhood threw up, but this…' He looked over at me, as if trying to gauge my reaction.

'All what shit?' I demanded. 'I remember nothing about Thomas, and I was actually born then. You were nothing but a glint in Dad's eye.'

Chris studied me, as if wondering how to respond. 'Okay.' Then, as if it was a huge effort, as if he'd just aged fifty years in the last five minutes, he got to his feet. And he held out his arms, palms up, as if offering himself to me. His eyes saying I want to help you. 'My memories are there. Solid and absolutely irrefutable.'

'What on earth are you on about?' I felt my head spin.

'I can't do this.' Chris threw his hands up and then left the room.

'Chris,' I shouted after him. 'Chris?'

From where I was standing I could hear Chris open the front door.

'Great,' I shouted after him, feeling close to losing control and not caring. 'Do what you usually do and fuck off, why don't you?'

Chris came back to the door of the living room, his face dark, as if he was about to let rip. With a visible effort, he turned and left again.

When I'd heard the door slam shut I sunk back down on to my seat and wondered why almost every interaction between us ended in a similar fashion. We needed to learn how to be better for and to each other.

Half an hour or so later, Chris walked back in the flat holding a bottle of single malt out towards me. It looked like expensive stuff. Way better than the cheap bottle I had in my cupboard.

'Peace?' he said.

I accepted the bottle and twisted the top off, offering Chris what felt like a tired smile. 'Peace,' I replied.

Chris left the room and returned with a couple of glasses. I poured a generous measure into each glass and held one up to Chris in a toasting motion. 'How is it we both irritate the fuck out of each other?'

Then, wondering just how many families in the country behaved in this manner, disguising their inability to communicate via the noise and sights blaring out from a TV set, we settled down in front of the screen, just like we did once upon a time with Mum and Dad. Then, it was the news, the soaps and comedy shows. Fake news, fake drama and canned laughter.

Now, like then, we were allowing the sounds and actions of other people pretending to have relationships to act as a balm on the wounds we didn't have the courage to face.

As the evening wore on I became aware of how many times Chris looked over at me, and I could sense he was building up to something. In a feeble attempt at a distraction, or perhaps to bolster myself against what was coming, I filled my glass, pointed the bottle in his direction.

'Top you up?'

He shook his head, opened his mouth briefly and I *knew* he was going to pass judgement on my drinking, but then he thought better of it and said nothing.

Chris reached for the remote and switched off the TV.

'Hey,' I complained, on the brink of a yawn. 'I was watching that.' I'd no idea what had been on the TV, my mind had been wandering for most of the time we'd been sitting there.

'We need to talk.'

Chris studied me and in a rare moment of self-awareness I wondered if he could still see the boy he once knew behind the pale, doughy skin and the drink-numbed eyes. Because if he could, I couldn't. I was too tired by the dark thoughts in my mind, the constancy of the heavy, sour weight in my gut, and not knowing who to blame for it, other than myself.

Fuck it. Fuck it all, I thought, and took a large swig of whisky.

'Maybe you're comfortable hiding, but I'm not,' Chris said, his mouth curved into a brittle smile.

'What the hell is that supposed to mean?'

'Sometimes I wish I could hide behind a shit memory as well,' Chris mumbled as he leaned forwards, his head in his hands.

'Would you stop speaking in riddles. What are you talking about?'

Certain I didn't have the energy to go wherever Chris was heading with his comment, I made an effort to divert the conversation. 'We've made a huge step in finding Thomas and all you can do is—'

'You really remember nothing?' He asked, and I could see he was keeping his voice low as a tactic to keep the energy in the room low.

'I don't know what you want from me, Chris.'

'A brother. That would be a start.'

'What?' I was on my feet. 'You're the one who's always running away. How can I be a brother when you're never here?'

'You've never asked why I'm never here. You rarely contact me. And when I am here it's like I'm nothing but a massive boil on your arse.' Chris sprung up, his eyes wide, saliva spraying from his mouth, his attempt at dialling down the energy in the room abandoned.

'Nothing's ever good enough for you, is it?' I said. 'You were always on at Mum and Dad. Complaining. Bitching. Acting like a spoilt brat…' I knew I was out of line but I couldn't help myself. I needed an outlet for the anger sparking in every cell of my body. Chris was the only one available to me, and it was some sort of relief not to aim that fury inwards for a change.

'Fuck you, *brother*,' Chris said, as if he was investing the word with as much spite as he could manage.

'No, fuck you.' I was in Chris's face, my right fist raised in readiness for a punch.

'Ah, there he is. Mr Angry. Just like when we were kids. Be warned, John. Now I hit back.'

I could see a war raging in my brother's eyes. He was readying himself to block and hit back if I threw a punch. But then something softened in his face, as if he'd reached the edge and with what looked like a huge effort he'd managed to mentally back off.

I pushed Chris away from me and turned to the side, feeling shame at how close I had come to striking out. 'I think you should go,' I said, quietly at first, but Chris just stood there.

I roared, restraint gone, my mood swinging back to rage, my mind melting into something beyond fury. 'Get out. Go!'

27

I'm dreaming.

A glass of whisky is on the table in front of me. A squat, heavy-bottomed crystal tumbler half full of liquid gold. I reach for it, saliva a shine on my tongue, thirst a desperate need in my throat.

I reach out and register a tremble in my fingers. I discount this as a concern – it's because I'm stretching, isn't it? The idea that I might be dependent is ridiculous.

I can stop any time.

The colour of the liquid in the glass changes, from amber to deep red. Fine. I can take some of the grape. It's healthy isn't it? Just look at those French and Italians with their olive-toned skin and silky dark hair.

But it's no nearer. Just a little.

More.

Effort.

My fingertips tingle with anticipation as I reach, but now that I am closer my fingers fail to wrap themselves around the glass.

I smell the odour of rum and see the liquid is now the colour of burnt sugar. And finally I manage to grasp at it, pick it up and feel the satisfying weight of the tumbler, just as a writer might appreciate the snug fit of a pen.

I moisten my lips, tip my head back, and nothing.

The glass is empty, and my father is standing in front of me, a disapproving look studded on his face.

Mum is behind him pointing at me furiously, her mouth a blur of accusation. They both look like they're ready to go out. He's in a dark suit. She's wearing high heels and a blue polka-dot dress that stops mid-thigh. I momentarily long for this version of her, acknowledging the ruin she has become since her stroke.

'Why can't you be more like your brother?' they chant in unison, and I have flipped back into being a child.

Dad's hand is at his waist. He pulls the belt from his trousers in one smooth, practised motion, and I can feel the tender skin on my backside sting even before he begins.

28

The urban sprawl of Glasgow melted behind us and our surroundings began to take on a gentler hue. The traffic thinned along with the density of housing and the green of grass replaced the brown of brick.

Chris drove the car down the M8 towards Gourock, where we would catch a ferry at MacInroy's Point. He focused on the road ahead, saying nothing.

After our blow-up he'd moved into a nearby hotel – a Hilton – using his ex-girlfriend's credit card. Then, a week later he'd got in touch via Facebook messenger:

Still playing private detective?

This was typical of our interactions after any arguments. Behaving as if nothing had happened was all but in our DNA.

What are you on about? I began to reply, but then deleted it before I could press send. If he was reaching out, I could at least sound more friendly.

Still looking for clues as to what happened to Thomas, yes, was the best I could manage.

I finally put that journalism degree to good use, he replied within moments. *Fancy a wee trip doon the watter?* – something Glasgow holiday-makers would say when venturing down the Clyde coast on high days and holidays.

He explained what he had planned and we arranged a time and date. And here we were, our previous row unmentioned, but not forgotten, like a pot placed on a quiet simmer.

'Nice car,' I said as part of my attempt to show that I was the bigger man. This elicited a hint of a smile.

Chris patted the wheel of the BMW he'd rented for the occasion.

'I reckon I have another few weeks of credit-card use before the ex freezes it.' He laughed and shot me a cheeky smile. I couldn't help but respond with laughter of my own, and felt a thawing.

We settled into a more friendly silence as we both watched the scenery go past.

'Do you not remember *anything* about Thomas?' Chris asked at last. 'It still all feels surreal to me.'

'Nothing,' I replied instantly. 'Even when I look at that photo of us down at the beach there's nothing there. It's as if that infant isn't me.'

'Do you recall Mum and Dad ever talking about him?' he asked.

'Never.' I trawled my memory. 'There were a few conversations that were shut down when I entered the room…'

'Yeah, me too, but that could have been about anything.'

'Knowing this, how do you feel about them?' I asked.

He took his eyes off the road and stared into mine for a moment. 'I'm furious. Aren't you?'

When I went to where my feelings about my parents should reside there was a whole stew of emotions – anger being just one. 'Of course I am. How could they think this was protecting us? What on earth from?'

'Exactly,' Chris replied. 'They were protecting themselves from their own memories. It had bugger all to do with us.'

I nodded in agreement, feeling relief that in our shared frustration with regards to our parents, Chris and I had something to build our relationship on, even though that was not the most solid of foundations.

'Did Dad ever belt you?' I asked, recalling the dream that had now visited me on several disturbed nights.

'Of course he did. Do you think he stopped at you?'

'Yeah, right enough, that was a stupid question.'

'Man, did they fuck us up,' Chris said with a harsh laugh.

My mind pushed an image of my father at me. I'd dropped something. An ornament. He loomed over me, his face dark with fury, and his fists so tight his knuckles were pale. Beyond him Chris was cowering in a corner of the sofa, his eyes on anything but me, as if keeping his own eyes diverted would mean no one could see him.

We waited in the line of cars for the ferry and soon we were being ushered on board by one of the crew.

'The sailing takes twenty to twenty-five minutes, apparently,' Chris said. 'So just relax and enjoy the view.'

Across the wide body of the Firth of Clyde lay a spread of mountains and glens. The opposite coastline was punctuated with buildings, which I followed with my eye until I could see a concentration of them: Dunoon.

'Quite a view isn't it?' said Chris.

'Aye,' I answered. 'And only an hour from the heart of the city … it's like a different world.' I heard myself say the words and my toes all but curled – I was talking to him as if conversing with a stranger.

The ferry began its glide into the middle of the channel and from there slowly navigated its way across to the far shore.

We were on our way to meet a man called Tom Coulson. Dusting off his old journalist's skills, Chris had found an article about Benny Marinello in a business magazine online. The article was discussing the value of mentors to young business people. According to the writer, Coulson started with the old man, then went out on his own and became extremely successful. He credited Benny with giving him valuable advice to help get him on his way.

'Here…' Chris reached into the side pocket of the car door and pulled out a folder. He handed it to me.

The article was overwritten and full of corporate jargon and success cliché. What did intrigue me was the photograph used to illustrate the piece. Two men in dinner suits and bow ties wore fixed smiles while shaking hands and staring at the camera. The look on Marinello's face suggested that all was not well. He looked as if the moment Coulson let his hand go he was going to douse it with an anti-bacterial spray.

Too soon, with a lurch we drew into the quay and cars began to drive off. Chris drove to the end of the quayside, took a right and took us along the loch side. I kept my eyes on the view, wondering why I hadn't visited this part of the world before now.

We left the main road and were soon on a single track that dipped and rose and turned for what seemed like miles and miles.

Eventually there was a small loch on our left, visible through a row of conifers, a lone yacht berthed on its calm waters, begging to be photographed. Soon, a signpost snagged my attention. Ormidale, and we began to climb. We reached the top of the hill and as the scene unfolded before me, I ran out of adjectives.

'Wow,' I managed.

'Aye. No bad,' Chris said with classic Scottish understatement.

The hills, clothed in every hue of green and brown imaginable, sloped down to the sea. We were high above it and could see small islands dotted about the coastline, and just beyond them a ferry plied its trade. The tiny islands, Chris informed me, were known as the Burnt Islands, the remains of an old land bridge that led to the Isle of Bute.

We drove the rest of the way in silence as Chris negotiated the winding single-track road, a couple of sheep sparing us a glance as they nibbled the greener shoots nearby. The road then began to wind its way down the hill, becoming a double track and then again, a single track. The road then took a wide bend and we were at a T-junction. Chris turned to the left and several hundred yards along the road he pulled over, in front of a small white bungalow. A wooden gate led onto a long drive, bordered by a row of rose trees and a neatly manicured lawn.

A white, Nissan Qashqui with a fairly recent number plate sat in the drive.

'He's at home, then.' I said.

'Let me do the talking,' Chris said as we walked up the path. 'And keep a close eye on how he reacts to you.'

As we reached the front door it opened and a genial face peered out at us.

'Mr Coulson? asked Chris.

'Aye.' He peered over the top of a pair of dark-framed spectacles.

'Wondered if we might have a word?'

'About?' he asked as he studied me.

'You worked for the Marinellos way back?' Chris asked.

'That I did,' Mr Coulson stated, furrowing his brow. 'And?'

'We're sorry to bother you,' Chris said. 'This is going to sound strange, but we're desperate. You see, our brother disappeared around the time the Shows were in Glasgow, almost thirty years ago. We're trying to trace his last movements.' As he said this last sentence he dug his hands into his pockets, as if suddenly feeling that this was a colossal waste of time. I realised Chris was hamming it up, and I focussed on Coulson to see how he reacted.

He raised his eyebrows, but there was sympathy in his tone when he spoke. 'That was a long time ago, lads, so I doubt I can help. But I'm happy to talk with you, see if my poor little brain cells can come up with something.' He stepped to the side. 'And let's not stand out here where all the neighbours will be thinking I'm an unwelcoming host. In you come.'

As I stepped into the small porch I took the opportunity to look the man over. He was of average height, and appeared to be in his mid-sixties. His hair was a mop of unruly silver and his complexion weather-beaten and relatively unlined.

'Go into the sitting room on your right there and I'll go and put the kettle on.' I tried to work out the different notes of his accent. London or Essex? He took our drinks orders and left the room.

The front wall had a huge window that offered a panoramic view onto the Kyles and over to the Isle of Bute. Another two were lined with walnut bookcases, adorned with family photographs and paintings of wildlife.

Our host arrived shortly with two mugs of coffee. He handed us one each. We all sat. Then as we sipped, Tom moved his eyes back and forth between us. Each time I met his gaze, he moved his eyes away. Was there a look of recognition there?

'We're trying to find out what happened to some of the old Marinello workers. See if anyone remembers anything,' Chris said.

I reached into my jacket pocket and pulled out the photo of me and Thomas.

'Our brother went missing when I was just a toddler,' I began, then explained how I'd found out about him. 'Dad went to his grave knowing nothing about what happened to his son; and before Mum goes it would be nice to put this to rest for her.' I explained about the connection we'd come up with – around the funfair, but only so far as it pertained to Thomas. I was worried that mentioning the other boys might make him defensive.

Tom studied the photo as I talked, and when I stopped the room fell into silence. 'You're the little one here, right?' he asked me eventually.

I nodded.

Tom put his mug down on a coaster, ran his fingers through his hair then let out a long sigh. 'Let me digest this a little.' He studied us both before continuing. 'You came to see me in case me or any of the team at Marinello's ever came across a boy who may or may not have been abducted and killed by someone who may or may not have worked with us at Marinello's thirty years ago?' Tom asked, his tone incredulous. 'Guys, I can't remember what I had for breakfast yesterday, let alone what shady characters hung around the Shows.'

I changed the subject, trying to win the older man's confidence. 'You have a beautiful home here, Tom. How did you get from that kind of work to a small village in the west coast of Scotland?'

Tom narrowed his eyes as he looked at me before answering, as if he was trying to decide if there was an angle to the question.

'What, you're thinking this house must be worth a few bob, so how could someone from my background afford it?' The man may have been smiling but there was needle in his tone; it made me wonder why he was being so defensive.

'No slight intended, Tom,' Chris said, shooting me a look that said *if that's the best you can do, let me do the talking.* 'You've done well for yourself. This is lovely.' He nodded in appreciation. 'It's nice when people realise their dreams. Good for you.'

Tom sat back in his chair, appearing a little mollified. 'The old man brought me fishing up here when I was a kid.' He looked out of the panoramic window. 'You don't get much of that in Manchester, and I fell in love with it at first sight. Promised myself I'd retire up here, and I made that happen,' he finished with a satisfied nod.

Manchester? I was no expert in accents but even to my ears, despite the odd Scottish note, he sounded as if he came from much further south.

'Your dad would be proud of you,' Chris said.

'My father was an arse. He disowned me when I wouldn't go into the family business. So I ran away. Got a few labouring jobs here and there, and somehow, I can't remember quite how, Mr Marinello saw me, liked what he saw and gave me a job.' He paused as if memories were rising up inside him. 'That was a hard life – long hours – but I loved it. I'd found my people, you know?' He looked down at the cakes, as if debating whether or not he should have one. He picked one up and pointed it at us. 'That's what life is all about, boys … people and the relationships you have with them.' He bit down on the sponge and then, mid-chew, continued to speak. 'You do that when you get older, don't you? Lecture people. It's on the continuum with walking into a room and forgetting why you're there.'

Chris and I both made agreeing noises.

'You know, I should write a book about my life. Would be much more interesting than some of the celebrity crap we get served with … Anyway, father never spoke to me again. Mother kept in touch, though. When the old man died, he left his run-down shop to me, and it was in such a mess that it felt like a punishment from the grave. But I decided to show the old bastard. I left the Marinellos, built up the business using the lessons I'd learned there, and sold it five years ago for two million pounds. And that' – he looked at me – 'was how I managed to end up here.'

'That's quite a story,' I said.

'Yep, it is, and I couldn't have done it without my Jane. Just a shame she didn't get to enjoy it.' He looked off into the distance as if he was fighting back his emotions.

'You should definitely write that book,' I said, sensing that the atmosphere had chilled a little again. 'Would be a bestseller.'

'You know, I might just do that, lad.' He leaned back in his seat and clasped his hands over his belly, as if he had made his point, whatever that was. 'Might teach you young 'uns a thing or three.'

'And when you write your book, what characters from your days at the Marinello Fair will make it into the story?' I asked, and caught a look out of the side of my eye as Chris reacted to my unsubtle question.

'I'd be here all day if I began to tell you about the folk I met,' he said, his eyes cool on mine. 'I met all sorts while I worked there – good people, great people, lazy people, stupid people, bad people, but I can assure you I didn't meet anyone who would abduct and murder a child.'

Rain lashed the car as we set off back towards the ferry terminal at Hunter's Quay. It was still early but the clouds had darkened the sky to the extent that Chris had to switch on the headlights.

'Notice that there were no photos of Jane anywhere?' Chris asked, as he performed a U-turn to get us back in the right direction for the road out of the village.

I looked over my shoulder at the house to see Tom Coulson standing at his door, like a sentinel, both hands behind his back. 'Man, I could do with a drink.'

Chris snorted. 'Keep your mind on the job, Docherty.' He stopped speaking while he negotiated a junction. 'I'm not buying the ditsy old-man thing…' He made a face. '"It's on the continuum with walking into a room and forgetting why you're there." He's hiding something.'

I laughed. 'Yeah, that made him sound like a bit of a wanker. You were watching him while we talked, did you get the impression he recognised me or Thomas?'

'I don't think he knew you from Adam.'

29

A phone rang. It was answered quickly.

'It's me.'

'I know who it is. I told you not to get in touch and never to use this phone.'

'Someone's snooping around.'

Silence.

'Then you know what to do.'

'I can't. I put all that behind me.'

'Let me remind you of what's at stake here.'

Speech stilled. There was nothing but breathing from either end of the phone.

'I can't.'

'You have no choice. None.'

'But…'

'Nip this in the bud. Deal with the loose ends. All of them. You should have done that years ago.'

'But—'

'No buts. Sort this out now.'

They cut the connection.

30

On Sunday I woke to the smell of coffee and bacon. The other side of my bed was now empty. Relieved any awkwardness had been avoided, I pulled on a pair of shorts and a T-shirt and pressed two fingers hard at my forehead in the hope that it would alleviate my headache.

In the kitchen Chris was at the table, an iPad and a pot of coffee in front of him.

'Anybody I know?' he asked.

'Eh?'

'The woman who let me in as she was leaving…'

After Chris dropped me home the previous evening I went for a drink in town. Got talking to a woman. One thing led to another.

I poured myself a coffee, swallowed a mouthful and sighed with pleasure, signalling that was the only answer he was going to get.

'By the way, we have a couple of viewers for Mum's house.'

'We do?'

'They're coming next week.'

When was I going to have the time to see to this while I was at work?

'Don't worry,' he added when he saw my reaction. 'I'll take care of everything. I'll do the grand tour with them all.'

'Okay,' I said, pleased. 'Thanks.'

'And…' He leaned heavily on the syllable. 'I posted that photo of you and Thomas on my Facebook page,' Chris said.

'You did? Why?'

'Got to cover all the angles, right? I know we're doing the private dick thing, but lots of stuff happens online these days. Who knows what will come of it?'

'Probably attract a lot of weirdos.'

'Yeah, totally, but nowadays social media is like that old saw: if no one is there to see the tree fall in the forest, did it really fall?'

'You're saying if it doesn't appear on social media…'

'…it didn't really happen.'

'Jesus, the world is fucked.' I scratched at my forehead.

'Every silver lining has a cloud.'

'I can only take so many messy aphorisms this morning. Anything turned up?' I drank some more coffee.

He reached for his iPad and opened it up at his Facebook entry. I peered over at it and read a few comments.

—*Cute kids.*

—*Sorry for your loss.*

—*Wish you well in finding him.*

—*Man, your parents were careless.*

'Arsehole,' said Chris. 'There's always one.'

'Ach, well, worth a try.'

'It's been shared about a dozen times, so who knows what will come from that.'

'Okay,' I said trying to inject some enthusiasm into my voice. I used the Internet, of course I did, but I saw how much damage social media did every day to my kids so I was pretty sceptical about its use in our situation.

Chris looked at me as if he was about to say something, then changed his mind.

'Remember D.I. from school?'

'D.I.?'

'Sandy Taggart? He was in my year. Good footballer.'

A tall, skinny lad hove into my mind's eye. He had the misfortune of sharing a surname with the most famous TV detective of the time and consequently copped a silly nickname.

'Oh aye. What about him?'

'He saw the post and got in touch. So, I'm meeting up for a few beers with him and a couple of the lads. School reunion.' He looked pleased with himself. 'See. Social media ain't such a shitshow after all.'

I waited for him to add that I was welcome to come along, but he got to his feet, rubbing his hands. 'I have another couple of avenues I'm looking into.'

'Yeah?' I sensed a note of excitement.

'I'm thinking there's another visit you and I could make,' he said.

'Just bloody tell me.' My head was too sore for his games.

'The Lochwinnoch kid that went missing – Robert Green; he was the only one who was with someone at the time. The other two were on their own.'

'That's right,' I tried to recall what I'd read on the microfilm. 'He was with a girlfriend, wasn't he?'

'That's significant on its own,' he said. 'If Elsa is right and kids were being picked up and moved on, the fact the kidnappers changed their methods and went for someone who was in company could be worth investigating.' He paused. 'And while you were getting up to whatever' – he waved his hands in the direction of my bedroom – 'I tracked her down.' He looked so pleased with himself I almost wanted to slap it out of him.

'Just tell me already.'

He turned the iPad round so I could see the screen. What appeared there was the face of a woman I'd been speaking to a few weeks earlier.

'Is that…?' I looked over at Chris, my mouth hinged open in surprise.

'Yup,' he replied. 'Benny Marinello's granddaughter, Gina.'

31

A day at work was the last thing I wanted. All I could think of was what Chris and I would learn from Gina Marinello.

Chris arranged to pick me up from school on Monday afternoon and we'd drive to her house in Johnstone.

'Gina's in her mid-forties, lives in the house she grew up in. Her parents died when she was in her early twenties and she inherited the family home,' Chris informed me as we parked in front of an upmarket white semi-detached house. It had a portico and a broad, curving drive, the windows were wide and tall, and the paintwork looked pristine.

'She inherited this in her twenties? Wow.'

I looked at a pair of massive conifer trees that sat either side of the entrance to the drive. 'Did you get a chance to look into Gina?'

'From what I could glean online, she's had one long-term boyfriend. Met him at university. But he died in a car crash a week before they were due to get married.'

'Poor woman.' I looked from the house to Chris. 'Don't you feel a wee bit creeped out about how easy it is to find out all this stuff about someone?'

'It's the information age, bro,' he said, looking pretty pleased with himself. And I could see that if he had been reluctant at the start he was fully engaged in this search now. 'She's the only grandchild. The old man brought her into the business after she'd completed an MA in business and economics.' Chris released his seatbelt, and put one hand on the door handle. 'Lesson over. Let's go.'

At the door, I turned to gaze at a gold-coloured Lexus sports car resting in the drive.

'Business must be good,' I said.

Chris held a hand up to the heavy wooden door, but before he could knock, it opened and Gina stood there in a tan cashmere coat.

'Oh,' she said. 'Mr Docherty and…'

'Mr Docherty,' Chris added, reaching across to shake her hand. 'I'm his younger brother, Chris,' he added with a smile.

'Sorry, guys, I was just on my way out. Is there anything I can help you with?' She looked at Chris and then settled her eyes on me. Warmed by her scrutiny, I smiled at her.

'We just had some follow-up questions from the other day…' I said.

'I really have to go, gents. Sorry,' she said with a hint of impatience.

But I didn't want her to leave – and not only because I wanted to find out about her old boyfriend. 'Robert Green,' I said. 'You were with him the day he went missing.'

Her mouth fell open and she stared at me.

'We tracked down a couple of lads who vanished at the same time as my brother. Robert Green was one of them.'

She held a hand to her mouth, her eyes wide. 'Oh my God. Poor Robert. I haven't thought about him for years.'

'Mind if we come in for a quick chat about him?' Chris said.

She began to unwind her scarf from her neck. 'Sure,' she said and took a step back into the hall. For a moment it looked as if she was uncertain where she was. 'Come in. We'll go into the front room.' Her heels clipped on the dark parquet flooring as she walked towards a door on the left.

Inside, she directed us to sit on a large, white leather sofa as she sat on a matching armchair to the right of us. A massive fireplace took pride of place in the middle of the far wall, a lion's head carved in to the wood at either side.

'Sorry about this,' said Chris. 'We won't take up much of your time.'

She nodded in acknowledgement, and then looked over to me, studying my face. 'Sorry if I said this when we last met,' she said, 'but I have this weird feeling that we've met before.'

'Not as far as I'm aware,' I said.

'You really do look familiar.' She shook her head. 'Sorry. I meet so many people in my work…' She turned her attention back to Chris. 'So, about Robert. How can I help you?'

'At the time our brother disappeared there were a few other young boys who vanished. And each of their disappearances seem to tie in with a visit from the Marinello Funfair.'

'You can't be suggesting…' She sat forwards, her face stern.

'We're not saying your grandfather's business had anything to do with it. On the contrary' – Chris held a hand up – 'these kinds of places attract all kinds of people. And where kids congregate, sadly, so do predators.'

'I haven't thought about what happened to Robert for years.' She crossed her arms. 'I feel guilty about that.'

'Don't be so hard on yourself,' I said, but realising this woman's good regard was too high on my agenda, I coughed. 'It was a long time ago. Besides, you've had other, more recent tragedies to contend with.'

Chris gave me a hard stare and a frown.

'Have you been checking up on me?' Gina asked as she narrowed her eyes.

'Just a quick Google,' I said, hoping I wasn't digging myself in deeper.

'Jesus, I hate the Internet. Everything's up there *forever*,' she replied and seemed to relax a little.

'What can you tell us about Robert?' Chris asked.

'He was the first boy to ever kiss me,' Gina replied looking wistful. She tucked her hair behind an ear. 'A sweet boy who was in my class at school. He was a couple of inches smaller than me actually.' She made a little grimace. 'And always trying to make up for it, the daftie.' She stared off into the middle distance. 'He had beautiful blond hair … he was really pretty. He would have grown into a handsome man if…' She paused. 'Other than that I can't remember much, to be honest.' She scratched at her right cheek as if a memory had just become clearer. 'Of course, Mum and Dad hated him, the old snobs. They thought he wasn't good enough for me because his dad was unemployed and his mum was a cleaner.' She pursed her lips and blew out some air. 'We were inseparable that year. I remember standing out in that hall' – she pointed and smiled – 'shouting at Mum because she wouldn't let me answer the door to him. I told her that he was the boy I was going to marry and now that I was sixteen she couldn't stop me.' She laughed. 'I really was insufferable. And probably determined enough to do it … if he hadn't disappeared.'

'What do you think happened? Did you ever come up with any theories over the years?' Chris asked.

She shook her head. 'I had to get the bus back home from the Shows on my own that day. I was furious. To be fair, I could have gone to Gramps and got one of his guys to give me a lift, but I didn't want Mum and Dad to get more proof that Robbie wasn't to be trusted.'

'What can you tell us about what the two of you did before he disappeared?' I asked.

'I loved the place, you know? When the Shows came to the area I couldn't wait to show off to Robbie. Take him round everywhere, let him see that I knew lots of the cool people, and perhaps get him free rides on stuff.' Chris and I stayed silent, allowing her space to relive those moments. 'We got a free go on the dodgems and then Robbie won me a little teddy bear at a dart-throwing stand … think I've still got it in the loft somewhere … And then this boy fell in with us.' She stopped speaking as if her recall had run into a brick wall. Then she looked over at me, staring. 'That's how I know you!' She was on her feet. 'On my God. After all these years. How dare you?'

'Gina,' said Chris, trying to interrupt her.

Her face was red, and as she shouted she stabbed the air in front of her with her index finger.

'You utter creep. How could you come in here like this? You went and visited my grandfather, for God's sake. I'm calling the police.' She reached for her handbag and pulled out her phone.

'Gina, think about it,' said Chris raising his voice. 'This was nearly thirty years ago. John was just a toddler.' He fished in his pocket and pulled out the photo of me with Thomas and handed it to her.

'This child is you?' She looked over at me and sunk back down onto her chair. Her face flushed a little as if she'd realised how badly she'd misread the situation. 'Jesus, I'm an idiot. This child is you.'

I nodded.

'And he's your missing brother?'

Again, a nod.

She studied the picture for a long moment. 'Dear God. This is the boy. This is him. He said something about getting us drugs, and whispered something in Robbie's ear. Then they both ran off.'

We sat in silence.

Then Gina asked out loud the question that was on all of our minds.

'This can't be a coincidence. What was your brother doing with Robbie just before he went missing?'

32

1990

'So. A bright kid like you has got to be wondering what a man like me wants from him.'

Ben studied his shoes and took a step back.

'You seen that *Oliver Dickens*?' The man asked him.

'Twist,' Ben said correcting him, and then ducking as if the man might take a swipe.

'What you on about?'

'*Oliver Twist* is what the book's called. Dickens wrote it.' They got it at school recently. Ben didn't like it. Couldn't see the relevance to his life.

'I like a fucking smart arse, I do,' the man said and his smile seemed genuine for the first time. But Ben instantly realised it was only because the man saw that his quick mind could be of help to him. 'Well, anyway…' The man's hand shot out before Ben could duck again and caught him on the back of the head. It was enough of a blow to make him stumble, but he knew the man wasn't really trying to hurt him, he was just playing a part. Keeping him right. Telling him there was more – and far worse – where that came from.

'Ow,' Ben said and rubbed the back of his head.

'I was saying,' the man continued, making a face that suggested maybe he did use more force than he intended. 'Dickens wrote about kids being … used back in the day to help wiv criminal enterprises.' Smile. 'Nuffinks changed, mate. They're all' – he adopted a posh voice – 'this is 1990 and we expect better of people, but it's utter bullshit, mate. Show me an angle and I'll work it. If there's some-thing wot a kid can do wot I can't, then the kid's going in. Get me?'

Ben had only a vague sense of what Seth was on about but nodded anyway. 'And this morning's job was only the start. You still owe me. A lot.'

Ben reared back. He owed this guy? How? He'd been drugged, transported to … wherever this was. He felt a cold chill rise up his spine. Felt a pressing in his bowels. What was going to happen to him? And what about that boy?

He'd gone up to the boy and girl as directed by Seth, assessed them both, saw the boy's thick head of blond, almost-white hair, read how the girl was taller than the boy, who looked a year or two younger. But he revised this estimate, thinking they must be the same age or they wouldn't be going out together. He told them he had some wacky baccy, knowing the boy would want to impress his girl with how grown up he was.

'You don't even smoke, Greeny,' the girl said.

'What do you know?' Greeny replied, hopping from one foot to the other. 'I've done lots of stuff.'

The girl snorted a 'yeah right'.

'Only Greeny can come,' Ben said, thinking how easy this was. If this was all he had to do for Seth, life would be a dawdle. He looked at the girl. Long, straight, dark hair, large eyes, and one big yellow-headed spot on the point of her chin.

Then Ben turned and began walking away, shaking at the thought of what Seth might do to him if this didn't work, praying that the boy would follow him.

He did. His eyes flashed with excitement when he drew shoul-der to shoulder with Ben. 'I've only got a tenner on me, pal,' he'd said.

'You said you'd win me a goldfish, Greeny,' the girl called to them. 'There's only a couple left.'

'I'll do that when I get back,' he shouted over his shoulder and offered Ben a shrug that read: *Girls, eh?*

Ben turned round to see the girl's reaction. He'd been told to separate them; if he didn't Seth would be furious, and he'd get another
whack on the head. Or worse. To his relief the girl simply stamped
her foot, turned and stormed back down the hill.

'It's Seth who's got the stuff. He'll let you know what it costs.' Ben
turned to the other boy, and dipped in between two stands, moving
in the direction of the van that brought him here, wherever here
was. He almost asked the boy what town this was, but decided that
would make him look suspicious and that he'd leg it. And then Seth
would be pissed off. And he didn't ever want to see what a pissed-off
Seth looked like.

Seth's voice sounded just behind him. Ben ducked automatically,
afraid that the man was going to hit him again.

Seth gave a little snort of pleasure at Ben's reaction. 'I'll take things
from here, sunshine. You go and sit in the front of the van.'

Feeling like he'd just committed an act of betrayal, Ben did as
he was told. He had no other option if he wanted to get away from
home, and stay away. From his seat in the front of the van he saw
Seth walking with the boy, arm over his shoulder. The boy looked
tiny beside the man – completely at his mercy.

As if that thought somehow transmitted to the other child, he
chose that moment to look over his shoulder and threw a panicked
stare towards Ben.

Shit, what have I done? Ben asked himself, praying that the boy
was going to be okay.

Seth and the boy returned ten minutes later, and Ben could see
that the boy was holding something in his hand.

Seth had a flask in his.

As he reached the van Seth signalled with his head that Ben should
come and join them. Then he led both boys to the back of the van,
opened the doors and bade them have a seat.

With an uncertain look at each other the boys sat down.

'Young Robert here has his stuff…' At that Robert held out his
hand and showed that he was holding a little packet. As he smiled

at him, Ben could see that his earlier bravado had vanished and that he was hoping and praying that whatever this was it was going to be over soon.

'Before you go back to your girly,' Seth said to Robert, 'You need to seal the deal wiv a little drink, alright?'

Robert nodded. It looked like he'd agree to do anything, so long as he could then get as far away from here as possible. Seth gave the lid of the flask a little twist, removed it and handed the flask over to the boy.

'Drink up,' he said.

'What is it?' the boy asked, looking from Seth to Ben.

Ben opened his mouth to speak but closed it again, unsure of what to say. His mind was at war with itself. He was sure the drink contained the same stuff the big woman had given, whenever that was – he'd lost track of time – and by drinking it Robert was going to find himself in the same position as Ben. Ben felt weak with guilt. He didn't want this boy to come to any harm.

As if he could read what was going through Ben's mind, Seth shot him a look of warning. 'Ben will have a little drink too, to show you how it's done.'

Seth took the flask from Robert and handed it to Ben.

Ben knew he'd be in trouble if he didn't comply, so took a large gulp and added a little dramatic noise to the action.

Reassured, Robert took the flask and had a long drink from it. He wiped his mouth with a sleeve. 'That was…' he tried to think of a word '…nothing really.'

'Of course it was,' Seth replied. 'Do you think I was after giving you something poisonous?'

'Right,' Robert said. 'I eh … need to be going. Thanks for the…' He held his hand up, the one holding the little packet. And then with a cheery, and relieved, 'see ya' he climbed out of the van and started to walk away.

Ben was now starting to feel the effects of whatever was in the drink and wondered when it would show on the other boy.

The answer came quickly. Robert had only taken a few steps before he stopped and turned. 'I don't feel good,' he said, his face pale.

Seth clambered out of the van and in a few strides he was alongside the boy and with little effort he swooped him up into his arms and carried him back up to the van. There, he laid the boy on the floor.

'You might as well join him, lad, before the stuff kicks in,' Seth said to Ben.

Wordlessly, and hating himself for it, Ben did what he was told.

Just then he heard movement down the side of the van – heavy breathing and the swish of one leg passing the other, as if a large person was walking there. He tried to lift his head, tried to assess if there was any way he could get out of here, but his thoughts were too slow. Then he heard the voice of the woman who'd passed him on to Seth.

'What are you doing, you idiot?' she asked. 'That stuff can be brutal, you have to be careful with it.'

'He just took a little sip. Don't be stressing, woman.'

Through the mist that had settled in his mind Ben was aware of the back of the van being pushed down a little as if someone was leaning on it, and even through the mist of whatever drug he'd been given he felt a surge of fear. He needed to get out of here. He needed to get them both out of here.

'You've got another one,' the woman said, and even from the distance the drug created Ben could hear the disgust in her voice. Then in a thoughtful tone she said, 'I recognise his face from somewhere.' There was a pause. 'I know that kid. He was with the old man's granddaughter. He's her boyfriend.'

'And?'

'Mr M hears about this and you are toast, man. Whatever you think you're doing here you need to stop it now, and get that kid out of your van.'

'What's done is done,' Seth said his tone suggesting he didn't have a problem with crossing whoever Mr M was. 'I'll be hitting the road soon, and Mr M can kiss my hairy arse. Besides, he's a special order. Blond wanted, if you know what I mean. That lad's going to earn me a fortune.'

Ben listened to this conversation with mounting horror. If it hadn't been for him this boy would be safe, going home to his family.

However, there were two of them now in this situation. Two would be more difficult for Seth to handle than one. They just needed to be brave. And as soon as the situation presented itself, they'd run for it.

33

Chris and I walked back up the drive in silence, save for the rhythmic crunch of gravel.

When we were sitting inside the car Chris turned to me with a hopeful expression on his face. 'Looks like we're making progress.'

'Why would our brother be selling drugs?' I asked as I thought through what Gina told us.

'He disappears, then the next time he's seen he's a dealer. There's something wrong with that picture,' said Chris with an anxious expression.

'What do you mean?' I was puzzled.

'It's quite common for criminals to use children to trap other children. Robert would trust another kid but run a mile if an adult approached him.'

'But why trap him?'

'Well, according to Gina, Robert was a small boy – pretty, with blond hair.'

The implication of this crystallised in my mind. 'No,' I said.

Chris's face took on a slumped, grey expression. 'There's a market for everything, John.' With that, he switched on the engine and we drove off.

Soon we were on the M8, driving past the airport and on into the city.

'Fancy a detour before I take you home?' Chris asked.

'Depends,' I said.

'Elsa Brown. In that brain of hers there's going to be a detail she's overlooked. Something that might help us find Thomas. And Robert.'

Twenty minutes later we were walking up Elsa's path, a fine drizzle settling on our heads and shoulders, our breath mingling in a cloud in the air in front of us.

Chris knocked at the door, setting the dog off.

'No one's getting in here unnoticed,' I said.

We heard Elsa's footfall approaching the door and her voice as she talked to the dog. 'Who the hell is knocking on my door at this time of night?' The chain was rattled into position, then the door opened a little and a portion of her face appeared.

'John Docherty? Everything okay?'

'Got a minute, Mrs Brown?' I answered.

She threw the door open wide and ushered us in. 'Quick, before anyone sees you.'

We did as we were asked. The dog was silent now, as if it recognised us.

As we sat down in the living room I spotted a small bunch of flowers on the mantelpiece that weren't there when we visited earlier, and a birthday card.

'Happy birthday, Mrs Brown,' I said.

'Thanks, son,' she replied. 'I try to forget birthdays now. They feel more like a harbinger of doom than a reason to celebrate.' She motioned to the dog and it jumped up on to her lap, circled and then lay down.

'You helped us make a connection the other day, Mrs Brown,' said Chris. 'We went to see Gina Marinello.'

'Oh.' The dog gave out a little bark, as if it was a fur-covered weather vane for Mrs Brown's emotional state.

'Do you remember her?' Chris asked, casually.

'A little,' Elsa replied. 'She was a pretty wee thing. Her grandad doted on her.'

'She took over the business, eh?'

'And sold it,' Elsa replied. 'Clever woman, right enough. There's few that can make that game work nowadays.' The dog lay its head back down.

'When we were here, we said that we had found the names of other boys who had vanished around the same time as Thomas. One of them was called Robert Green.'

Elsa's hand stilled in its movement over the dog. 'And?'

'Turns out he was Gina Marinello's boyfriend.'

The dog gave off a low growl, and Elsa shushed it.

'Did you ever meet him?' Chris asked, head tilted to the side, hands relaxed on his lap.

Then Elsa's demeanour changed, as if she'd briefly run out of patience. With us or with herself, I couldn't say.

'So that was his name,' she sighed and with some effort shifted in her seat, as if accessing these memories was causing her physical pain. 'Robert Green? You know how some kids have "victim" written all over them?' she asked. 'It's in the way they walk. The way they hold themselves? He was one of them.'

The dog issued a series of high-pitched yips. 'Dolly, quiet,' Elsa said sharply. I'd thought I'd had the measure of the woman, but now I wasn't so sure. When she continued talking, her reserve was back, and the frightened, frail woman we first encountered was back in the room.

'Seth, he called himself. The man who took your Thomas.' She held a hand to her mouth, fingers trembling as if trying to stop the words from flowing. 'He'd disappear for months on end and then suddenly appear, demanding I set him up with more children.' Her head fell forwards and she started crying.

Neither Chris nor I made a sound. There was nothing we could say to make her feel better about what had happened in the past.

When she recovered her composure she began to talk again. 'Green, you said his name was? Robert? He was a really pretty wee boy. I didn't like to think about what Seth had in store for him. But your brother...' she looked at me '...he had street smarts, Seth said. He liked the boy's gumption. My impression was he intended to move Robert on. He said something about having an order for a blond boy.' She paused at this and slowly shook her head as if disbelieving that she had stood by and done nothing to stop this from happening. 'But it looked to me that he was grooming Thomas for something else.'

At this, my hope for Thomas was rekindled. 'What do you think that could have been?' I asked.

'Didn't matter,' she replied with a weak grin. 'The last service station before London, Seth stopped to allow the boys a chance to go to the loo, and they legged it.'

'Good,' I said.

'No, not good,' she replied. 'Seth was furious. I'd never seen him so angry, and there was no chance he was letting it go. He kept looking for them until he found them. Reason being, if the blond boy ever made his way back home and Marinello found out he was his precious little Gina's boyfriend and had been abducted, Seth was fucked.' As I heard the word I mentally recoiled from it. I didn't care about bad language, but coming out from this woman's mouth among the doilies and children's photographs it curdled in the air.

'So, next time he was back up this way, Seth took pains to tell me he'd found them both and…' She steeled herself before going on. 'He said they'd never be running anywhere ever again.' Her eyes had a look of finality about them.

'Jesus,' I whispered, shuddering at the implications of this. I opened my mouth to ask another question, while shrinking from the possible answer.

'He didn't go into any detail.' Elsa guessed where I was about to go. 'But he left me under no illusions.'

I closed my eyes, feeling emotion swell within me. Poor Thomas.

'About old man Marinello?' Chris asked. 'You said if word got back to him, Seth was fucked?'

'Mr Marinello was a businessman, first and foremost, but people learned the hard way never to cross him or his family.'

In the car, driving back along the motorway towards the West End, Chris looked over at me with a defiant expression.

'Seth didn't tell her definitively that Thomas was dead,' he said.

'Yeah, but you could see it in her face. She was left in no doubt.'

We fell back into silence for a while.

'You okay?' Chris asked at last.

'It feels like Elsa unburdened herself to us there. I hope she feels better for it.'

'Mmm.'

'What does that mean?'

He shot me a look. 'It means I think she was *acting* as if she was unburdening herself.'

'I don't get you.' I thought about her story. About the debt and being trapped in a hellish situation with this man, forcing her to pass on kids. Added to that her genuine contrition for her sins and her attempts to make reparation by taking up foster care.

'She was up to her armpits in all that stuff. Victim my arse.'

'Cynic.'

'Why not tell us all of that during our first visit? In my experience people who parcel out information like that are stalling.' He shook his head. 'Whatever went on back then she's up to her neck in it.'

I was back in that room, watching her tears, the way her hands slowly twisted round each other. To me her remorse seemed genuine.

'Perhaps she *was*,' I conceded. 'But she's implicating herself in a terrible crime. Why do that if she wasn't feeling guilty and looking to make some kind of amends?'

'It's her birthday, yeah?' Chris added, looking unconvinced.

'Aye.'

'Foster carers make a huge difference in their kids' lives. Huge. She told us she had dozens and dozens of kids through her door in all her years as a foster carer, yet she only had one birthday card.' He turned slightly and raised his eyebrows at me. 'One card. That was it. If she was so good with the kids why have none of them kept in touch with her?'

34

My dreams for the next few nights were fractured, but two moments lingered like a mental aftertaste, which soured my thoughts for most of the next few days. I had been in a massive vehicle gaining speed, thundering down a hill. A faceless passenger was screaming at me to hit the brakes, but as much as I stretched and reached down with my foot, I couldn't get near them. My speed grew and grew.

I reached, desperately stretching every muscle of my legs and feet but I could hit nothing.

The person beside me, their face twisted into a horrified mask yelled, 'Brake!'

That panic shifted and became something else. A discomfort every bit as sharp in my mind as my fright had been seconds before. A door opened. A man stood there. A slightly chubbier and older version of me. When he saw me his expression was tight and grim, and full of loathing.

'You're not my brother,' he said, and slammed the door in my face.

Over and over the same dream presented itself to me, and as it repeated my sleeping mind must have recognised the pattern because my unease grew with each viewing. A disquiet that pressed against the muscles of my back, making me want to turn and run. But I was powerless. I had absolutely no control over events. This loop would run for ever.

The door *would* open.

The man *would* stand there, motionless.

'You're not my brother.'

At lunch break, almost a week after we'd last visited Elsa, I made for the staff toilets and in there I splashed cold water over my face and studied myself in the mirror. My eyes looked haunted and I could barely meet myself in them.

A colleague paused beside me, going to drying his hands.

'You alright, John?'

'Didn't sleep too well last night, Dan,' I replied. 'Got so much on just now.' It was a common complaint among teachers, the workload, and that was enough for him to make a grunt of recognition and return to his own thoughts.

In the staff room, I pulled my lunch and my mobile phone from my locker. A quick check: I had no texts and no missed calls. Then I eyed my limp tuna sandwich, felt a twist of nausea and reached for the kettle. Just as I finished preparing myself a cuppa my mobile rang out. It was unusual for me to get a call during work hours so I answered it immediately. It was Chris.

'Yeah?' What on earth was he doing calling at this time of the day?

'It's Elsa Brown. She's dead.'

'What?' My mind presented me with a picture of her in her chair, head back, mouth open, eyes glazed.

'Apparently we were among the last people to see her alive, so the police want to speak to you.'

'Sorry, what's going on?'

'John,' Chris said loudly. 'You need to get your head in the game, mate. The police are on their way…'

'But I'm at work.'

'Best to get it over with, and appear willing.'

'Right,' I said uncertainly, already worrying about what the head would have to say about this.

'Nothing to worry about, they think it was an accident. Just be completely honest and tell them what we were doing there and why.'

'She's really dead?' I asked, unnecessarily. Someone I was speaking to just a few days ago was deceased. A thought entered my head like a sniper's bullet. Did my appearance in her life have something to do with it? 'They think it was an accident?'

'Take a breath, John,' Chris said, and I realised I was in shock. My pulse felt rapid in my neck and I felt dizzy. I allowed myself to slump onto a chair.

How could she have had an accident in her own home that would kill her? She had been worried that someone would see Chris and me entering her home. Did her death have something to do with that?

'Oh my God.'

'You'll be okay in a second,' Chris said, and absently I wondered when he had become this calm and collected person.

Several thoughts hit me at the same time. Guilt – would she still be alive if I hadn't pursued my search for Thomas? And disappointment – she was one of the last people to touch Thomas's life that I knew. What else was in her head that would have helped me find him?

A school secretary entered the room, slightly out of breath. Mary Quinn.

'Ah, Mr Docherty. There you are.' Her expression was questioning. 'There are a couple of police gentlemen who are asking to speak to you. Her voice was loud enough for Chris to hear it at the other end of my phone.

'I've already given my statement, so just tell them what happened and you'll be fine.'

'I've put them in Mr White's office for now,' Mary said. 'He's out at a meeting this morning.'

I nodded to Mary, but then a thought occurred to me. 'How did they know to get in touch with you?' I asked Chris.

'One of the neighbours must have reported my hire car being there. Make and model and there is a sticker on the inside back window for the car-hire company. Would have been dead easy to find us.'

'Mr Docherty?' Mary persisted.

'Better go,' I said to Chris and hung up.

One of the police officers standing waiting for me barely looked old enough to shave, while his partner looked like he had one hand reaching out for his pension pot.

'John Docherty?' The younger one said.

'The very same,' I said, and stood at the side of White's immaculate desk.

Without any preamble the older one began to speak. He gave me both their names, then got straight to the point. 'We believe you visited Mrs Elsa Brown at her home last week?'

I nodded. 'I did, yes.'

'Her dog,' he replied, 'wouldn't stop barking. Was doing it all night apparently, so her next-door neighbour, who had a spare key, let herself in and found Mrs Brown prostrate on her living-room floor. She phoned an ambulance, but she died on the way to the hospital.'

'Jesus,' I whispered.

'I'm sorry for your loss,' the younger cop said.

I shook my head. 'I barely knew … I'd only met her once or twice.'

The young cop pursed his lips and gave a short, sharp nod as if I'd just confirmed something.

'What time did you leave her house?' asked the older man.

'Can't have been late,' I thought and scratched at my face. 'When I got back home it couldn't have been much later than eight.'

'You were visiting her with your brother, Chris. May we ask why?'

I explained about trying to find my brother.

'Was Mrs Brown able to help you with that?'

'Not sure,' I said, reluctant to give too much detail to these men. They were cops after all, and I had promised Elsa we'd keep her confidence. 'These are events from about thirty years ago. Feels like I was wasting my time, to be honest.'

On a silent signal both men shifted their position, shoulders angled towards the door 'We won't waste any more of your time, Mr Docherty. Thanks for talking to us.'

I followed the men to the office door, thinking, *Is that it?*

'If there's any follow-up questions we'll be in touch.'

'Can you tell me anything about how she died?' I asked.

'Blow to the side of the head,' the young cop said.

'Really?' I recoiled. That didn't sound accidental.

'She was found on the floor beside the fireplace. It's possible she fell and hit her head on the marble hearth. We'll have to wait for the post-mortem to confirm cause of death.'

'Yes, sir, we can't speculate at this time,' the older cop said with a quick look at his colleague. I had a vision of Mrs Brown escorting us to her front door then making her way back to her armchair, tripping over the dog and hitting her head as she landed.

Would that be enough to kill her? And would that be enough to satisfy the police?

35

Chris was waiting for me by my car when I came out of school after a distracted day's teaching – I had been unable to stop thinking about Elsa Brown. An image of her stuck there, dying on the carpet played continuously across my mind.

It wasn't helped by the detail one of the police officers had provided. She'd died on the way to the hospital. That meant she'd been lying there on her own as her life ebbed away.

'You've been thinking about this all day, haven't you?' Chris said.

I nodded.

He put a hand on my shoulder. 'You can't go there, John.' He offered me a small smile. 'It was an accident. And if there is anything nefarious going on, it's past actions coming home to roost.'

'How can you be so callous?' I asked.

'Pragmatic I'd call it.'

'But...'

'But nothing, John. Let's not forget we're dealing here with people who were trafficking children. As far as I'm concerned she got what was coming to her...' he paused '...if it wasn't an accident.'

My boss, Alex White, appeared, with his briefcase under his arm, pointing a key fob at a large silver Ford.

'John,' he acknowledged me with a nod. When he looked at Chris his expression soured. 'I hear the police interviewed you today?' His mouth was a tight line of reprimand.

'I do some charity work in the evening.' I had no idea where the lie came from but I had no intention of telling White the truth. 'And one of the old ladies I visit now and again died in the early hours of this morning.'

'That's terrible,' he said, but he appeared mollified at the idea that one of his staff was doing some form of community work. 'Well, be sure to have some rest tonight so you're back in tip-top form for your pupils in the morning.'

'Will do,' I said.

Ten minutes later Chris and I were facing each other at a table in a nearby coffee shop. The shop window was covered in a net curtain, the Anaglypta walls were decorated with postcards, and there was a giant aluminium urn instead of a proper coffee machine. The baristas of the West End hadn't quite reached this neighbourhood.

'What are you thinking?' I asked.

'I can understand if you're feeling a bit wobbly about all of this, but the most likely explanation is that Mrs Brown actually did trip over her dog and hit her head on the marble hearth. We both saw the mutt was always under her feet.'

'And if it *wasn't* an accident?' I said.

'There's nothing about this that suggests it wasn't, John.'

'Yeah, but what if? What if someone killed Elsa Brown to keep her silent, and we've kicked a hornet's nest? Are we in danger?' I had an image of me going home that evening and crawling across the living room floor to close the curtains in case anyone could see in and take a shot at me.

'Why would they come after you? You don't know anything.'

'Tell me to shut up,' I said. 'I'm being paranoid.'

'If – and it's a big if – we *have* prodded a bear, what do you think? Take a step back for a while and let it go back to sleep?'

'I just…' Exasperated I threw myself back in my chair. 'I can't help thinking Elsa Brown would still be alive if we hadn't gone to visit her. And the logical conclusion from that is someone is going to extraordinary lengths to keep their secrets hidden.' I crossed my arms, feeling small and regretting that I'd ever found that photograph in my parents' loft. 'If they're crazy enough to kill a defenceless old woman…'

36

I awoke the next morning to light streaming in through the half-shut curtains. Trying to ignore the sour aftertaste of another weird dream, I went through to the kitchen to see Chris sitting in front of a pot of coffee.

'Want some?' he asked.

I nodded in reply.

'When did you get here?' I asked. 'You should check out of the Hilton and move back in,' I said.

'I'm actually booked in to a modest wee place just off the Great Western Road. The Hilton thing is really taking the piss.' He grinned. 'Besides it gives me somewhere to mince off to when we have one of our rows.'

I laughed in recognition.

He grew sombre, pulled his iPad close to him, looked at it and then me. 'After yesterday, where's your head on continuing to look for Thomas?'

'Not sure,' I replied. 'I keep worrying about poor Elsa, but then I go back to thinking that we need to do this.'

Chris looked at the table top, then into my eyes. 'It kinda worries me how intense you've been about all this.'

'What do you mean?'

'It's like an obsession.' His eyes strayed to a large wine glass and empty bottle by the side of the sink.

'Rubbish,' I replied trying to fight my irritation that he thought my drinking was a concern.

'What is all this really about for you, John?'

'I want to find out who my brother is and what happened to him? Is that so strange?' How could I explain to Chris something that I had barely articulated to myself, that this was as much about me as it was about Thomas. I had spent so much of my adult life keeping an emotional distance from my family, frustrated by our dysfunction, that I found it easier to chase a possibility that I knew to be remote in the extreme, than to find the courage to face my thoughts and re-establish a relationship with those who *were* present.

'Okay, because … I couldn't sleep last night and went online … and I think I've found Robert Green,' Chris said.

37

We were sitting in Chris's car looking down a long street of four-storey sandstone tenement buildings, fronted with black iron railings. It was early evening, the nine-to-fivers were home and the kerb was a long line of expensive metal and engine.

'How did you track this guy down then?' I murmured.

'Painstaking online work,' Chris turned and gave a smile.

I looked down the street, a little shocked as to where we were. 'This is only a few streets over from my place,' I said. 'I could have walked past this guy a million times.' I rubbed at my thighs aware that my nerves were building.

We got out and walked along to the correct door number and paused at the security entrance. Chris pressed the buzzer to the flat we were looking for.

It was answered after a delay of about twenty seconds.

'Hello?' asked a female voice. As she spoke I could hear a small child chanting something in the background.

'Is that Mrs Green?' Chris said. 'I was just passing this door and found a bank card on the street here with your name on it. Should I just leave it here and you can run down and get it?'

'Oh my God,' she said, and I could make out an English accent even though she sounded electronic and distant. 'Gosh, that's so kind of you. I can't…' A child was crying now. 'Would you mind if I buzzed you in and you came up. I'm only on the first floor.'

'No problem,' Chris said, turned to me and smiled. The buzzer went and he pushed the door open.

'Why the elaborate ruse?' I asked when we reached the bottom of the stairs, our feet echoing in the stone stairwell.

'Shh, voices carry,' he said in a low voice. 'I doubt she would have let us in if I told her the truth.'

We made our way to the correct floor and found the door open. A woman stood there with a child at her leg, her hand out while wearing a smile.

'This is so kind…' Her smile halted when she saw us both standing there. 'Who are you?'

'Sorry, Mrs Green,' Chris said before he introduced himself properly. 'We would like to speak to your husband, please.'

She stepped back with her hand on the door as if she was about to slam it shut, but then she looked at me and stopped. The child at her leg looked up at me and smiled. I gave him a little wave.

'Daddy's at work,' the kid said.

His mother shushed him then asked. 'Why do you want to speak to my husband?' A strange look passed over her face, and I had the feeling that I'd seen her before, which wouldn't be a stretch given that we lived just a few streets apart.

'We think he might be a young boy who was abducted from a funfair in Renfrewshire about thirty years ago,' Chris explained.

'Along with our brother,' I added.

'What are you talking about? My husband was never abducted. Who are you people?' Her anger was part bluster, as if she had to work her way up to it. As if she was playing a part. But in among the emotions that raced across her face, there was fear, and I was sure we were not the source of that concern. 'You need to go.'

'My brother's name was Thomas,' I said in a rush, sensing this woman knew more than she was letting on. 'My father died thinking he'd been murdered. We just want to know the truth.'

She winced at the word 'murdered' and held a hand out to the child as if to protect him from those two syllables. 'I'm sorry for your troubles,' she said, her attitude softening a little. 'But my husband isn't in and he certainly wasn't the victim of an abduction.'

'Mrs Green, if you could tell us when he'll be home from work…' Chris asked.

'I'm sorry,' she interrupted, her eyes fixed on me. 'You need to go.'

We were silent as we walked back to the car. Once seated inside, Chris spoke.

'Thoughts?'

'I didn't do too well at reading Elsa Brown, but that woman is hiding something.'

'Agreed. But what?' Chris stared down the street towards the address we'd just left. The streetlights were on now and the far end was fading into gloom.

'Worth waiting around to see what happens next? She's going to be straight on the phone to her husband telling him to get his arse home.'

'If,' Chris said with a mixed note of caution and agreement, 'she is indeed hiding something.'

At his words I reined in my sense of expectation.

'Tell you what,' he shot a look at the clock on the dashboard. 'I'll set up shop here and give you a shout if anything happens.'

'You sure? I don't mind waiting with you.'

'I'm the layabout here. You've got work in the morning. You don't want to be going in there like a half-shut knife.'

'True,' I replied, and watched while Chris hunkered down into his seat. 'Doesn't matter what time it is, if something happens you call me, right?' Suddenly I felt keener than ever to find out what had happened to Thomas.

We were onto something here, I was certain of it.

At home I surfed TV channels, unable to keep my attention on any programme for longer than a minute. With a groan, I switched the

TV off and moved to my laptop, opened it up and checked my emails. Nothing of any interest.

Angela popped into my head and I picked up my phone. Scrolling through my contacts my finger hovered over her name. With a sigh I threw the phone onto the sofa. The last thing she'd want was to speak to me.

Then I brought up YouTube and scrolled through my recent views, looking for something to keep my mind occupied.

From time to time I checked my phone in anticipation of Chris calling. I wondered how he was coping and if he'd ever had to do any doorstepping when he was a journalist.

Finally I went to bed, but just as my head fell onto my pillow, my phone rang.

It was Chris. There was a strong sense of excitement in his voice.

'You need to get yourself over here now.'

38

Looking at the man standing before me was like staring into my future, if I didn't cut my hair for a few months, and grew a goatee beard, and even more of a belly.

'You need to get the hell out of here,' he said, as he held two children by the hand.

The older one, who could have been about four or five, looked up at his father with big eyes. 'Daddy,' he cried. 'What is it?'

The smaller child stood there rubbing his eyes as if all he wanted was to go back to bed. Mrs Green stepped forwards, bent down and picked up the little one, while the man stooped to pick up the older child, who began crying the second he was in his father's arms.

'Hey, buddy,' the man said and nuzzled the boy's cheek. 'Everything's going to be fine.' The tone in his voice suggested otherwise. He was worried. Very worried.

'But you're shaking,' the boy said.

'Shh.'

As soon as I'd put the phone down with Chris I'd dressed and run as fast as I could the few streets over to where I'd last seen him. When I got there, panting, Chris was standing in front of an old, silver people carrier with his hands up, not letting it leave.

The man who had been trying to drive off jumped out and began to remonstrate with him when I turned up.

We both caught sight of each other in the same moment. I was expecting to see someone who could be Robert Green. Instead I was greeted by the man I'd been seeking for months.

'You need to fucking go,' he said again, his voice rising in panic. He turned and pushed the children towards the woman who'd opened the door to us a few hours previously. I could hear the children crying as their mother tried to cajole them inside the vehicle. 'Liz, get them in the car. Quick, honey.'

'Thomas, it's me,' I said. 'Your wee brother, John.'

'Why are you doing this?' He moved closer to me, hands clenched into fists. 'What did you think was going to happen? Happy fucking families?'

I hadn't taken much time since I'd started this search to think through what our reunion might look like. I'd thought the chances of it were remote.

'You *are* Thomas Docherty?' Chris asked.

'Thomas Docherty died a long time ago,' he said quietly, his gaze dropping to the ground. Then he looked at Chris as if he had managed to steel himself to face whatever was coming. 'And who the hell are you?'

'Chris Docherty,' he replied. 'I wasn't born when you disappeared.'

'Jesus,' Thomas said, his expression carved through with worry. 'Look, this is all very nice and shit, but we need to get the hell out of here.'

Chris held his hands out. 'If you really want to go we can't stop you. I only delayed you so John could see you before you vanished.' With that he stepped back onto the kerb. I wanted to scream at him, *What the hell are you doing?* But his words had the desired effect; Thomas's anxiety seemed to drop a level.

'I'm sorry, John,' Thomas turned to me. 'You look like you've turned out alright. You both do,' he said as he glanced at Chris. 'But I'm not the…' He shook his head. 'I'm no longer who you think I am.' Then he looked into my eyes. 'Thomas died and became Rob Green a long time ago. And that can't change.'

'Okay.' I stepped back, feeling small. 'I hear you.'

'Before you go,' Chris said, and his words and tone again felt like they were calculated to put Thomas more at ease. 'Can I ask: are you running away from the Marinellos?'

Thomas huffed. He looked into the distance and back to Chris, his expression suggesting to me that Chris had not quite hit the mark, but that he was close.

'All I'm going to say is I can't be here.' Then he looked at me. 'You *both* can't be here, or things will come out that will land me in jail.' His face was pale under the neon streetlight. 'It took us long enough to have kids. I can't not be a dad to them … after what happened to me.'

I let that roll across my mind.

'Where are you going to go?' I asked. I'd found my brother only to lose him all over again.

'I can't say,' Thomas said, his eyes heavy with apology. 'To be honest, I don't really know yet. I was just going to get in the car and drive. But these people have eyes everywhere. I just need to be gone, I knew it as soon as I'd heard you'd been here. As soon as I knew someone had found me.'

'I'm really sorry,' I said, but I was finding myself overwhelmed. We'd found our brother. He was alive. And by the looks of him he'd been thriving. I studied him, seeing myself and Dad in his gestures, the shape his mouth made as he listened, the angle of his shoulders. I had to put a hand on the vehicle to steady myself.

'You okay, John?' Chris asked. We exchanged a look and I could see he was every bit as thrown by this development as I was. But he was handling it much better.

I managed a nod while keeping my eyes focussed on Thomas, as if shifting my attention would mean this event would end.

'You need somewhere to hide, right?' Chris turned to face Thomas.

'Well … yeah,' Thomas replied.

'You've been hiding…' Chris turned around and with an outstretched arm he indicated the family's recently departed home '… in plain sight for a while now. Why change a perfectly good tactic?'

'Meaning?' Thomas asked.

'I know a place,' Chris replied.

'I'm not sure…' Thomas tailed off as his wife left the car and came to stand by his side.

'You okay, honey?' she asked.

He replied with an uncertain nod of his head.

'What do you know about Elsa Brown?' I asked.

Chris glared at me and both Thomas and Liz looked alarmed.

'Please don't tell me you've been to see Elsa?' Thomas demanded.

'She died,' Chris said, after shooting me another look.

They gasped, but they looked more concerned for a friend than scared.

'How?' Thomas asked. He and Liz looked at each other and it was clear even in the weak light that her eyes were already heavy with tears.

'She had a fall in her house,' Chris replied and gave them the full details.

'Poor Elsa,' Liz said, her hand at her throat.

Chris and I looked at each other.

'She was your friend?' I asked.

'Wouldn't say that exactly, but we wouldn't have made it back up here without her,' Thomas replied.

'What exactly was her part in—' I began to ask, but Chris interrupted.

'Not the time or place, John. We need to get these people off the street.'

'We can trust you?' Thomas looked from Chris to me, as if my opinion carried more weight. It said to me: *You are the family I remember. There's a connection, you won't mean me or mine harm.* And I was taken aback by the burst of love I felt for this man I'd only ever seen before in a photograph.

'Yes,' I replied, emotion clenching my throat. 'Absolutely.' I turned to Chris. 'Where are you taking them?'

'They can have my room at the hotel. I'll move back in with you.'

'Right,' I said and made to go home for my car. 'I'll join you there.'

Chris held a hand up. 'No, I don't think that's wise.'

'But…'

Chris moved in close, speaking quietly. 'They've have had a bit of a shock, and they are clearly worried about what is happening next. A big family reunion on top of that is just too much stress for anyone to handle.'

'You're family too.'

'Yeah, but…' he began.

I understood: he'd managed to maintain an emotional distance in all of this so far, and would therefore be less of a drain on everyone. I looked from him to Thomas, hoping he'd ask me to come with them. But Chris put a hand on my chest. 'At this point, this is not about you, John, or us. Let them settle in, get a night's sleep and you can come over tomorrow.'

Thomas nodded, his expression harried. 'You must have so many questions, John,' he said.

'Understatement of the year,' I replied.

'Chris is right,' Thomas said. 'As Chris says, let us settle in and I promise you, when we meet up, I'll tell you everything you need to know.'

39

Going to bed was a waste of time. I couldn't relax in any one position. On my side I didn't know what to do with one arm. On my back my pulse thumped in my neck. And the quilt was too heavy. The room was too warm. The traffic outside too noisy.

Thomas was *here*. He'd been here all this time. Just a few streets away.

Each time I closed my eyes he appeared, his eyes tight with worry, telling me to go. What kind of danger was I putting him in by simply being there? By being aware of his existence?

Frustrated at the constant rumble and tangle of my thoughts, I got out of bed and made my way into the kitchen. Locating my laptop, I made my way through to the sofa where I opened it and brought up a Word document.

Writing helps you to access parts of the brain that otherwise might lie dormant. Or so I read somewhere. Perhaps if I started to write about my earliest memories some of them might actually enter my head?

I stared at the screen, and then hit a few random keys. Nonsense filled a line of text.

Once upon a time, I wrote, *there was a boy who couldn't remember much of his childhood. His life was a mystery to him. His brother was also a mystery.*

How could that be true? I thought, I didn't even know I had an older brother. I carried on writing whatever came into my head; words, feelings, impressions, colours, sounds, but nothing new appeared from memory. Moving from Word to Google I put in a search for memory loss to see if there was anything I could find there that might help. The first article I read suggested that thinking of memory as an accurate recording, like a piece of video film was flat-out wrong, mainly because it promotes an unrealistic level of accuracy and suggests permanence.

Our memories, it pointed out, actually represent a distorted version of what happened, and importantly, they change over time. Also, memory doesn't only record what happened, it records what we *feel* about what happened. And those feelings can be affected by mood, beliefs, biases and even your individual brain structure. Meaning you are recording your individual perception of the event, rather than objective fact. What's more, perception that can be altered by time and the adult mindset through which you view the memory.

The implications of that were beyond me, so in frustration I closed the lid and lay back in my seat. What was it with me and memory? Why was it that whenever I searched within myself I mostly came up blank, with nothing to reward me but a pain drilling deep between my eyes.

I closed my eyes, thought of Thomas, Liz and the kids and fantasised about how our lives might be from now on: family visits, long dinners ... and the next thing I knew my alarm was sounding from my bedroom.

The clouds were heavy and dark enough to hold back most of what was left of the day's light. Rain bounced off the concrete and gathered in rivers at each side of the road. A tiny torrent of rain water washed along each kerb carrying its urban flotsam – fast-food wrappers, cigarette butts, and empty drinks cans. After another day's distracted teaching, I stepped out from under the canopy at the school door and ran across the car park to my car. The rain was so heavy that by the time I sat inside it I was soaked.

Pushing my wet fringe back and wiping the water from my eyes I turned the ignition key and started the engine. The windows clouded quickly from the heat of my breath. I fired off a quick text to Chris to let Thomas and family know I was on my way to the hotel, and once the windows had cleared I drove off.

Every driver must have, at many points in their driving career, turned a corner and wondered how they had arrived there. Unable perhaps to remember the last couple of minutes of their journey. That evening I pulled up just outside The Hamilton without any recollection of any part of the journey.

My stomach lurched as I released the seatbelt. This was it. There was no going back now. I was about to learn one of the great truths of my life.

Out on the pavement, reluctance was a weight all but gluing my feet to the ground, but I pushed myself towards the door of the hotel. Hand on the wood I waited before I entered. Straightening my back, I swallowed deeply and took a step forward.

Chris was the first person I saw. He was leaning against the bar sipping from a white cup, and Thomas was on a stool beside him. He was wearing a pair of dark jeans, a zipped sweat top, and his hair was slicked back as if he was just out of a shower. He looked tight across the shoulders and there was a distinct shadow under his eyes.

'John,' Chris said and gave me a nod.

I responded with a nod of my own, and opened my mouth to say something, but nothing came out.

'You guys go sit in the corner and I'll order us a drink,' Chris said, his voice purposefully energetic.

I stood where I was and fidgeted with the car keys in my pocket, unsure what to say, or do – even how to be.

Thomas jumped off his stool, approached me and placed a hand on my shoulder. 'Come on. No one will hear us over there.' He led me to the far corner of the seating area and chose a chair.

I joined him, and without at first realising it pulled my chair away from Thomas, increasing the distance between us. He ran his fingers through his hair.

'Truth is, we were kinda expecting this,' he began haltingly once

Chris had joined us. 'Liz mentioned the day that she met you in the shop. The day the wee one called you Daddy…'

I looked at him, wondering what he was talking about. Then recall slipped in.

'Oh my God.' I rocked back in my chair. 'When I saw her yesterday I was sure I'd met her before and couldn't think where.'

He nodded. 'Liz came home in a total panic that day. She knew who you were straight away, because of the…' He pointed towards my face. 'The Docherty genes and all that.' He paused. 'It did set us back and we debated then if we should move. But we heard nothing more and convinced ourselves that you must have just been visiting the library and couldn't be local.'

'I *was* visiting the library, and I *am* local.'

There was silence for a moment. Then we both opened our mouths to speak.

'You first,' I said.

'No. You,' he replied. 'After all I'm the one who resisted this.' His voice was deep and well modulated with a touch of English across some of his vowel sounds, but mainly he sounded just like Dad. I said so. He recoiled.

'Sorry,' I held a hand up.

'It's okay,' he gave a weak smile. 'I understand this must be really strange for you.'

'And likewise.'

He nodded and placed his hands on the table, clasped as if in prayer. His nails were clipped and thick, blue veins were prominent on the backs of his hands.

'The kids are cute,' I said, thinking I should start with something safe.

His eyes lit up. 'Angels one minute, demons the next,' he said. 'It took so long to … because, you know…' He looked into my eyes, apparently expecting understanding. But I wasn't sure what he was alluding to. 'I had to learn to trust. Myself as well as others.'

'Right,' I said, but I had no idea what he was talking about.

'Two boys,' he added. 'Seems like boys run in our family. The oldest, Andrew, is four and the wee one, Jack, is eighteen months.' Then he paused. 'Go on,' he said with his head tilted to the side, and he was so like Dad it nearly broke me. 'Ask me. It's okay.'

'Why?' I asked softly. 'Why did you run away?'

'Looking back I can see it was always there. In fact I can barely remember a time when it wasn't. Just a bit too much contact, sexual remarks, lingering hands…' His eyes glazed in memory. 'Birthdays and Christmas were always a special time.' He gave a rueful laugh.

An image pushed through in my mind. A bath full of water. Steam and bubbles and a row of little ducks. What age was I there? I shook my head against the memory and felt the familiar pressure build between my eyes.

'Nothing happened to you did it?'

'No,' I answered, and it sounded too quick even to my ears. 'What do you mean?' I added.

He swallowed. 'Years of therapy and I still find it difficult to go back to that time.' Then he stared at me for a long moment. I broke contact first, feeling heat build in my face. What was he getting at?

'I'm sure you can join the dots,' he said. 'Are you sure…?' Again he studied me. I reared back from him, feeling anger build in me.

Chris coughed at my side, but I couldn't look at him.

'I went to one of Dad's colleagues, cos that's what you do, eh?' Thomas continued. 'You go to the cops. The first guy told me to piss off. I went back the next day and the next guy took me into a side room and made me give him … he unzipped and made me…' For a moment his eyes were full of loathing, for himself or this cop, I couldn't be sure, then the look in his eyes shifted, as if he'd self-corrected, as if he was mentally administering hard-learned good advice.

While he was speaking I started to become aware of a noise in my head, like a persistent buzzing. I had to concentrate hard to hear him.

It all seemed too much.

Much too much.

'Anyway,' he continued. 'There was nowhere to turn. Nowhere I could go where I was sure I was safe, so I ran away.' He paused and gave a small smile. 'I tried to join the travelling funfair, how clichéd is that? That's where I first met Elsa. But you know that already. How was she when you last saw her, before she died?'

'Getting on a wee bit. Doting over that wee dog of hers. And vague,' Chris replied.

I was pleased that Chris spoke, because the connections between my brain and my tongue felt like they'd been severed. Thomas had just told us that he'd been abused at home, and then abused by a cop he'd gone to seek help from. That had happened in the house I grew up in? I wasn't sure I could handle more of that without challenging it – in a way that would mean he'd probably never want to speak to me again. After a great deal of effort I managed a question I hoped would help us veer off that conversational track.

'Do you have much of a memory of me?'

He smiled. 'I remember this cute kid following me around. Tom, you called me. You were always wanting to play football with me.' As I listened I was disappointed that his words prompted no recollection.

'Remember this?' I handed him the photo of him and me down at Portencross beach.

'Wow, that would have been just before...' His voice became so quiet I could barely hear him. Then he spoke as if the words were meant for him and him alone. 'That's the boy I have to console in my mind every minute of every day.' He coughed. Closed his eyes tight. When he opened them he looked like he'd gained a little control again. 'Sorry. This is tougher than I thought it would be.'

'Did you know Dad died?'

He nodded. 'Saw it in the *Herald*.' His expression darkened. 'Pillar of the community, my arse.'

'Why have you never been back in touch?' I asked.

'Jesus, where to start?' He studied the back of his hand, rubbed the knuckles. 'Stuff happened after I ran away. Stuff that still has consequences today.' He took a deep breath. 'Someone died. And if the truth of it ever came out, I'd rot in prison for the rest of my life.'

'The real Robert Green?' I guessed.

He nodded.

I recalled what he'd said the day before. 'But what has that got to do with me? Why does it put me in danger?'

'It's complicated.'

'Try me.' I offered a half-smile. 'I'm smart, I've got a degree and everything.'

'A sense of humour, too,' he said and smiled back grimly. 'Good. It's probably best you don't know too much, but it was part of a deal I made to get out of … my previous life, that I remain anonymous.' He shrugged. 'Not that it was difficult. I never wanted to see anyone from that house ever again.'

That house.

The home we grew up in.

A life that was even now a mystery to me.

After a long silence he said, 'I came up from London once. I sneaked back to see you on the day of your fourteenth birthday.' He glanced at Chris. 'Don't remember seeing you there.' Then he paused, searching my face to see if I would show a flicker of recall. 'I came back to warn you, but I couldn't get close. I was terrified … terrified it would happen to you too.'

'What the hell are you talking about?' Pain exploded in my head. 'Terrified about what?'

'I felt so guilty for years. If I'd tried to get help you'd be safe.'

'Safe from what?' I demanded.

'Are you sure nothing happened to you?'

'Yes, I'm fucking sure,' I shouted, then immediately lowered my voice, looking around the bar to see if anyone had heard.

From the look on his face he didn't know if he could believe me or not.

A cloud passed over his eyes. 'The first time was when I was in the shower … helping me wash myself.' His eyes drilled into mine.

'I knew it was wrong, but I froze and couldn't stop it. I tell myself I was just a kid. I had no power, no control over what was happening. But I was nearly a man, wasn't I? I should have been able to do something.'

40

Daybreak found me by the sea. The brass band inside my head had abused its instruments all night, to the rhythm of my pulse. The pain didn't abate as the night wore on, and Thomas's words wheeled around inside my mind.

I hadn't been able to take any more of what he was saying and had run out of the hotel. After several long hours of driving around the city, as if sense was to be found in its dark, empty streets, I went home.

Chris called me from outside my bedroom door, but I ignored him, just lay there, silently praying he would just go away.

'Your car's outside, John. I know you're in there,' he said.

I said nothing.

'We need to talk.'

I could say nothing.

Then after more hours of struggling for sleep, I struggled into my clothes and drove to the seaside.

The ocean was a wide wedge of blue at the end of the car park, and as I trudged towards it I wrapped a rug around my shoulders that I kept in the car boot for just such an occasion. When I reached the water's edge I sat on a large boulder and looked out across to the Isle of Arran.

The sea was lapping at my left foot, and I wondered how it might be just to immerse myself, to let myself fall in, allow the waves to fill my lungs and the current take me away to far shores where none of this would matter. It would be easy enough, just a small movement and I'd be in the water. Then my clothes would be too heavy, pulling me under, and the chill sea would fill my lungs.

It wouldn't take long to die in a cold sea like that.

But doing nothing is a form of decision, isn't it? So, that's what I did. Watched the sun rise into a frigid, colourless sky, feet, hands and face numb, my mind stuck in a place where nothing and no one would ever make sense.

The conversation of the previous night still played on in my head, taking its tempo from the fall of the waves. I had refused to listen to any more of Thomas's explanation. How could he say such things?

Then Liz had appeared. 'The kids are napping.' She gave me a little smile, but it froze on her lips as she read the atmosphere between us.

'How can you say these things?' I had hissed. 'Nonsense. Utter fucking nonsense.'

Thomas shook his head, and looked like he was going to retort until Liz took his hand and sat down. Then she turned her attention to me.

'John, you need to listen to what your brother has to say.' Her voice was calm and certain. 'It has taken him years to be able to talk about what happened to him as a kid. If you'd been by his side all these years and witnessed the effect of some of his nightmares, then you wouldn't doubt for a second the truth of what he's telling you.' There was a certainty in her voice and body that stilled every thought in my head.

'Please listen. It may be uncomfortable to hear and it will hurt you, but it is what you have come here for, isn't it?' She then kissed Thomas on the forehead and left.

'This is all a bit … I just…' My words tailed off as I struggled to explain my feelings.

'I don't blame you. It's how I would react if I were you.' Thomas held his hands out, palm up. 'Please. Just listen, ok?'

His hushed and sincere tones as he went on to explain how the impact of what had happened had affected his life, his honest pain and his open body language, convinced me that he was in fact telling what he knew to be truth. Every syllable that he uttered rang clear with it. I just didn't want to hear. He spared me no detail and answered any questions that I interposed into his soliloquy with a quiet calm, as patiently as any father would answer his child.

'The day after the cop forced me to give him a blowjob, Mum asked me to go the shop. So I grasped my opportunity. I took nothing with me; I wanted nothing, not even the clothes on my back. I was terrified, to be honest, but determined to get away. I wanted everyone to think I was dead. I didn't want anyone to try and find me, so I cut my finger a little and I let the blood drip onto my shoe and left it down by the railway in the hope that everyone would think the worst.'

'I've got that shoe,' I said quietly. 'I found it in a box in the loft. Dad had a stash of stuff to remember you by.'

'He did?' His surprise at this was genuine, as if he couldn't believe the man cared for him.

'So did Mum. I found a wee box above her wardrobe. That's where I found your birth certificate.'

'Jesus,' he said. 'I don't know what to do with that.' His mouth was open.

As he continued to talk our conversation was punctuated with long, deep silences, as if that hush held the meaning of his words and allowed them to be carried deep into our minds. At times I dipped out of hearing, the buzzing was so loud in my head, the pain building deep in my skull so that I lost focus.

'God, I could tell you some stories. Teenage boys can be pretty popular on the streets.'

'Jesus.' What else could I say? There was a whole world of trauma in those few words.

'It was a complete mind-fuck. Was I gay? Is that why this was happening to me? Was it all my fault? I was completely confused. What was my actual normal sexual response? And what came from fear and necessity? You do what you need to survive, right? Sex wasn't really a pleasure for me; it was a commodity, something that I could use to put food into my body and clothes on my back. I had no education and no skill, just a mop of dark hair, a warm hand and a willing mouth.'

'Oh, Tom,' I croaked, my sympathy for him a vice around my throat.

We sat in silence as I fought for words that might offer support. Words that might count for something. He broke into the quiet before I could say anything more.

'Liz has been a godsend. I don't know what I would have done without her.' The force of his emotion tugged at the corners of his mouth. He laughed. 'You know, I spent so much of my life denying myself any emotion. I couldn't admit I had any feelings for anything or anyone. I couldn't admit that I liked someone. I couldn't even let myself feel any anger. Anger was an emotion, therefore it was not allowed.' I squirmed in my seat at a description that could have been about me. 'I put on this tough persona that no one could reach and no one could read.'

'How did you meet Liz?'

'When Robbie and I got to London someone told us to hang about outside Euston. Lots of Scots got off the train there and they'd maybe be kinder to a kid begging with a Scottish accent.' He smiled. 'First person we bumped into was Liz. She was begging and took exception to our plan. Told us to fuck off.'

As he continued to unburden himself I just sat there, meeting his gaze, my expression as neutral as I could manage, while my mind was a whirl of shock. This was almost too much to listen to, and if that was the case, how awful must it have been to live through?

'Sometimes I feel so angry that it is all I can do to keep sane, but you can't go on like that. You can't let the bitterness eat you up. The best revenge is a life well lived, eh? I came across something that Buddha said and it helped.' He clasped his hands before him as if in prayer. '"If you pick up a hot coal with the thought of throwing it at someone, you are the one who gets burned." Every time the hate overwhelms me, I think of that.' I was getting the impression he had a store of such aphorisms, and a mental box full of other techniques that would help pull him out of the black fog in his own head.

He then began to question me about myself and my life. But my answers were sharp, to the point. Although he had been extremely open, in the manner of someone long used to sharing what had gone on in their most secret of moments, I wasn't quite ready to share.

'I went to Dad's funeral.' He said after a particularly long silence.

'You did?' I scanned my memory for faces. Came up with nothing. 'How did that go for you?'

He shrugged. 'I felt nothing.' He fiddled with his glass. 'That's a lie. I felt a whole lot of things: sorrow, relief, anger … it brought back all of those confused and conflicting emotions that I thought that I had dealt with.' He put his glass down and ran his fingers through his hair, his eyes pools of weariness.

Just then a memory slid in. I was a boy. Only eight or nine. A dinosaur toy in each hand. A wisp of steam obscured someone leaning over me in a bath.

'Are you alright?' Thomas asked, his voice full of concern. 'You went all white there.'

'Yes … I'm fine,' I replied, wondering what the hell was happening to me. 'I've just got a bit of a headache.'

I was brought abruptly back to the present by the sound of a large dog, scrabbling across the rocks. He was a yellow Labrador and when he noticed me he ventured over to investigate, his tail high in the air on a slow wag. A pink tongue lolled inches from my face as he sat back on his haunches and tried to work out what the man thing was doing sitting down at the edge of the sea. He leaned his head to the side, quizzically. Then a male voice shouted 'Bob!' and with a spurt he was off. How I envied that dog his simple life. Food, a walk, somewhere warm to sleep. Wouldn't it be nice if life were that easy?

For the millionth time within the last twelve hours I continued my inner battle. How could I reconcile what I knew about my parents with the obvious agonised truth I had just heard?

'Christ, you look like shit,' Paul said when I met him in the pub later on that day.

I raised an eyebrow at his honesty. 'Thanks, mate … and thanks for coming to meet me.'

'Are you okay?' His voice was heavy with empathy. 'And should you not be at work?'

'Migraine,' I said, holding my head in my hands.

'So what the hell are you doing here?'

'I don't know if it's a migraine. All I know is my head hurts like fuck.' I looked over at him with eyes squinted half shut. 'Enough about me. How are you?' He looked disgustingly healthy.

'Have you taken any pills?'

'No, Mum,' I answered. 'I hate taking pills.'

'Don't be such a man. Take a bloody pill for chrissake.' He leaned forwards on his chair as if something had just occurred to him. 'Remember those headaches you had while we were at school? You went for all those brain scans and stuff.'

'I did? I was?' How much of my life had I forgotten?

'You were in some state then, mate. Did they cure you or what?'

I could feel my head spin. My pulse racing. How could I have forgotten something like that? 'No, they … eh … just stopped. I don't know. I can't remember, it was years ago.'

As if trying to give me a moment to marshal my inner resources Paul handed me a lunch menu from the stand in the middle of the table. 'What do you fancy?'

I took it from him and pretended to read it, aware that he was studying me from behind his.

'I fancy a good old burger. You can't beat a burger,' he said with false cheer, and then began to recount something of little importance that had happened to him. But he trailed off.

'If you want to talk…' he began.

'I was down by the sea most of the night.' I shook my head slowly. 'It would have been so easy just to fall in, you know?'

Paul's face was bright with alarm. 'Jesus, John, you should have called me.'

'It's alright. The moment passed. I wouldn't really have topped myself.'

'Talk to me,' he said.

'I thought it would do me good. Get out of the house…' I said while getting to my feet. 'I can't … I need to go.'

'But…' he began to reply, then read something in my face that stopped him. 'Go home, buddy. Gimme a shout when you feel up to it, eh?'

While I sat with Paul, memories had jumped into my mind, like photographic stills. They must have been my memories, for I was their centre, but each announced a surprise that my heart and conscience could hardly bear. I forced my mind out to the present and, like a startled fawn, scared from the brush by a predator, I caught myself looking around me, abruptly reminded of my surroundings.

I knew Paul would listen. Would believe. But finding the right words and saying them aloud would mean that all of that *had* happened and that was a truth that was too terrible to contemplate.

When I arrived back at the flat, I quickly drew the curtains in my bedroom, swallowed I'm not sure how many painkillers along with a generous slug of whisky and collapsed onto the bed. The pain crushed at my head and I curled up in the foetal position, my knees pushed against my elbows, which in turn pressed the heels of my palms into my tightly closed eyes.

Each eye squeezed a tear out from behind my hands. I gave in to them and gave myself up to them. Great heaving sobs wracked my body as I ceded myself more and more completely to my sorrow.

I wept for Thomas and Chris. I wept for Angela, but most of all I wept for me. The tears poured fast now. My past could no longer be ignored. It was there in sharp, incomplete fragments, which now demanded that I face them, deal with them and put them back in their proper place.

Unsure that I had the courage for the task, I swung violently between denial and acceptance. I had to face my past if my future was to have any worth. If I wanted to live my life productively, I would have to look, to recognise, to remember fully.

Tears had been my solace only twice in my life before that night. Each time I had watched from afar as my emotions took over, like a spirit watching over its near-dead host. This time, however, I didn't have the luxury of that detachment. My last thought before troubled sleep took mercy on me was for the other two episodes when tears occurred. One was on the night I severed my relationship with Angela. The other was on the night of my thirteenth birthday.

41

He's staring at me from the silvered glass. Enquiring. Demanding. I can't meet his stare, and I look away.

Am I awake, or in a dream state? Or am I permanently roaming the corridors of this halfway house for disturbed souls?

My skin chafes.

My mind is blistered.

My heart is withered for the want of blood soaked in honesty.

I lift my head and look back at him and I recognise the way I tilt my head, the way my mouth opens slightly, the way I look like a man who from time to time visits his own haunting, and demands of himself, will it *ever* stop?

This is my secret self. My real self. My lost self. The version of me that lurks behind the welcoming smile, the solid handshake, the attentive nod. But it's only in this place I see him. It's only in this place I can acknowledge he exists.

He's here. Oh, he's here.

He's been hiding among splintered memories.

In the space behind the mirror.

The persistent, shrill scream of the telephone leaked through to my somnolent brain. Stumbling from the bedroom, I moved through to the living room to answer it. But the call ended before I could press the accept button. The name I read there made me stumble.

Angela.

I held the phone away from me, then looked at it again. Yes. It had been Angela.

Why had she called me? My finger hovered over the redial button before I stopped myself. I couldn't speak to her in this state. She'd know instantly I was in a bad place, and if she came over it would be out of sympathy rather than genuine affection.

On the way through to the kitchen, I caught my reflection in the hall mirror. My face was gaunt and my eyes, squinting against the pain in my head, were puffy and ringed in red. I looked about ten years older.

Then with a charge of guilt, I looked back at my phone. What day was it? What time was it? I should be at work. With a massive sense of relief, I realised that it was Sunday.

What kind of state had I been in that I didn't even know what day it was? I had several faint memories of Chris's head appearing at my door. Me telling him to go away. His almost pleading reply each time. 'Okay, let me know when you want to talk.'

Strong coffee did little to revive me. So I tried a shower. Leaning against the wall under it, I turned the water from hot to cold, giving my skin shock after shock. Feeling a little more awake after this ritual, I stepped out of the shower, rubbed myself dry with a towel and dressed.

Back in the living room I reached for my phone. The screen I had last visited appeared at the press of a button, Angela's name hanging there like a promise. My imagination brought up a myriad of reasons for the call. I pressed a button to return to the main phone screen and saw that I had ten missed calls in total. One from the school, and nine from Paul. Why was the school calling? And why was Paul being so persistent? I checked the time of his calls, and was shocked to see that they'd been over a thirty-six-hour period. I'd slept that long? How come I hadn't heard any of the calls?

Then the doorbell went. It couldn't be Chris, he should have his key. Where was he anyway? I wondered. He'd probably given up trying to get some sense out of me and gone over to spend some time with Thomas.

'Hello?' I asked when I arrived at the intercom.

'John, its Angela.' She was outside my flat. I felt such a pang for her I almost doubled over. This was followed by a touch of panic. I couldn't let her see me in this state.

'Hi, Angela,' I tried to sound like nothing was wrong.

'Can you buzz me up? It's freezing out here.'

A series of excuses scrolled across my mind, none of them plausible.

'John?'

'Come on up,' I replied, pressed the buzzer to let her in the main door downstairs and then went to stand by my internal door, feeling pleased that at least I'd had a shower. However she saw me, at last I would be clean.

Her face formed a faltering smile when she arrived on my landing. 'Oh goodness, I'm so unfit,' she said, and took a couple of deep breaths, while I drank in the sight of her. She looked amazing. Even more beautiful than the first time I saw her.

'In you come,' I said, rubbing my hands on the sides of my jeans, not sure what to do with myself. Should I give her a hug? Would a kiss on the cheek be inappropriate? I held a hand out as if to touch her shoulder, but let it fall to my side.

She stepped past, and made a little nod of apology as she did so, as if she was sorry she'd stood too close.

'You know where to go,' I said. As I followed her into the living room I drank in every detail. From the gloss of her hair to the pace of her feet hitting the carpet.

In the living room we sat on either side of the settee. Angela almost hugging its arm, as far away from me as she could possibly sit.

She looked around her, trying to ascertain my mental state from the condition of my living quarters, I thought. The place was in a mess. Angela crossed her legs, her shapely knees pointing away from me.

'How are you, then?' Angela asked.

'Oh, you know, fine.' I settled for the platitude.

'I thought that I would just pop in and see how you were.'

'I'm fine,' I repeated. Then I paid attention to what she just said.

She just thought she'd pop in? Last time we spoke it was well and truly over. Why on earth would she decide just to *pop in*?

'That's good.'

'How are you?' I asked when she had been silent for a long moment. 'I'm fine too.'

'What have you been up to?' she asked.

'Oh, I found my brother. He's alive. I actually had … coffee with him the other day.' As the words tripped from my mouth I couldn't believe I was being so matter of fact.

'What? Really? You found him?' Her mouth was a perfect O of surprise.

I recounted the whole experience.

'Oh John, that's fantastic … I can hardly believe it.' She looked genuinely pleased for me, and relaxed for the first time since she'd entered my flat. Which made me think she had not just popped in, but had some other motive.

'Did Paul put you up to this? Or was it Chris? He's been conspicuous by his absence. Has he cleared out to give you a chance to talk to me?'

'What do you mean?' She shook her head, her face a blank of confusion.

'I'm not daft, Angela. I…' I rubbed at my forehead. 'I appreciate the visit more than you can imagine, but it's been weeks since we last spoke to each other. Why would you suddenly decide to visit?'

'Okay, Paul came to see me at work and asked me to look in to see you,' she admitted after a pause.

'Oh, he did, did he?' My heart sank a little. I'd still held out a little hope that this visit wasn't someone else's work. 'Why?' I wasn't sure whether to be pleased with Paul or mad at him.

'He's worried about you. He said that you wouldn't talk to him, but maybe I could reach you.'

'I don't look that bad, do I?'

She clasped her hands in front of her, twisting her fingers, as if deciding how honest to be.

You look fine, John. Just … like you've not slept for a month.' She warmed this comment with a smile. 'But it was more your mental state that Paul was worried about. He said you guys met for lunch the other day and that you kept shaking your head, as if you were trying to get rid of something, and that you kept fading in and out of the conversation. He also said something about you possibly being … suicidal.' She looked over at me, assessing, eyes heavy with concern. 'I told him not to be daft. But he was really spooked, John. He must have thought something serious was up if he came to me.'

I wasn't used to this. People caring. I didn't know how to handle it, or how to be when offered help. My habit when hurt was to retreat, find the closest thing to a cave that was possible and keep to myself until my mind began to quest outside my own head – when my thoughts once again turned to what was outside of me.

'I appreciate the concern. I do,' I said, aware that I was sitting bolt upright with arms crossed. 'But Paul shouldn't have called you, and you shouldn't have come.' I felt distant from my body, as if watching from the side. I could hear how irrational I was sounding, and how my tone was edging into anger.

'Really?' Angela said, her face tight. 'I shouldn't have come. I'm told the man I thought I was in love with could be suicidal and I shouldn't do what I can to help?'

'I don't need your help.'

The sensible, held-at-a-remove part of my mind recognised I was becoming defensive and knew that would lead to anger. But I was incapable of controlling the impulse. The switch had been flicked to self-destruct.

'Yeah, right,' Angela responded and it was clear some hurt that still lingered from my rejection of her and her child was feeding her energy. 'Look at the state of you.'

'Well, thanks very much.' Anger was like a hot lance. 'If that's what you came to say then you can piss off. I don't need Paul and his sympathy, and I certainly don't need you.' The speed of my rage took me by surprise. Heat blazed from me, but was immediately quenched by the sight of Angela lifting herself from her chair and leaving the room. Like a pauper chasing a gold coin, I rushed after her.

I caught her at the front door and held her arm. Angrily, she pulled it from my grasp, eyes blazing.

'This was not my idea of a fun afternoon, John. I was doing a favour for your friend because he was worried sick about you, but as you so succinctly put it, you don't need or want anyone's help. So let me go and I'll piss off out of your sight.'

'I'm sorry,' I said. 'I am. I shouldn't have spoken to you like that.'

She let me lead her back into the living room.

'Sit down, please.' I was almost grovelling in my attempt to make her stay.

'Can I get you something to eat or drink?'

'No, thanks.' Her voice was tired. But Angela could never stay angry with me for long, her voice softened. 'What's wrong with you, John? You've never spoken to me like that before. I've never seen you in such a state.'

I breathed out a deep sigh. Where was I to begin? I wasn't sure if I was even capable of saying any of it out loud. If anyone could help me in this situation, I would rather it was Angela. I was struck afresh by her beauty. That someone like her would care about me gave me a sliver of hope. Pulling at my fingernails, I decided to start with something safe. As I told my story, Angela listened quietly, rarely interrupting, her face a study in concentration.

'It began with me trying to find Thomas, and then the headaches, or was it the other way round?' A stabbing sensation came from behind my left eye and I pressed against it with the heel of my hand. I groaned and took a moment, waiting for the pain to subside. 'Like that. Paul reminded me I had these headaches when I was about fourteen. I'd forgotten all about them. I went for every kind of test that you can imagine and they found nothing. Eventually they just went away of their own accord. That's why I haven't been to a doctor this time…'

'What about Thomas?' she asked. 'How did you meet him?'

I told her how Chris had found him.

'I'm so pleased for you.' Then she looked into my eyes and reached out for my hand. 'There's more, though, isn't there?'

How should I tell her? There was no 'right' way. I just needed to open my mouth and speak and trust my mind would push out the words.

I told her everything Thomas had told me.

Angela's mouth fell open. She sat in stunned silence. Then she rose from her seat and knelt at my feet. The compassion on her face nearly undid me. I struggled for control. She held my hands tightly. The question must have formed instantly in her mind but it came out of her mouth haltingly.

'Did … the same thing … happen to you?' She looked up at me.

I could only nod.

With a supreme effort of will I formed the word 'yes' with my mouth but heard no accompanying sound.

'Oh, John.' She sat on the settee beside me and held me in her arms. The silvery trail of a tear ran down her cheek. The pain and emotion inside me crested and something broke. Breath caught in my throat and was released into the air in a loud sob.

For a long spell my chest and shoulders heaved, pain twisted and tore at my chest, my gut, I could hardly breathe, and my face ran with tears. I honestly thought I could have had no tears left after the previous night, but on they flowed as if they would never stop.

'Oh, John,' Angela said, over and over again, those two syllables sounding like a lament.

Eventually I cried myself out – for the moment at least – straightened my posture and looked over at Angela, head up, as if putting myself on display. This is me. This is me in all my weakness and vulnerability and stain. How could you ever have thought you loved this?

Angela reached out and placed the palm of her hand against the side of my face. It was such a tender and thoughtful gesture I started sobbing again.

'How could you bottle all of that up? How could you go through life with that in your mind?'

'I think the technical term is disassociation. You're a child. You're helpless. Your betrayal is so deep you don't know who you can trust, and in the absence of a miracle, the mind learns to protect itself. Everything is buried deep. It took meeting Thomas and hearing his story to dredge all of the memories up.'

Angela paused before speaking, as if she was trying to make sense of her own thoughts. She turned to gaze out of the window. The world outside held a weak light, and I was so lost I wasn't sure whether a new day was rising or one was ending.

She swallowed as if a pebble had been stuck in her throat. 'It never ceases to amaze me, what humans do to each other. Their own children, for chrissake. What makes people do that? They're not people, they're monsters … and your Dad was a policeman as well, a trusted member of the community. How could he do that to his own sons?'

'My dad's sin was one of blindness. Of being in a position to stop this but being unable to see what needed to be seen.' My voice was so quiet I'm sure Angela could barely hear me.

I breathed in deeply, as if to cleanse the dark thoughts I was harbouring in my heart. My voice, when I answered her question, was filled with a sadness so heavy and profound it settled on the whole of the room like dust.

'My father wasn't the guilty one,' I answered. And the fog cleared, just a little.

'It was Mum.'

42

1999

I woke early on the morning of my thirteenth birthday, excitement like a family of ferrets under my skin. Would I get those football boots I asked for? And the Scottish football team tracksuit? A warning had been given though, before I had gone to bed, that if I was up before eight o'clock, I would get nothing. My parents were veterans of my excited gabble in the early hours of birthdays and Christmases.

Eventually, I heard movement from my parents' room, so I bounced through to see if it was time to get up. Before entering, I knocked on the door and waited for my dad's gruff voice to give me the all clear to come in.

'It's the birthday boy,' said my dad, sitting up in bed with a broad grin as I entered their bedroom like an express train.

Their room was an essay in tidiness. A large antique wardrobe was deployed to cover one wall, a dressing table stood to attention under the window and the two single beds were in regimental order, looking as if they had just been made, despite the fact that they were still occupied.

Standing at the foot of Dad's bed I asked, 'Can I get up now? I'm bored. I've been awake for hours.'

'Is Chris up yet?' Mum asked.

'Yeah,' I lied.

'Give us five minutes, John. Go back up to your room and we will give you a shout when it's time to come downstairs,' Mum said as she slipped out of bed. As the reason for this delay was to set up my birthday surprise, I was more than happy to comply.

My birthday present that year was, as I hoped, new boots and a new tracksuit. As well as the usual new socks and pants pile that arrived at all such occasions. And as this was a weekend I was allowed to make my own agenda, looking out of the window to see that it was pouring, I asked to go to the swimming pool with my friends, followed by a trip to the cinema to see *Star Wars: The Phantom Menace.*

That evening, Mum served all of my favourite food for dinner – sausages, mashed potatoes – real potatoes, not that powdered muck – and a mountain of beans, and then she brought out a huge birthday cake with thirteen lit candles for me to extinguish. This I managed with one fierce exhalation that made my eyes bulge, and then I made a solid effort to eat as much of the cake at one sitting as I could.

'Have you had a nice day, son?' my Dad asked afterwards, when we sat watching the television.

'Not that you had much to do with it,' my mother's words were accompanied by a jagged little smile. A barb doused in perfume.

'Brilliant, Dad. Absolutely brilliant,' I answered. 'Can I stay up late, seeing as it's my birthday?' It was worth a try.

'Once you see your new bedroom you might not want to,' he replied.

I looked at both of my parents quizzically.

'We've been busy,' Dad said with a big grin. 'And your Mum added the finishing touches while you were in the cinema, son.'

'I've cleared out the back room just for you.' She smiled. 'You're a big boy now and you need your own space.'

The back room was a room on the ground floor that had been filled with all kinds of junk for as long as I could remember. Every couple of months, or so it seemed, Mum would say to Dad that he needed to clear it, that the boys would soon be of an age when they would each need their own space. Seemed like Mum got fed up asking Dad and decided to do it herself.

The door closed softly and I was on my own. I had my own space in my own home and I loved it. Moving so I had my back against the door, I turned back and with a whoop dived onto my bed. From there, both hands under my head, I scanned a small bookcase tucked into the corner, to the left of the door, and noticed that all of my books had been brought through and placed in alphabetical order. Even my football posters had been stuck on the walls. This was easily the best birthday ever.

Grabbing a book that Chris had given me, I settled myself on my stomach and began to read.

Mum's head appeared at the door. 'That's ten o'clock, young man, time to get some sleep. Have you brushed your teeth?' she asked.

'Yes, Mum,' I lied in a bored tone.

'Fibber,' she said with a small smile. 'C'mon.' She stepped to the side and pointed up the stairs towards the bathroom.

With a long drawn out, 'Muuuuuum,' I did what I was told, and walked upstairs, into the bathroom, and brushed my teeth. My mother stood at the door watching me, a strange look on her face. She took the two steps required to stand behind me.

'Look at you, a big teenager now,' she sighed. 'Getting so big.' She traced the width of my shoulders with both hands. And then squeezed my bum. 'And firm,' she added. 'All the girls will be fighting over my big boy. But they needn't bother. You're mine.' She mussed my hair.

Back in my bedroom, I wondered if Mum'd had any wine with her dinner and sat on the edge of the bed and began to undress. When I was naked, I jumped under the covers, foregoing the pyjamas. I was determined to enjoy my newfound privacy. Growing up in a home where even partial nudity was frowned upon, I wanted to experience the freedom of having no clothes on while I lay in my bed. The clean cotton sheets caressed my skin and quickly absorbed some of the heat from my body. Running my hands down my chest and down to my thighs, I fully examined this new sensation. I felt unfettered and for the first time free to be sensuous without fear of a younger brother rushing in to spoil my fun. My body responded and blood rushed to my groin. Just as I was beginning to tentatively touch myself, the door opened.

'Just thought that I would come and say goodnight, son, before I go back out to work.' It was Dad's turn to appear at the door.

The blood rushed from my groin to my face. Had he noticed anything? Did he know what I had been doing? If he had, he gave no indication.

'How was the *Phantom Menace*, son?' he asked as he came over and sat on the edge of the bed.

'It was cool, Dad,' I answered, trying to hide my mortification.

'That's good, I'm glad.' He ruffled my hair. 'Listen, I'm sorry I couldn't spend more of the day with you,' he said and a shadow passed over his eyes, like he was disappointed in himself. 'You know how it is with work…'

My father was a taciturn man, and struggled with any form of close physical contact. I have often wondered, while nibbling at the few crumbs of my past that I would allow myself access to, whether my father's dedication to his work, and his efforts to protect the local community, was his way of telling us how much he cared about us. If so, he lavished attention on us by proxy.

'It's okay, Dad.' I had been having such a good time that I really hadn't given much thought to his absence. It was what I was used to.

'Good. I'm glad you had a good time,' he repeated and walked to the door. Just as he opened it, he looked back and said in a stage whisper, 'It'll make you go blind.' Then he closed the door and flicked the light switch, leaving me in the darkness.

Wondering if he'd said what I thought he had, I felt my face heat again. Then I let my eyes adjust to the darkness. This was great. I was lying in my own bed in my own room, but I was too wide awake to sleep just yet. Locating my torch in my bedside cabinet, I dived under the covers with my book. This way, if someone happened to check up on me, they wouldn't be able to guess what I was up to. The torch illuminated the pages and the words pulled me into the story.

Soon, fatigue tugged at my eyelids and the words faded from my brain. I fought for as long as I could, but sleep was impossible to ignore. Pushing my torch under the pillow along with my book, I surrendered to its pull.

I dreamt of my new bedroom. It was the universe and contained everything that I could ever need. It was huge, with corridors that led to other rooms that were also mine. Each new room that I travelled to contained more new delights. I didn't walk or run, I glided. Moving as fast as I wanted to, I had only to think of something and the next room contained it. A huge bed, draped in white furs. Someone lay in the centre, lost among the white cloud of soft fur. Her hair was as black as night and her skin tan and bare.

Noticing my arrival, she sat up, somehow managing to look shy and welcoming at the same time. My eyes travelled slowly down her body as I enjoyed the sight, while simultaneously being nervous about what might be expected of me. Blood pounding in my ears, I ached for … for something. I wasn't sure exactly what but I knew the answer lay on the bed.

But something wasn't quite right. The feeling nagged at the back of my mind as I moved through treacle onto the bed. Soft hands caressed me, touching me everywhere and I pulsed in response. The feeling of wrongness persisted and the pleasure began to subside. A hand moved down across my thigh. I awoke with a start. Feeling another person's weight on the bed beside me, I strained in the darkness to recognise them.

'Mum … what…' A finger pressed against my lips to quieten me. Panic fluttered in my chest like a caged bird.

'Shh, we don't want to disturb anyone,' she whispered.

'But…' I was silenced with a kiss on my forehead. 'This is our special time, darling. Don't worry, nothing's wrong. This is Mummy's treat.'

After the pleasure had subsided and was but a distant memory, disgust and shame rose to the surface, crowding my mind with accusations. How could I let this happen? I enjoyed it, so I must be guilty. I had to be in the wrong as even with my limited experience of sexual matters I knew that the male had to be aroused for anything of a sexual nature to take place. Didn't they?

Guilt surged up from my belly like bile, and I spun away from her to vomit over the side of the bed.

She rushed out of the room and came back with a bucket and cloth. Soon she was finished cleaning and she leaned over the bed to kiss me goodnight. I shrank from her, as far into my pillow as I could manage, but I couldn't avoid her lips. In a perverse form of benediction, she kissed my forehead and my mouth before leaving the room.

My new football boots lay discarded in the corner of the room, neither in nor out of their box, their sheen dulled by a patina of pain that no amount of polish would ever succeed in lifting.

When she was gone, in the darkness of the room I began to doubt that anything had actually happened. Nothing had changed. Horns hadn't sprouted from my head. Everything in my room was as it was. The dark would hide the truth and I would be its willing accomplice. Nothing had happened. It was just a bad dream, but for the rest of the night her last words to me just before she went to get the cleaning materials rang through my mind.

'Wee lamb,' she said. 'You just must have eaten too much birthday cake.'

43

Angela and I fell asleep on the sofa together, both emotionally wrung out. When I woke up some time later, I found she was studying my face in the weak light offered by the streetlights.

'Hey,' she whispered and kissed my forehead. 'You looked so peaceful.'

'Time is it?' I croaked. My eyes, nose and throat felt sore.

'No idea,' she said, 'but do you think you could move? My left arm has gone completely numb.'

I shifted to allow her to pull it from under me. 'You should have woken me up,' I said.

'I didn't have the heart to.' I could see the white of her teeth in the gloom as she smiled.

'Thanks for being here,' I said and stretching forwards I kissed her cheek. The softness of her skin felt wonderful and I paused there.

She leaned back from me. 'Don't be getting any ideas, Docherty.' I could hear both firmness and humour in her tone. 'There's no sympathy shag on offer here.'

I laughed. She joined me and we were both soon helpless with it, as if the laughter was another form of release.

When the giggles abated I gave her another kiss. A quick peck this time. 'I'm not sure where that came from but I needed it,' I said. 'I wasn't sure I had any laughter left in me.'

'Course you have. You have huge reserves of strength, John. You must have or you wouldn't have been able to hold that in all of these years.'

It was on the tip of my tongue to say that perhaps it wasn't courage that had me holding on all these years, but cowardice. I couldn't accept her summary because, as I saw it, I'd walled everything up and refused to even accept it was there, hiding behind a façade of normalcy.

'Listen,' she said. 'I need to go. Dad's got the wee one and I had no idea I'd be here so long.'

We got to our feet, both groaning as we did so. We laughed again and it felt like this sound could help bolster me in the coming days and weeks.

'Do you have to go?' I asked, aware that I sounded like a child.

She touched my hand then turned and picked up her coat and handbag. I walked with her to the door, already missing her before she had even left the premises. At the door she looked deep into my eyes.

'We have something, John, but for it to work it needs a stronger base than me wanting to help you move past this. In the difficult moments you'll think I'm only here out of sympathy and drive me away.' Her eyes were moist. 'I won't be able to deal with that.'

'But…'

'And there's Cathy…'

She left that hanging.

How I managed to get myself to work on the Monday I would never know. Once there, I sat in my car, stared at the building, felt the weight of this new knowledge and wondered if I could deal with even a minute in the classroom.

A knock at the window pulled me from my thoughts. I turned to see Mr White peering in at me. I opened the door a crack.

'Mr Docherty,' he said. 'Can I see you in my office, please?'

Shit.

'Of course,' I replied and pulled myself out of the car.

Silently we walked into the building, me following him like a recalcitrant pupil. Once inside his office I sat on my usual seat, but he remained standing, his eyes on me like lasers.

'What the hell is going on with you, Mr Docherty? This is just not good enough. You're either late or you don't turn up at all. And when you do turn up, you're stinking of booze. I've really had about enough.'

As his rant continued I just sat there, allowing his words to wash over me, all my muscles slack as I mentally retreated from his list of charges. A part of my mind was able to recognise this state. I used to do this when Mum came into the bathroom to watch me shower.

Eventually he stopped, as if he'd read something in my face that brought him out of his frustrations at me and my behaviour. He sat down.

'John,' he said, his elbows on the desk and his face now full of concern. 'How about you tell me what's really going on?'

'What?'

This new solicitous approach was not what I was expecting, but the expression on his face suggested it was genuine. This was not a side of this man I had seen before, and it was that more than anything that set me off. Before I knew it I was crying. Head in my hands, breath rattling through my mouth, my body wracked with sobs. I couldn't stop. I tried several times to speak but nothing intelligible made its way through.

Moments later I managed to get myself under control. This was completely unprofessional. How could I ever look at this man again?

'Sorry,' I managed to say while wiping at my face with a sleeve. 'I...'

'John, you don't need to explain anything at the moment. It's plain to see that you're dealing with something traumatic here. I might be a wee shite at times...' he gave a small self-deprecating smile at this '...but even I can see all is not well.'

The sympathy in his face and tone almost set me off again. I took a long, wavering breath and opened my mouth to speak.

'Have you been to your doctor?' he asked.

I shook my head. It was all I could manage in that moment.

'Okay. Get an appointment today, or as soon as your surgery can fit you in. Get yourself signed off *officially* from work, and then we'll see where we are. Just, please stay in touch – let us know what's going on. Okay?'

A wave of emotion surged through me and I bit down on my top lip in an attempt to hold it at bay. I couldn't keep crying in front of this man.

'Do you need help getting home? I'm not sure you should be driving in this state.'

'I'll be…' I managed a breath '…fine.'

'And don't worry about it,' he said as if he'd just read my mind. 'I've seen grown men cry before.'

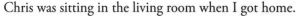

Chris was sitting in the living room when I got home.

'What are you doing home at this…' he began to ask, but one look at my face and his question froze on his lips. 'John,' he said, and that one quiet syllable carried a world of understanding and empathy.

And that one word was enough for the tears to start again. I stood there, in the middle of the room, head bowed, arms limp by my sides, shoulders heaving, frozen in position, giving myself up to my grief for the second time within only a few hours.

A part of me registered that his arms were around me, and that he was also crying. And at that a sense of responsibility rose up in me. A sense of blame. I was the big brother. I should have protected him. I should have found a way to keep the focus on me. I shouldn't have been relieved when she turned to him.

And the same thing shouldn't have caused me to be jealous.

I managed to lift my head up, and moved out of his arms.

'I can't do this,' I said, feeling the weight of that guilt and not sure how to deal with it.

'If not now, when?' he asked.

I could only shrug.

He caught me by the wrist and pulled me over to the sofa. We talked for hours. Until I thought there could be no more words. Until the first hint of morning light appeared in the sky.

'Man, I need to sleep,' I said eventually.

Chris stretched. 'Me too.'

'How have you handled all of this?' I asked. 'How have you managed to appear so together?'

He shrugged. 'I got better at acting the part.'

Luckily, my doctor's surgery had an emergency slot available the very next morning, so, after another sleepless night of trying to ignore the pain that drilled through my head, I made my way there.

The waiting room was almost full and I picked a seat beside two middle-aged women who were chattering in tones that suggested they didn't care who was listening in. They broke off from their chat to give me a little nod of acknowledgement. For a moment I felt self-conscious, certain that they could read from my face what was wrong with me, but their attention was brief and they went back to their conversation.

My name scrolled across the appointment board, telling me to go to Room 4. Inside, I gave the doctor a nod and sat down.

He had the air of someone who had just come straight from university, his clothes looked as if they had just been airbrushed for an advert and his eyes burned bright with a commitment that the constant war of cash versus patients was yet to extinguish.

He clasped his hands before him and asked, 'How can I help you, Mr Docherty?'

'It's my head,' I replied while examining my nails. 'I've got constant headaches.'

'Is it a stabbing pain or a dull throb?'

'Mostly a dull throb.'

'And you have it all the time?'

I nodded.

'Does it vary in intensity?'

Again a nod.

'Any other physical ailments? Sore throats, weight loss…?'

'No, nothing like that, but I do feel tired all the time. It's a struggle to get out of bed most mornings.'

'Is that because the headaches mean you don't sleep? Or is it something more than that?'

'Probably a bit of both.' I tried to ignore the tremor in my voice.

He pursed his lips in thought.

'Headaches are funny things to diagnose,' he began. 'To help you understand, the brain itself has no nerve endings and therefore cannot feel any pain. The pain itself must come from external stimuli. We'll send in a request for some tests…' He made a smile of apology and scanned through the notes in my folder. 'You seem to have been in fine health so far, John, but when I go right back to your childhood I can see references to headaches that you suffered then. You were sent for tests in 2002 and 2003, nothing was ever found and … they went away of their own accord.' He looked up at me. 'Can you think of anything that might have triggered them?'

I held my thoughts for a moment. Did I have to go through this again? Then I realised if I wanted to begin the process of moving towards health what had gone on and how it had affected me could not remain unexamined. So I told him. Everything. He listened with cool, professionalism and without letting anything I said to him trigger anything remotely like judgement show on his face.

'What age were you when this started?' he asked, and I could see his mask of professionalism slip just a little.

Mum on her knees facing me. My football shorts discarded. One of my little friends had kicked me between the legs. Her mouth on me. Saying she was just going to kiss it better.

'I can't remember a time when it wasn't happening,' I answered.

Once I stopped speaking he sat upright in his chair. 'We have a counsellor linked to the surgery and the NHS are able to pay for six sessions. But there's a massive waiting list.' He scratched at his chin. 'It's likely that your employers will only be able to offer something similar.' He turned and rifled through a drawer, then turned to face me with a pamphlet in his hand.

'Survivors Scotland is a charity who help male victims of sexual abuse…'

As he said those words I froze.

I was a victim of sexual abuse. Despite the process I had gone through in facing and admitting what had happened to me, those words hit me like a hammer.

44

Angela phoned me that evening. 'Up for a coffee tomorrow?' she asked.

'That would be nice,' I said and we arranged to meet the next morning in a café just along from the Kelvingrove Museum. Part of me was dismayed at the fact this was a morning meet and in a public space; the other, less selfish, part of me realised it was a clever move on Angela's part. She could continue to be a friend to me without sending out signals that I might misconstrue.

Across a table from each other in that large space it was difficult to be too personal, but it hopefully showed Angela that I was still able to function as a human being.

'Have you been in touch with Survivors Scotland yet?' she asked me. In our phone call I'd filled her in about what happened at work and my subsequent visit to the doctor.

'Not yet,' I replied, studying the sugar bowl in front of me. 'I will though. I will definitely get in touch with them.' Even I could hear the reluctance in my voice, and I wasn't sure where it came from.

'Okay. Good,' she smiled, and pretended to be satisfied with my answer.

We fell into silence. The coffee machine ground out beans and spat out steam. The chatter from the people nearby hung in the air. I looked around me, noting a smile here, a pair of linked hands there, people eating, people talking, people just getting on with everyday life, and I resented them for it.

Staring into my now-empty cup, I thought about Angela and our future. Did we have one? Pleasant as the chat was, and no matter how much I enjoyed just being in her presence, I could feel her keeping a distance. There was a child-shaped space in the air between us, and until I reconciled with that we didn't have a future.

I sneaked a look over at her, just as she sneaked a look at me.

'Penny for them?' she asked.

'I was just thinking how nice you looked.'

A faint flush filled her cheeks, and she ducked her head as if she felt unable to take the compliment. Or perhaps she saw it as the deflection that it was.

I should walk out that door and out of her life, I thought. Save both of us a lot of pain. But I loved her. I knew that now more than ever. I would have to find a way to keep her in my life.

The silence we fell into then was a little more awkward. Angela fiddled about with her bag, and then got to her feet.

'I really should…'

'Sure,' I replied and did likewise. 'It was nice to get out of the flat.'

'Good,' she said, holding her bag in front of her like a shield. 'When you're ready to talk…' Her eyes were brimming as she gave me one last look and walked away.

When Angela left I went out to my car and contemplated what I should do next. I wondered about Thomas. Would he welcome a visit from me? Would he be wondering why I had stayed away for the last few days?

Then it occurred to me how selfish I had been. I'd pulled him out of his safe existence and forced him to seek refuge in a stranger's hotel room. Then I'd abandoned him to whatever happened next.

The Hamilton was only a few minutes away, so, feeling guilty and dreading more awkwardness in my life, I fired up the engine and set off.

After a quick phone call from the young woman at reception, Thomas joined me in a quiet corner of the bar.

'I don't know whether to be pissed off at you for just leaving us here, or pleased to see you,' Thomas said as he sat down.

'The first is probably a legit reaction,' I admitted. 'Sorry.'

He studied me for a moment. 'By the looks of you this hasn't been easy,' he said quietly.

'And then some.' I gave a little nod, and trying to look as if I was relaxed I sat back in the seat and crossed my legs. 'Liz and the kids?'

'They went out for some fresh air. It's not good for them to be cooped up inside all the time.' He clapped his hands on his thighs, a move that was so like Dad I started. 'Where are my manners?' he said. 'Can I get you something to drink?'

'Glass of water would be fine, ta,' I replied.

He rushed off and returned moments later with a glass.

I sipped. We studied each other. No sound inside the room, but passing traffic from the busy road outside was audible through the double-glazing.

'Your memory has returned, hasn't it,' Thomas said at last, his face full of empathy.

I opened my mouth to speak but nothing came out save a little croak. I took another sip of water, swallowed and said, 'How could you tell?'

'I see those same haunted eyes every morning when I look in the mirror.'

'Does it get any better?'

'With help, it will.'

I looked at him, then looked away out of the window. Who could understand better than him, so why was I reluctant to say any more?

'Believe me, John,' he said. 'It's better out than in.'

45

1991

Hunched together in the back of the van as it trundled ever closer to the big city, the boys made a pact. They agreed that Seth was a scary guy, so they'd keep their heads down, do everything he told them to do, never question him, always look if they were sure of what they were doing, then once he started to relax a little around them, give them just that bit of leeway, they'd grab their chance and do a runner.

It came at a service station just outside London. All three of them went to the toilet, where Seth announced loudly that he needed a shit. Wait for me at the sinks, he told the boys. They nodded. And as soon as Seth snibbed the door on his cubicle they were out of there.

In the car park they approached a number of lorry drivers, most of whom told them to beat it.

After what felt like hours, and feeling anxious that Seth would be out of the toilets and making his way into the car park, Thomas approached one more driver.

'Who are you running away from?' he asked. Everything about this man was plus-sized. His head, his chest, his beard.

'Not from. To,' Thomas said. 'Our dad took us away from our mum, and we want to get back to her, so we're…'

Whether the man believed his story or not, he didn't say, but after looking the boys over, as if assessing whether they might be more trouble than they were worth, he gave a little nod. 'My old man was an arsehole as well,' he said. 'We're over here.' He started walking towards a large lorry.

On the way to London the driver got chatty. When they told him why they'd really run away he told them to make their way to Euston Station. 'That's where the Jocks get off the train,' he said. His thinking was that they might give the boys a little more cash when they heard their Scottish accents.

In the absence of anything else, this seemed a reasonable course of action to the boys, and after some persuasion the lorry driver agreed to a large detour and dropped them there.

'Why do we have to beg?' asked Robert. 'Why don't we just go to the cops and explain what happened?'

'Brilliant idea,' replied Thomas, his voice heavy with sarcasm. 'Then they'll arrest me for helping to kidnap you. I'll get banged up, but you'll get a chauffeur to drive you all the way home.'

Robert saw the sense of this and rather than have his only friend in the world locked up, he agreed to do the begging. He was the youngest and was better looking. People were more likely to feel sorry for him and empty their wallets.

On the first day they raised five pounds, and with the naivety and optimism of youth calculated that they'd only get better at this, raise more money and have enough in a few days' time to get them both back up to Scotland.

Trouble was, Seth had the same thought regarding their location and caught up with them just a couple of days later.

He waited until after midnight, then pulled them out from under the cardboard box they were sleeping in and hauled them over to his van. There, he punched them both full in the face before throwing them in the back. Then he drove through the streets of the city for what felt like hours, before parking, and then dragging them both up the path of a house and throwing them into a room, where the floor was covered in thin mattresses and the glass in the window was painted over with black paint.

'There's a bucket in the corner,' Seth said. 'Do your toilet in there. And get some sleep, we've got work to do tomorrow.'

Next morning, he took one look at Robert and cursed his bad temper.

'Look what you made me do, you little shit. No one's going to buy you looking like that.'

Thomas hadn't really looked at Robert the whole night; he'd been too full of his own pain and frustration. When he took in the other boy's face now, he gasped. Robert's nose was badly swollen and he had heavy bruising around both eyes.

Robert wheezed.

'Got a broken nose, eh?' Seth said. 'The people I was going to sell you to want someone who's perfect. You won't do at all, my son.' He sighed, cursed and then gave out a loud whistle. Two other men appeared at the doorway.

'Hold them, will ya?' Seth said.

The boys protested, kicked out and squealed but they were helpless against the strength of Seth's new allies. They were held down and injected with something.

'What are you doing to us?' Thomas yelled.

'Just a little something to make you more biddable,' said Seth with a satisfied look. 'You little shits won't be doing a runner on me anytime soon.'

What followed was then a nightmare of muddled sleep, horrific dreams, strange hunger and continued injections. It was only a few years later that Thomas realised he'd been forcibly fed heroin and set firmly on the road to addiction.

46

Even in my dreams the shame is still there. It burns through every action, every decision, every moment in my life. I walk into a room and I'm certain everyone can see its stain.

He allowed his mother to do terrible things to him. How can they not be thinking this?

Shame tells me I'm not worthy. It haunts like an invisible shroud, a net that encircles me and is tethered to my mind by hooks of inadequacy and self-condemnation. I conceal what I feel because shame does not make a distinction between an action and the self. Therefore, with shame, bad is not separate from self, it's integral. It's as much a part of me as my brown eyes.

What human being wants to broadcast their shame? No, we hide from it, deflect it, call it out in others, not caring that it will have hugely damaging implications for them, passing it on like a diseased baton.

But it was time for that cycle to end. Without being asked I told Thomas of the first time that it happened and of the subsequent times. I told him of my anger, my guilt, my hate, and my love for the woman who abused me. And while I spoke, Thomas said nothing, simply nodded and offered the occasional grunt of recognition, his expression one of grim understanding.

'The doctor gave me a leaflet for a charity who deal especially with men who've been…' I tailed off.

'That's good,' Thomas said. 'In my day there was no such thing. In fact the first therapist I saw refused to believe me.'

'What?'

'She tried to tell me I must have been mistaken, that it must have been my father who abused me … women don't do that sort of thing.' Bitterness at his treatment was strong in his voice, as if it had just happened days ago. 'I thought I was going around the twist, you know, I began to question my own sanity. It was almost as if I had been abused all over again. But…' he found a smile '…Liz was better for me than any counsellor.'

'Have you ever wanted to go and confront Mum?' This was a thought that was entering my head more and more. Would facing up to her once and for all help me in my recovery?

'I dreamed about it. Revelled in the thought. I had so many day-dreams where I tore strips off them both, Mum and Dad.' His reply was all the more powerful for the bold, unemotional way that it was stated. 'I know that Dad couldn't have known anything about it and he didn't have a hand in it, but I can't help thinking that perhaps if he hadn't spent so much time at work it might never have happened, or not happened as much.'

My head moved in agreement.

'And as for that woman, if I saw her again I don't know how I would react. I don't know if I could keep my hands away from her throat.'

It was clear that Tom was still fighting the demons of his child-hood and this frightened me. The root of that fear lay in my selfish concern that I would never be free of the horror either. He showed the face of a well-adjusted family man, but beneath the paper-thin mask he wore were the scars of decades of internal turmoil.

I wondered how this affected his family life. That anger had to go somewhere, didn't it?

'Did Mum ever hurt you?' I asked.

'No, she never actually physically harmed me. It was always under the guise of love and affection. Her touch was always gentle…'

'Pleasurable?' I asked hesitantly.

'Yes.'

'That's something I am having huge problems dealing with. I mean it took me a long time to actually admit this, but I found … I enjoyed the contact with Mum, it was the only time she ever gave me any affection.' I felt a surge of nausea as I said this. 'But I had to physically respond before the abuse could happen … Does that make me as sick as her?'

'Bloody hell, no, John,' Thomas said. 'You were only a child. She abused the power she had over you. Don't feel guilt over your sexual response. When you're tickled, you laugh, don't you? When someone flings pepper up your nose, you sneeze. These are all involuntary physical reactions that you have no control over, just as a sexual response to contact is. This is all on her, please believe that.'

'I hear you. And I kind of understand in here.' I held a finger to the side of my head. 'But … I can see now that as I grew up, on some level I saw an erection as proof of how sick I was, not of how healthy or normal I was.'

'What about relationships?' Thomas asked. 'Have you been able to…'

I gave a grim laugh. 'Lots of one-night stands. But when it means something?' I thought of Angela and my failed attempts to make love to her after I'd proposed. Just then I heard the approach of rapid feet and Thomas's oldest boy rushed in.

'Daddy, Daddy, Daddy,' he shouted as he ran. Then he jumped into his father's arms, swung round to face me and studied me from his perch.'

'Mum said you're my uncle,' he said.

'I am so,' I replied.

'Baby,' Liz said as she joined us, holding the younger child in her arms. 'Don't be giving Uncle John a hard time.' She gave me a little smile of acknowledgement before stooping to kiss her husband on the cheek. 'You guys okay?' she asked.

We both nodded and said yes.

She then handed the child to his father and straightened up. As she did so she put a hand in her pocket, her face forming a quizzical expression. 'I don't remember putting anything in…' She pulled out a square of paper and looked at it, her face forming into a look of horror.

'What is it, babe?' Thomas asked as he got to his feet. I joined him and looked down at the sheet of paper. It was a photograph of Liz and the two children at a swing park.

'That's the park just round the corner. Oh my God, someone's been following us.' Eyes wide in shock, she held a hand to her mouth.

'How on earth did that get into your pocket?' I asked.

'Oh my God. Oh my God, ohmigod,' Liz cried.

'Right. Let's not panic,' Thomas said. 'We're safe here. This is a public space. No one's going to try anything. They're just trying to scare us.'

'And it's bloody working,' cried Liz.

The children picked up on her alarm and both of them started to cry.

'I'll text Chris,' I said, pulling my phone out of my pocket:
Can you get back to The Hamilton? Need you.

'It would help us if we knew more about what we were dealing with here,' I said to Thomas. 'Who are these people and what kind of hold do they have over you?'

47

1991

Living became incidental for Thomas. His next hit was the thing, and what he had to do to get that fix. Seth pushed them both into doing small jobs – delivering parcels or standing watch while deals were made, picking pockets, acting as decoy, acting as bait.

Then, as the boys became more and more in thrall to their addiction, the jobs became more and more demeaning.

'Good lad,' Seth said to Robert one day when they came back in from a delivery, hand on the back of his neck. 'That guy on the corner could have been a copper; you might just have saved our bacon.'

Robert's spine seemed to straighten under this praise and his eyes shone.

'Here you go, son.' Seth handed him a small packet, and it quickly vanished into Robert's pocket. 'Just rewards.'

Robert shot a sly, sideways smile at Thomas. A smile that said, *See, I'm his favourite.* With a great effort of will Thomas held himself in check. He wasn't going to give Robert any satisfaction, but inside he seethed. No way that man on the corner was a copper. He stank, and his long beard and the front of his coat were littered with food fragments. And besides, Robert couldn't spot an elephant with a pink bow on its neck so deep were his cravings.

'What about me?' Thomas chipped in, hating how he could hear a whine in his voice. 'I managed to get in and out of those loos without anyone seeing me.'

The blow came before he could react.

'You're such a little pussy. Give it a rest.' Seth's tone was scathing. And Thomas promised himself he'd be the one getting rewarded the next time, and sent Robert a look of pure loathing. His life would be so much better if the little shit would just die. Any connection the two boys had managed to foster during their brief time of freedom was long gone.

Thomas could see that Robert was desperate to get to his filthy mattress and cook up whatever substance Seth had given him. And his own craving went into overdrive as he imagined Robert on his back, staring at his ceiling with wide-open, unseeing eyes as the drugs took over.

Everything was subservient to the pay-off provided by the drug. Even as men lay on top of him, pushing his face into the pillow, their breath hot on his neck while they thrust, all Thomas could think about was the moment the needle pierced his skin and the substance was released into his blood stream.

Degradation became the normal. When you can't get any lower, what does anything matter? And there was always safety in the warm cocoon of the drug.

Robert became a physical representation of his shame. Thomas could ignore it, bury it deep, but not when Robert was by his side, because then the yellowed skin, almost toothless gums, and hollowed-out expression of the other boy was a reflection he could not ignore.

Nor would his conscience allow him to forget his part in Robert's debasement. And that was his greatest shame – a shame he allowed to transform into hate. A hate that grew until it was second only to the next score, and he began to dream of a time when the boy no longer existed.

At the beginning, by way of a warning, Seth told them about a boy who'd been killed. Seth had been paid, he crowed, so a man could fuck and kill the child, then his body was thrown in the river, discarded like a piece of trash.

Rather than serve as a caution, Thomas began to fantasise that this would happen to him. Better to be dead than suffer this living hell.

But then, as the cravings took hold, and the tactics Seth used to set the boys against each other took effect, he placed Robert at the heart of this sick dream. This twisted his mind so much it was all he could do not to grab him by the throat and choke the life from him every time they were in the same room together.

His chance came one evening when they had some rare time off. He didn't even have to get his hands dirty.

Thomas was on a chair, in the corner of a dark room where the shabby curtains were permanently closed, his mind lifting from euphoria into drowsiness. His limbs were heavy and he felt unable to lift his head. Then the itchiness began; on his thighs, his arms. No amount of scratching could satisfy it. He used the pads of his fingers, rather than his nails, to rub into his flesh, pressing down as if trying to reach through layers of muscle.

A loud gasp distracted him. Then the sound of a strangled breath. As if someone was fighting to breathe through a collapsed throat. He looked over to see that Robert was on his mattress in the middle of the room. Even in the gloom Thomas could see that something was badly wrong. Robert's hands were at his own neck, his mouth was wide and his back was arched as if his next breath was beyond hope and prayer.

Thomas could have called for help. Instead he watched for a moment more as Robert's face turned blue, as his attempts at breathing became more agonised. Then, without a backward glance, he went in to another room in the squat, found an unoccupied mattress, curled up into a ball and fell asleep.

Sometime later, Seth prodded him awake.

'Oi,' he said, his booted toe nudging at Thomas's ribs. 'Wot happened with your mate?'

'What do you mean?' Thomas croaked, momentarily forgetting, his mouth and lips painfully dry.

'He's only gone an' croaked, the little shit.' Seth looked down at Thomas, his expression knowing. 'You could have saved him, couldn't you?'

'What do you mean?' Thomas sat up, suddenly alert.

'You let him die, you little bastard.'

'No … no … I…' Thomas struggled to find any words, so worried was he about how Seth might punish him.

'Never mind,' Seth said as he tapped the side of his nose. 'Here's a little something to tide you over until your next hit.' He handed him a small pill and a glass of water, with a strange light in his eyes. As if Thomas had passed some kind of test.

While he swallowed the pill and drank the water, Thomas heard a series of clicks in his ear. He was sure it was the muscle of his heart slowly turning black, and the blood in his veins being reduced to dust and ash.

48

I felt wrung out by Thomas's story. How anyone could go through all of that and come out the other end while functioning as a husband and a parent was beyond me. Where did his capacity to endure come from? I prayed I possessed even the tiniest amount of his resilience.

'Oh, honey,' Liz said as she studied her husband's face. This was a surprise to her, clearly. He raised his eyes to meet hers. 'Why didn't you ever tell me this?'

'I couldn't.' Self-loathing and relief warred across his face. He had been honest, and it was costing him.

Liz got to her knees in front of him and held both his hands in hers. 'You know it was the drugs, don't you?'

Thomas gasped, as if breathing fresh air for the first time in a long time.

'Every step of the way you were being manipulated by grown-ups. None of this was your fault.'

The two kids made their way over to their father, the smaller one on hands and knees. Once they reached him they both crawled up into his lap, and the four of them huddled in warmth and mutual comfort. Solace sought and found from the people who loved each other the most.

The sight of the four of them together caused a lump to grow in my throat and made me feel I shouldn't be there. I wasn't that connected to my brother that I could join in and share in the hug. It was such an intimate moment that I felt I should leave the room.

At the door I was met by Chris.

'You okay?' He asked, and there was such naked concern in his expression, I almost burst into tears.

'Getting there,' I managed.

He looked over my shoulder at the other four.

'What's happening?' he asked in a low voice.

I motioned with my head that we should leave them.

Out on the street, Chris led me to his car. We sat inside and with cars and buses passing, people going on with the humdrum of their lives, I went through everything Thomas had told me.

'Jesus,' Chris said. 'Bad enough he went through all the addiction and sexual abuse, but to add in the death of the other boy?' He shook his head slowly.

'What's the actual crime here, though?' I asked. 'How could these people hold this over him all these years?'

'This is in England, yeah? It might fall under the crime of manslaughter,' Chris said. 'What you've got to remember is he was just a kid when this happened. Ripe for a bit of mental torture, particularly given what else he'd gone through. Whether a court would charge and convict is almost immaterial, what matters is that Thomas was convinced enough to stay away.'

'And his guilt and shame about Robert's death would do the rest, ensuring his silence.' I shrank from the enormity of this situation. How could he have held that in for all of these years?

'But what's in it for these guys now? This is all ancient history.'

'Unless they're scared Thomas has something on them – something solid that will blow up in their faces.'

'He needs to get in front of them and reassure them it's still in his interest to keep schtum.'

I ran through everything I knew. Thomas managed to escape that life on the proviso he kept to himself, and didn't in any way encourage questions into his past. Questions that would demand answers. Answers that would place these people and their past under the microscope.

'This is all my fault,' I said. 'If I'd just left everything alone, Thomas and Liz and the kids would be fine, getting on with their lives. And Elsa Brown might still be alive.'

'You don't know that,' Chris said. 'And the police are going with an accident as far as Elsa is concerned, so don't beat yourself up on her account.'

'There's something else,' I said, and told Chris about the photo Liz showed us. 'It could only have been taken since they came here. They've never visited that particular swing park before.'

'The photo was in her coat pocket?'

'Yeah.'

'And it was just the photo? There was nothing else? No note?'

'Just the photo.'

'Someone could have brushed past her and easily slipped it in there,' Chris said.

'What should we do?' I asked.

'What else can we do but wait?' Chris said. 'The people who dropped the picture will want to get in touch and make their demands. If that's their game.' He stopped as if something had occurred to him, and looked back at the hotel. 'Look, there's a couple of cameras. Wonder if…' He tailed off.

'If what?' I asked.

'Leave it with me,' he said. 'I'm on good terms with the night guy at the hotel.'

As I studied him, I was both humbled by his pragmatic approach and feeling guilty that I hadn't been a better brother. Which led my mind to my other brother. The danger he was in was all on me.

Thinking through everything I'd learned so far about Thomas, I was once again struck by his resilience. That kind of fortitude served as an example to me. My big brother had dealt with so much.

And so could I.

Before I knew it, I was striding back towards the hotel, and my parked car just beyond.

'There goes a man on a mission,' said Chris as kept stride with me. 'Anything I can do to help, bro?'

'I need to go and visit you know who.' I turned to him and put my hand on his shoulder. 'And face up to her at long last.'

49

My mother was propped up on a bank of pillows, staring out of the window, when I walked into her room. I could see that the ravages of her stroke had receded a little more. What that meant for her recovery I would need to ask her doctors, but not now. This meeting was about something else entirely.

All the way down in the car I'd questioned the wisdom of visiting her while I was in my current state of mind. What if I set off another stroke? Each time the question rose in my head I answered: *So be it.* This was the moment I had to do this, for my own sanity. If her reaction caused further damage to her health – if she became collateral damage – I was not responsible.

The justification of the morally compromised.

'It's been a while, son,' she said. Her words were clearer. They didn't run into each other as they had when I first visited her, but one of her eyes was still shut and her left hand was still frozen in a claw.

Before her stroke, and certainly since Dad died, my mother appeared to hold everything in tight control. Her short, grey hair was thick and always beautifully cut, her clothes precise. Time had trod carefully around her, imposing on her only a gentle ageing.

But time's kindness had now deserted her. Although she had recovered somewhat, the stroke had aged her. It was there around her eyes, in the dull grey-white of her hair, the slackness of one side of her mouth, and the tremor in her arm as she tried to hold my hand.

I shrunk from her touch.

'What's the matter?' she asked, her voice sharp with worry.

'You must have known this day would come,' I said. The words were out before I could stop them. All of my carefully rehearsed speeches lost in the sudden wind of my anger.

She looked stunned. 'What's going on, John?' she asked.

'It's a process, apparently, Mother,' I answered. 'Face your fears. Name them, and they no longer have a hold on you.'

Puzzlement creased her eyebrows, deepening her wrinkles. She opened her mouth as if to question me, her face adopting a benign expression.

'Why?' I asked.

'Why, what, son?'

I reared back from the title. But, mindful of her health, I fought to keep my tone even. 'I'd prefer you didn't call me that.'

She reached out with both hands, looking unsure of herself.

'You abused me, Mother. Repeatedly, when I was a boy.' Somehow I managed to keep my voice level, while inside my guts were twisting.

'What on earth…?' she shouted, and I was surprised at the loudness of her voice. I didn't think she had the strength. 'How dare you—?'

'How dare I? How dare *you*?' I interrupted, each word clipped, my voice deliberately quiet.

'John, son,' she said, her voice low in an attempt to cajole me out of my anger. 'What's happening? Where's this coming from?'

'I remember everything. My new room. The birthday cake…'

'Pfft,' she said. 'You never liked birthday cake. You were such an odd child.'

'The birthday cake I vomited all over the carpet after you abused me.'

Her voice just above a whisper she said: 'How dare you come in here and accuse me of such vile things, while I'm lying here in my sick bed? What kind of a man have I raised?' Her lips were a thin, tight line, her skin puce.

'A man in your own image, perhaps? How could you, Mother? What on earth could have happened to you that you'd think what you did to us was appropriate?'

'I refuse to listen to this. Have you gone mad? Or is this where you blame all of your problems on your parents, but conveniently Dad isn't here, so Mum will do?' Shaking with anger, she managed to lift a hand to her mouth and wiped at the saliva she'd sprayed down her chin. 'Is that it, son? Let's conjure up some false memories and dump the crap on Mother Dearest.'

'Do you know what it does to you when the person that you first run to for love and safety is the one that you most fear?' A solitary tear was slipping down my cheek. I wiped it away with the back of my hand. 'Yes … I was terrified of you, but I also wanted you so much that the ache was…' I shook my head as if that would rid me of the memory of that sensation. 'And don't try to tell me that some shrink planted false memories, when you provided very real ones.'

I straightened my back and looked away from her. As I did so I noticed a group of photographs on a low table in the centre of the bay window. They were photos that had previously taken pride of place in our house. Someone must have gone in and brought them to her. One of the neighbours, perhaps. An image in the middle of the row snagged my attention. It was framed in silver and showed me having just reached thirteen, filling my lungs in order to blow out the candles on top of my cake. The colour had faded somewhat, but my eyes sparkled with youth and promise. A promise that was to be extinguished as quickly and as callously as I extinguished those candles. I walked over to the window and nudged the top of the frame so that the photograph fell on its face.

My mother took advantage of my moment's silence. 'Time for you to go, John. And don't come back until you've got this stuff out of your system. I don't know what has come over you. I never harmed a hair on your head. I gave you nothing but unconditional love. If your father could hear you now he'd be turning in his grave.'

I turned to face her. 'How did you keep it from him?'

'Shut up and get out! I refuse to listen to any more of this.' Her lower lip trembled and tears shone in her eyes. Her upset was so convincing I almost doubted myself.

'Please, Mum, please admit it. You need help. We need help.'

'Get out.'

'I'm begging you, Mum. Help me make sense of this. Please…'

'Get out!' The sinews on her neck stood out like rope around a maypole as she screamed at me.

At this point the door opened behind me and I turned to see that one of the staff had come in.

'Please,' she said to me. Her voice was respectful but I could see in the way she was holding her hands rigid by her side that she was outraged on my mother's behalf. 'You have to leave. Your mother is not well. You can't be—'

'Don't worry, I'm going.' I made my way to the door, feeling animosity bristling from the woman who'd come to my mother's rescue. Her opinion of the situation was plain in her stare. Big strapping son verbally abusing a frail, old lady. 'Don't let appearances fool you,' I said to her.

When I reached the door I remembered that I hadn't told my mother everything that I'd intended to, so I turned and faced her one more time. What came out of my mouth next was pure spite, but I couldn't help myself.

'Oh, by the way – remember your firstborn? He's living in Glasgow. And not that you'll ever see them, but he made you a grandmother.'

50

The view of the sea was obscured by the fine mist of my breath on the car's cold windows. Muted colours and indistinct shapes reared up in front of me, hemming me in. I filled my lungs slowly, hoping the oxygen would go straight to my brain and clear my thoughts. Pushing the car seat back to its furthest position, I pulled my feet up and placed my chin on my knees, then tried to make sense of my recent conversation.

None of my mental discussions with my mother had included her actual reaction. Now the vision of her straining neck and bulging eyes was painted on the car windows' fog. Her rage had been terrible, and I was beginning to doubt if it was the act of a guilty person. Should I have expected her to confess straight away? Surely a guilty person couldn't have met my eyes with such a stare.

Had I imagined the whole thing? Was she right? Was I having false memories?

Absolutely not! I pounded on the steering wheel. False memories wouldn't appear with such clarity. All of my senses were involved in those memories; surely that wouldn't be the case if this was all a result of an overactive imagination.

Doubt seeped through my mind, making it a swamp, the silt of uncertainty smothering all my convictions. Screwing up my eyes, I tried to force all doubt from my mind. There was no doubt, I told myself; my mother was guilty and her performance had been borne from the panic of discovery. She had been rehearsing that scene for decades.

When the #MeToo movement kicked off, she must have been worried it would encourage me to face my memories and I'd tell someone I'd been abused. She must have thought a day of reckoning would come. Or perhaps she had been reassured by the number of articles and comments online that said this was the time at long last for men to shut up and listen to women? Even though my memory of my own abuse had been locked away, this was a notion I'd rejected as soon as I heard it. If female abuse victims hadn't been listened to before now, neither had men. This was the time for everyone to be heard.

Or perhaps the lag in time since that phenomenon broke had her reassured that she was safe, that her manipulation of my mind as a boy had been successful – my silence was guaranteed.

I tried to examine my feelings for my mother. Did I hate her? Did I love her? Could I ever forgive her?

The answer to these questions was a limp: *I don't know*.

51

A text alert sounded on my phone. I ignored it. Then it rang.

'Did you get what you needed?' It was Chris. I could hear he was worried about me, and I was touched. I coughed to release the tension in my throat.

'Not really,' I said with a bitter laugh.

'It will take time, John,' he replied. I could hear a lot of unexpressed emotion in that sentence.

'Are you not tempted to have it out with her yourself?' I asked.

'Other than getting things sorted out with the house, I don't want to see her ever again,' he said firmly.

'I wish I could be more like you,' I said. 'But I need to know why. How she could even think it was…' I coughed again. Having this conversation with Chris over the phone was far from ideal. I broke my chain of thought. 'You had an idea earlier. Did you get anywhere?'

'Luckily, Billy, the night guard, was in a wee bit earlier this evening. All it took for his help was a couple of joints and the contact deets for my supplier,' he said with a smoky laugh. 'When will you get here? We could do with a hand going through the CCTV feed from outside the hotel.'

'Give me an hour.'

Thomas seemed a decade older since I'd first seen him just days before, as if the weight of his admission had aged him. When I walked into the hotel I found him and Andrew sitting in a corner sofa just beyond the reception area, in front of a large TV showing a cartoon channel. He gave me a nod of acknowledgement, but his eyes wouldn't meet mine.

'Liz was putting them down for their afternoon nap, but this one wouldn't go to sleep.' He jiggled the little boy in his lap. 'So I brought him down here so his mum and brother could get some peace.' At this, Andrew ducked his head, and then placed it against his father's chest, his large blue eyes full of love and concern. He looked as if he'd barely left his father's side while I'd been gone.

'Okay?' Thomas asked as he looked up at me.

'You?'

He sighed. 'Been worse.' He kissed the top of Andrew's head. 'This little man is making me feel better by the second,' he said raising his energy and inserting cheer into his voice.

The teacher in me reared back from this, and an internal voice chided: *Please don't put that burden onto your son. Your emotional health is not his responsibility.* But, of course I said nothing. In his clearer moments I was confident Thomas would realise this.

Chris entered and gave us both a nod. 'John, the office is just along here…' He beckoned me to follow.

'Anything I can help with?' Thomas asked.

'The more the merrier,' Chris said with a smile. 'But perhaps it might not be ideal to have small eyes looking on?' He added looking down at Andrew.

'Gotcha,' Thomas said. 'Give me a sec.' He picked Andrew up and kissed his forehead. 'Let's go and see what Mummy's doing.'

A couple of minutes later, Thomas returned and Chris led us from reception along a short corridor towards a door. He pushed it open and when we walked in Thomas gave a small whistle.

A broad-shouldered bald guy wearing tiny round glasses, looked over from a computer monitor tucked away in the corner of the small office. Above him on a shelf sat another screen, which was divided into four, each of them displaying the view from a different camera out on the street.

'You must be Billy,' I said.

He tipped his chin at me, and then, following my gaze, said, 'It's not the worst part of the city but we've had the odd issue with drunks and junkies.' He looked at the screen. 'The boss thinks this keeps us all a wee bit safer.' Then he looked over at Chris. 'This didn't happen,' he said with a look of warning. 'Or I'm in serious bother.'

Chris made reassuring noises as Billy got up from his chair and walked to an industrial-sized printer in the other corner of the room. 'I pulled a number of pictures from the feed. Unfortunately, there's no one person in particular who looks like they've placed the photo in the pocket of the woman ... Liz?' He looked at Thomas for confirmation. 'But there are a number of people who got close enough to.' He took a large pile of paper from the printer. 'You guys want to look through these?'

'Sure,' Thomas took the photos from him and fanned them out on the desk. One caught my eye. Liz was in the centre of the image, head turned slightly as if something had caught her attention. Her hands were on the handle of Jack's pushchair. The top of Andrew's head was visible but there was no one else in the frame. As I studied the picture I could see how easy it would have been for someone to drop something into her pocket.

Thomas slid another image across to me. And so the process went. One image after another, all of us checking carefully to see if there was anything of note.

But nothing.

'Shame,' Chris replied. 'It was worth a shout.'

I looked up at the line of small screens, my attention caught by a passing white van. Everywhere on each of the screens there was movement. Except ... I leaned in closer.

'What is it?' asked Billy.

In the weak evening light we could see a man in a pale raincoat standing at the corner. Everyone else was going somewhere except for him. Which was not that unusual really, he could simply have been waiting for a friend, or any number of things.

I pointed, thinking that I might as well satisfy my curiosity. 'Can you zoom in on this guy?'

'Sure,' Billy said and pressed a couple of commands on his keyboard. An image filled one of the large monitors. The man at the corner raised a hand to his face, scratched his cheek and slowly looked up and down the street.

'I know him,' I said. 'It's David Collins.'

'Who?' asked Thomas and peered closely at the screen. Then he stepped back, hand to his mouth, eyes wide as if he'd just been presented with a face from a nightmare.

'What is it?' I asked, looking from Thomas to the computer screen and back again. Then the penny dropped.

'That's him,' said Thomas. 'That's the cop I went to for help.'

52

Thomas barged past me. I stood in the doorway for a moment, bewildered at his speed.

'Where's he gone?'

'He's gone for Collins,' Chris said with urgency. 'And as soon as Collins sees him charging at him, he's going to leg it. There's a back door that will bring me out just behind where Collins is standing. I'll go and cut off his escape. You follow Thomas out the front and make sure he doesn't do anything illegal.'

I charged down the stairs and arrived in the reception area just as Thomas pushed open the front door. 'Thomas,' I shouted, hoping to delay him just a moment so Chris could get into position.

He turned to me, his face wild. 'I need to get that bastard. Don't even think of trying to stop me.'

I reached him and grabbed a handful of his T-shirt. 'I'm not going to stop you. I'll be right beside you.'

He smiled, a grim feral thing that I shrunk from.

'But harm this guy and you'll end up in prison…'

'I'll gladly do time for that prick.' His face was in mine as he struggled to free himself from my grip. It took all of my strength to hold him back. 'Let me go,' he hissed.

'I'm on your side, Thomas, but think of Andrew and Jack. Think of Liz. I know you need to confront this bastard, but you let go of that anger and you'll likely end up killing him. Then you'll be in prison and not able to see your kids for years. Is that what you want?'

'Don't fucking stop me,' he snarled and with a sudden movement he was free and out on the pavement.

I followed quickly after. And there, thirty yards away, was David Collins. He saw us move in his direction. At first he misjudged our intent and moved back against the wall, as if to avoid our eyes. But then, realising we'd spotted him, he turned … and walked into the brick wall that was my brother, Chris.

With a roar, Thomas launched himself at Collins, grabbing him and throwing him against the wall. Collins fell to the ground and Thomas lashed out with his feet. One kick. Two.

'Enough,' shouted Chris and grabbed hold of Thomas. 'Get Collins,' Chris shouted at me as he twisted Thomas's arm up his back.

People were now gathered around, shouting at us to leave the old man alone.

I moved into professional mode, as if I was dealing with a playground full of feral teenagers. 'Nothing to see here, people. Thanks for your concern, but it's all under control.'

Chris moved towards the back exit of the hotel, still holding on to Thomas's arm. I could see that his grip was one Thomas wasn't getting out of soon. 'Bring Collins,' Chris said to me. 'Less people to see what's going on around the back way.'

'I was just minding my own business, son, and then that guy started kicking me,' Collins said. His eyes were wild, his white hair sticking out in every direction, and his expression one of a wounded victim.

'Sure you were,' I said to him and grabbed him by the upper arm, braced for him trying to escape, but I needn't have worried – he was as meek as a lamb.

We'd got them both through the back exit and into a corridor that fed the kitchens and the office when Thomas lunged for Collins again. He managed to connect with the side of his face before Chris pulled him off.

'Enough,' Chris said. But Thomas had lost it. He was screaming, windmilling his arms, trying to make contact, any contact with Collins.

'Enough,' Chris said again.

Then he moved so fast I couldn't make out how he'd done it, but

Thomas was bent over, his arm out to the side and his hand pushed into an angle that had momentarily incapacitated him. Chris was barely even breathing.

'If we're doing this, we're doing it right,' he said to Thomas. 'Okay?'

'Okay.' Thomas snarled.

'You sure,' Chris demanded. 'Cos I can keep this up all day. Can you?'

Thomas hung his head, and let out a long groan. 'No,' he said.

Chris let him go, and Thomas moved over to a chair, glaring at Collins and rubbing at his hand.

'Sit,' Chris told Collins.

I sent Chris a look, wondering where this version of him came from.

'What's going on here,' Collins said staring at me. 'I've not done anything.'

'What were you doing outside?' I asked.

'Waiting for a friend. We were going to come into the hotel for a drink.'

'Why here?'

'My mate likes it.'

'Who's your mate?'

'You won't know him.'

I could sense Thomas becoming agitated again. 'What the hell is that achieving? What are you up to, you old prick?' He stepped closer.

'Thomas, do I need to force you out of the room?' asked Chris.

At that moment Billy arrived, so agitated he was hopping from one foot to the other.

'Guys, guys, what the hell? We can't be having this here. You need to take it somewhere else.'

'Got any spare rooms?' Chris asked.

'Aye…'

'Charge it to my account will you? And get me the key?'

'But…'

'Everything's fine now. All the children are behaving.' He looked over at Thomas and Collins. 'Aren't we?'

'These guys have abducted me, son,' Collins shouted to Billy. 'You need to call the police.'

'Chris, I can't have this. You're getting me into trouble,' Billy protested, reaching into his pocket and pulling out a mobile phone.

'Don't Billy, please,' Chris said, holding his hand up and moving closer to him. He quickly explained what was happening, and who Collins was.

Billy's expression darkened.

'We just want some answers from him and then we'll cut him loose,' Chris continued.

'I can't have violence going on in my hotel,' Billy said.

'You want your junk? You want your boss to know you're buying junk from a hotel customer?' he asked in a low voice.

'Chris, you wouldn't,' Billy said, a look of heavy disappointment on his face.

'Don't be daft,' Chris replied. 'I never dob in a mate. However, this guy has some answers we really need. If I promise nobody gets hurt will you let us take him up to one of the rooms out of the way?'

Billy looked at him for a long moment, then he threw his hands up. 'If this comes back to bite me, Chris I'll fucking have you.' As he said this his mouth and fists tightened, and looking at the figure he cast I was pretty sure this was no idle threat.

After some more protests from Billy and some more persuasion from Chris, we were directed to a small conference room beyond the function suite on the first floor. Not wanting to draw more attention to ourselves, we took Collins up the back stairs.

The room was large enough to hold a long, dark wooden table with seating for ten, a drinks cabinet on the far wall, and a floor-to-ceiling window that looked down on the Glasgow traffic. At the sight of this I could see Collins relax a little. As if the thought occurred to him that nothing bad was going to happen to him in full view of the city. He allowed Chris to direct him to a seat.

'Thomas,' Chris looked over at him. 'Put the snib up on the door. We don't want to get interrupted.'

With a look that suggested he was pleased with this request, Thomas did as he was asked.

'Taken any nice pictures recently?' I asked Collins.

'Eh?'

'Empty your pockets, please,' asked Chris.

'I'll do no such thing.'

'Oh, empty your fucking pockets.' I felt my agitation rise. I was not comfortable with bringing this old man up here and was unsure how far Thomas might take things.

Chris shook his head at me slightly, telling me to dial it down a little. I ignored him and leaned over to go through Collins' jacket. He struggled to get out of my reach. 'We do this the easy way, or I release the angry guy there…' I indicated Thomas with a nod of my head.

'Fine, fine, fine,' said Collins and began to go through his pockets one by one. A small pile soon built up on the table in front of us. A packet of cigarettes, a lighter, a brown leather wallet, two pounds thirty-six in change, a handkerchief, a bus ticket, a receipt for a Tesco Express that was just two doors down.

'You live about thirty minutes from here,' I said. 'Why are you shopping at a local Tesco?'

'I was hungry, for chrissakes. Is it illegal to buy snacks?'

I looked at the date on the receipt. 'This was for two days ago. Were you just a bit early to meet your pal?'

'Something like that,' he replied, trying to look defiant, but instead seeming worried that his flimsy cover was blown.

'Where's your phone?' Chris asked.

'Cannae be doing with those things,' Collins replied. 'Waste of money.'

Chris nodded at me, so I leaned across and stuck my hand into the inside pocket of Collins' jacket. Bingo. I pulled out a large smartphone and handed it to my brother.

He looked down at the phone, and then, before I could blink, he reached across, pulled Collins' hand over and pressed his index finger against the screen. It unlocked.

'Hey,' Collins protested, and pulled his hand back and cradled it in front of his chest as if Chris had broken his finger.

Ignoring him, Chris located the photo gallery on the device and quickly found what he was looking for.

'Why are you taking photos of this man's wife and child?' Chris held the phone up so Collins could see what was on the screen.

'I've no idea what you're talking about,' Collins said. As he spoke he shrunk a little in his seat.

'And look,' Thomas said as he stepped forward and placed the paper version his wife had found in her pocket on the table with a thump. 'The exact same photo was placed in my wife's jacket pocket.'

Collins said nothing, but shrank further into his seat.

'Okay. Cards on the table,' said Chris. 'You were in the force long enough to know we have enough to raise suspicion, but not enough for the police to charge you with anything. However' – he pointed beyond him – 'that man is willing to testify that he came to you as a child to ask for help because he was being abused at home, and you took advantage and abused him all over again.' Chris turned to Thomas and asked. 'That about sum it up?'

Thomas's mouth was a tight line of hate. It was all he could do to nod.

'Now, how about you tell us what is really going on and we might be able to do a deal with you.'

'Oh aye?' Collins sat upright.

'First, I need to talk to my two brothers here.'

Chris took us over to the window and started to mumble incomprehensibly. Thomas and I looked at each other, wondering what the hell was going on. Chris had positioned us so that he had his back to Collins. The old man was studying us keenly.

Chris was still holding Collins' phone and I saw he'd accessed a note-making app and was typing out a short sentence:

We've got this guy. Play along with whatever I say, okay?

Then just loud enough for Collins to hear he said, 'We really need this guy's help. You need to think about the bigger picture here, Thomas.'

Chris showed him the screen again: *Play along.*

Then he said, 'If we get this guy to call off the dogs, your family is safe for evermore, aye? Or you call in the police, make your statement, he gets arrested, does nothing to help us, your family have to go through the whole court thing with you, and then you'll be looking over your shoulder for the rest of your life, wondering when whoever is behind all of this is going to come for you. Or your kids.'

'You're saying I should let this guy get off?' Thomas demanded, but I could see he'd brought the intensity of his reactions down a notch, as if he understood and was playing along with Chris, but not making it look too easy.

Chris give a little nod of satisfaction. 'I'm saying we find out who is behind all of this and we save your family a lot of grief.'

'That prick gets off?' Thomas turned around and kicked out at a chair. It shot across to the other side of the room and I looked at Thomas with concern. A look that I could see out of the corner of my eye was picked up by Collins.

'It's not an easy decision, Thomas, but it's one you've got to make, for everyone's sake,' I said, wondering what Chris was really up to.

'Who knows how many kids that evil bastard abused. You're telling me...' He turned away in disgust, and then stormed out of the room.

Chris twisted round and shrugged at Collins. 'He needs a minute,' Chris said. 'I'm sure he'll see sense.'

Collins was sitting upright, hands on the table in front of him, an apparently neutral expression on his face. But I could see his eyes shifting back and forward from me to Chris, to the window, to the door. He was calculating his odds of getting out of this intact. If he gave up the people he was working with, what might happen? If he kept quiet and faced charges of child abuse, what would happen then? He licked his lower lip. His nostrils flared. He crossed his arms, then released them, palms down as he drummed on the table top with both thumbs.

A couple of minutes later the door flew open and Thomas charged towards Collins, who backed up nervously against the wall.

'If whatever you tell us doesn't pan out, I'll take a full-page ad out in the *Herald*, and on every social media site possible with your details on it and ask everyone who was infected by you to come forward. I'll build up such a case that you'll spend the rest of your worthless life in prison getting butt-fucked by every convict who wants to make a name for themselves. You hear me?'

Collin's eyes were huge. He was clearly frightened of Thomas, but I could see that he was doing a lot of mental calculations.

'What I'm about to tell you, you could have found out without my help,' he said as if he was preparing his defence for when his cohorts demanded an explanation. He looked at me and took a deep breath, as if bracing himself. 'Before we start. I need a whisky. Single malt. Make it a double.'

53

Collins took a sip of the amber liquid.

'Jesus, I needed that.'

'Before you begin,' I said, and placed my phone on the table, located the voice recorder and then activated it. 'Insurance,' I explained.

Collins shrugged as if he didn't care. Then he took another sip and looked over at Thomas. 'You're lucky you're still alive, buddy.'

'How so?' Thomas asked, his expression sharp.

'There's some people who got out of the shit you guys were up to and made a nice life for themselves. Got wives, kids, grandkids. And they don't want what's in your head to come out and jeopardise all of that. They were satisfied you'd gone underground, but then this little detective' – he looked at me – 'goes digging up all kinds of stuff, and that has got these people worried.' He crossed his arms. 'I'm the vanguard, if you like. They wanted me to make you a little nervous to see how you reacted, to see what that might throw up before they did something…' he looked at Thomas with dead eyes '…irreversible.'

'And we're in a Mexican standoff cos Thomas is worried they'll go to the cops with the stuff he's done,' Chris said.

'We know all of this,' Thomas said, his tone betraying his impatience. 'They're worried. I'm worried. Tell me who we're dealing with, for chrissakes. We'll arrange a meeting to persuade them that it's in everyone's interest to keep quiet.'

'Knowing who they are could be enough to seal your death warrant, buddy. These people might be in a different life now but … old habits and all that.'

'We have a deal, old man,' said Thomas. 'It doesn't take a genius to work out that one of them is my old friend Seth. But let me worry about what happens once I know who the others are. So where's Seth and who else is involved?'

'It's just him,' Collins said.

'My arse,' said Thomas.

'No lie,' he said, arms wide, palms up. 'Except he changed his name.' He raised his eyebrows and looked from me to Chris. 'And these lads have already been to see him.'

I had an image of a house on the side of a loch.

'Coulson,' Chris and I said at the same time.

'You fairly set the cat among the pigeons, visiting him,' Collins said.

'You met Seth already?' Thomas asked. 'How on earth?'

'I think we got lucky,' said Chris. 'An old article in a business magazine where he credited Benny Marinello with helping in his success.'

At that name Collins visibly flinched and his face whitened.

'What's the real connection between Coulson and Marinello?' I asked him.

'That's above my pay grade,' he replied, but it was clear from the way the skin tightened around his mouth that he was worried. Really worried.

'That's the link,' Thomas said, his eyes bright. 'That's what confused me all along. I know Seth – Coulson. Whatever his name is now. Why would he be bothered? I know he's too bloody lazy to come after me. But if…' he looked at Chris '…Marinello is involved…'

'Marinello's a mess. He's not going to be orchestrating anything,' I said, recalling the mental state of the old man in the nursing home.

'He's not in a good way,' Collins agreed. He paused as if making a decision. 'But Coulson reckons he lays it on thick. He's immobile, but not senile. Not yet anyway.'

'No way,' I said. 'That old fella's beyond caring about all this shit. What are you leaving out, Collins?'

'I swear to you, I've never met the guy, but he's the one pulling Coulson's chain. The way he describes it, the old man has him on a retainer in case something from the old days comes back to bite him on the arse.'

'And what do you know that's going to be such a worry to Marinello?' I asked Thomas.

'Buggered if I know,' he replied. 'I did all kinds of stuff down in London that I'm ashamed of, but that was all on Seth – Coulson. Marinello had nothing to do with it.'

'You sure?' Chris asked.

'Certain,' Thomas answered. 'Elsa told me years later that Seth trafficked troubled kids and Marinello turned a blind eye as long as Seth gave him a share of the proceeds now and again. But everything I was involved in down south was all about Seth and his mates down there.'

'Then, what are we missing?' I asked.

54

An hour or so later we were all still sitting there, trying to think this through, and getting nowhere.

Any time there was a silence we could hear a growl coming from David Collins' stomach.

'Do you guys not need a feed?' he asked. 'I need to get regular scran or I get a right painful belly.'

'Shut up,' Thomas and I both replied at the same time. Collins huffed and crossed his arms.

'Would be nice to get some food in me. There's a pizza place just up the road,' he said and looked hopefully at me. I studied the man and was struck by how humdrum the human face of evil appeared. That was twice he'd asked for food now, demonstrating how little he was really affected by his confrontation with Thomas. Either he'd been preparing for this day for years, or he didn't care. Thomas the boy had simply been a piece of flesh with which he'd attempted to slake his twisted desire.

The nature of evil. The evil in our nature. The good and the great have debated for millennia what caused that corruption of the human spirit. I wasn't going to come up with any answers. But I spent a second sending a prayer skywards that my own soul didn't carry the same taint.

'I can't bear being in the same space as this piece of shit for much longer. And I'm fucked if I'm going out to buy him a pizza,' Thomas said as he got to his feet and left the room. A couple of minutes later Liz entered.

'It's gone six p.m.,' she said. 'I hear someone's off for pizza? I'll come along.' She looked at me.

'I'll go,' I stood up, getting the message. I couldn't bear to be in the man's company a second longer either. 'What do you all want?' Everyone shouted out their orders and I grabbed a pen and paper from the cabinet to write everything down.

We walked along the street towards the pizza place. It was raining; that famous Scottish smirr that is so fine it feels like the atmosphere around you is two parts water, one part air, and before you know it you are wet through. The pavements were wet and shining, the street-lights a string of bright blurs above our heads. Traffic was loud and fast and constant, people surrounded us, each of them locked in their own thoughts, unaware of the trauma Liz and I were facing in that moment.

'Despite what's going on,' Liz said, throwing me out of my melancholy. 'I'm glad you came looking for Thomas.' She touched my arm. 'He thought of you often, you know. Wondered how you had turned out. Worried that your mother had turned her attentions to you…' Her smile was an offer of commiseration. 'You do understand why he didn't seek you out?'

'Completely,' I said. 'Besides. He got away; why would he want to come back and be reminded of everything he despised?' We reached our destination and I pushed at the door. It opened with a jingle and a whoosh of conditioned air.

Inside, I walked to the counter and gave the server my order.

'You're talking ten to fifteen minutes,' the man said. 'Want to come back or you happy to wait?'

'We'll wait,' I said, spotted a bench along the window and Liz and I took a seat.

I looked across at her and smiled. 'You guys have been together a long time. Been through a lot, eh? What's your story, Liz?'

She laughed. 'If they ever made it into a movie it would need to be a trilogy.'

The bell above the door jangled, someone else came in and made their way to the counter.

'There's so much I want to say to you, John,' said Liz. 'But I don't know if it's appropriate yet.' She held me by the wrist. 'How are you dealing with all of this?'

'Oh, you know.' I felt my eyes brim with tears. 'It's not been easy.'

'Do you have someone close to you?'

'Not really,' I replied. 'There was someone recently, but that hit the buffers.'

'If it's okay to ask, what happened?'

'You don't shy away from the personal, do you?' I laughed.

'Sorry,' she ducked her head slightly, but her small smile demonstrated that she wasn't sorry at all. 'We've got a lot of time to make up for, why waste any more?'

Strangely, I wasn't threatened by her asking, or uncomfortable. Her manner and the affection inherent in her questions was a bridge between us – two people who had until very recently been complete strangers. And I knew this wasn't just idle curiosity, but a genuine quest for connection and empathy.

'Her name is Angela. She's beautiful. And she has a lovely daughter.' I heard myself falter as I said this last sentence.

'Ah,' Liz gave a nod of understanding. She looked away, then back, as if she wanted to say something but wasn't sure how it would be received.

'Just say it,' I said, having no idea what was on her mind.

'You're not your mother's son, John,' she held both my hands in hers. I pulled away.

'Sorry?'

'You know what I'm saying.' She looked into my eyes. 'Men who've gone through what you have are often scared they're going to turn into the thing they most dread.'

I crossed my arms, uncomfortable with the fact that she'd voiced my biggest fear. 'Haven't most abusers been abused themselves?'

'Yes, but the vast majority of victims never ever go on to abuse. And here we're faced with the inadequacy of words…' She looked at me as if the force behind her eyes would better convince me. 'Tell me this: if you want to keep your distance from children, why become a teacher?'

'Good question,' I replied, and before I knew it something I'd never articulated appeared in my mind, then began to form on my tongue, and in an all too rare moment of self-awareness and honesty I spoke my thoughts. 'I think I wanted to find the damaged boy I'd locked in my memory in the kids that came through my class-room, and make a positive contribution to their lives.' I shrank from the earnestness of my words while recognising the absolute truth in them.

'That's lovely, John. You are a sweet man.' She reached over and gave me a little hug.

I could feel my cheeks raise a blush.

'And tell me this as well.' Liz moved back so she could stare into my eyes. 'Have you *ever* been sexually attracted to children?'

'Jesus, no,' I answered, disgust a roiling, wreaking thing in my gut.

She raised an eyebrow in response. 'There's your answer. Why on earth would you start now?' She paused, then asked in a low voice. 'You're still in love with Angela, aren't you?'

I looked away for a moment, turned back and nodded.

'Let me repeat: you are not your mother's son. Don't let the fear of something that's not real stop you from living your life. It's time to start giving yourself a break, John. Real happiness is such a rare commodity in life. Why distance yourself from that?'

'I'm quite content as I am,' I said, and as the words hit my ears even I could hear the defensive tone.

'Content,' said Liz, with an eyebrow raised. 'That's an interesting choice of word. Reeks of compromise.'

'Oh, shut up, you,' I nudged her side with my elbow. 'You're far too clever.'

She nudged me back and laughed, her eyes full of warmth. 'Nah, not really. Just, been there, seen it, and I wring the T-shirts out on a daily basis.'

We delivered the pizzas to the group back at The Hamilton, and we all chewed down on the food in silence. Once we'd finished Chris tidied away the boxes and gathered us all together. And as I watched my young brother take control yet again, I sat with the thought that he'd become a huge credit to himself.

'Where do we go from here?' he began, and glanced at his watch and then at the door.

'Let me go and I'll tell Coulson you guys want to meet up for a talk,' said Collins.

'No one asked you for your opinion,' Thomas replied.

'Apart from the letting him go part, he's making sense,' I said. 'We need to speak to Seth, and if it is Marinello who's behind all this, we need to work out why he's so bothered and let him know he's got nothing to worry about.'

The door opened and Billy ushered in a couple of uniformed policemen.

'We got a call?' The one on the right scanned the room to see who would answer.

'Jesus,' Chris said, 'I thought you guys were never going to arrive.'

What was this all about? I looked at the others, but the only person who appeared to know what was going on was Chris himself.

Collins stood up so fast I wondered why he didn't faint.

'You bastard.' The penny dropped with him before anyone else.

'Officers: this man' – Chris pointed at Collins – 'is a former policeman. He sexually assaulted this man here,' he indicated Thomas – 'when he was only a boy, looking to escape abuse in his own home. And I'm sure a concerted campaign will unearth a few more witnesses. No way is Thomas his one and only.' He looked at Thomas. 'You'll be happy to give a statement?'

'Absolutely,' Thomas said. He was also on his feet as if preparing to launch himself at Collins should the old man decide to try to run.

'You bastard,' Collins repeated. 'I thought we had a deal.'

Chris's grin had 'fuck you' written all over it. Then he shrugged and said, 'I lied.'

55

Realising that Thomas's allegation would only start the process I told the policemen about Collins' attempt at intimidation, showed them the printed-off photo and the corresponding item on Collins' camera phone. From the look on their faces this was sufficient to remove him from our presence. Whether they took him back to their station for questioning, or they'd pay him a professional courtesy and just let him go outside the hotel, I didn't care. His impact on the situation was finished and as soon as the other players found out he'd been compromised, I was sure their reaction would be more robust than ours was. If I was him I'd be heading for the nearest airport.

The policemen took all of our details, the phone and the photograph, and after they'd elicited promises that we'd all be willing to make statements they accompanied Collins out of the hotel.

'How did Collins and Coulson ever get involved with each other?' I asked when we were on our own.

'A child abuser,' Chris said, 'and a child trafficker? Their kind always seem to find a way to get together. Perhaps Collins passed some of his victims on to Coulson to keep them quiet? Who knows? But to stay in the job and off the radar for so long, I wouldn't put it past him.'

We drifted into silence.

I considered the look of relief and pleasure on Thomas's face when the cops took Collins away. Of course, only one of his abusers was on track for some kind of justice. Would I ever see something similar? Did I even want that?

'Are you thinking you need to get some kind of closure now with Mum?' Thomas asked as if he had been reading my mind.

'She all but spat in my face the last time,' I replied.

'What about you, Chris?' Thomas asked.

'The woman is dead to me.' Chris's voice was flat and brooked no argument.

'Sounds like you need more, though, John. Worth another go?' Thomas asked.

'I don't know. Is it wise?'

'Only you can answer that. In this case it wouldn't work for me. I don't want to ever see that woman again. But you've had a lifetime with her … What do you want to get from it?'

I sat with his question for a moment or two, not quite sure how to articulate the charge of emotion that rose through my mind and body whenever I thought of my mother.

'Honesty. I want her to be honest. I want her to see what she did to me. To us. I want an explanation. I want her to say she's sorry. I want penitence, tears and snot.' The pitch of my voice was rising. 'I want her to beg forgiveness and to throw it back in her face. I want to know why. I want to know how she hid it from Dad. I want to get all of this…' I stabbed at my forehead with the stiffened fingers of my right hand three times '…out of my head. I want to take this black, fucking cloud and shove it down her throat…' I tailed off, surprised at how quickly my anger had risen up in me.

'All very understandable, John,' Thomas said as he reached across and placed a hand on my knee. 'But be prepared for the fact you might not get any of that.' He looked over at Chris. 'You're awful quiet.'

'What can I say?' He looked away from us for a second, and as he did so he wiped a tear from his cheek. 'I thought I'd dealt with this. I thought I was through the other side. But Jesus,' his voice broke. 'This is bringing it all back.' He looked up to the ceiling and exhaled a long, wavering breath. 'Fuck.'

'Hey,' I said, feeling my own sadness rise in response to his. 'Why did you never talk to me about this? And why didn't you shake some fucking sense into me?'

Chris wiped another tear away, and raised an eyebrow. 'You kidding me? Mr Shitty Memory? You had to come to this in your own way, John. In your own time. Any attempt to force you to go there would have caused nothing but grief, and I didn't want to fight you on this.'

'Did you guys fight a lot as kids?' Thomas asked, and I could see he was processing the fact that he should have been there, been our big brother.

'Some,' Chris and I both said at the same time, and we each gave a small, self-conscious laugh.

'Did you each know the other was being abused?' Thomas asked.

Chris and I both looked at each other, and then each gave a small nod of recognition.

'Oh, it ranged from bitchy comments to full-on fist fights,' Chris said. 'Looking back it feels like we never stopped having a go at each other.'

'I was so jealous,' I said.

'Me too,' Chris said. 'I wanted Mum to myself. I knew it was off-the-chart wrong, but at the same time it was really the only thing that mattered. How twisted is that?'

'She was playing you; you know that, right?' Thomas asked. 'She would be getting off on pitching you against each other.'

'Yeah, but we were fighting each other well into our teens,' I said. 'By that time we should have grown the hell up.'

'You're being too harsh on yourself. The patterns had been set in concrete when you were little boys,' Thomas said shaking his head. 'And that shit is difficult to get past.'

'Isn't that the truth,' Chris said quietly.

'Oh man, I'm so sorry, guys,' Thomas said, his eyes heavy with self-recrimination. 'If I'd stayed. Talked to someone else. Shouted from the fucking rooftops. *Done* something else, you guys might have been okay.' He jumped to his feet, looking about him as if the solution to all of this was still just out of his reach.

Chris stood up too. 'This isn't on you. None of it is. You were just a kid yourself.'

I got to my feet. 'You can't blame yourself, Thomas. That's crazy.'

Thomas looked at me, hands out, as if begging me to take away his pain, his eyes red. He began to shake his head, as if the thoughts it contained were too much to bear. 'I should have done something instead of just running away. I fucked everything up.'

'Hey,' Chris repeated. 'This is not on you.' Tears were running down his cheeks. He reached out and pulled Thomas into a hug.

I joined the hug, resting my head against a curve of bone where my brothers' foreheads were touching, my arms out wide, resting on each man's shoulder.

I've no idea how long we stood there for. Each of us weeping, processing, healing. I only knew a connection was being made.

Despite everything, we were brothers, at last.

Sometime later, Chris excused himself.

'I need a lie down in a darkened room and some paracetamol,' he said with a weak smile. 'You guys okay?'

Thomas and I both nodded. And I could see that we each needed to be on our own for a time. So we said our momentary goodbyes and agreed to meet up soon to sift over everything we'd learned, each of us knowing we'd made a start on learning how to become real brothers to each other.

Outside, on the street, as I walked to my car I heard rapid footsteps nearing me and Thomas shouting, 'Hang on a minute, John.'

I turned to face him. 'What's up?'

'Coulson,' he said. 'Where is he?'

'He's … eh, what do you want with him?' As I asked I read his dark look and felt something dark uncoil in my belly.

'That's nothing for you to worry about,' he replied.

'For your own sanity you don't want to be messing around with that man.'

'I thought I'd dealt with all of the stuff he did to me, but…'

Thomas turned to the side, his neck bent, his arms rigid. 'Coulson has to pay.'

'Pay? Pay how?' I asked.

Thomas met my eyes and I could see his were swimming with the threat of violence. There was an atavistic anger pulsing from him that caused me to step back. Reading my reaction, he exhaled and gave himself a shake.

'I need to confront him, that's all. And give him a wee scare.'

'Jesus, Thomas, that's not a good idea.'

'Let me decide what is or isn't a good idea, John. Where is he?' Thomas asked as he stepped closer to me.

Momentarily cowed, and recognising that he was using his physicality to intimidate me into giving him what he wanted, I steeled myself. I would not go on in this relationship with such a formative moment. I placed a hand on his chest, pushed him back a little and looked him in the eye. 'If you go, I go,' I said.

'Not a good idea,' he replied.

'Let me decide what's a good idea,' I said, throwing his own words back at him.

'I like your style, little brother,' Thomas said, his eyes shifted slightly as if he was making a quick calculation. He placed a hand on my shoulder. 'Tomorrow, then. Come and get me just after nine and we'll go and speak to him.'

At home I poured myself a large whisky and sat on the sofa and ran through everything that had been revealed that day. I was determined I wasn't going to allow myself to push everything into a dark corner of my brain again where it could be forgotten, and fester. If I was ever going to overcome my past I had to face it and own it.

Sometime later, perhaps an hour, my mobile rang. It was Liz.

'Do you know where Thomas has gone?'

'He's gone?' And I knew instantly where he was headed. 'Shit.'

'Where is he, John?' She sounded close to tears.

'He said he needed to confront Coulson.'

'Fucking idiot,' she said. 'Right. Pick me up in five minutes. We need to stop him before he does anything stupid.'

'How does he know where to go? I didn't tell him.'

'Perhaps he asked Chris?'

'Listen, I don't think it's wise for you to come along, and, besides, who's going to watch the kids?'

'Billy's grown quite fond of them. He's in here every five minutes playing with them.'

'Sorry,' I said, remembering the look on Thomas's face earlier that day. 'You really don't want to...'

'John, you better come and get me or—'

I hung up. A minute later I was out the door, down the stairs and in the car.

56

When I arrived at Coulson's cottage, an early-evening calm had descended on the loch that fronted the road leading to the house. A pair of small boats were moored just off shore and the water was so still it looked as if the craft had simply settled on top of a stretch of glass. The grass verges were full of daffodils, crocuses and tulips, and the moor grasses and heathers on the far hills were being burnished gold by the setting sun.

In the drive was Coulson's car. And just behind it sat Thomas's ancient people carrier.

I'd expected to see it there, but nonetheless I still felt a surge of fear and disappointment. Pulse heavy in my neck, I got out of the car and walked as quietly as I could up the slope to the door. Should I knock? Should I just go in? What if Thomas really had come here to simply confront the man who'd done so much harm to him all those years ago? Who was I to barge in? But what if he was intent on a final revenge? No one walks away from that kind of act unmarked.

I put my ear to the door, and heard shouting, but the words were unintelligible through the wood. Hand on the door handle, I turned it slowly. It was unlocked.

Judging from the sounds there were two people talking, so if Thomas was planning on violence that hadn't happened. Yet.

I pushed the door closed again, and settled my back against the wood. If I heard something worse than shouting, I'd go in and separate them.

I didn't have long to wait.

There was a loud crash, followed by some grunts, another crash, and a scream. I opened the door, and rushed in to the front room, but what I saw was not what I expected.

Thomas was on the floor, holding his head, while Coulson glowered over him with a hammer in his hand.

'What the hell?' I shouted.

'Good,' said Coulson turning his face towards me – a beacon of satisfaction. 'I can see to you as well.'

'You touch him and I'll…' Thomas began.

'You'll what?' Coulson kicked him in the ribs. 'You're done, boy.'

'Nobody's done,' I said and edged my way into the room, palms up.

Thomas twisted and looked up at me from the floor, and as he moved his head I could see one side was coated in blood.

'Jesus,' I whispered and reached for him.

'Stay where you are, Mr Docherty,' Coulson said as he brandished the hammer.

'Get the fuck out of here, John!' Thomas shouted, and then gave a groan as if the effort caused him huge pain. If he'd taken a hit to the head from that hammer in Coulson's hands he needed help and soon. I could only guess at what harm it had done.

'Sit down,' Coulson said to me, indicating the sofa and holding the hammer over Thomas's head, suggesting what he would do if I didn't obey him.

I complied.

Thomas groaned. 'You should have left when you had the chance…'

'Love it,' said Coulson. 'You two already have that brotherly love thing going on.'

'What do you intend to do, Mr Coulson?' I asked carefully.

'Collins called me…' he took a step back and looked over his shoulder. I followed his line of vision and saw a small, blue suitcase '…I was going to leave for a while, until everything blew over.' He kicked Thomas's leg. 'If you hadn't come here.'

'I only wanted to talk,' Thomas protested.

'With this…?' Coulson held up the hammer. 'That's the kind of conversation I only get into when I run out of options.'

'Yeah, so it is. You're the picture of restraint.'

'I'm a changed man, Thomas. Or is it Robbie?' He smiled as Thomas winced at the name. 'I always thought that was a bit sick – how you took your dead friend's name.'

'You guys gave me no choice, I had to go under the radar so they…' he looked over at me '…wouldn't come looking for me.'

'And yet…'

'Can I at least get up?' Thomas moved into a sitting position, still holding his head.

'Stay where you are,' Coulson said and kicked out at his foot. He turned slightly and rubbed at his face, and as he did so I saw that there was some swelling there. So Thomas had managed to get something on him during their brief struggle. That cheered me a little.

'I get that you wanted to be incognito, but why take the boy's name?' Coulson asked.

'It was Elsa's suggestion,' Thomas replied. 'She'd read something in the papers about undercover cops taking the names of dead people and thought it would be a good idea for me.' Thomas pulled his legs up towards his chest. 'And it seemed a good thing – a kind of homage to Robbie,' he added quietly.

At the mention of Robbie's name, Coulson's eyes took on a strange light, and his mouth curved into a smile. It didn't last long, but it was there long enough for me to see it, and read the satisfaction in it.

Realisation struck me.

'You sick, sick, bastard,' I said.

Thomas looked over at me, questions in his eyes.

Coulson raised an eyebrow. 'At least one of you brothers got some smarts.'

'Thomas didn't let Robbie die. You killed him.' I pointed at Coulson, anger sparking through every cell in my body.

'What?' Thomas said and tried to get to his feet.

'Stay where you are,' Coulson snarled and raised the hammer in threat. 'Jesus, you were such a sucker.' He grinned, and there was such evil on his face I took a step back from him. 'Memory's such

a tricky thing, innit? And it was such an easy suggestion to plant.'
He shifted the hammer in his grip, as if preparing to put it to use.
'What's the harm in telling you the truth now. You're not going to
see tomorrow.'

'What did you do, Seth?' Thomas demanded, using the man's
former name, and I could see Thomas was back in that moment, a
boy, discovering his friend was dead. The horror of it bleak in his face.

'He was on the way out anyway,' Coulson said with a sneer. 'None
of the men wanted him anymore. He was used up, washed out, the
drugs were wasting him away. He wouldn't have lasted the month.'

'What did you do, Seth?' Thomas shouted.

'Wasn't nothing,' Seth shrugged. 'Like putting a mongrel out of
his pain.'

I could see that Thomas was readying himself. I was sure he was
going to charge at Coulson, and when he did I would too. So I sur-
reptitiously scanned the room for something, anything, I could use
as a weapon. We just had to keep him talking.

'Elsa's dead,' I said, aware that Coulson was in a talkative mood
and needing to know if he had a hand in that as well. 'In case you're
thinking of going to see her after you've dealt with us.'

'Poor Elsa. Couldn't handle the guilt of handing over all those
kids,' Coulson said. And something in the way he said it gave me
pause. He knew already. There was a little bit of pleasure in his tone
and in the slight twist of his lips.

'How do you know?' I asked, frowning.

'Goodness me,' said Coulson with a camp little grimace. 'You
got me.' Then he grew serious. 'What does it matter. I'm going to
end you two as well.' His smile was tight, baring a set of stained and
broken teeth, the light in his eyes a flare of danger. 'She always was
a mouthy cow.'

'Wait,' Thomas said. 'You killed Elsa?'

'Well, I went back, didn't I? The old man said no loose ends.' He
said like someone reporting that they'd taken some trash to the local
dump.

'What did you do to her?' I asked.

'It was quite easy to set up, really. I take it the police had it down as an accident?'

'You bastard.' With a roar Thomas was on his feet and propelling himself the short distance at Coulson. But in his damaged state he was no match for the older man. In moments, Thomas was on his back on the floor and Coulson was astride him, hands around his neck. Squeezing for all he was worth.

The vase. It had a heavy glass base. Without thought, but with every bit of malice I owned, I picked it up and brought the thick glass end crashing down on the back of Coulson's head. And I was back in the woods, with Paul, striking him with the stick and exalting in the loss of control, feeling stronger than I ever had, feeling I'd at last taken some power back.

Coulson fell on top of Thomas and between us we managed to flop his slack body to the floor – it was as if every muscle in his body had been switched off.

'Jesus, Jesus, Jesus,' I intoned, bending over him while making sure not one part of me touched any part of him. 'Is he dead?'

'I fucking hope so,' said Thomas as he got to his feet. He staggered a little before righting himself.

'Fuck. I've just killed someone. Fuck.' I felt as if I was outside my body. Numb. And hot. And drenched in sweat. My pulse was a metronomic thump battering through every cell in my body.

'John. John. John!' Thomas was in my face. He shook me. 'We have to go.' He shook me again, more violently this time, and this brought me back to myself.

'Jesus. What do we do? We should call the police.'

'Not happening, brother.' He bent over the body, and checked Coulson's neck. 'Still a pulse.'

I breathed out. 'Thank you, God.' Then. 'We should call an ambulance. Say we just arrived and found him like this?'

'And why are we here? Two total strangers just popping by on the off-chance we can make a friend? Get real, John. No one can know why we were here. And anyway, he got what was coming to him.' He bent down and picked up the vase in one hand and the hammer in the other. 'We'll get over to the ferry at Hunter's Quay and phone in for an ambulance from there, if that makes you feel better.'

I nodded. I could see the sense in what Thomas was saying. We didn't want to be associated with this, but neither did I want to be responsible for the man's death.

'What are you doing with them?' I asked, nodding at the vase and hammer.

'Evidence,' he shrugged. 'In case the bastard dies, we'll drop them over the side of the ferry into the Clyde. No murder weapon. Less chance they catch us.'

At the thought of being caught by the police I winced. 'We need to wipe everything we touched.'

'Yeah,' Thomas nodded. 'I like the way you're thinking. Cool head in a crisis. Who would have thought it?' he said, and we set to work.

Outside the house, on the doorstep, I rubbed vigorously at the door handle with my sleeve. Then we both scanned the surroundings to see if anyone might see us. There was no one about, thankfully.

'We were never here,' Thomas said.

'Never happened.'

I shuddered at the memory of me wielding that vase as if it was an axe. Hearing again that thump as it connected with Coulson's head. It was either him or us, I told myself. I turned towards my car, pushing my hands deeper into my pockets as if burying my shame over my all but forgotten capacity for violence.

57

I phoned Chris on the way back from Coulson's to get him up to speed.

'You did what?' he demanded. 'Is he dead?'

'There was still a pulse when we left.'

He paused for a moment as if digesting this.

'Fuck him,' he eventually said. 'The man got what he deserved. Let's hope there's a bleed in his brain and he croaks it.'

'I'd rather not be a murderer,' I said, feeling a shiver throughout my body at the idea.

'You did what you had to do, John. Don't be feeling guilty. If what you say is true…'

'It's true.'

'Then your conscience should be clear.'

'It would be clearer if I phoned for an ambulance. Regardless of what the old prick has done I wouldn't want his death hanging over me.' I made a mental note to call 999 after we stopped talking.

We sat quietly on either end of the line for a few minutes, both of us lost in our own thoughts, as if we were reluctant to break the connection.

'Oh, you need to know,' Chris broke into the hush. 'We got an offer in for the house. I forgot to say in all the drama. A very good offer.' He gave me a number, a number that would pay for Mum's care for a good number of years. And with a sense of relief that any last shreds of duty we had to her as sons would be satisfied by managing this arrangement for her, I offered him my thanks.

My mind then returned to the situation with Thomas. 'All of this means that Marinello no longer has a hold over Thomas. It was

Coulson who killed poor Robert Green. Thomas didn't have anything to do with it.'

'Yup. We need to go and visit Marinello. Find out what he was so worried about and make sure he doesn't have Coulson Number Two on standby.'

Next morning at ten o'clock Thomas, Chris and I were sitting in Chris's car outside Marinello's nursing home.

'Anything on the news?' asked Thomas, and I knew instantly what he was talking about.

'I phoned for an ambulance,' I admitted.

He nodded. 'And?'

'Anonymously,' I said. 'So I don't know the outcome.'

'If he'd been found dead surely there would have been something on the news about it,' Chris added.

'Fair enough,' said Thomas as if he didn't care one way or the other.

'Why are we here?' I asked, unsure why we were bothering and keen just to have this whole thing over and done with. 'With Coulson no longer a threat, do we still need to talk to the old man?'

'Yes,' Thomas said firmly. 'Coulson got one thing right. No loose ends.'

'But he's done,' I said, remembering what the old man was like when we visited him.

'We don't know if he's got other people on his books like Coulson,' Thomas said.

'And, don't you want to know why?' Chris added. 'Why he was frightened of Thomas?'

'Collins seemed to think that the old man was more incontinent than senile, so I'd like to test that out,' replied Chris.

'Why would he put on an act like that?' I asked, remembering how the old man's mind wandered when we last visited.

'To mess with us?' Chris suggested. 'Anyway, will they even let us in?'

'Maybe not mob-handed,' I said. 'I think it's important Thomas goes in. And I got nowhere the last time. Why don't you two go and I'll wait here.'

They got out of the car and made their way to the front door. I leaned back in my seat, turned on the radio and waited for them to return.

Half expecting them to see them walk straight back down the path, having been refused entry, in fact a full song had played and they were still inside. Then another song. And another. They had to be getting somewhere, I reasoned.

Some minutes later I saw a familiar car draw up, and Gina Marinello get out.

Shit.

I couldn't sit there any longer, not with Gina now in the picture. I had to know what was going on. I got out of the car and followed her up the path to the main door. I walked in just a few strides behind. She went past the reception desk, seemingly unaware of my presence, and took a left down a carpeted corridor. As I passed the desk the woman behind it gave me a smile.

'Sir, if you would just like to sign the—'

'I'm with her,' I half whispered and winked, and continued to follow Gina.

She entered a room about halfway along the corridor. I arrived just as the door clicked shut, but that was enough to catch a glimpse of Chris and Thomas sitting by the old man's bed. I caught the door before it closed and stepped inside.

'And who are you?' the old man in the bed asked. Everyone else in the room looked at me.

'I couldn't—'

'What on earth is going on here?' Gina looked from me to Chris, and then to Thomas. 'Oh my God,' she said, hand to her mouth. 'They found you? You're still alive.' Then, as if old emotions she had suppressed took over from her surprise, she demanded, 'How come you're here? And what do you want with my grandfather?'

'Now, Gina,' the old man said. There was a defensive edge to his voice, and perhaps even a little fear. 'Let's hear the boys out.' He was propped up on a bank of pillows and I couldn't help but compare him to my mother: two people at the end of their lives, with their pasts catching up with them.

Of course, the old man's guilt was currently supposition, but the more I considered the situation the more I was convinced he was involved in all this.

'This man helped abduct my first boyfriend, Grandad. I'm not going to roll out the red carpet. In fact' – she rummaged in her handbag – 'I'm going to call the police.'

'No one is calling the police,' Benny said in a surprisingly strong voice. 'I want to know why these men barged into my room, and what they have got to say for themselves.'

'If I can talk, please?' Thomas looked from Gina to Benny. 'Whatever happened, it was a long time ago. And it needs to stay in the past. I have no wish to bring it all up again. I just want to be left in peace to bring up my kids. I've got a new life now. I won't do anything to harm that.'

'Who's asking you to harm anything, son? And what is it that you think you know?' As Benny spoke his eyes narrowed.

'Do I need to spell it out?' Thomas said. 'Cos I'd rather not.' He gave Gina a quick glance.

'My granddaughter knows all my business. All of it,' Benny repeated. 'There's no need to be coy on her behalf.'

'What, the stuff that Seth did?'

'Seth who?' Benny asked.

'If that's the way you want to play it, fine,' Thomas said.

'Oh my,' said Benny. 'I suddenly feel quite tired.' He closed his eyes.

'If that's the way you want to play it, I'll just keep on talking,' Thomas said, as if he found Benny's fatigue a little bit too convenient. 'Seth was trafficking kids from your fairgrounds, Mr Marinello.

You knew. You took a cut of his proceeds by way of a licence, I guess. At least, that's our information.'

'Oh, come on,' said Gina. 'That's bloody ridiculous.'

'But I won't say anything' Thomas said firmly. 'I want to forget the whole thing happened. I just want to be left in peace.'

'Don't we all, son,' Benny said. He looked over at his granddaughter as if judging how she'd received this news. 'You should just go, Gina,' he said. 'Get on with your paperwork, or whatever it is you do here on a Wednesday.'

'What's he talking about, Grandad? Did this Seth person actually traffic kids from the Shows?'

'It was all so long ago, darling,' Benny wheedled. 'Don't you worry yourself about any of this. It's all just a bit of confusion. I'm sure it can all be…' He looked as if he was struggling to find the right words, and it occurred to me that in his stronger days he would have been able to talk Gina down much more easily.

'And how did this Seth pick his victims?' Gina asked.

'These kinds of places attract a lot of troubled kids. Loners. Kids that wouldn't be missed. Kids who wanted to run away,' Chris said. 'Like Thomas here.'

'That doesn't explain Robbie,' Gina said, her face pale. 'He wasn't a runaway. He wasn't a kid who no one would ask questions about. And he certainly wasn't alone. Why was he chosen?' She looked from Thomas to Benny.

'As I remember it,' Thomas said, 'Seth said he had an order for a young, blond boy.'

Gina shuddered. 'Jesus.' Her hands were over her stomach as if she was finding this new information to be physically painful. 'But still. Not your typical victim…' She stared at her grandfather.

He met her eyes for a moment, before looking away. His bottom lip trembled.

'Tell me you had nothing to do with this, Grandad.'

Benny closed his eyes tight, and then exhaled slowly. When he opened his eyes again it looked as if he had come to a decision.

'He was only supposed to give him the frighteners,' the old man spoke in a way that suggested he no longer had the energy to maintain his secret. 'Your mum and dad were worried you were going to run away with the wee creep.'

'Mum and Dad? What do they have to do with it?'

'Darling, you don't want to go there. This is all ancient history.'

'Oh my God,' Gina said, her voice raising in volume and pitch with each word. 'Who was it? Mum or Dad?'

'Your mum,' Benny said in a whisper.

'The witch couldn't bear seeing me happy.' Her handbag slipped off her lap and fell to the floor. 'We were sixteen. I knew I went on and on about running away with him. I was just trying to piss her off. I would never have done it.'

'Your mum was pretty convinced you were only days from packing a bag. She had the boy looked up, and found out his uncle was a panto ... pardo...' He struggled to find the right word. 'She was inconsolable. No way were you going to bring a kiddie-fiddler into our family, she said.'

'So based on hearsay she had an innocent boy abducted and sold into God knows what? Jesus, this is like a bad movie.'

'The boy escaped, or so I heard. Made his way down to London,' Benny said. 'Whatever happened to him after that wasn't down to us.'

'He escaped?' Gina asked, her mood now laced with a sense of hope.

Thomas opened his mouth to respond, but paused before doing so, and I guessed he was editing events in his mind, hoping to give her a more palatable version.

'Please tell me the truth,' Gina said. 'I at least deserve that.'

'I felt bad about what happened, about my part in ... so I ... We escaped from Seth. But he found us again and...' The truth was evidently still too painful for Thomas to tell.

'And?' Gina was wringing her fingers.

'He got us both on smack. Made us addicts. And then one day Robert got a bad batch.' Thomas looked down at his hands, his face etched in shame. 'He died.'

Gina just sat there and stared at him. Then she began to sob.

'Honey, don't be getting upset,' Benny said. 'This happened a million years ago. So much good stuff has happened since.'

'How can you say that?' Gina sat forwards, wiping the tears from her face with the heel of her hand. 'Because of me, because of my hateful mother, a beautiful boy died.' She then seemed to have a thought. 'What about Peter?'

'Peter?' Benny asked.

'My fiancé. He had a car crash just before we were due to get married. Did my parents have a hand in that as well?'

'Now, now,' said Benny. 'You're letting your imagination get the better of you.'

Gina stared over at her grandfather. 'So, Mum just wanted Robbie frightened off. You put Seth on it, and instead of, what, giving him a kicking or something, he got this guy here' – she indicated Thomas – 'to lure him somewhere private and then he was…' She shook her head. 'I can't even say it,' she whispered.

'Honey, please, don't do this to yourself,' Benny said, and by the way he was leaning forwards in his bed, he wanted nothing more than to console his granddaughter with a hug – and felt his inability to do so very deeply.

'Did you carry on dealing with Seth after he came back from London?'

'What do you mean?'

'Did Seth continue to traffic kids and did you continue to take a cut?'

'Darling, it's not as simple as that…'

'Actually, it is … and don't call me darling.'

Marinello fell back on his bed and for the first time since we'd entered the room he looked every inch the old and infirm man he was – as if his granddaughter's good opinion had been the one thing holding him together, and now it looked to have been withdrawn, there was no reason to go on.

'You are my grandfather and as such I have a duty of care. Your needs as far as being warm, fed and dry will continue to be met, just like any client of this home. But that is it. Our relationship is over, because frankly you disgust me. The sooner you die the better.'

I gasped at the brutality of her statement.

Gina got to her feet, smoothed down her skirt, and looked at the three of us. 'What did you hope to accomplish by coming here this morning?' Her stance was rigid. Only the slight tremble in her hand betrayed the fact that she was only just holding it together.

Thomas explained about Collins, the photo in his wife's pocket and the threat this implied. And restated his intention to forget that the Marinellos ever existed, provided he had assurances his family would be left alone.

'You can be assured that my grandfather's interest in your family is over. I will see to it.'

'Thank you,' said Thomas, relief in his voice.

'I no longer care about the old man, but I care about my family's reputation, so if I get a whisper that any of this is coming out, you will wish you never fucked with me.'

She stared at each of us in turn. And I saw a whole other side to this woman. She may have been innocent in this situation, but the ruthlessness that informed her grandfather was there in the straight line of her shoulders and the determination of her gaze. 'I don't want to see any of you ever again.'

58

There's a small boy. He's waving. All those people on the train and I *know* the wave is meant for me. The train passes and there he is again, and again, ahead of us, standing behind a fence, waving.

I lift a hand, but hold back on any movement as I become acutely aware of the people around me. Can they see him? I cross my arms, tucking my hands under them, reluctant to appear the fool.

The train moves on.

He's in the seat beside me. His small, warm hand in mine. He climbs onto my lap and leans his head against my chest as if he's sharing my heart beat.

We breathe the same air. The silk of his hair a balm against the rasp of my unshaven cheek. Like a benediction.

I send him a silent thank you: beginning to understand that because he endured so can I. With a short, tight, squeeze of his hand, and a smile, he's gone. Small gestures that leave their message, and as I wake into a new day I feel the realisation lodge in my mind, and become aware of the challenge it represents.

It's kindness that brings us back to ourselves.

There are two sounds that I have always loved. The first is footsteps in crisp snow and the second is the crunch of gravel as I walk or drive over it. The former is easily understood – what child doesn't love to be the first person to walk on a virgin piece of snow. The latter is not so easily explained. Perhaps the reason is buried in my past. Perhaps the enjoyment I find in this sound is the whisper of a memory of better times. Whatever the reason, whenever I hear this noise my face lifts into a smile.

My passenger looked over at me quizzically. I declined to answer the obvious question in Angela's eyes, simply enjoying the noise of small stones being crunched together by the passage of my car.

The week before, the day after Thomas and I visited Coulson, I had phoned Angela. Strangely, something about that act of violence helped to clear my mind.

'Hey,' she had said, her voice tentative. And that one syllable was enough to make me realise I couldn't not be with her.

'I've missed you so much,' I said, my voice cracking.

'Me too,' she replied.

'I want to make this work. I want to get to know Cathy. I want both of you in my life,' I babbled. 'Can we try?' I'd never felt so nervous as in that moment, as I tried to read her silence.

'You cheated on me, John,' she said in a small voice. 'That kind of trust is difficult to earn back.'

'I'll do anything,' I said, not caring that I sounded desperate. 'Anything.'

'The drinking needs to stop.'

'Already working on that.'

We met.

We talked.

We fell in love all over again.

As soon as she heard that I was planning on confronting my mother again, Angela offered to come with me. She made the suggestion carefully, with eyebrows uplifted, her whole body leaning towards me as if to protect me. Admitting that her company would be a comfort, I accepted.

Inside Lennox House, Angela took a seat in reception. 'I'll wait for you here,' she said, allowing her hand to linger in mine before letting go.

Up the stairs, feeling that my heart was about to burst out of my ribcage, I knocked at my mother's door and entered.

'Hello, John.' A weak, tremulous voice came from the bed. A bony hand fidgeted with a gold chain. My mother's gaze held mine for a fleeting second. She was the first to look away. 'How are you, son?' she asked, her voice edged with false cheer.

We were in full denial mode again, then. Only that brief fidget suggested my previous visit was on her mind.

'Fine,' I said. 'Fine,' I tried again after clearing my throat. 'Are you being looked after?' I asked, with a politeness normally reserved for strangers.

'Speech therapist says I'm doing well.' She held up her damaged hand. 'The physio is less confident.'

For several minutes the conversation continued in this vein as we carried on our charade of loving mother and dutiful son. A lapse in the conversation then followed as we both fought for something to say. The quiet was even less comfortable than the dialogue.

'Have you had many visitors?' The word 'Mum' stuck in my throat like a solid lump of bile.

'Yes.' She tried to sound bright. 'Mrs Johnstone has been really kind; she's been in and out of here a couple of times a day since I arrived.'

'Good.' I smoothed down an imaginary bump in the bedclothes, and then withdrew my hand as if I might be burned. I had gotten too close to touching her. 'It's a shame it's not a nicer day.' I said looking out of the window. 'That's quite a view you've got.'

'Beautiful,' she agreed. 'The change in the weather gives it that little something extra. No two minutes looking out of this window are the same.'

This was a safe conversation, and a light like a remembered happiness smoothed out some of the lines on her face as she took in the view.

As I watched her speak I remembered past joys. Moments when she had been a good mother, when her affections weren't tainted. I was that small boy again, needing her love, craving her attention and touch. I was that boy again whose anger was a black surge in his mind. It was wrong, all wrong, but she told me it was special. I was special.

And then it stopped.

The relief and the disappointment warred within me. The shame that I wanted more. The gut-scouring guilt as memory provided a view of her going into Chris's bedroom, knowing what was about to happen, being powerless to stop it, and feeling that tiny nub of envy prodding at my heart.

Why hadn't I gone to Dad? He would have stopped it.

The memory of her voice in my mind was a whisper and a song. 'This is love. The purest form, between a mother and a son. I'm taking you back into myself … and it is beautiful.' Her eyes shining with tears, her expression beatific.

If it made her so happy how could it be wrong?

'Dad won't understand how unique we are. He'll break us up. You'll be sent to a home. Do you want that?'

Panic, bright and harsh burst in my mind. 'No.'

'Then this has to be our secret. No one can know.'

But there, before the shame crashed in, a second of affection, a touch that was driven by love, not power and lust. I closed my eyes against this yearning, disappointed in myself, feeling that shame all over again. And in that moment, sorrow, rage and longing tumbled over and under each other. Aware that my hands were shaking I placed them under my thighs.

My mother looked back towards me, and my attention shot back to the view She continued to speak – inconsequential stuff, gossip she'd learned from Mrs Johnstone, the quality of the food here. As she spoke her eyes were fixed on the glass. My eyes darted back and forth from her to the window. The muscles of my jaws ached as I forced myself to stay calm. Willing my shoulders to relax I walked over to the window and filled my lungs with the clean air that seeped through the small opening at the bottom of the sill.

'The doctors say I'm making good progress,' she said.

'Right,' I said and fell silent.

The shrill quiet then sounded in our ears. It was broken briefly by the squeak of a wheelchair passing by the door. I could sense that my mother was building up to something. It took all of my courage not to fill the silence with another inane comment about the weather. I cursed myself for being a coward.

'Would you fill up my glass with some water please, John? All of this talking is giving me a thirst.'

'Sure,' I replied. As I handed her the glass, the warm paper of her hand brushed against mine. She caught my involuntary shudder and her eyes clouded in pain.

'How's Thomas? I really do have grandchildren?' she asked, her voice a tremble of absence. I could see she was bracing herself for my answer. She knew I would withhold the information, but still she couldn't help but ask.

'You have some nerve,' I replied, each word clipped with anger.

'Sit here, beside me, please,' she pleaded. A bubble of rust formed on my mental shield and I sat. Her hand gripped mine with a force that surprised me.

'What have I done to you, John?' she whispered.

My hand remained limp in her grip. Now that the moment had come, I found myself unable to speak. I wanted to rail at her, to scream and expel the last of the poison that lingered within me. I wanted her to feel my hurt, my confusion, my loss. Instead I said nothing. Freeing my hand from hers, I scanned her from head to toe and once again wondered at how one person – someone now so frail and tiny – could have had such a pervasive effect on my life.

There was one difference now, though: I was the one in the position of power. But I was unsure of how I should use it. Retribution or forgiveness? How could I possibly forgive something so terrible? How could I act as if nothing had happened? Questions crowded my mind like a babble of desperate children.

A tiredness so profound that it leached from me even the power to speak stole over me. All I could manage was 'Why?' My voice seemed to come from the end of a long tunnel.

My mother's chest rose painfully as she prepared herself for my judgement. Her eyes moved back from the window to me and bore nothing but truth.

'Why?' she repeated. 'It was the only way I knew how to love. You were my sons. Part of me. You came from me. You were mine. I'd never had anything that wonderful and beautiful before. Can't you understand that?'

'Jesus. You get something new and beautiful and wonderful, and you want to fuck it, is that how it works?'

'John, don't be so coarse.'

'Yeah, cos the f-word is infinitely worse than sexually abusing your children.'

She shrunk from that and in a small voice, asked. 'Was that how you saw it? At the time, wasn't it loving, comforting? What we had was special, John. Can't you see that?' As she spoke she was stroking my thumb and with a charge I remembered that little movement, and I couldn't remember an age when she didn't do it. It was her habit to sit at the side of my bed and as a prelude she'd hold my hand, stroke my thumb, the touch warm and soothing.

I jumped to my feet. 'It wasn't loving and comforting, Mother. It was dirty and shameful. And twisted.' I could feel a sensation, like a heavy metal cap being tightened around my head. 'And…'

Tiredness had me slump against the window. And I had a sense of wishing the glass wasn't there and I could slip from her vision, let her watch and worry that the fall might kill me.

I exhaled. Forced myself to feel my feet on the carpet, my back on the solid glass. I recognised the destructive force of my thoughts and how ultimately it would be aimed inwards if I didn't change the focus.

'Wait a minute,' I said. 'It was "the way you knew how to love"? What does that mean?'

She opened her mouth as if to speak, and stopped herself as if unsure quite what to say. Her gaze turned to the window and the seascape beyond, but she looked like she was seeing nothing of the beauty contained there; instead her eyes shifted from side to side as if she was having a debate with herself.

Slowly, carefully, she brought her eyes back to meet mine, a movement that felt like an act of supplication. In response I could feel the muscles of my face stiffen. Forgiveness was the furthest thing from my mind. She looked away first.

'On my fourteenth birthday, Grandad took me down to the seaside. Just me and him. He was a lovely man. Then we stayed at a bed and breakfast. Dad was gone. Mum was cold and distant. She was jealous, I could see that. She wanted to keep me and Grandad apart. And I knew I was special, cos Grandad never, ever slept with either of my sisters.' Her eyes were wistful, as if she was remembering a golden era in her life. 'That was why I made sure all of my boys learned from me. I didn't want any of you to feel left out.'

I shook my head, trying to understand what she meant by all of this, but I gave up. How can anyone comprehend how people like her justified their actions to themselves?

'What happened to your sisters?'

She nodded. 'We lost touch when Mum kicked me out after I got pregnant.'

'You were? … What happened to that child?'

'I called him Thomas, after Grandad.'

'But … Dad?' Thomas wasn't my dad's child?

'He was a decent man. He knew Thomas wasn't his, but loved me enough to take us both.'

'Whoa,' I said as I shook my head. The level of deceit and manipulation inherent in that last sentence was impossible to compute. What did that make Thomas – my brother and my uncle? I recoiled from this new piece of information. I imagined what Thomas's reaction would be if I told him. I shook my head; that was a truth that would have to stay hidden. What other lies did this woman harbour?

'Don't you see how wrong all of this is?'

She shook her head sadly, continuing to speak as if she hadn't heard me. 'I knew I was wrong, dirty, because my dad left us. But

Grandad was nice to me. Bought me lots of lovely dresses, and jewellery and stuff. And that helped turn me around.'

'Mum, none of that makes sense.'

Silence again reigned. I had suspected that something terrible may have happened to my mother, but suspicion and certainty sit at either end of an emotional chasm.

'Surely, being a victim of abuse, you would never want to inflict that kind of torment on your own children … surely.' I was desperately trying to understand.

'I can't begin to understand it myself, so I can't make you, John. While I was in that situation it felt loving. It was only later that I felt shameful and dirty. And later, when I was with you there was this…' she paused as if fighting to find the right word '…compulsion, I rationalised it, talked myself into accepting my behaviour as normal. I saw you beautiful boys and each of you took my breath away. Your purity and innocence was my last chance to make myself whole … by taking my sons back into my body, I was trying to make myself complete.'

'My God,' I exploded. 'Can you hear yourself? Can you hear just how sick that sounds? We were your sons, surely if we were so beautiful and pure' – I doubted that the two adjectives could have been uttered with such venom – 'then you could have given yourself a pat on the back for having a hand in its making instead of destroying exactly what you thought was so amazing.' Demanding an answer but expecting none, my eyes bored into hers.

'I'm sorry, son. Can you ever forgive me?' Her shoulders moved as she sobbed.

She leaned her head forwards to hide the passage of her tears, and then resolutely lifted it up. She offered me her tears as an act of contrition. Holding my stare, she was bare of artifice and empty of pride. Every score that life had left on her face, every line of her weakened form begged for my forgiveness. But it was clear she was sorry about my reaction, not the act.

I shook my head slowly.

And still, to this day, I'm hostage to her actions as I have a niggling sense that until I can forgive my mother I will never know complete, untrammelled happiness.

But that afternoon, I sat at a distance of both miles and inches from her as she attempted to explain and atone for her actions. Out of the window lay one of a plethora of breath-taking views that the inhabitants of this hauntingly beautiful country have been blessed with. Inside the ivy-covered building hewn from local rock, two disparate people attempted to make sense out of their lives. To find peace.

I knew I had help in that regard. Thomas and Liz were coming over later for Sunday dinner, a dinner that Chris had suggested he cook. Angela would also be there with Cathy, who had already met and had been completely enchanted by Andrew and Jack. And I was looking forward to having them all squeeze into my little flat.

Despite the worst efforts of the woman lying in a bed facing me it looked like we had a future, as a family.

I stood over her one last time, aware of the switch in power, cognisant of how powerfully her body had been wrecked by her illness, and despite my better self, I felt a sense of satisfaction that she'd been punished in this life for her actions.

In an echo of how she used to begin her seduction of me, I slowly traced the feeble purple vein on the back of her hand, down her thumb to the brightly polished nail.

And with a backward glance, I left the room to begin the rest of my life.

Acknowledgements

This book has been a long time in the making. I wrote the first draft in 1996–1997 and during that time there were a number of people who offered encouragement and advice. Chief cheerleader on the project at that time was the amazing Margaret Thomson Davis. Aside from making herself available to me whenever I was stuck, she arranged lunch at her house with a social worker and a psychologist so I could discuss with them the issues raised in the book. Sadly, Margaret died just a couple of years ago, at the age of ninety – but she would have been absolutely delighted to see this manuscript (eventually) make its way onto the published page. Thanks are also due to friends who read chunks of the text as I wrote it and chivvied me along until I finished it: Nan, Stuart, Jackie and Wincey – made it at last, eh?

Long story short, the manuscript sat on a computer for a couple of decades until I mentioned the story to the wonderful Karen Sullivan. With her blessing I had another shot at bringing John Docherty's tale to life, and to an audience. And here, once again, I have to acknowledge her superpower as an editor. Karen has the BEST eye to help develop a story. And along with her talented copyeditor, West Camel, they helped me focus and tighten the book so that it would sit better in your thoughts and in your imagination.

Thanks also to Sharon Belshaw and Sharon Bairden, for helping when I needed last-minute clarification around my research.

And finally, to the readers, bookshop staff, reviewers, bloggers, librarians, fellow scribes, and everyone who has read, enjoyed and championed my work: without you I'd be a madman screaming into a void. Thank you for your attention, support and wisdom.

EXTRACT FROM *A SUITABLE LIE*
(Orenda Books, 2016)

Prologue

I don't know how long I walked for. My heels slammed on to concrete until they almost went numb. Fists tight in my pockets, I walked and walked.

And walked.

Light from a shop window spilled on to the pavement just in front of me. What was a shop doing open at this hour? For the first time I noticed my calves were so cold they had no feeling in them. My watch read 6.30. What the hell was I doing? I had been walking for hours wearing only boxer shorts and a t-shirt under my coat; on my feet, a pair of mule slippers.

What the hell was I thinking?

The shop door opened, a small, bald man came out and propped an advertising board for a newspaper against the wall. He stared at me as if I was an idiot searching for his village.

'Looking for my dog,' I muttered, feeling as if I had to offer this total stranger an excuse for the way I was dressed. He shrugged and walked back into his shop. The newspaper headline on the board read, 'DIVORCE DAD KILLS KIDS'.

As I turned and walked away from the shop, I realised just how weary I was. Each step was an effort and each time my heel jarred on to the ground, shockwaves reached my spine. The banner had sapped what strength I had left. What kind of a world did we live in where someone would think such a crime was their only way out? What kind of a god would countenance such an act? I stumbled to a halt. What on earth would drive a man to do such a thing? Only an extreme emotion would result in such a dreadful action. Was it desperation, anger, jealousy? A disturbed mind's version of an act of love?

I willed myself to continue walking and my own situation pushed its way to the front of my thoughts, like a small child in a crowd shouting, 'What about me?' What about me?' Would I ever feel that desperate?

The banner blazed like a warning.

I would have to find a solution. I would have to find a way out of this trap.

At last, my circuit brought me home. The door was unlocked, I pushed it open and walked inside. Pausing by the living room door, I saw her curled up in a chair. Fast asleep. Even in the weak light I could make out the silted lines of mascara that ran from her eyes and down the pale expanse of her cheeks, almost past her nose.

She had obviously fallen asleep waiting for me.

And that was the first time I thought about murder.

1

It was a Sunday, the day we met; Sunday 7th July 1996. I've no idea why I remember that. It just stuck. And it would be nice to say our eyes lit on each other across a crowded dance floor, cos that's romance, eh? But, no, it was a smoke-filled bar at the local rugby club.

I've no clue why she was interested in me, I was one of a type. The room was filled with broad-shouldered, thick-limbed, flat-bellied young men, so why would she pick me? My first thought was that it was ghoulish curiosity. After all, it wasn't like I hadn't encountered it before. Being a widower with a toddler before you reach the age of thirty does have a certain appeal, as my young brother Jim told me when he dragged me out that night.

'You need to get out of the house,' he said. 'All work and Disney movies makes for a dull life, brother.'

'Suits me just fine, Jim.'

'You'll thank me for it,' he countered. 'The ladies love a tragedy. They'll be throwing their knickers at you soon as you walk in the door.'

It was an image that filled me with horror. Having lost the only woman I'd ever loved, the thought of a group of women looking at me with wide-eyed, open-mouthed sympathy was more than I could bear.

'C'mon, Andy,' he pleaded. 'I told Mum I'd drag you out tonight. You know what she's like if I let her down.'

'You'd think she'd get used to that,' I grinned.

'It's been arranged anyhow.' He shrugged. 'Mum's coming over in...' he stretched his right arm out in such a way that his silver Tag wristwatch edged out past the cuff of his Thomas Pink shirt – my brother is a slave to the high-end brands – '… in forty-five minutes to put the wee fella to bed.'

I groaned. Once Mum was here it would all be over. Mrs Boyd doesn't take no for an answer.

Jim wore a sly grin like it was a badge of honour. 'Game's a bogie, big man. Go get your good jeans on. And wear that light-blue shirt I got you at Christmas. Makes you look less like a morgue assistant.'

'Do I have to?' I made one last effort at resistance.

He winked. 'Your nutsack must weigh a ton, brother. What is it, over four years since Patricia died? Time to get them emptied.'

I shook my head. Looked him up and down and made a face. 'You look so refined. But you've really just stepped out of a cave, haven't you?'

When we walked in the door of the club an hour later, the smell of my son, Pat's Thomas the Tank Engine pyjamas still lingered in my nostrils and that tuft of hair on his crown stuck in my mind. I'd have given anything to be back there, tucking him in, reading *The Gruffalo* to him one more time. Instead I fought the churn in my stomach and allowed Jim to push me inside.

A few of the guys came over, slapped me on the back, told me it was good to see me. Like it had been a long time, even though I had played a game with them just the previous weekend. But I knew what they meant. Since Patricia died it had been nothing but work and Pat. And the occasional game of rugby when injuries meant they were struggling for players.

As Jim led me through the crowd to the bar, a Spice Girls song came on and I was for turning and leaving. Jim sensed my movement and with a hand on my back he pushed me forward. What the hell was I doing here? A lot of nods were sent my way. Ayr was a fair-sized town with a village mentality. Everybody knew everybody. I'd gone to school with most of these guys. Their parents knew my parents.

My parent.

Another tick in the Andy Boyd tragedy box. Father died of

a massive heart attack just when the boys were approaching the troublesome teenage years.

'You know Louise, don't you?' Jim said over the babble.

I hid my reaction. Two minutes in the door and he was already trying to set me up. To be fair, he'd made a good choice, I thought as I looked at Louise. I recognised her. She'd been a couple of years below us at school and had grown into herself rather nicely in the intervening time. I remembered a shy girl: look at her and she'd try to hide her blush under her long fringe.

I gave Louise a nod and a tight smile. No point in misleading her. There was as much chance of me hooking up with anyone that night as there was of Ayr winning a European championship.

Next up on the DJ's version of a fun night was somebody singing what sounded like *Ohh, ahh, just a little bit.* Yeah, I'm all over that, I thought as I turned away from Louise, faced Jim and asked for a pint of lager. He gave an almost imperceptible shake of the head and waved at the barmaid.

Pint in hand, heart feeling as solid as if someone had poured fast-setting concrete into my chest cavity, I took the chance when Jim was distracted by Louise's blonde pal to walk across to the far corner of the room.

I took a seat, crossed my arms and legs and surveyed the crowd. I was in a room full of people – most of whom I knew – but I'd never felt so alone.

That was when I saw her. Shoulder-length blue-black hair; black turtle-neck, short-sleeved sweater. Very little jewellery. Minimal make-up. Yet she was easily the most attractive woman in the place. She was surrounded by guys, but she was looking at them as if they held as much attraction for her as a pile of dung.

She took a sip of her red wine. Looked away as one of her would-be suiters cracked a joke. Judging by the way he threw his head back in laughter, he thought it was hilarious. Her cheeks barely budged in response.

She saw me looking.

I looked away.

Moments later, as Celine Dion was chuntering away, she sat beside me.

'Fancy helping out a bird in bother?'

I sat with that for a moment.

'Cos a damsel in distress doesn't sound Ayrshire enough?' I asked at last.

She made a 'well done' face. 'You're about the only guy in here who would have got that.'

'And what's bothering you?' I asked. 'Or who?' I added, thinking about the guys who had been surrounding her earlier.

'New girl in town. I know nobody,' she said as she looked around the bar. 'I was asked here by some guy. Ken something. And now he's creeping me out.' Keeping her arms straight, she tucked her hands between her knees and gave a dramatic shudder. 'Wouldn't be surprised if his mum's called Norma and he stabs shower curtains in his spare time.'

I followed her line of sight. Saw a guy who grew up on another estate. We used to play football with him. The jumpers-for-goalposts kind. He would have been better taking the place of one of the jumpers.

Never took to him. His gaze would meet yours for less than a second before it slid off, as if he was afraid you would read his mind. We found him one day down the River Ayr throwing stones at the swans and avoided him from then on.

'Ken Hunter,' I answered. 'His wife, Sheila, works in my office.'

'What a prick,' she said, leaning back and to the side, as if this would make her less visible to him. 'Didn't say he was married.' She looked at me. Her eyes were large, clear and an intoxicating blue. 'You'd rather be somewhere else, eh?'

I gave a non-committal shrug.

She stood. 'Let's go. We can rescue each other.'

Thinking, *why the hell not?* I followed her outside. 'Where are we going?' I asked when I caught her at the door.

'I don't know. You're the local.' She scanned the playing fields and the tall, full-leafed trees beyond. 'Is the beach far from here?'

Half an hour later we were walking alongside the low grey wall that holds the sands of Ayr beach from being blown into the town. The tide was in, the waves had their lazy on and we could see the sweep and curve of the bay ahead of us. And out to sea, holding up the skyline, were the hills of Arran. A cool breeze was coming in off the water and, despite the early summer evening sunshine, I could see her arms stipple with the cold when she crossed them.

'Nice,' she said. 'No wonder you've never left town.'

'How did you…?'

'It's written all over you,' she smiled. 'Born, bred and buttered Ayrshireman, eh?'

On the way down here our chatter had been light and unaffected, and, to my surprise, without any awkward silences. She was an easy girl to talk to.

'It's Anna, by the way,' she said as she took a seat on the wall. I sat beside her, being careful not to get too close.

An elderly couple walked past with a yellow Labrador. Judging by the colour of its coat it was just out of the sea and it chose that moment to give itself a shake, spraying us both with droplets of sea water. Anna's laughter was loud and unrestrained.

The couple were profuse in their apologies. The dog approached us and nudged Anna's hand with its nose. The woman tutted. 'This is Dave, by the way.' Her pride in the dog evident. 'Greedy bugger's looking for a treat.'

'Not the only one,' the man said and gave me a wink. 'Jeez, hen, you're all wet. You'll catch your death. Here have my fleece.'

'No,' Anna stretched out the syllable. 'I'll be fine. Honestly.'

The man offered her it again. It was clear he was momentarily caught up in the glamour of her. I glanced behind me at the sea and thought of mermaids and their siren call.

'C'mon you,' the woman said and gave him a nudge. 'Offering

young women your fleece. They'll be calling the cops on you.' She set off, and with a regretful air, man and dog obediently trotted after her.

Anna waited until the couple were out of earshot. 'At least the natives are friendly.' As she said *friendly*, she looked into my eyes.

Discomfited and flattered, I looked away. She was way out of my league. What the hell was she doing with me?

'We were getting round to the introductions, before Dave showered us…' The pause at the end of her sentence a request for my name.

I told her. 'And what brings you to my home town?'

'I've just been sent here. Work.'

'What do you do?'

'Nothing special,' she smiled at me. There was a light in her eyes and a blush to her lips and I felt my thawing into the human race continue. 'I work for the Royal Bank,' she explained. 'But don't be asking for a loan. I'm just a teller.'

'Wait,' I sat up. 'The Royal? Which branch?'

'The one at the top of the High Street.' She cocked an eyebrow at my sudden interest.

I mentally reviewed the staff there. We were expecting a new team member, but that wasn't until next week.

'I don't start until next Monday. I've got a few days holiday to take first.' She held her hands out. 'Thought I'd take in the sights first.'

A file had arrived on my desk the day before. The name came to me.

'Anna Reid?'

'How the hell do you know that?' She straightened her back.

'Andy Boyd,' I reached out, shook her hand. 'I'm based at the branch at the other end of the town. I'm your new boss.'

She threw her head back and laughed. 'You're at it.'

I shook my head slowly. 'Nope. Not long promoted.'

'Wow. What are the chances?'

'It's a small town.'

'Hope I made a good first impression?' She tilted her head to the side.

'I think your new boss is already thinking that HR have been very kind to him.'

'Bet you say that to all the girls.'

'Only the ones that laugh at my jokes.'

'You tell jokes?'

'On high days and holidays. Maybe the odd funeral.'

She lifted her legs up and swung round on her backside so that she was facing out to sea. I followed suit and in a silence usually only possible between long-time friends we stared into the distance and watched the sun as it painted the distant Isle of Arran and its crown of clouds in shades of red, amber and gold.

I sneaked a look at her. She caught me, nudged me in the side and gave a little giggle. I couldn't help but join in.

My sensible voice warned that our employers might not take kindly to any fraternisation between us. My usually unheard devil voice was louder. It said: fuck it.

Our shoulders were all but touching. My hand was on the wall, within centimetres of hers. I felt the heat of her skin on me as she slowly moved her pinkie and linked it with mine. I looked down at how our little fingers were joined and looked up and beyond the horizon.

A smile warmed my face. My heart gave a little twist and I couldn't help but feel, maybe, I was about to get a second chance at happiness.